The Road to Revolution

Book 1

Chris Bennett

The Road to Revolution

ISBN: 978-1-955100-14-4 (Trade Paperback)
ISBN: 978-1-955100-13-7 (eBook)

Map of NE USA:

Names: Bennett, Chris (Chris Arthur), 1959- author.
Title: The road to revolution. Book 1 / Chris Bennett.
Description: [Wadmalaw Island, SC] : [CPB Publishing, LLC], [2025]
Identifiers: ISBN: 978-1-955100-14-4 (trade Paperback) | 978-1-955100-13-7 (ebook)
Subjects: LCSH: Teenagers--United States--History--18th century--Fiction. | Fathers-- Wounds and injuries--Fiction. | Pioneers--United States--History--18th century--Fiction. | Soldiers--United States--History--18th century--Fiction. | United States--History--Revolution, 1775-1783-- Fiction. | LCGFT: Historical fiction. | BISAC: FICTION / Historical / Colonial America & Revolution. | FICTION / World Literature / American / Colonial & Revolutionary Periods. | FICTION / War & Military.
Classification: LCC: PS3602.E66446 R631 2025 | DDC: 813/.6--dc23

To sign up for a
no-spam newsletter
about author
CHRIS BENNETT
plus
exclusive free bonus material
please visit my website:

http://www.ChrisABennett.com

Revolution [rev-*uh*-**loo**-sh*uhn*] noun:

1. A fundamental change in the way of thinking about or visualizing something: a change of paradigm.

2. A sudden, radical, extreme, or fundamental change in social structure, especially one accompanied by violence.

3. An overthrow, repudiation, or renunciation and complete replacement of an established government, ruler, or political system by the people governed, often using violence or war.

Dedication

To
Daniel Morgan:

"Fought everywhere,
was beaten nowhere."
- Inscription on his statue
in Winchester, VA

Contents

*"The wave of Brits advanced towards us
in order to swallow us up ...
but they found a choaky mouthful of us."*

– Private Peter Brown
on the Battle of Bunker Hill

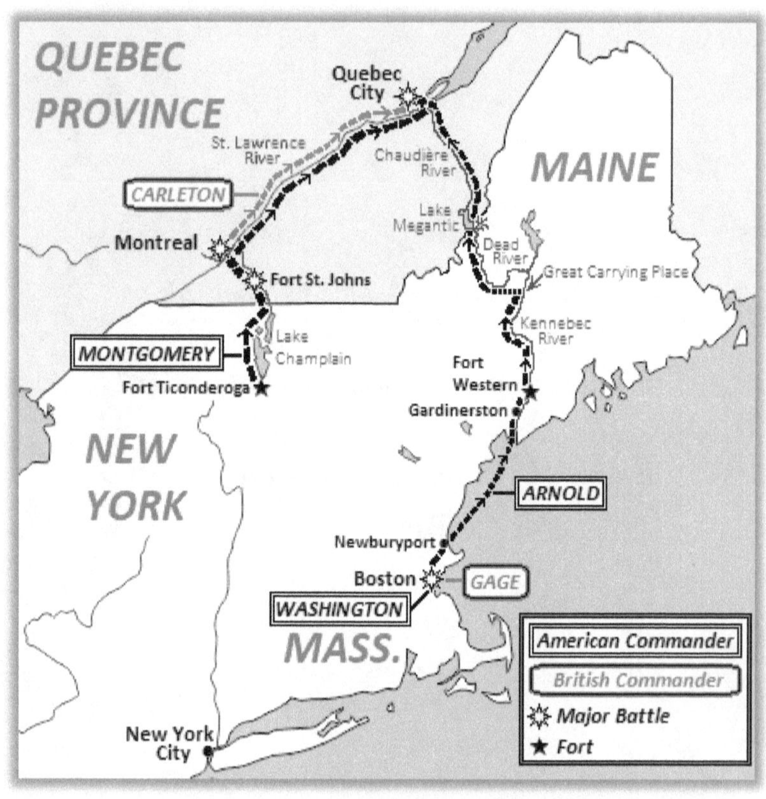

American Invasion of Canada, 1775

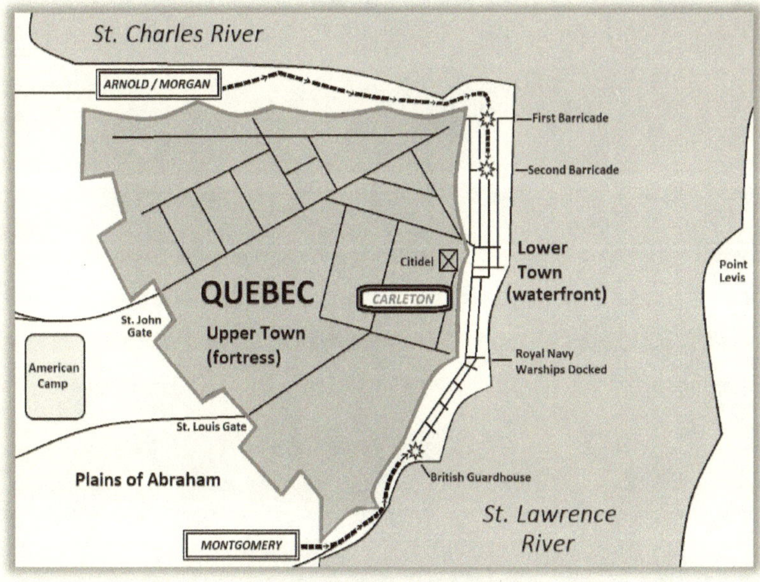

Battle of Quebec, 1775

CHAPTER 1. TRYING TIMES

"These are the times
that try men's souls ..."
- Thomas Paine
The American Crisis

Thursday March 30, 1775 – Winchester, Virginia Colony:

"Ah, *dagnabbit!*" Ethan swore as the log tumbled off the stump, a chunk cleaved from one side rather than the full split he'd intended.

"*Hah.* You need more practice, Ethan." Levi Miller laughed from where he sat, leaning his back up against the wall of the house. Seth Taylor, who sat next to Levi, snorted a chuckle of his own, but said nothing.

The three teenage boys, who'd been friends for as long as they could remember, were a contrast in physical appearance: Levi was built short and wiry, Seth was more stout—bordering on pudgy—and Ethan was tall and lean. But despite their differences, they were together so often they might've been mistaken for brothers.

Ethan scowled as he leaned down to retrieve the fallen log with his left hand while still gripping the axe in his right. "I'd like to see you do better, Levi. Or *help*, maybe?"

"What? And deprive you of your fun?" Levi grinned. "I'm too good a friend to do that to you."

"That goes double for me," Seth agreed, nodding mockingly with a playful grin.

Ethan gave them a derisive look, then reset the log on the stump, quickly giving it another whack—this time more successfully.

"See? Better already," Levi grinned.

But despite his mild annoyance at his friends' teasing and their unwillingness to help, he was happy for their company as he went about the wearisome task. Their good humor and playful banter helped to pass the time and distract his mind from the tiredness in his arms and back. He'd finished up all he could do on the plat maps days ago, and today he was working on chores around the house. He wanted to get this particular task done before his father returned from his trip, which may or may not be later today.

He picked up another log, set it upright on the stump, and took a swing. This time it was a perfect hit, splitting the log into two neat sections. Ethan looked over at Levi, intending to give him a satisfied grin, when he noticed his friend was no longer looking his way; Seth, too, gazed out past Ethan toward the street in front of the house.

"What the …?" Levi muttered.

Ethan turned and saw an open-bed wagon coming up the street, drawn by two horses, with a large man up front in the driver's seat. There was nothing unusual about that. But what immediately caught Ethan's attention was the driver himself: a tall, muscular man, whose youthful vigor and obvious strength belied his actual age of forty years, made known only by his almost completely white shoulder-length hair. Ethan had only seen him from a distance before, but every young man for miles around knew the stories of adventure and heroism surrounding the long and colorful career of "the old wagoner," Daniel Morgan.

To Ethan's greater surprise, the wagon came to a stop in front of his own house. So he dropped the axe and strode toward the front gate to greet their unexpected and most prestigious visitor. Levi and Seth jumped up to follow.

Before Ethan reached the gate, Morgan called out, "This the Chambers' place?"

Ethan opened the gate as he answered, "Yes, Mr. Morgan … I'm Ethan Chambers, I—"

"Good," Morgan interrupted, immediately turning to climb down into the bed of the wagon. Ethan noted that the man held a stern look on his face. "Come 'round here, Ethan, and bear a hand. Your daddy's been hurt. You other two fellas come too."

"Oh!" Ethan ran around to the back of the wagon, looked inside, and gasped. His father, Gideon lay on top of a wool blanket, his eyes closed, seemingly unconscious. Both of his arms were wrapped tightly in white cloth, but Ethan could see blood soaking through in several places.

"What happened, Mr. Morgan?" Ethan asked, clambering up into the wagon bed.

"His wagon flipped, back up the road a ways, in the hills outta town. Thankfully, me an' my man Will happened by to pull him out.

"Grab the edge of the blanket there, Ethan, and let's get him in the house. You other boys grab the sides once we're out of the wagon, so's he don't spill out."

The boys did as they were bid, and soon they were approaching the front door, even as it popped open. A woman stepped out and went wide-eyed at the sight of them, placing her hand over her mouth in shock.

"Mrs. Chambers … Please hold the door open, ma'am," Morgan ordered.

Without a word, Hannah Chambers held the door back as Morgan and the boys carried Gideon into the house, down the short hallway, and laid him on his bed.

◄◄◄◄◆►►►►

Daniel Morgan took a seat, removing his wide-brimmed felt hat as he did. "My name's Morgan, ma'am—" he began.

"Yes, of course, we know who you are, Mr. Morgan," Hannah immediately answered, taking a seat opposite him in the small sitting room in the house. Ethan stood behind her chair with his hand resting on her shoulder. His younger sister, Elsie, stood behind Ethan holding his other hand, her face tucked into his shirt. Ethan could feel her body shuddering as she wept, the wetness of her tears soaking through the fabric. Levi and Seth had respectfully taken their leave after offering any assistance they might.

Hannah wiped the tears away from her face and sniffed, trying to maintain a brave front for their distinguished visitor.

"Mrs. Chambers … I've already sent my man Will to fetch Doc Adams up in town … I expect he'll be here shortly," Morgan said as he leaned forward and met eyes with her.

Hannah nodded. "Much obliged, Mr. Morgan."

Ethan, seeing Morgan up close for the first time, was impressed by the intensity of his steely blue eyes, and at the same time, the concern and compassion shown on his rugged face.

"Mrs. Chambers … I am a man who tells things as they are … Some folks may find that a bit off-putting." He shrugged. "But such is how I am. So, I'm just going to say it: your husband's hurt *bad*, ma'am. I seen plenty o' terrible wounds out fighting in the wars and driving wagons … and this here's one of them kind. If he lives, he's like to lose his right arm at the least. Maybe he'll keep the left … Hard to tell. But it'll likely be crippled and of little use hereafter."

"Oh, dear," Hannah gasped, tears welling in her eyes once more. She buried her head in her hands and began to softly sob.

"We'll know for sure once the surgeon arrives—" Morgan was interrupted by a knock on the door. "Ah … speaking of …" he concluded.

Ethan rushed to answer the door. When he pulled it open, he recognized the short, gray-haired man who stood there as the local doctor, though thankfully he'd not had reason to call at their house in several years. Doc Adams held a sour expression on his face and a black leather bag in his left hand. He removed his felt hat politely with a slight bow as Ethan ushered him inside.

"Mrs. Chambers, Mr. Morgan," the doctor greeted the two adults in the room with a quick nod but retained his severe expression. "The patient is—"

"Down the hall, first door to the left," Morgan answered. The doctor turned and followed the directions without further ado, as Morgan, Ethan, and Hannah resumed their seats to await the results of the doctor's examination. Elsie continued to stand behind her brother.

Morgan turned and met eyes with Ethan for the first time since entering the house. "What work does your daddy do, son?"

"He … he's a surveyor. Mostly been working for Lord Dunmore these past several years. Drawing up plats for the lord's lands so he can sell them off in parcels. Also drawing up maps of the valley for his lordship."

Morgan nodded, but said nothing.

"I ... I've been helping him ... He's training me as his apprentice. But I'm still learning ... Not much good at it, to be honest. And ... I'm not sure it's what I want to do, anyhow. I've been planning to attend school down in Williamsburg at William and Mary College next year. It's where Father got his education. He said the money from his current map for Lord Dunmore would pay the cost ..." Ethan realized he'd said more than he'd intended or had been asked, and suddenly felt self-conscious and could no longer meet Morgan's intense gaze.

"I see ..." Morgan nodded. He glanced over at Hannah, who continued to cry.

Morgan then seemed to notice Elsie for the first time, peering over Ethan's shoulder. She'd stopped crying, though her eyes were still red and puffy, and she continued to sniffle.

"What's your name, darlin'?" he asked her, gracing her with a gentle smile.

"Elsie, Mr. Morgan."

"Pretty name ... Did you know I have two girls about your age? Nancy and Betsy."

"Oh. No, sir, but they sound very nice."

"Well, perhaps you'll have to get to know them. I'll wager you three would get along famously."

"I reckon we would, thank you, sir," she answered, and managed a slight smile for the first time.

Morgan continued to converse with the girl, asking her various mundane questions about her friends, things she enjoyed doing, and so on. Ethan realized that Mr. Morgan was likely only trying to ease Elsie's discomfort and help pass the time while they all awaited the doctor's pronouncement—kindness for which he was grateful.

After several minutes, which to Ethan felt like hours, the doctor stepped back out into the sitting room. Ethan's heart sank as he saw that the man's previous sour expression was now even more severe. Doc Adams did not immediately speak, but instead looked at Morgan for a long moment before slowly shaking his head.

Morgan nodded and sighed.

He turned and gave Ethan a hard look. "Well, son ... apprenticeship's over, and so is schooling. Time to be a man."

◄◄◄◄◄◆►►►►►

Doc Adams reached over and picked up something metallic and shiny from the leather satchel he'd unrolled onto a side table in the bedroom. Ethan glanced at the thing, then quickly looked away. It was a long, slender blade that appeared to be razor sharp.

Adams looked at Ethan a moment, then over at Morgan, "Is the boy up to it?" he asked.

Morgan shook his head, "He's a boy no more, Doc. Starting today, he's a man."

The doctor nodded, then looked over at Ethan who'd been stationed by his father's feet and nodded once more but said nothing.

"All right, though he's unconscious at the moment ... he may awaken from the pain ... and even if he doesn't, he'll likely thrash reflexively. You two must hold him still, or he will be harmed far worse, perhaps even fatally."

Then he looked at Ethan, and locked eyes with him. "Do you understand, son? No matter what he does or says, you *must* hold his legs firmly, or it will go badly for him. Mr. Morgan will hold his chest and upper arms."

Ethan swallowed a lump in his throat that threatened to choke off his words. He felt a twisting pain in his stomach and a cold bead of sweat running down his brow. But he nodded and said, "Yes, Doctor Adams. I understand ... Hold him still, no matter what ..."

Adams looked back at Morgan. "Ready?"

Morgan nodded and leaned into Gideon, pinning him to the bed.

Ethan couldn't look at what the doctor was doing, only focused on his father's legs in front of him. At first Gideon's legs only twitched slightly. And after a few moments, Ethan heard something metallic dropped into a bowl.

"Soft flesh is now cut away," the doctor announced, which made Ethan wince at the thought.

"Now is the difficult part, and most painful. I must remove the jagged bone with the saw. You must be ready, young man. Here goes …"

Ethan leaned down on his father's legs and gripped tighter. Suddenly Gideon's legs went stiff, then thrashed violently, and he cried out in agony. But Ethan held on tight, and he could see Morgan doing the same, preventing Gideon from pulling away from the doctor's painful ministrations.

Again Ethan heard the metallic clang.

"Good, good. Arm's off, now I need to tie off the artery. Don't relax yet, this part is the most delicate, and deadly …"

But this time Gideon did not thrash, and Ethan suspected he had simply passed out again from the overwhelming pain caused by the saw.

"Done," the doctor announced after several minutes.

Ethan felt a sudden, almost palpable, relief that the ordeal was over.

But then the doctor said, "Now … Ethan, you stay put, and keep holding those legs. Mr. Morgan, you switch sides with me, and we'll see what we can do about setting those broken bones in his left arm and hand."

Ethan inwardly groaned, but said nothing.

Once the two men were repositioned, Adams began feeling Gideon's left arm, starting at the shoulder and working his way down. "Hmm … clavicle feels fine … but the shoulder's out of the joint. We'll need to get that back in." He looked up at Morgan, "You done that before?"

Morgan nodded, "Oh, yeah, sure. It's a common enough injury when you're dealing with horses and wagons, as I've done. Hurts like the devil, but pops right back in with a good hard pull. Usually heals up fine in a week or two."

"Good, cause I'll need your strength to do it. Now … let's pray the humerus is intact, else it's going to be a whole lot more difficult …" he felt carefully down the upper arm.

At the thought of his father's arm out of its socket, the knot in Ethan's stomach twisted harder, and he feared he might vomit, but he continued to hold on as he'd been instructed.

"Good news. The humerus feels fine … Elbow … good … Radius … there's one break … two … that's it. The first one's offset and will need to be reset. The other'n not. Ulna … one break, but still fairly lined up. Think we'll leave that one as is."

Then he felt around the hand, slowly shaking his head. "Bit of a mess." He sighed, "We'll just have to do the best we can with that … Hopefully he'll be able to figure out how to work with it once the bones stitch and the pain subsides."

Once again, Gideon's legs thrashed and he cried out in pain when Morgan pulled at his upper arm to pop it back into the joint, and again when the doctor pulled on his lower arm to straighten the larger of the two broken bones. But by the time Adams started working on Gideon's mangled hand, it seemed as if all his strength was gone. His legs only twitched slightly, and he whimpered quietly.

Finally, Doc Adams stepped back, looked over at Ethan, and for the first time since his arrival his features had softened. "Well done, son. But you look a bit pale. We can take it from here. Mr. Morgan can assist me with the bandaging. Why don't you step outside and get some air. Perhaps sit down for a bit."

Ethan did as he was bid, leaving the bedroom. But the thought of facing his mother and sister, feeling like he did, was unbearable. So he turned and went out the back door.

As soon as he shut the door behind him, he could feel his stomach finally giving up the battle, and he leaned over to vomit on the grass. Then he sat down, put his head in his hands, and cried.

◄◄◄◄◆►►►►

As Daniel Morgan stepped out the front door, Hannah followed, pulling the door closed behind her.

"Mr. Morgan … I can't thank you enough for pulling my Gideon out from under that wagon and bringing him home to us. Without you coming along, I hate to think of what might've happened," she said, still sniffling, but having regained much of her composure.

"Happy I was there to help, ma'am," he answered with a quick smile, tipping his hat to her, preparing to depart. But then he paused, as a thought occurred to him.

"Uh ... look here, Mrs. Chambers ..."

"Hannah. Please call me Hannah, Mr. Morgan."

"Miss Hannah ... I know these present troubles are a bitter hard blow for you and yours ... so whatever I can do to help y'all, I will.

"I'll just have a couple o' my men run over tomorrow and fetch your wagon from out o' that ditch, bring it back to my farm. We'll fix 'er up there for you."

"Thank you, Mr. Morgan. That is very kindly of you," Hannah answered.

"And if there's anything at all you need while Mr. Chambers is recuperating and young Ethan is taking over the trade—food, supplies, equipment, what have you—you just go ahead and send your young man 'round to the farm to fetch it. If I'm not there, just have him call on my wife, Miss Abby, and she'll see he gets whatever he needs."

"Oh, I can't ask you to do *that*, Mr. Morgan."

"You ain't asking, Miss Hannah ... I'm just gonna do it. I reckon that's what neighbors are for, ma'am. And ... well, to be honest, our family has fared well in recent years; made a good profit running and then selling my freight-hauling venture, and the farm's now doin' a good business. It truly ain't no inconvenience to help y'all out for a spell, and this old wagoner is more'n happy to do it."

Hannah graced Daniel with a quick smile, followed by a long thoughtful look, "Much obliged, Mr. Morgan. You know ... you've always had the reputation around town for being a rough character. But now, I no longer believe it."

Morgan chuckled, "Oh, I'm still a rough character, Miss Hannah, despite my Abby's best efforts to smooth me over. But ... it turns out I *do* have a heart."

"That I can clearly see, Mr. Morgan. That I can clearly see."

The day after Gideon's accident, Ethan and his friends met in the barn at Levi's family farm. And as expected, it was a glum, downcast gathering, as Ethan's family issues now cast a pall over the usually happy crew.

"Doc had to amputate his right arm, just below the elbow," Ethan explained, then shuddered. "It was—" but he choked up and couldn't continue for several minutes. The thought of the horrible surgery still haunted him.

"Sorry, Ethan …" Seth said, reaching over to pat his friend on the arm. But Levi just slowly shook his head, for once at a loss for words.

"Doc says Papa shouldn't lose the left arm, but whether or not he'll be able to write or do any work with it is doubtful," Ethan continued.

There followed a long silence, with none of the three young men eager to broach the subject hanging over them. Finally, Ethan broke the silence.

"Look, fellas … I know we were planning on striking out for Boston as soon as Papa finished his map and he wouldn't be needing me for awhile, but …"

"We know, Ethan … You got to take care of your momma and Elsie now," Seth responded. "We already talked it over, and it's what you gotta do. So, if you ain't going, we ain't going neither."

Ethan shook his head, "No … no, that's not fair. Just 'cause I can't go doesn't mean you guys have to stay and miss out on all the excitement. After the fighting up at Lexington and Concord, I hear nothing much has happened. If you wait too long, maybe they'll just meet and settle the matter, and then the whole thing'll blow over and you'll not get to see anything at all."

"You sure about this, Ethan?" Levi asked. "We can stay and help you out …"

"No, there's no need of that. Papa's already taken all the notes for the surveying and the maps, so I'll just have to get everything written up neat and drawn out for his lordship. Nothing for you guys to do ..." Then he turned and gave Levi a wry grin. "Unless you wanna help me split firewood, Levi ..."

Levi chuckled, "Not now ... not *ever*, Ethan."

◄◄◄◄◄◆►►►►►

Despite Daniel Morgan's words, Ethan still didn't feel much like a man in the present circumstances. After a long couple of weeks, in which Gideon had suffered a high fever that threatened to finish the job the wagon accident had started, Ethan's father was finally on the mend. He now sat up in bed, and was able to move slowly about the house with his left arm in a sling and the missing stub of his right arm hidden within the sewn-up sleeve of his shirt.

That good news was offset, in Ethan's mind, by his father's almost obsessive drive to finish the work promised to Lord Dunmore. And since Gideon could not do the work himself, his anxiety was re-directed at his young son, who was now the only person available for the job, inexperienced and inadequate though he may be.

Finishing the write-up for the surveying work was fairly easy for Ethan; Gideon's clear, concise notes made the work mostly mechanical and mathematical in nature. Still, Ethan's inexperience meant it required a good deal of correction and re-work, which took almost two weeks.

But when it came time to draw up the map, Ethan gazed at the pile of notes and measurements his father had compiled, along with a stack of rough sketches, and felt completely overwhelmed.

"But, Father ... I've never done anything like this before," he argued. "I don't know if I can do it."

Gideon frowned and shook his head, "You can, and you will, because you *must*. There is no other choice, Ethan. I can't do it myself, clearly, and our family's fortunes are dependent upon delivering this map to the governor. He is our largest client by far, and not a man who will accept any excuses. If we lose his business ..." Gideon left the rest unsaid, but Ethan could imagine it would be a devastating blow to their income.

"All right, Father ... I will do my best."

"I know you will, Ethan. You've always been a good boy. And your momma tells me that Mr. Morgan told you it's now time for you to become a *man*, and I agree."

Ethan nodded, then went right to work. It was a tedious, exhausting task, which Ethan worked at tirelessly from dusk to dawn for nearly three weeks. At the end, his exhausting efforts were rewarded by an unenthusiastic, "Adequate; it'll have to do …" from his father.

◄◄◄◄◆►►►►►

Wednesday June 7, 1775 – Williamsburg, Virginia Colony:

Ethan was up at sunrise, bathed, and dressed in his finest clothes, which had been carefully packed and kept meticulously clean during his weeklong ride from Winchester to the Virginia colony's capital at Williamsburg. He'd arrived in town the night before, but had resisted the urge to ride straight to the governor's palace to deliver the map; he'd been warned by his father that one didn't show up in filthy, travel-stained clothing to meet with Lord Dunmore. So, for the first time on his long, tiring trek, he forked out the money to stay under an actual roof, eat a hot meal, and take a much-needed bath.

But Ethan had enjoyed the adventure, he had to admit to himself—the first time he'd done anything of the kind without his father. And the ride had been a welcome break from the tedious work he'd been doing and the gloomy mood that had pervaded his home ever since his father's accident. He'd either slept outdoors in a small tent or, on occasion, under a roof, generously offered by strangers along the way. The only troubling aspect of the journey had been the continual rumors, whenever he encountered travelers coming from the opposite direction, of growing unrest between angry colonists and the governor in Williamsburg.

As he rode up the street toward the palace in the early morning sunlight, he reflected on all that had happened since his father's accident, and realized for the first time the truth of Mr. Morgan's words at the time: that it was time to step up and be a man. Now, after having completed his father's work and having traveled alone across most of the Virginia colony, he was starting to feel like it might be true.

When he arrived at the palace gates, he was surprised to find them closed. And rather than a red-coated soldier standing guard, he found a man who wore no uniform and held a normal hunting rifle instead of a musket.

"Good day, sir," Ethan said, tipping his hat, but still sitting on his horse.

"Good day, young feller. What can I be doing for you?" the man, who appeared to be in his mid-thirties, answered amiably. Ethan thought the fellow had the look of a common laborer.

"I'm here to see Lord Dunmore ... on business," Ethan answered.

But surprisingly, the man chuckled at this response, as if it were humorous for some reason. "Oh? And what *business* would that be, if you don't mind my asking, sir?"

"Uh ... the lord had commissioned my father to survey his lands out in the Shenandoah Valley. I'm here to deliver the documents the lord has requested."

The man frowned, "So ... y'all are on the governor's side?"

"Side?" Ethan responded, not understanding the question.

"Yeah, the way things stand here at Williamsburg, you're either on the side of the damned Brits, or you're a good American. Ain't no other choice, son ..."

Ethan just stared at the man, open mouthed. "But ... I really know almost nothing of such matters, mister," he shrugged. "I don't wish to pick *any* side in the argument. I'm only here on my father's business ..."

The man slowly nodded, "Well, I understand you're still a boy ... but time will come where you *will* have to decide, same as every other man. There won't be no choice to stay out of what's coming."

Ethan didn't know how to respond to this statement, so he thought to turn the conversation back to accomplishing his mission.

"So … may I please pass the gate that I might carry out my duties with his Lordship the governor?"

The man chuckled at this, and slowly shook his head.

"Is there … something *humorous* about my question, sir?" Ethan asked, trying to decide between confusion and annoyance.

"Well, no … not normally, but … as it turns out, his Lordship is not currently at home."

"Oh?"

"Yes, it seems he had a little … *disagreement*, shall we say? With our most esteemed gentleman, Mr. Patrick Henry, and several hundred of his militiamen … including myself, I might add—part of that 'choosing sides' matter I was speaking of. As Mr. Henry and the rest of us approached the governor's palace, the lord and his family developed a sudden desire to go on a hunting expedition."

"A … *hunting expedition* …?"

"Yes, so it seems, my good lad … I heard he fled the palace in great haste and has taken up new residence at his hunting lodge a few miles north of town—a place called Porto Bello."

◄◄◄◄◆►►►►

Later that afternoon, after a pleasant ride through the Virginia countryside led to a tense encounter with a troop of suspicious, red-coated cavalry soldiers, Ethan was left to wait for several tiresome hours in the foyer of Lord Dunmore's two-story brick hunting lodge.

Having seen the governor's grand palace back in Williamsburg, Ethan could imagine the governor was none too happy about being forced to retreat with his family and staff to this modest-seeming home in the country—a place clearly intended only as bare essential housing for men intent on indulging in the rough pleasures of the hunt.

When he was finally led into the governor's makeshift office by a butler, whose fanciful attire sharply contrasted with the humble furnishings, Ethan was greeted cooly by his Lordship, the Royal Governor of Virginia, John Murray, Fourth Earl of Dunmore.

Lord Dunmore reclined in a deeply padded leather chair, a frown knitting the brow of his lean face. Ethan thought the governor appeared tired. His shockingly red hair stood up at odd points on his head as if he'd recently tousled it.

Dunmore finished reading the sheet of paper he held, then set it down and gazed across at Ethan.

"I'm told you are here to deliver some documents?" he finally asked, in a flat voice that seemed entirely disinterested.

"Yes, Your Lordship. I am here on behalf of my father, Mr. Gideon Chambers, who has been performing certain surveying and mapmaking activities on your behalf over in the Shenandoah Valley."

"Chambers ...? Ah. Yes ... *Chambers*. The surveyor. You're late."

"Yes, my lord, for which I apologize most sincerely. Unfortunately, my father has suffered a fairly serious accident ... which has critically delayed the matter, I'm afraid," Ethan answered. He'd already decided to make no mention of the severity of his father's injuries, as it would likely only cause issues if the lord knew that a mere apprentice had been forced to finish the work that he'd commissioned.

"I see. Well, you're here now, so I may as well have a look at what you've brought ..."

"Yes, my lord," Ethan answered, handing across a stack of papers. "The plat maps for the requested parcels ..."

The lord took the papers and flipped through them one at a time, glancing briefly at each and seeming to make a count before setting them down on the desk in front of him and looking back up.

"And *this*, my lord," Ethan handed over the large, rolled-up map.

Dunmore took it and now stood, unrolling the map across the table before placing several heavy objects on the corners to hold it open. He gazed across the paper for a long moment, seeming to focus on various points for extended periods of time. "Hmm ... uh-hunh ... good ... good. Yes, this is what I wanted, to be sure ..."

Then he removed the weights, rolled the map back up, and sat once again, gazing up to meet eyes with Ethan, as if really noticing him for the first time.

"But it's too late, Chambers," Dunmore said, scowling, as he slowly shook his head. He handed the map back to Ethan, along with the stack of plat write-ups. "That damnable scoundrel, *Patrick Henry!* The insufferable demagogue has run me out of my own home and has put his villainous rogues in control of the government offices at Williamsburg."

Dunmore stood and slammed his fist into the table, as his face turned beet-red. "I'll boil his blood to make my pudding, the knave! Just wait 'til the army arrives in force. We'll hang the lot of treasonous vermin, mark my words." Ethan was shocked by the vehemence of the lord's display, and didn't know what to say or do.

Lord Dunmore slowly sank back into his chair, then sat gazing at the surface of the table for several moments, trembling in his rage, before looking back up at Ethan.

"It's too late, Chambers ..." the lord finally responded in a calmer tone. "What use have I of plat surveys or maps of the Shenandoah Valley when I can't even enter my own capital city for fear of being accosted by rebels?"

"But ... my lord ... the payment ...?"

Dunmore frowned, "Have you not heard a word I've said, man? The map is *late ... too late ...* so late as to be entirely worthless to me."

Ethan's heart sank with the now certain knowledge that it had all been for naught, and there was nothing more to be done. "Yes, my lord ..." he answered.

Dunmore went silent again for another long moment, staring unblinking at the table in front of him. Ethan wondered if he should quietly take his leave, or if he was supposed to wait until he was dismissed.

But then Dunmore seemed to come back to himself. He looked up and once again met eyes with Ethan. "I can see you're a good, loyal subject of the king, Chambers, as is your father, no doubt. So, I'll make you this bargain: once the current troubles are over—

and I promise you, as God is my witness, they *will* be soon—you call on me once again, and I will happily pay for your father's work. Minus a fair deduction for its lateness, of course ..."

Chapter 2. A Call to Arms

"To arms, to arms!
The British are coming,
the British are coming!"
- Paul Revere

Saturday June 17, 1775 – Charlestown, Massachusetts Colony:

"Jesus, Levi … how the hell did we get into the middle of *this?*" Seth gasped out, as he shoved the ramrod down into the rifle barrel. With a dull thud, the lead ball set down tight on top of the wadding and powder. Dust caked his face as sweat streamed down from under his straw hat in small rivulets.

Levi shook his head but could think of nothing to say in answer; he saw his own mind-numbing, abject fear reflected in his friend's eyes.

The two teenaged boys sat with their backs to a low mound of dirt, haphazardly shoveled up against the base of a split-rail fence—a meager redoubt that was now the only thing standing between a few hundred Americans with hunting rifles and the oncoming red-coated British Army, bayonets fixed. They'd just endured a quarter hour of deafening artillery bombardment, hunkered down with their faces pressed against the earth and hands covering their heads as coin-sized metal balls—which someone called "grapeshot"—screamed through the rails of the fence, sending deadly splinters flying, and tearing through the bodies of anyone unlucky enough to get in their way. But now the big guns had gone silent, and the Americans figured the assault would soon begin again in earnest.

Despite the terror of their present circumstance, or maybe because of it, Levi's mind wandered back to the day they'd started out on their adventure, hearts light and minds swimming with excitement for the journey ahead. At the time, they had little thought about the bigger issues of the conflict, and bore no strong opinions as to the wrong or the right of them. To the boys, it was just a wild lark, a chance for a little excitement in an otherwise humdrum existence. The idea of soldiers marching in file, rifles on their shoulders, was a thing that set their minds awhirl. And when Levi thought about watching actual cannon fire, he became so excited that he had trouble sleeping at night.

They'd brought their rifles along, of course, but hadn't thought much about using them for actual fighting; rather, they planned to supply much of their food along the trail by hunting small game. And, unlike their friend Ethan, who'd been raised in towns, Levi and Seth had grown up on their folks' farms; they'd been hunting since they were big enough to hold a rifle.

Levi gazed back up Bunker Hill away from the approaching enemy, toward where Charlestown should've been visible but for the cloud of dark smoke engulfing it. The word was that the British had burned the town as a prelude to their assault on Breeds Hill. Whatever the reason, Levi decided it well fit the hellish inferno they presently found themselves in.

The two young men, who'd never before even considered firing a gun in anger, had already fired two volleys into the British lines as the redcoats marched up the hill toward the American redoubt. Levi tried not to think that he had very likely killed at least two men today; for a boy who regularly hit moving squirrels at more than a hundred yards, hitting a full-grown man marching upright in a straight line, wearing a bright red coat at only fifty paces, was simply ... *murder*. He shuddered at the thought, and pushed it from his mind with an effort of will.

The slaughter had been horrific, and shocking. The British Army, expecting a quick rout of a ragtag rabble of farmers and merchants, had been devasted by the close-up rifle volleys unleashed by the rebels. Hundreds of redcoats had gone down in rows. Twice they had tried it, and both times the result had been the same: absolute butchery that stopped the assault dead in its tracks. Especially devastating to the British had been the loss of their officers; the Americans, having little notion of the niceties of European-style warfare, had especially targeted the enemy's commanders, easily identified by their elegant uniforms.

But despite the courage and determination of the Americans, they'd not come prepared for an extended battle; ammunition was almost entirely depleted, and a formal chain of command was non-existent. After the second failed British assault, men began streaming away from the redoubt, back up Bunker Hill, away from the fight.

Levi still couldn't quite fathom why he and Seth, who'd never planned on being there to begin with, had stayed when so many others had fled. *Maybe just stubborn, farm-boy pride*, he decided. Also, many of the men had retreated for the simple fact of running completely out of ammunition. But Levi and Seth had brought plenty of powder and bullets for their hunting, so they couldn't in good conscience invoke that excuse.

Peter Brown, an older man in his thirties, who'd fought next to the boys all day, poked his head up for a quick look, then ducked back down. "Here they come again, boys. Looks like they've learned their lesson; they thought to swallow us up quick-like before, but they found we was quite the chokey mouthful!" he laughed at his own grim humor, despite the circumstances. "This time they's comin' in wide-spread columns, not broad rows. Harder to target that way ..."

Levi and Seth just nodded as they cocked the hammers on their rifles and pulled their legs up under their chins, preparing to rise and fire. They waited for orders ... but none came.

After several minutes, Levi rose up cautiously and turned to gaze out toward the enemy. He gasped instinctively squeezing the rifle's trigger just as a red-coated soldier stepped up to the fence and thrust a bayonet at him. The rifle barked, and the soldier crumpled forward onto the fence.

The other remaining Americans, realizing what had happened—that there'd been no officers left to give the command to fire—were now on their feet, firing their rifles, then tangling with the oncoming red tide in desperate hand-to-hand combat.

Levi felt, rather than saw, something hit Seth hard next to him on his left. He glanced over to see a snarling, blond-haired Brit yank his bayonet free from Seth's stomach. Without conscious thought, Levi slammed the butt of his rifle into the soldier's face, where it hit with a sickening crunch that knocked the man backward onto his fellow soldiers.

Levi threw down his rifle, grabbed Seth under his right arm, and began dragging him away. Peter grabbed Seth's other arm, and the three fled from the deadly fence.

Halfway up Bunker Hill, American resistance once again stiffened, and there were men who took charge and organized a fighting retreat that prevented an all-out slaughter. By then, Levi and Peter had been carrying a now unconscious Seth for several hundred yards uphill through knee-high pasture grass, and were beginning to suffer the strain. They finally paused, and laid Seth down. Levi stood, hands on knees, trying to catch his breath, gazing down at his friend as Peter knelt and placed his hand on the side of Seth's neck. After several moments Peter looked back up at Levi and slowly shook his head.

Seth was gone.

◄◄◄◄◄◆►►►►►

Saturday June 24, 1775 – Winchester, Virginia Colony:

Ethan had been home from his unsuccessful mission to Williamsburg for just over a week when the shocking news reached Winchester: a major battle had been fought between American militiamen and the British Army just across the harbor from Boston at a place called Bunker Hill. And, although the British were claiming a victory, having pushed the colonials off the hill and entirely out of the Charles Town peninsula, from all reports the American militia had remained intact, retreating in good order. More importantly—and most shockingly—it seemed as if the British had actually suffered much higher casualties in the engagement than the Americans had. The news triggered an excitement throughout the town such as Ethan had never felt before.

But Ethan's initial reaction upon hearing the news was a sinking sense of dread. Levi and Seth had gone to Boston to watch the soldiers on both sides, assuming it would be a lot of posturing and squabbling, but no serious fighting. That clearly had not been the case. And Ethan had heard nothing from his friends, nor had their families when he visited them to inquire.

He forced these ill thoughts from his mind by reminding himself that neither Levi nor Seth were especially scholarly, so he'd not expected any regular correspondence. Still, it was worrisome, and he prayed that they had stayed safely away from the fighting and that he would hear something from them soon.

Two days after the news of the battle began to circulate, fliers were posted around town that the Second Continental Congress, meeting in Philadelphia, had authorized the creation of the Continental Army, and had commissioned George Washington, a fellow Virginian, as its commanding general.

When Ethan heard the news, he immediately went to his father, remembering having met Mr. Washington once when they were passing through Richmond on the way to see the governor.

"They selected George Washington, you say?" Gideon responded. "I'm not surprised. He's a good man; helped me out a lot when I was first getting started in the surveying business. Very smart, good leader, a real military man."

"I remember you talking about him before, Father. I just recall from meeting him that he seemed very kindly for such a large, serious-looking gentleman."

Gideon nodded, then looked down and became quiet.

Ethan could tell something was amiss. "Are you not feeling well, Father?"

"No, no ... I feel fine ... considering," he held up his crippled left hand, then shrugged. Ethan gave him a reassuring smile, resisting the urge to grimace at the unsightly appendage.

"It's just ..." Gideon continued, "I wish it wouldn't come to a shooting war ... It seems so *unnecessary*. In the end, we're all Englishmen, subjects of the king. *Taxes on tea?* Why do we care? I don't even *like* tea, for God's sake!"

Ethan shrugged. He understood it even less than his father did.

"I wish men like George Washington would find a way to work things out with the king," Gideon slowly shook his head.

"Look what's already happened with Lord Dunmore ... The whole thing's bad for business."

◄◄◄◄◆►►►►►

The next week, following the news of the establishment of the new Continental Army, a group of prominent citizens representing Frederick County met in downtown Winchester to discuss forming a rifle company. Nobody in town was surprised when the committee unanimously nominated Daniel Morgan to recruit and lead the unit, and they commissioned him as a captain in the new army.

The following day, Ethan came upon a flier nailed beside the front door of Allason's Shenandoah Store on Main Street. Captain Morgan had just posted these fliers around town to announce that trials for the new rifle company would commence a week hence, on July 13th, at the Berry's Tavern grounds just north of Winchester.

Ethan shook his head as he read. Even had he felt inclined to fight, which he didn't, he knew he'd never qualify, his age not withstanding; he'd grown up in the city and had never even owned a rifle. He'd only gone hunting with Levi and Seth on occasion, during which his skills had proven woefully inadequate, to Levi's amusement and Seth's consternation. There was no way he would even consider embarrassing himself in front of the rugged frontiersmen who would no doubt answer the call.

But ... like most of the other young men in town, he imagined himself heroically marching off to war, a rifle slung over his shoulder, led by Captain Daniel Morgan.

◄◄◄◄◆►►►►►

With all the excitement surrounding the upcoming rifle company trials, and given Daniel Morgan's new role, Ethan was surprised when a small, one-horse carriage pulled up and he recognized the driver as the same man who'd helped Morgan pull his father from the toppled wagon.

Sitting next to the man was a woman with blonde hair tied up in a bun and a blue bonnet shading her face. She was dressed in the clean but simple dress of a farmer's wife, and despite the fact she appeared to be nearly old enough to be his mother, Ethan thought her one of the prettiest women he'd ever seen. The driver helped her down from the carriage, then stood by the horse as the lady turned and approached the house alone.

With a slight bow, Ethan opened the low front gate for her. She paused and smiled. "You must be Ethan."

"Yes, ma'am. And do I assume correctly that you are Mrs. Morgan?"

"Yes," she beamed, "have we met before, Ethan?"

"No, ma'am. But I recognized your driver from when Mr. Morgan helped rescue my father. So I just assumed …"

"Very perceptive of you, Ethan. Daniel said he thought you were a bright boy … but I can see now that you are *hardly* a boy … a *young man*, Mr. Morgan should've said."

Ethan could feel himself blushing. "Thank you for saying so, ma'am." And then, remembering his manners, "Won't you please come inside, Mrs. Morgan?"

"Abby. Please just call me Abby, Ethan."

"Thank you, Miss Abby. Won't you please come inside, ma'am?"

Once inside, Ethan introduced Abby to his mother, Hannah, and was then amazed at how quickly the two women relaxed and launched into a lengthy, good-humored conversation, comparing notes on all the various ladies in town, as if they'd been lifelong friends.

Then, sticking to his theme of attempting a display of proper manners, he went to the kitchen, lit the stove, and boiled a pot of water before serving tea to the ladies. He chuckled to himself when he remembered his father's comments about the British tax on tea, and how he had little use for the stuff. He briefly wondered where his father was, fearing he was once again retired to bed early, as had been a too frequent habit since his accident.

The two ladies sat across from each other at the kitchen table sipping their tea while Ethan watched and listened, offering more tea whenever it seemed appropriate.

Then, at the end of more than two hours, Abby stood and announced it was time for her to return home, that she had greatly enjoyed their visit, and that she hoped Hannah would come to her house sometime soon.

Then she turned to Ethan, looked him hard in the eye, and said, "Ethan, you just hitch up your wagon and come on out to the farm tomorrow morning ... say seven o'clock. My men will load your wagon with a few items your family may be needing."

But when Hannah tried to object, Abby gave her a serious look. "Now look here, Hannah ... I know your family has suffered a grievous blow through no fault of your own—not only from Mr. Chambers's accident, but also Lord Dunmore's inexcusable lack of common decency in not paying the money he rightly owed.

"There is no shame in accepting help from a loving neighbor. And ... I am certain that were the shoe on the other foot, you would do the same for me and my family without the least hesitation."

Hannah teared up, thanked her guest, and the two exchanged an embrace before Abby departed. Hannah, eyes still watery, looked over at Ethan and said, "That's one of the finest ladies I ever hope to meet."

Ethan could think of nothing to add to that assessment, so just nodded his agreement.

◄◄◄◄◄◆►►►►►

When he arrived the next morning at the Morgan farm, Miss Abby greeted him warmly before sending him around to the backside of the house, where a couple of her farmhands had gathered the things he was to pick up.

Ethan pulled up to the back stairs of the veranda, where he saw two men standing by a large pile of goods. They greeted Ethan warmly, then one jumped into the bed of the wagon while the other remained on the veranda next to the pile, where he proceeded to heft items and toss them to his comrade, who stacked them neatly in the wagon. When Ethan tried to help, they waved him off, the one on the veranda grinning. "Don't try to take our jobs away now, sir," he said, to which Ethan laughed and shrugged.

He was amazed at the bounty the Morgans were gifting them: whole hams wrapped in white cloth, large sacks of flour, beans, and corn, and smaller bags of sugar and salt, among various other items.

But when Ethan tried to thank the men for everything, they just laughed, and this time the one in the wagon answered, "Hell, son … don't thank *us* … *we* didn't pay for the stuff."

As Ethan stood watching the men work, he caught a movement out of the corner of his left eye, up on the veranda. He turned to look and saw a pretty young girl, he guessed about twelve, gazing out at him from around a corner of the house. She had blonde hair, wore a pink dress patterned with white flowers, and she held a yellow daisy in her hands. Ethan immediately recognized a strong resemblance to Miss Abby.

"Hello," he said, tipping his hat. "My name's Ethan. What's your name?"

"I'm Nancy," she said, making a neat little curtsy and smiling brightly as she did.

"Nice to meet you, Nancy," he answered.

"She's too young for you, Ethan," a deep voice boomed from behind him. Ethan turned to see Daniel Morgan striding toward him from one of the barns, a few dozen yards away. "And … she's my daughter," he added.

Ethan flinched at the implied accusation—that he had designs on Morgan's young daughter—but was relieved to see that Morgan was smiling, and likely only meant the comments in jest.

"Oh, yes sir, Mr. Morgan. I … can see the family resemblance all right … which was what I was thinking on just now. Like Miss Abby … if you don't mind my saying so."

Daniel stepped up in front of Ethan and held out his hand, which Ethan accepted and shook. It was a hard, firm grip, and the skin was dirty and rough with calluses, but the gesture had a friendly feel to it, which helped to put Ethan at ease.

"I don't mind at all, son; everyone says so. The two o' them'll look like twin sisters once Nancy gets a mite older. Now my younger daughter, Betsy … she takes more after me, though a whole lot better looking, thankfully," he chuckled.

Ethan returned the smile, though he thought Morgan a fine-looking man, despite the wicked battle scar on the left side of his face. Downright heroic, even. But he wasn't about to argue the point.

Morgan turned toward the girl and gestured, "You run along now, Nance. Go see if your momma needs any help up at the house. Me'n Ethan have some business to discuss."

"Yes, Daddy. Goodbye, Ethan. It was nice to meet you."

"Goodbye, Nancy."

They watched the girl retreat around the corner of the veranda, headed toward the front of the house.

Morgan glanced over at the loaded wagon, then looked over at Ethan again, "Abby get you everything y'all were needing, son?"

"Oh, yes, sir. That and more. Thank you ever so kindly. My momma wanted me to be sure to thank y'all profusely. And … to tell you we shan't need any more help, though …" he shrugged.

"Yep, I know … Times're tough right now. Not much work to be had, I'm guessing …"

"Yes, sir. Seems folks don't want to part with their pounds and shillings, not knowing what's going to happen."

Morgan nodded. "I'd hire you to do some work around here, but I'll not be around for a spell, I'm afraid."

"Yes, so I've heard, Mr. Morgan. But it's all right; I'll find some kind of work. And you've done plenty enough already for our family. We are forever grateful and in your debt, sir."

"Never mention it, my boy. It's my pleasure to help out a neighbor, as I've said before. Oh, and speaking of … how's your daddy doing?"

Ethan frowned, "Well, he's *healing* okay, I'd say. Still can't use his left hand for much, but it's stopped hurting for the most part — at least that's what he says."

Morgan nodded knowingly, *"But?"*

"But … I think it's hard for him to feel like he can't do any work … that he no longer has a purpose, if you understand …"

"Yes … I'd say that's just about the worst thing for a man to endure. Well, let's hope he discovers something new he can do."

"Yes, sir."

They were quiet for a moment, and the farmhands had finished their loading and returned to their other duties. So to fill the awkward silence, Ethan decided to ask the question that'd been on his mind ever since his return from Williamsburg, and for which no one seemed to have a good answer.

"Mr. Morgan, can I ask you a question?"

"Certainly, Ethan. Ask away."

"Sir … what's it really all about? Why are folks so mad at the king and his men? Mad enough to start a war? I hear about taxes and whatnot … but there've always been taxes as far as I know. I really don't understand it."

Morgan grunted, then gestured toward the veranda steps and moved in that direction. Ethan followed, and the two of them sat on the second stair.

"Never mind taxes, laws, rules, and so on … or even whether old George the Third is a good king or a bad one," Morgan began. "In the end, it ain't about any of that. It's about men who live in a whole other country, thousands of miles and a month o' ocean travel away, who think they know best for us that actually live here. And when we try to tell 'em how it *really* is, over here in America, they ignore us, and go right on telling us what to do, and how to do it, even if it means they ignore their own laws. And if we don't like it, they threaten life and limb."

"Ah …" Ethan answered, noncommittally.

Morgan was thoughtful a moment. "Let me give you a 'for instance,' Ethan. They tell me there's a fellow up at Boston named John Adams …"

"I've heard of him."

"Yep … a real scholarly, decent man, they say. And he knows the laws here in the colonies and back in England, like you and me know the scars on the backs of our hands. Anyway, this fellow Adams—who couldn't be a more respectable fellow, from what I hear—has been trying his best to make the king and his parliament understand the way things are over here, and how we want to live. And do you know how they've made answer to this decent, honorable man? With the point of a gun, that's how. That's what all the fuss up at Lexington and Concord was all about—the Brits sent their troops out to track down Adams and his friends and arrest them, intent on hanging the entire lot. That's when the shooting started; the folks up there weren't going to just stand back and let it happen."

"*Oh*. That's awful. Why would the British do that?"

"Because they can … Because they think we here in America are lesser men, just 'cause we weren't born over in England, though we all come of the same stock."

"Well that's just … *stupid*."

Morgan smiled. "Worse than stupid, Ethan. But they're gonna learn—to their everlasting regret—just how wrong they are about us. All they're gonna do with their guns and bayonets is to wake up a country that's been long asleep. Hell, it's already started, just look at what's happened up at Bunker Hill.

"And once we figure out just how strong we can be if we all stick together … well, I reckon the Brits're gonna wish they'd listened to the wise, gentle *words* of Mr. Adams rather than the *guns* of cruder men … hard men … like this here old wagoner, Daniel Morgan."

◄◄◄◄◄◆►►►►►

Friday July 7, 1775 – Winchester, Virginia Colony:

A carnival atmosphere pervaded the green surrounding Berry's Tavern, with the proprietor and longtime friend of Daniel's, Ben Berry, marching around shouting orders with two pistols tucked into his belt. Ethan thought Berry more comical than admirable, basking in his newfound attention as if he were the lord of the manor.

Dozens of tents of all shapes and sizes had been pitched out on the pasture next to the tavern, and hundreds of people of all ages and genders milled about. But it was easy to spot the men who were there for the trials—these men had a hard, rugged appearance to them. They dressed in buckskins or other sturdy frontier clothing and walked with long rifles slung over their shoulders and knives tucked into their belts.

Ethan and a dozen other boys his age, who'd been drawn by the excitement of the day, stood around joking and telling tall tales, waiting for the action to begin.

Though the sun had been up for more than an hour, and those gathered waited expectantly, conspicuous in his absence was the man who would be the event's focal point: Daniel Morgan.

And then, as Ethan leaned in to hear the punchline of the latest joke, the boy speaking suddenly stopped and his eyes widened, "Oh. There he is!"

None of the boys needed to be told who "he" was. Ethan pivoted and saw Daniel Morgan trotting up on his great black horse. A cheer rose up from the crowd gathered as Morgan rode into their midst. Though Ethan had, of course, been around Morgan several times recently, and had even had the honor of getting to know the famous man a little, he still looked on in awe. Daniel Morgan, sitting tall in the saddle, loomed larger than life.

He wore a fine, light-colored buckskin suit, almost white, with the typical leather fringes and short white fur trim around the seams, cuffs, and collar. Angled over his broad, handsome face sat a black wide-brimmed felt hat, rakishly pinned up on one side with a large white feather sticking out of the hat band. His perfectly contrasting white hair flowed out from underneath the brim.

Upon his shoulders, and pinned at the collar by a large, brass broach, hung a full-length cape, navy blue velvet with a natural-colored suede inner-lining. It had been a parting gift from his wife, made by her own hand, though no one but Morgan knew it.

Around his waist he wore a red sash. Upon his belt, he carried a large, utilitarian hunting knife in a sheath and an authentic Shawnee tomahawk—a hard-earned souvenir from the French and Indian War—tucked in next to it. Across his left shoulder he carried a beautiful long rifle, its burled walnut stocks fancifully carved, with sparkling brass kickplate, and richly engraved brass hardware around the lock plate and trigger guard.

Ethan stood gazing with mouth agape. In that moment, he thought Morgan more magnificent than any man he'd ever seen or imagined. Not even the British officers, in all their elegant finery, came anywhere close. Next to Daniel Morgan, those English gentlemen looked effete and foppish, Ethan decided.

Morgan stopped his horse in the middle of the crowd and gazed about as the cheering increased in intensity.

"Morgan! Morgan! Morgan!" the crowd began chanting in unison.

Morgan smiled at them for a long moment, gazing slowly about as if meeting eyes with each person in the crowd, until he finally raised a hand for silence. But so enthusiastic was his audience, that several more minutes went by before it was quiet enough for him to speak.

"Thank y'all for coming," he began. "Those that know me, understand I'm not a man given to speeches; more inclined just to get things done. But I reckon today is a solemn one … maybe the start of a road that'll lead to the end of all we've known. So, I figure a few words won't hurt.

"The men I'm fixing to take with me must prove skill with the rifle, and other kinds of fighting. I'll also need men of loyalty and honor. I can only bring along the best o' the best. That means many of you, sadly, will *not* be joining us this time."

This last statement elicited a groan from a number of voices in the crowd.

Morgan raised his hand for quiet, then continued, "Before you get your britches all in a twist … I reckon we may be in for a long, hard storm. There'll be plenty o' time for the rest of you to step up and do your part, and I know you men of Virginia will do just that."

Then he removed his hat and placed it over his heart, "Reckon a gathering such as this, rightly ought to start with a word from our Lord. This here's my favorite passage from the Good Book, and seems fitting … It's in the Twenty-Third Psalm; 'Yea, though I walk through the valley of the shadow of death, I will fear no evil … for *thou* art with me … *Amen.*'"

"Amen!" the crowd repeated back at him.

Then Morgan replaced his hat, and Ethan could see that his previous dour expression had turned to a bright smile. "Now, men … though this is a serious event, still … I believe we should have some fun with it. Who's with me?"

The men let out a great shout at this challenge, and many tossed their hats in the air. Morgan dismounted, greeting Ben Berry, and handing him the reins to his horse.

With that, the trials for the honor of serving among "Morgan's Riflemen" had officially begun.

◄◄◄◄◆►►►►►

The trials began with a test of marksmanship, each man attempting to shoot an apple off a split rail fence at a hundred yards. Anyone who couldn't hit the apple in two attempts was immediately disqualified, though Daniel Morgan personally greeted each such man, shook his hand, and thanked him for coming.

Ethan, watching from his roost atop a branch in a tall tree near the field, decided he'd not be able to hit that apple no matter how many shots they gave him, though he thought his friends Levi and Seth could do it.

Those who passed the rifle test moved on to a whole series of different trials: foot races, lifting of heavy rocks, knife throwing, and even wrestling matches, which regularly turned into fisticuffs.

Morgan watched the proceedings intently, making regular comments, urging the men on to greater efforts, and complimenting them when they did well. Despite the seriousness of the endeavor, it seemed to Ethan that Morgan was thoroughly enjoying himself, smiling and laughing boisterously on a regular basis.

The trials lasted for ten days, though no single contender participated for more than two days. Men kept arriving from the far reaches of the county, and Morgan refused to call a stop while they still did. Ethan was there watching nearly every day, though his mother tried to dissuade him. But he ruthlessly invoked the one argument that he knew she dared not oppose: that he was

32

only going there to support Mr. Morgan's efforts, after all that the man had done for the Chambers family.

At the end of the trials, Morgan posted a list of ninety-five men who had made the roster of Morgan's Riflemen, though the Continental Congress had only authorized ninety.

The men packed their gear and prepared for the 500-mile march to Boston. The day before their departure, Daniel Morgan led the new rifle company in a parade down Main Street in downtown Winchester. Ethan and the other boys lined the street to watch, along with nearly everyone else in town. As Daniel Morgan marched past where he stood, Ethan caught his eye, and the great man nodded in recognition as he passed, calling out, "Hello, Ethan. Give my best to your momma and daddy."

"Thank you, sir, I will. And Godspeed to you and your men."

◄◄◄◄◄◆►►►►►

Sunday July 16, 1775 – Winchester, Virginia Colony:

Daniel Morgan tucked little Nancy into bed, then leaned over and kissed her on the forehead, pulling the covers up under her chin as he did. Her little sister Betsy was already fast asleep beside her.

And though Nancy's eyes were heavy, she was not yet finished with him for the evening, "Daddy …"

"Yes, darlin'?"

"Daddy, Momma says you're leaving tomorrow. Off to fight a war again …"

"Yes, it's true. I'll be gone for a spell this time, I reckon."

"Why you gotta go, Daddy?"

"Well, darlin' … it ain't a thing a man wishes for, but it's his duty. A man's sometimes gotta do things he don't want for the good of his family and his country. I reckon this is one o' them times."

"Oh. You'll be back as soon as you can?"

"Yes, darlin'. That I will, I can promise you that."

"Before Christmas, maybe?"

"Don't know … We'll see …"

"Good night, Daddy. I'll pray for you."

"You do that, Nance; that'll be just the thing. Good night."

Daniel slowly backed out of the room, quietly closing the door behind him.

He went out to the kitchen where Abby sat at the table, gazing up at him as he sat down across from her, settling into his chair with a heavy sigh.

"Nancy's none too happy about you leaving?" Abby asked, picking up on his cue.

He nodded, "Yep … I'm not happy about leaving y'all either. But …"

"Yes, I know … you've got to go. There's no man better to lead our boys in battle, and you know it. And Mr. Washington has been a good friend to you over the years; sounds like he could use your help right about now."

"I reckon so."

Daniel gazed at the table and a silence fell between them for several moments. Abby reached across the table and took his hands in hers.

"Daniel … you're a good man, and you are doing what you have to do for us all. We couldn't be more proud of you. And … I choose to believe that all will be well; it will work out as the good Lord intends—that he will watch over good men like you and over the righteous cause of our colonies."

Daniel looked up, met eyes with her, and smiled. "I really don't deserve you, Abby, darlin'. But I thank God every day that I have you."

"Me too, Daniel. Me too."

He could see a sadness in her eyes, but she was a strong woman, and refused to break down and cry, for which he was grateful.

"Now, Dan … there is a serious matter I wish to discuss with you before you leave."

"Oh?"

"Yes … I am concerned that out in the war, with all the marching and fighting and whatnot, that your lessons will languish."

"Oh, *that*." Daniel felt some relief that her concern wasn't anything more serious than her ongoing efforts to teach him to read and write, beyond the very rudimentary level he'd attained during childhood. "I don't reckon, with the war going on and all, that my *lessons* are the biggest concern I'll have."

She frowned at him, "Now, you listen here, Daniel Morgan … whether you know it or not, you're a *great* man. One of the greatest in the colonies, I'd wager—if betting weren't such a sin. You are a natural-born leader of men, and a fearless fighter. But where you're going, over to Boston, you won't be out on the frontier anymore amongst your rough friends. You'll be among high class men like Mr. Washington and Mr. Charles Lee. Men who're college educated and at home even amongst the high lords and ladies from England."

Daniel shrugged, "So?"

Now her frown turned to a scowl. "Don't '*so*' me. You know of what I speak … By rights, you should be a general in this new army, but as of now you're only ranking as a captain."

"Well, I'm sure it'll change once the real fighting starts. George knows what I can do. We served together against the French, you know …"

"And if you can't write out orders … or write messages to the other officers, or to the army headquarters …? And you can't write to the Congress asking for supplies and ammunition for your men …? And you can't even read what's sent to *you* by any of those people? What *then*, Daniel?"

"Well, I … I guess I never thought about that …"

"Yes, I should say *not*. And I don't expect you're wanting to go around asking the men you just selected for your rifle company if one of them is willing to teach you?"

"No … I expect not …"

"Nor is it likely anyone you find in Mr. Washington's army camp up at Boston will be wanting to spend their time teaching you, much less to read and write for you whenever you need it …"

Daniel was quiet and thoughtful for several moments, mulling over the challenge his wife had just thrown out to him, something he'd not previously considered in all his planning and preparation for the coming march to war.

He then recalled seeing a particular someone along the parade route earlier in the day, and an idea began to form in his mind. And the more he mulled it over, the better he liked it. It not only addressed Abby's concerns, but it had the benefit of also helping a neighbor in need.

"I can see you're considering something ..." Abby prompted.

"Yes ... I'm now thinking I should add another man to our company."

"Oh? Is one of your old fighters is a bit more learned than the others?"

"No ... not one of my old men ... A *young* man. And he's not any kind of fighter. But he *is* well educated, and he's got some experience reading maps—and *making* them, which could come in handy, now that I think on it."

Abby frowned, "The *Chambers* boy? Is he old enough? And is he ready to march off to war with you tomorrow?"

Daniel nodded, "He will be ... And with his father no longer able to work, and Governor Dunmore no longer paying for any surveying, Lord knows the family could use the money, even if it's only a soldier's pay."

"True ... true ... But I wonder how Hannah will feel about it."

"She's a mother; she'll hate it and she'll hate me for it. But she knows she can't keep him from growing up. In the end, she'll pack him a bag, kiss him goodbye, and push him out the door."

◄◄◄◄◆►►►►

Monday July 23, 1775 – Winchester, Virginia Colony:

It was still black as night outside as Ethan sat across from his mother at the table eating a meager breakfast of toasted bread and butter and a few slices of bacon. His father and sister were still in bed, but Ethan had risen before dawn with the intention of walking downtown to see if anyone would hire him for some manual labor for the day. It was also common knowledge that Daniel Morgan's riflemen would be starting their long march to

Boston this morning, and he had a mind to watch them depart before he went to look for work.

He'd just stuck the last piece of bacon in his mouth, wistfully wishing there were more, when there came a loud knock on the front door. He glanced up at his mother. He assumed her look of surprise was mirrored on his own face; nobody ever knocked at this hour.

He stood and went to the door, immediately pulling it open. Daniel Morgan stood on the front step clothed in his buckskins, as he'd been during the parade the day before.

"*Oh*. Good morning, Mr. Morgan."

"Good morning, Ethan. May I come in?"

"Of course, sir. Of course, please ..." Ethan stood aside and gestured for Morgan to enter.

Morgan removed his hat and stepped past Ethan, stopping in front of Hannah. "Good morning, Miss Hannah."

"Good morning, Mr. Morgan. We were just breaking our fast ... Would you care to join us?"

Morgan glanced at the table, which now held only two empty plates containing a few stray breadcrumbs and some bacon grease. "Oh, thank you ... but no, Miss Hannah. I've already eaten this morning."

"Very well ... And to what do we owe the pleasure, Mr. Morgan?"

Ethan was surprised when Daniel Morgan didn't immediately answer, instead looking down at the hat in his hands for a moment. Then he looked back up at Ethan's mother and said, "Miss Hannah, ma'am ... I'm very sorry to tell you this, but ... I'll be needing your boy now."

Chapter 3. The Siege of Boston

"War is our scourge;
yet war has made us wise.
And, fighting for our freedom,
we are free."
- Siegfried Sassoon

Monday July 23, 1775 – Winchester, Virginia Colony:

Ethan had barely noticed the weight of his pack across his shoulders and the strain on his back as he'd marched with Morgan's Riflemen down Main Street in Winchester. And it hadn't bothered him a bit that he'd been placed at the very rear of the formation; better there than not being included at all, he figured, knowing the other boys in town would be green with envy when they saw him.

It'd been a heady experience, with people lining the streets to cheer them on their way. He'd worked hard to keep a serious expression on his face, though with every fiber of his being he'd wanted to break out into a broad grin, his family's tearful farewell already swept from his mind in the excitement.

But now, two hours later and several trudging miles down the road, he was beginning to realize this was not going to be all cheers and glory. The pack hanging from his left shoulder, with its load of spare clothes, food, bedroll, and ammunition, already felt like it weighed a ton. And the long rifle lent to him by Daniel Morgan, slung over his right shoulder, proved even worse. Both straps dug into his shoulders mercilessly.

And now his legs were beginning to tire, a dull ache spreading from his heels up through his thighs. He realized with a sudden sinking feeling that he'd never hiked more than a few miles at a time in his entire life. Even on the few hunting expeditions he'd been on with Levi and Seth, they'd carried only the bare essentials of food and water, with very little ammunition. And they'd stopped and rested regularly. So far, Captain Morgan had shown no inclination to stop for rest.

So Ethan gritted his teeth and soldiered on. He knew he was the lowest man in the company: the youngest, the weakest, the worst marksman, and likely the least skillful by almost any measure. But this made him determined not to fall behind, so he forced himself to keep going, focusing on the feet of the man ahead of him and matching his strides. *As long as he keeps going, I'll keep going too*, he decided. But then a voice inside his head argued, *Yes, but what if you can't?* To this he had no answer, so he did his best to ignore it.

By the end of the day, when the company finally stopped to make camp in a farm pasture just outside the town of Martinsburg, Ethan was so exhausted he lay down on the grass and was immediately asleep. Sometime during the night, he woke up shivering and hungry, so he dug into his pack to retrieve a hardtack biscuit and took a swallow of water from his canteen. Then he unrolled his bedroll, slipped inside, and was asleep again almost instantly.

And then someone was shaking him awake. He looked up and groaned, "Why are we getting up in the middle of the night?" he asked the figure looming over him in the darkness.

The man laughed, "'Cause it ain't night, lad. It's mornin', so get a move on. Cap'n don't suffer no stragglers."

Ethan looked over at the sky and saw it was true. Off to the east the rim of the earth glowed with the imminent arrival of the sun. He sat up, wiped the sleep from his eyes, and reached into his pack for something to break the fast.

Within a quarter hour, he was once again striding along at the back of the column as dust swirled around him in the growing heat of the day. Several hours later, soaked through with sweat, coated in dust, legs leaden, and stomach growling, Ethan wondered what in the world he'd gotten himself into.

When he sat up in his bedroll at the start of the third day, he felt an aching, stabbing pain all through his body. Just reaching out to grab food from his pack hurt in various ways, such as he'd never imagined possible. And when he tried to stretch, his calf muscles locked up into an agonizing cramp that took several minutes to subside.

Once on the road, the march was much the same as the two days prior, though someone said they'd now passed into Pennsylvania. But there'd been no sign nor marker, and to Ethan it all looked the same: hills, trees, and the occasional stream that, if they were lucky, might have a bridge across it but most often had to be forded.

By midday, Ethan was completely done in. His head spun from heat and exhaustion, and his legs barely responded to his commands. His face was on fire, and he felt out of breath, like he simply could not get enough of the thick, humid air into his lungs.

All he could think of was an overwhelming desire to step off the road, lay down to sleep, and never get up again. He made up his mind that when they reached camp that evening, he would tell the captain he was quitting and going home. But for some reason, the thought, which by all reasoning should've brought a feeling of relief, instead filled him with dread. Dread of disappointing the great man—the man he admired, respected, and who had saved his father's life. He shuddered at the thought of the captain's reaction.

Ethan groaned as he forced himself to his feet. Every muscle in his body hurt, and every joint ached. Aside from that, his clothes were soaked through with sweat, and he was caked in a thick coating of dust that had turned to mud from the combination of humidity and perspiration. His sunburnt face felt like it was on fire. And though it was now evening and the sun was beginning to set, there was not yet any respite from the relentless heat that had pounded him since just after sunrise.

But despite his considerable discomfort and exhaustion, he was determined to speak with Captain Morgan before hitting his bedroll for the night. So he stumbled through the camp, weaving precariously between various groups of men already laid out in bunches across the field of dry, knee-high pasture grass. Morgan had ordered a halt at a place that held nothing better than a broad meadow beside the road. Ethan had been hoping for a place with a nice little stream, so he could slake his burning thirst with cool water and dunk his head to soothe his burning face, but such was not the case; he'd have to make do with warm canteen water and a hot dusty face this evening.

When he was about halfway across the field and the edge of the encampment was in sight, he spotted Captain Morgan at where he'd expected to find him: at the front of the formation. Morgan was standing on a large stump, arms folded in front of him, gazing out at the grand vista of ridgelines and trees below them spread across the valley ahead. And it was not lost on Ethan that Morgan was the only man in camp, other than himself, who wasn't already seated on the ground eating his hardtack and jerky or laid down to sleep.

He stepped up behind Morgan and said, "Excuse me, Captain Morgan, sir ..."

Morgan, turned. "Ah ... hello, Ethan."

"Sorry to disturb you, sir. But I ... I wished to speak with you for a moment."

"Certainly, Ethan. What's on your mind?" Morgan asked. Ethan noted that Morgan held a mild expression, and if he were suffering under the strain of the long day's hike, he showed no sign of it. But Ethan also noticed that Morgan didn't smile at him as he'd done whenever they'd met back in Winchester.

"Sir, I ... I don't think I can do this."

"Don't think you can do *what*, Ethan?"

"This march, sir. Today ... even before midday ... my head was swimming, and my legs hurt so bad I felt like I could not take another step. I felt like I was just going to collapse by the side of the road and never get up again."

Morgan nodded. "And *yet* ... here you are, Ethan," he answered in even tones, raising a questioning eyebrow. "Not dead *yet*, clearly."

"Yes, sir ... But—"

"Ethan ... do you remember what I told you when we first met, the day I brought your daddy home after his accident?"

Ethan looked down at his shoes, no longer able to meet Morgan's intense gaze. "Yes, sir … You said my childhood was over."

"Yep, that's right, son. I reckon this here's part of that: being a man. A man's got to do things that's painful and uncomfortable, and he's got to endure suffering such as he'd never imagined he could. And the *why* of it boils down to this, Ethan: when things get tough, a man either endures what's set in front of him, or he quits and dies. There ain't no third choice."

Ethan couldn't think of anything to say in answer, so there was a moment of awkward silence.

Then Morgan grumbled, and said, "I know you reckon me for a cruel taskmaster, or like some of the others, figure I'm pushing us hard just to prove we can beat ol' Hugh Stephenson and his boys from Berkely County to Boston so's to get some sort of bragging rights on 'em."

He chuckled, "I have to admit, there is *some* truth to that … I would love to wipe the smug look off'n Stephenson's face when he marches into Boston and finds we've already been there for a few days." He grinned for a moment, turning once again to gaze out at the vista, as if enjoying the image in his mind. But then he turned back to Ethan, a more serious expression returning.

"But there's more to it than just pride. Aside from the fact General Washington is in dire need of men, and every day that goes by is a day the Brits may choose to try 'n crush him, the truth is, we're marching off to war against the hardest army on earth. So it's bound to get a whole lot tougher before it ever gets easier again. This here march is one way to make sure our men are even harder than our enemy's men. We're gonna *need* to be."

Ethan nodded his understanding, but could think of nothing to say. His heart sank at the growing realization that his previous wishful thinking, that Morgan might just acquiesce and send him home, was never going to come to fruition.

Morgan gazed at Ethan for a long moment, then said, "Go get some rest, Ethan. Tomorrow ain't gonna be any easier, I promise you that. But at the end of the day, no matter how hard the going, you ain't gonna quit, 'cause I don't allow no shirking nor quitting in my company. Understood, son?"

Ethan nodded, "Yes, sir." Then he turned and started back to find his pack and his bedroll.

"Oh, Ethan …"

He stopped and turned back to look at Morgan, who now seemed to have the hint of a grin at the sides of his mouth.

"It may ease your mind to know … though these other fellas all seem hardened frontiersmen to you—and many of them are, no doubt—I seen in their eyes that many of 'em are suffering this march just as much as you are, maybe more so on account o' they ain't got your youthful vigor."

He laughed, "They're just too proud and Goddamned stubborn to say so in front of their fellows."

Ethan returned Morgan's grin and nodded. "Thank you for *that*, sir."

But then to Ethan's surprise, Morgan frowned, and adopted a more serious tone, "There's one more thing, *Private* … I'll not have any men in my company who're poor marksmen. And you bein' a city-raised fella, I suspect such is the case. So from here on, once we make camp and until it's too dark to see, one of the sergeants is gonna take you out for rifle practice. By the time we reach Boston you're gonna be takin' the eye from a squirrel at 200 paces—*on every shot*—or there'll be hell to pay. Understood?"

Ethan suppressed a groan, wondering how he'd even be able to hold a rifle, let alone hit anything, after a full day of marching, but all he said was, "Yes, sir," then turned and staggered back to his bedroll.

But if he'd turned to look back, he would've seen Captain Morgan nodding and beaming at Ethan's retreating back.

◄◄◄◄◄◆►►►►►

"So … the secret to hittin' the target, lad, is holding the rifle steady," Sergeant Timothy Murphy instructed in his strong Irish accent as he knelt next to Ethan, who lay prone with his rifle rested on a low stump.

Well, yes, tell me something less obvious, Ethan thought, but resisted saying aloud. That had always been the challenge for him on the few hunting trips he'd been on with his buddies. No matter what he did, the rifle seemed to jiggle just at the wrong time when he pulled the trigger.

Boom! The rifle belched fire and smoke. Both men looked out and saw that the pinecone Murphy had set upright on another stump some distance away had not moved. Nor did the stump appear to have been injured in the least, to Ethan's further annoyance. A complete miss.

"All right … not too shabby," Murphy said, rubbing the stubble on his chin. "But you was a might high and a pinch to the right on that one."

Though Ethan saw him as a grizzled old veteran, whose hair was graying in places and thinning in others, Ethan knew from an earlier conversation that Murphy had only just turned thirty years old.

"First thing is, you're grippin' the trigger too hard," he continued.

"Gripping the trigger?" Ethan responded.

"Yeah … lookie here," Murphy said, holding up his own hand and extending the trigger finger. "You're restin' the trigger in the crook here, in the joint twixt the first two bones on yer finger. When you do that, your grip's too tight, see … Reload, then try 'er again; only this time, rest just the pad of the tip of your finger on the trigger. It'll feel odd at first, but it'll help to keep you from jerkin' the rifle as you fire."

"All right," Ethan answered, happy to have finally received some concrete advice to try. His friends had always just made fun of him and told him he needed to practice more, but had never shown him any useful techniques.

Ethan stood and began the tedious process of reloading, but Murphy held up his hand, "Do it layin' down this time, lad … and faster than before. We gonna be in some mighty thick battles, I reckon, and you ain't gonna want to stand up to reload, lest you get your bloody head blowed clean off."

Ethan nodded, "Makes sense."

So Ethan proceeded to load the rifle laying flat on his back. It quickly became apparent why Murphy wanted him to practice this maneuver, as it proved many times more difficult than standing; first, getting the powder down the barrel was a challenge, then he realized he'd lost all leverage when shoving the stubborn lead ball down the barrel against the pressure of the rifling. The gun kept slipping from the grip of his left hand as he shoved hard on the ramrod with his right. Murphy suggested he rest the rifle's buttstock on the top of his foot, and this made it work much better. Finally, after several minutes of effort, he had the gun ready for another shot.

Murphy chuckled and said, "Practice that'n *every* time from now on, mind. The other fellas can do it twice in under a minute. You're gonna have to be doin' it that quick in a battle, lad."

Ethan shook his head in disbelief, wondering how he would ever be able to accomplish such a seemingly impossible task.

"Why are we using these hunting rifles anyway, Sarge? I heard the British only use military muskets with smooth bores. That they can reload those in a fraction of the time it takes to load these long, rifled guns."

But if Murphy was put off by the question, he didn't show it, grinning brightly. "You know, I asked the cap'n that very thing afore we started on our march. I'll tell you what he told me, lad: It's on account o' these-here rifled guns are brilliantly accurate at long range, don't you know. While them Brits may be able to spew out a whole lot o' lead balls in a hurry, they can't hope to hit anythin' specific more'n fifty paces or so out. So, they count on volume of fire—always up close, you see. With these here long rifles, an experienced hand can unseat a Brit general at three or four hundred yards. Think on what *that* would do in a battle, lad. Helps even the odds when they got more men and guns. Them Brits ain't gonna know what hit 'em. Hell, they don't even *make* rifles like ours, much less use them in battle."

"Shoot a *general?* I thought there were rules against shooting their officers."

"*Pah!* The only rule in war is winnin'. If killin' their bloody general be gettin' the job done ..." he grinned and shrugged.

Ethan returned to the stump, rested the rifle across it, and this time made sure he only touched the trigger with the pad of his finger.

Boom! He looked out and saw a puff of dirt rising up in front of the target, but the pinecone still stubbornly stood its ground.

"Better. Next time, don't be yankin' the trigger so hard … just squeeze 'er slowly 'til she goes off. Don't be in such a gull-durned hurry. Better accurate than fast, boy. Keep them sights on target, and *SLOOOWLY* squeeze.

"Also … breathe. Breathe, half-out, then stop …"

"What? I don't understand …"

"Take a few good deep breaths, let the last one half out, then stop and hold it. Helps ya to relax and calm down. Slows the heart and keeps the breathin' from jigglin' the aim. Remember, lad … *accurate*, not fast."

"Accurate … not fast. Yes, sir."

It took three more shots and a good deal of concentration trying to remember all of Murphy's various instructions for a mind and body that were weary to exhaustion from marching all day in the hot sun, but finally Ethan scored a direct hit, sending the intransigent pinecone spinning off into the woods.

Murphy looked down smiling, patted Ethan on the back, and said, "Nice shot, lad."

Ethan looked up, returning the sergeant's smile. "How far you say that was, Sarge? A hundred-fifty yards?"

Murphy laughed, "No … no. That there's only … oh, fifty or sixty yards, give or take, don't you know."

"Oh …" Ethan felt crestfallen. He wondered how he'd ever hit those squirrels out at the 200 yards Captain Morgan had spoken of.

"Still … not bad for the first day. Go get ya some chow and some shuteye, now. I'll do the same. We'll pick 'er up again tomorrow."

"Yes, sir. And … thank you, Sergeant."

As he walked back to where he'd dropped his pack, the long rifle slung over his shoulder, Ethan's mood began to improve, despite the amount of work it had taken to hit what the other men would consider a ridiculously easy shot. His thoughts had turned to what Murphy had said about the weapons he and the other of Morgan's men carried. He began considering how these long-range rifles might be used to great effect in a battle. Then it occurred to him what Captain Morgan likely had in mind for his new rifle company—to wield it as a new kind of weapon that their enemy would not be expecting and would have no good way to counter.

The thought brought a smile to his face, and a new appreciation for the captain's subtle military mind. And, to his surprise, he also felt a sudden enthusiasm for mastering this most uniquely American weapon, despite his less-than-stellar first day.

◄◄◄◄◄◆►►►►►

Sunday August 6, 1775 – Cambridge, Massachusetts Colony:

"All right boys … I know y'all are worn to the bone from these last three weeks, but … over yonder lies the end of your hard labors, for a time at least. There, just beyond that hill, sits General Washington's camp," Morgan gestured toward a rise that loomed up behind him as he stood in front of the men facing them. He'd unexpectedly called the march to a halt in the middle of the road, and Ethan resisted the urge to unsling his pack and his rifle, rest his hands on his knees, and gasp for air.

"Now, listen here, men: we're proud Virginians … the best of the best, and the toughest of the tough. I'll not have us staggering into camp like a bunch o' midnight drunkards. Aside from which, we'll likely be the first Southerners any o' these Northern colonists have ever even seen, and the first to join them as brothers in arms. Just by being here, we make this truly a continental army, not just in name.

"So, form up now, men. Two abreast, rifles on shoulders, chests out, and smiles on yer sorry faces. Let's show 'em what we're made of, Virginians.

"Sergeant Murphy will call out the cadence, just like we practiced it back on the green at Berry's Tavern. Who's with me?!" he shouted, raising his rifle above his head and shaking it with great enthusiasm and vigor, beaming brightly, as if he'd not just slogged more than 550 miles in three weeks of non-stop marching.

But to Ethan's amazement, the entire company of ninety-eight men unslung their rifles, raised them above their heads, and shook them, shouting, *"Huzzah! Huzzah! Huzzah!"* before scrambling to form up into two columns, even as their captain had ordered.

Ethan realized that he had no idea what to do, as he'd missed out on the marching drills back at Winchester, only having joined the company at the last minute when Morgan had fetched him from his family's house just as the rifle company was heading out of town. And there'd been no formal marching en route to Boston; there'd been no call for it.

But Ethan watched what the others were doing, got himself lined up next to one of the other men, put his rifle over his shoulder, and then after a moment of fumbling, managed to get his feet moving in the right order, as the sergeant called out, "Left … right … left. Left … right … left." in a regular cadence that was repeated over and over and over again, until Ethan was sure he would hear it all that night in his sleep. And to his surprise and shock, he realized that for the first time since leaving Winchester, he no longer felt exhausted, and his muscles no longer ached.

And he did feel proud to be a Virginian, marching to the oh-so-desperately needed aid of their fellow American soldiers outside Boston.

◄◄◄◄◄◆►►►►►

As Morgan's Riflemen marched down the road through the center of the American camp, men rushed forward to line the way and get a sight of this unexpected martial vision. The first men to arrive simply gawked in amazement. But wide-eyed shock quickly gave way to excitement and enthusiasm; soon, a spontaneous hat-waving cheer arose from the assembled troops as the Virginians marched past, chests puffed out, and smiles on faces as if they'd just marched here from down the block, and not from half a thousand grueling miles away.

Ethan felt goosebumps on his skin; this was a thrill such as he'd never before imagined—being enthusiastically cheered as a hero by thousands of men whom he'd never met. Suddenly all the hard, painful hiking and deprivation was driven completely from his mind.

Captain Morgan called them to a halt in the middle of the camp and turned to the left to face a group of officers who were striding toward them down a gently sloping lawn. With growing excitement, Ethan recognized the leader, tall and strong, though the last time he'd seen him back in Richmond, he'd not been wearing a uniform: General George Washington himself!

Captain Morgan stood to attention and saluted. General Washington stepped up in front of him, stopped, and returned the salute, breaking into a broad grin even as he lowered his right hand.

"Hello, George. It's been awhile," Morgan said, returning Washington's smile as the two men shook hands.

"Daniel … words cannot describe how happy I am to see you," Washington responded. And Ethan could see that he meant it; the general had a look that seemed to spell a mixture of both joy and relief.

"We've been a bit shorthanded around here," Washington continued. "Your bold presence alone will be a great boost to morale and our fighting spirit, Daniel. And it looks like you brought some fighters with you."

"That I have, George. That I have. The best shooters Frederick County has to offer. And such as we are, we are yours to command, sir."

Washington continued to smile, reaching out to pat Morgan on the back. "Please, Daniel, give over your command to one of your officers and have him set up your camp while you come join me in my headquarters. I wish to get caught up with the news from Virginia, and discuss the best use of your men."

The day after their arrival at Washington's camp, Ethan and several other of Morgan's men trudged up the dusty, rutted road through camp to where hot food was being served out for the midday meal. Captain Morgan had warned them not to expect much, that it'd likely be little better than what they'd endured on their long march. But Ethan felt like any change would be for the better; jerky and hardtack, occasionally supplemented with some game meat, apples, or corn acquired along the way, had gotten tiresome to his palate.

As they neared the field where they could see soldiers queued up for food, Ethan noticed another group of men coming toward them and moved to the right to let them pass. He happened to be the first man in the line, so his sudden movement prompted the rest of his company to follow suit, giving the oncoming men plenty of room to march past.

But at the last moment, Ethan noticed the man coming toward him wasn't paying attention, gazing down at his feet, with the wide brim of his hat covering his face. Too late Ethan realized they were going to collide, and called out, "Woah there!" as the top of the man's head banged into his shoulder, nearly sending both men spinning to the ground.

"Hey! You fellas watch where you're going," one of Ethan's company growled, to which the opposing men grumbled and cursed in reply.

But when the man who'd bumped Ethan looked up and the two met eyes, all angry thoughts left him. "*Levi?*" Ethan asked.

Levi stood a moment, wide-eyed, as if not recognizing his longtime friend at first. And then, to Ethan's utter surprise and amazement, Levi began to tear up, and said in a voice barely more than a whisper, "Oh, my God, it's you, Ethan ..." then stepped forward and wrapped his arms around him.

◄◄◄◄◆►►►►►

After Ethan had collected his lunch, a bowl of beef stew, he and Levi sat on the grass. After their initial surprise encounter, Levi had said little, not even to answer Ethan's question about Seth's whereabouts, insisting that Ethan first get his food, after which they could talk. Ethan thought this odd, and strangely out of character for Levi, who was rarely at a loss for words.

And even after they sat, Levi stared down at the grass in front of him, as if struggling with what to say. Ethan was perplexed; clearly something had happened that had strongly affected Levi, but he couldn't puzzle out what that might've been. So, to break the silence, he once again asked the question that was foremost on his mind, a question he assumed was simple and innocuous. "So, where's Seth, anyway? Back at your camp?"

But when Levi didn't immediately answer, and continued to stare down at his feet, Ethan experienced a sudden feeling of dread. "What is it, Levi?"

Levi looked up and met eyes with Ethan, and once again his eyes were watery. "He's gone, Ethan."

"Gone? Gone where?"

Levi looked back down and mumbled something that Ethan couldn't understand.

"What's that?"

"I said, *he's dead*, Ethan." Levi snapped out. "Dead … Killed in the battle … over at Bunker Hill."

Ethan felt like he'd been punched in the stomach. "*Oh* … oh, my God …"

He slowly shook his head as he thought of Seth's warm smile and happy demeanor. Then he envisioned Seth's family back home in Winchester, not yet knowing they'd never see their son again. Tears welled in his own eyes, and he felt choked, like he couldn't breathe. In that moment he knew with a sinking certainty that the war was not some kind of glorious adventure … It was a deadly serious, excruciatingly painful calamity.

Several days after their arrival in Cambridge, Ethan sat cross-legged on the grass gazing at the thirteen cards he held, trying to decide if the hand he'd been dealt was good or bad. He was only just learning Whist, and had not yet grasped all the nuances—his mother had been adamantly opposed to gambling, so he'd never previously played any card games. But here in camp, with little or no money to be had, the gambling wasn't particularly high stakes—buttons, various food items, and other odds and ends were the only wagers.

Ethan pulled out a six of diamonds and placed it on the small board that'd been pressed down into the grass at the center of the four seated men to serve as their table. His card was lower than the jack of diamonds that the man to his right had played, so he knew he wouldn't win the trick, but he thought it best to save his trump cards for later in the round when higher cards might be at stake. And besides, his partner, Private Peter Carland, seated opposite him, hadn't yet played his card, so there was still a chance they'd take the trick.

The player to his left played a ten of diamonds, so the jack was still high. Ethan looked across at Carland and felt hopeful as he detected a slight grin on his partner's face. But even as Carland reached for a card, he paused and looked up just as Ethan heard a rushing noise behind him: the sound of a man running up out of breath.

Ethan looked over his shoulder and saw it was Adam Kurtz, a fellow private. He'd pulled up from his run and now leaned over with his hands on his knees trying to catch his breath. "Hey, boys," he managed between gasps, "looks like we got ourselves a tussle with some Connecticut fellers … *C'mon!*"

The four card players jumped to their feet, the playing cards scattering. A half dozen other men of their company, who'd been lounging nearby, rushed over to join them.

"Follow me." Kurtz said, then turned and headed back the way he'd come at a trot. Ethan followed along in the group, though he was puzzled as to what it was all about. *Why would we be having a fight with men from our own side?* he wondered.

But there was no time for him to stop and ask any questions; within a few hundred yards, they arrived at the scene of the "tussle," and a chaotic scene it was. A dozen or more men wrestled, rolled on the grass, punched, kicked, and yelled in a maelstrom of activity that was hard for Ethan's eyes to follow.

The men who'd accompanied Ethan threw themselves into the fray, almost gleefully, to Ethan's surprise. But he held back, mouth agape, still not comprehending what was happening or why.

But even as he stood at the edge of the scene, gazing in wonder, a man he didn't recognize stepped up to him, gave him a smile that was missing its two front teeth, tipped his hat politely, then punched Ethan hard in the stomach.

Ethan doubled over in pain and slumped to the ground on his hands and knees, struggling to clear his head and regain his breath. He could see the man's feet standing in front of him and glanced up in time to see a fist pulled back, ready to deliver another blow. Ethan flinched, but the man hesitated, a frown creasing his brow. He shrugged and turned away, as if disappointed that Ethan had so little fight in him.

As he gasped for breath, struggling not to lose his recently eaten lunch, something tickled the back of Ethan's mind. Like a tiny, annoying voice, it taunted him, saying, *Are you going to just take that, Ethan? Just lay there like a whipped cur ... or are you going to stand up and fight like a man?*

Ethan dragged himself to his feet and answered himself in a rasping, inaudible whisper, *"I'm going to fight ..."*

He stumbled forward, looking around for the man who'd hit him. In a moment, he spotted the man, now down on all fours, punching at another of Morgan's men who was underneath him on the ground.

With little conscious thought, Ethan stepped up and swung his balled up right fist at the side of the man's face. The blow hit hard, sending a jolt up through Ethan's elbow all the way to his shoulder. For a moment, his arm went numb, but to his amazement and great satisfaction, the man crumpled to the ground like a sack of flour.

The man on the ground, whom Ethan now recognized as Corporal John Gassaway, rolled the unconscious man off, then gazed up at Ethan and grinned. Ethan reached out to offer Gassaway a hand up, but before they could make the connection, Ethan was bowled over by two other men who were grappling and punching at each other. So Ethan scrambled to his feet and launched himself into the fray, swinging punches at anyone he didn't recognize while trying to duck the same coming back in his direction.

After several furious minutes, Ethan looked around for anyone else to punch and realized everyone standing around him was someone he knew. They were all smiling, and patting each other on the back, despite the blackened eyes, swollen cheekbones, and bloodied lips they now sported.

Of the Connecticut men there was no sign. They'd been driven completely from the field, bloodied and soundly defeated by the Virginians.

And to Ethan's pleasure, several men patted him on the back and said, "Well done, son," as they passed. Corporal Gassaway was particularly effusive, beaming as he said, "You sure as hell poleaxed that one fella, Ethan! Thought he was gonna knock my teeth clean down my throat. But you done stepped up and give him a whack such as he ain't like to forget anytime soon ... if'n he remembers it at all. *Ha!*"

◄◄◄◄◄◆►►►►►

A week and a half after the fight between the riflemen from Virginia and the soldiers from Connecticut, Daniel Morgan stepped into George Washington's headquarters office, politely removing his hat. "George ... you wanted to see me?"

Washington, who stood gazing out a window, turned toward Daniel, gesturing toward a chair. After Daniel took his seat, Washington moved over in front of him and sat on the surface of the table that served as his desk.

"Daniel ... I know we've known each other a long time, but in camp it'd be best if you addressed me as 'General' or 'General Washington' rather than by my given name ..."

"*Oh.* Yes, yes, of course, George ... I mean *General*," he smiled and nodded. "Sorry ... old habits. Won't happen again."

"Thank you, Captain Morgan," Washington responded. It'd been a mild rebuke, but Daniel assumed it presaged a change in their relationship, which was to be expected under the circumstances, now that he thought about it.

"Was there anything else, sir?" Daniel asked.

"Well, yes, in fact." Washington leaned over and picked up a sheet of paper from his desk. He read, "Connecticut, Vermont, Massachusetts, Rhode Island …"

"Sir?"

"Daniel … this is, as I understand it, only a *partial* list of the units your men have brawled with in the last week or so."

Daniel shrugged, "Sounds about right."

Washington scowled. "Captain, I expect you to keep better control over your men."

Daniel returned the scowl with a frown of his own, "They're fighters, Geor—uh, *General*. That's what they do."

"Yes, yes, I understand that. But don't you think they'd be better served saving their fighting for the British?"

"Well, sir, that's just the problem. There's been no action against the enemy since we arrived. With the British penned up behind barricades in Boston, with no end in sight, there's little enough *real* fighting to keep the men occupied, and so … men will find *something* to do," he shrugged.

"We both know this stalemate won't last forever," Washington answered. "In the meantime, will you *please*, do your best to discourage the fighting. I'm receiving complaints daily from the other commanders, and would dearly love to focus my energy on dealing with the enemy rather than trouble between our own troops."

"Understood, sir. I'll speak to the men on it. And I'll think on giving them some better things to do with their time."

"Good, good; you do that. And thank you, Daniel. That will be much appreciated."

"Never mention it, General."

◄◄◄◄◄◆►►►►►

"All right, Ethan … remember, just like we practiced it. A few deep breaths to relax, light grip on the trigger. Line up the sights, nice, easy squeeze …"

Ethan listened distractedly to the sergeant's words, by now so ingrained they no longer required conscious thought. Instead, he focused on the red uniform tunic of the man who stood two hundred yards away, alternating between gazing out at the Americans through a spyglass and shouting—apparently haranguing his troops. The man was clearly an officer; the haughty attitude, elegantly embroidered uniform, and tall, highly decorative hat were unmistakable, even at this distance.

Ethan took one last breath, let it halfway out, then slowly squeezed the trigger. The hammer snapped forward, igniting the powder, which exploded, propelling the lead ball toward the enemy faster than the speed of sound.

As the smoke wafted away, Ethan gazed out in time to see the red-uniformed officer slump forward onto the wooden barricade, his fanciful, feathered hat tumbling to the ground in front of him.

A spontaneous cheer went up from the half-dozen riflemen who'd gathered around to watch the shot. Ethan felt strong hands grip his left arm and shake him, "You got 'im, Ethan. You got the bloody peacock," Sergeant Murphy crowed.

Ethan turned to the sergeant and beamed, "I did it, Sarge. Just like we practiced."

"Yep, you done good, lad," Murphy answered as he continued to smile and nod.

But then a dark cloud passed over Ethan's elation at his successful shot: *I wonder who he was. Did he have a wife and children? Was he a good man?* The thought gave him a sudden knot in his stomach.

His gloomy reverie was interrupted by another voice calling out, this one deep, booming, and unmistakable, "Nice shot, Ethan."

Ethan turned to look back over his shoulder, and was not surprised to see Captain Morgan standing there, gazing out at the British barricade through his spyglass. "Right through the center o' the chest ... just under two hundred paces," Morgan added, "Yep, very nice shot, Private."

Ethan nodded and forced a smile he no longer felt. Then another man strode up to stand next to Morgan. But this man was not smiling. In fact, he held a dark frown. And this was a man instantly recognizable to everyone in camp, General George Washington.

"A word, Captain Morgan," Washington said as he stepped up next to Morgan.

"Of course, General," Morgan answered, remembering to use Washington's rank this time.

"Walk with me, if you please," Washington said, and turned to stride back up the hill, away from the American barricade.

When they'd moved out of earshot of Morgan's troops, Washington stopped and turned to Daniel.

"Daniel … I am concerned about this current campaign you've instigated."

"*Campaign*, sir?"

"Yes, you know … using your long-range rifles to fire upon the British soldiers in their barricades and back behind their lines."

"Oh, *that*. Well, you *did* say I should find something more useful for my men to do. And I can think of nothing more useful in a war than killing the enemy.

"A very successful campaign it has been, too, sir, if I do say so myself. Last count, we've killed thirty-four soldiers and five officers … No … make that *six* officers, counting the one Private Chambers just downed."

Washington seemed to wince at the mention of *that* killing. "Yes, that's precisely what I'm referring to. Daniel, I'm not sure I'm comfortable with this kind of warfare—killing unsuspecting men from a distance and then celebrating the fact like it was no more than a pheasant hunt. Doesn't seem … *honorable* … somehow. Especially targeting the officers. There've been longstanding—if unspoken—understandings between the European powers on *not* targeting officers. I'm not sure I want to break those conventions under the present circumstances."

Morgan scowled, looking Washington hard in the eyes. "George," he began, once again reverting to the general's given name, "my men know nothing of the *European* way of fighting, only the *American* way. They do know if you kill an officer, that's likely better'n killing a hundred regular soldiers. I heard the

British lost more'n fifteen hundred soldiers and over a hundred officers at Bunker Hill. And I'll bet you a year's wages we both know which o' those numbers caused them the most pain."

Washington nodded, but continued to hold a dark frown. Morgan locked eyes with the general, showing no inclination to back down.

"George, with our long rifles, we can sit back behind our barricade and kill Brits all the live-long day. And there's not a damned thing they can do about it other than to stay out of sight. They've no weapon to counter our rifles; their smoothbore muskets are only good for close-up, massed assaults; they can't hope to hit our men at any distance. Do you really want to forgo that advantage, just so's not to offend your sense of honor?"

Washington looked thoughtful, but said nothing.

"General, if we fight the Brits in the European way, we'll lose, simple as that. You want to keep your honor, or would you rather win?"

"*Both*, preferably," Washington answered, then turned on his heels and strode away.

Morgan watched him go, then shrugged, turned, and walked back to his men, arriving just in time to see another shot fired, this one knocking a British messenger right out of his saddle as he trotted up to the barricade to deliver an order. Another cheer went up from the riflemen, and Morgan smiled. As long as Washington didn't strictly forbid it, he had every intention of continuing the practice.

◄◄◄◄◄◆►►►►►

"You wanted to see me, sir?" Ethan asked as he lowered his hand from saluting the captain, a gesture that still felt awkward and unnatural, as he'd never been asked to do it until they'd arrived at General Washington's camp.

Captain Morgan had remained seated at a small, crude dining table in the rough cabin that served as the rifle company's headquarters in camp.

"Yes, yes, have a seat, Ethan," Morgan said, gesturing toward a simple wooden chair opposite him at the table.

Ethan removed his three-cornered hat and took his seat, looking up at Morgan expectantly.

But to Ethan's surprise, Morgan didn't speak for several moments, holding a frown and gazing intently at Ethan as if debating with himself about something.

Finally, he nodded, and said, "Ethan, you're a smart fella, so I reckon you've been wondering why I fetched you out from behind your momma's skirts and dragged you halfway across the colonies."

Ethan didn't know what to say to this, so he just shrugged and nodded.

Morgan smiled. "It's to your credit for not asking before now, and just doing as you were told ... even when it was tough going there for a bit."

"Thank you for saying so, sir."

The serious expression returned to Morgan's face. "I expect you already know it weren't on account o' your skills with the rifle. Though you've come along well in that regard, I have to say."

Now it was Ethan's turn to smile. "That's been as much of a surprise to me as it has been to you, sir. And, to answer your question ... no, I never believed you picked me for any kind of fighting skill, since I never had any. But, well, to be honest, sir, at first, I just wanted to go with you so badly that I never wanted to question you on your reasons, lest you change your mind on it. And then, after, when the going got tough, as you say, I was too exhausted to think much about it.

"But now that things have settled in a bit here at camp, I have to admit to a little curiosity on it."

Morgan nodded, and once again held a thoughtful expression. And then, to Ethan's surprise, Morgan's face turned a shade red, and the great man looked down at the table as if embarrassed.

"Ethan ... when I was a young fella, I cared little for book learning. Long as I knew enough arithmetic to count money, I figured that was plenty good. Out wrangling wagons and fighting Indians and Frenchmen there weren't ever much call for reading and writing."

"Yes, sir … I'd imagine *not*," Ethan answered, wondering where this was going, and why his captain would be confiding in him about something he obviously wasn't proud of.

"Anyway … after I met Abigail … uh, Miss Abby, that is … I wanted to become the kind of man other men looked up to. Not just for fighting and hard laboring, but … for being a proper gentleman … a man of means. A leader … you know what I mean?"

"I … I think so, sir."

"So, a few years back, Abby started teaching me school lessons. But …" he shrugged, "it's been slow going, I'm afraid. What with selling the freight hauling business, starting up the farm, and then off fighting the French, and more recently the Indians in Lord Dunmore's War … Well, seems like there's never been enough time for it to stick well, as you might say."

Ethan nodded, understanding of his own part beginning to take shape in his mind.

"But now, being an officer in General Washington's army … well, there's gonna be need of reading and writing orders, issuing reports, requisitioning supplies, and so forth." He looked at Ethan expectantly, as if waiting for a response.

"And you want me to … *teach you?*" Ethan asked.

"Well, yes, that's part of it: to continue on where I left off with Miss Abby, you could say. But that's gonna take some time, as you'd imagine." He chuckled again, "'Specially seein's how we got ourselves some fighting to do."

Ethan smiled and nodded, "Yes, sir. I reckon so."

"In the meantime, I need you to be my eyes to read, and my hand to write."

"Oh. Yes, certainly, sir. I would be very happy to do that."

"Only …"

"Sir?"

"Nobody else can know. It wouldn't do for the other officers to know of my … *disadvantage*. Reckon some men would use that against me."

Ethan thought about that a moment, then nodded. He could imagine someone who wanted to advance in the ranks using that deficiency in a rival to their own advantage.

"I understand, Captain. It will be my honor to help you in that regard, and I'll not tell another soul. You can rely on me, sir."

Morgan now smiled brightly, stood up, and leaned across to pat Ethan on the shoulder, "Good man, good man. I knew I could count on you, Ethan."

Ethan also rose, returning the captain's smile, "Thank you, sir."

"Oh, and speaking of ... before you go, Ethan, I need you to read out something for me. It's an order that just came in from the general," Morgan said, holding out a sheet of parchment paper.

"Yes, sir," Ethan answered, taking the letter and gazing at it a moment. It was written out in a bold, firm hand. He read:

An Order by
his Excellency George Washington, Esq.
Commander in Chief, Continental Army
Headquarters, Cambridge, Aug. 20, 1775

Captain Daniel Morgan, Virginia Rifle Company commanding — you are hereby ordered forthwith and until further notice to cease and desist long-range targeting of British military personnel in the current state of siege warfare at Boston.

Our quartermaster has reported to me a most serious and critical shortage of ammunition which, in my humble opinion, renders your current operations too costly in materiel to be continued under the present circumstances.

G. Washington

Ethan looked up and met eyes with Morgan, who smiled wryly, snorting a mirthless laugh. "*Ammunition*, he says ..."

Ethan returned the smile knowingly, then shrugged. He knew from General Washington's expression when he'd witnessed

Ethan's shot out on the barricade that their commander-in-chief disapproved of their tactics.

Morgan slowly shook his head, then sighed. "Ethan, just go fetch Sergeant Murphy for me so's I can have him spread the word to the men. Then come on back later this evening after mess. We'll get started on some other papers I need to go through."

"Yes, sir," Ethan answered, and turned toward the door.

"Oh … one more thing, son …"

Ethan turned back, "Sir?"

"Despite your new *duties*, I still expect you to fight … and *hard*."

Ethan smiled and nodded, "That I can do, sir. And, that I *will* do."

Chapter 4. The Fourteenth Colony

"You are a small people, compared to those who with open arms invite you into a fellowship. A moment's reflection should convince you which will be most for your interest and happiness, to have all the rest of North America your unalterable friends, or your inveterate enemies."
- Continental Congress
Official Address to Quebec Province

Thursday August 31, 1775 – Cambridge, Massachusetts Colony:

"General, sorry to disturb you, sir, but Mr. Arnold is here to see you. *Per your request ...*"

Washington glanced up from the document he'd been reading, another tedious letter from the Continental Congress, once again explaining why his current dearth of ammunition could not be rectified anytime soon. The good news, though, was that they were finally sending desperately needed hard currency, in the form of several strongboxes of English and other European coinage.

He was not surprised to see his young aide de camp, Lieutenant Colonel John Trumbull, dressed in a crisp blue officer's uniform, standing just inside the headquarters office, having quietly pulled the door closed behind him.

"*Arnold ...?*" Washington asked, still mulling over his response to the congressional letter and not yet focusing on what Trumbull was trying to tell him.

"Yes, sir. You may recall ... one of the fellows who helped take Fort Ticonderoga from the British?"

"Ah, yes. *Benedict* Arnold. Yes, yes, send him in straightaway, if you please. Thank you, Mr. Trumbull."

"With pleasure, sir." Trumbull gave a quick nod before exiting the room. He returned a moment later, once again opening the door, this time making a formal introduction. "General

Washington, may I present Mr. Benedict Arnold, late officer of the Massachusetts militia forces."

A gentleman in his thirties, dressed in fine civilian clothes, stepped into Washington's office even as the general stood from his desk.

"General Washington, an honor and a pleasure, sir," Arnold said with a genuine, friendly smile.

The two exchanged a firm handshake rather than the usual salute, since Arnold was not presently commissioned in the army. Washington towered over Arnold, but the general was impressed with the man's bearing and the intensity of his pale eyes.

Washington offered his guest a chair opposite him, then retook his seat as Trumbull took his leave and re-closed the door.

"Mr. Arnold ... General Philip Schuyler, our military commander in New York, speaks highly of you, especially in reference to the recent capture of Fort Ticonderoga and its guns."

"Very gratifying to hear, sir."

"Though, to be honest, I must admit I've heard conflicting reports about the engagement," Washington continued in a more serious tone.

"*Oh?*" Arnold asked. But despite the question, he did not appear taken aback by the comment.

"Yes ... seems there was some sort of disagreement, between yourself and a gentleman named *Ethan Allen?*"

"Oh, yes ... *that.*" Arnold was quiet for a moment and gazed down at his hands. He looked back up and met eyes with Washington. "Mr. Allen and I ... didn't entirely see eye to eye during the Ticonderoga campaign, though we did manage to cooperate at the outset. Don't take this the wrong way, as I have a good deal of respect for Mr. Allen as an individual, but ... he's not really a *military* man—not really *officer* material, if you get my meaning. Oh, he is brave and bold enough ... heroic even, one might say. A natural born leader of men, maybe.

"But he has no mind for discipline, nor logistics, and no respect for proper chain of command."

Washington nodded, but said nothing, so Arnold continued.

"A brief example, sir, if you'll indulge me … After we'd taken Ticonderoga, I received word that the British outpost at Fort St. Johns on the Richelieu River, which flows north out of Lake Champlain, was but lightly manned, and we might take it by surprise and relieve it of its supplies and munitions. But Mr. Allen was elsewhere at the time, and I had no information as to the timing of his return. So, I determined to launch my own expedition to take the post while we still held the element of surprise. This we did in good order, finding the fort was indeed scarcely defended. In addition to supplies, we found anchored there a small British warship, the sloop *HMS Royal George*, which we seized along with a number of small, flat-bottomed boats of the kind the French call *bateaux*.

"But as we were returning down lake, we passed Mr. Allen and his men rowing up the lake, intent on occupying the St. Johns outpost we'd just vacated. But he'd failed to bring any food stocks with him in his canoes, so I was obliged to share out our own goods to his near starving men. Then I warned him that surely our raid had already raised the alarm, and the British would be moving to reinforce the area. But he stubbornly refused to turn back and continued on. I understand he was met by a large contingent of enemy reinforcements, even as I had warned, and was forced to retreat."

"I see," Washington nodded.

"Mr. Allen does not seem to appreciate potential rivals, and outright refused to recognize my overall command, despite my colonel's commission from the Massachusetts Committee of Safety, at a time when he held no official commission whatever. So, the best I was able to accomplish with him was an agreement to cooperate. I understand he has since spoken ill of me before the Congress—I can only presume the purpose was to make his own efforts seem the more heroic and noteworthy."

Washington nodded, but if he had any thoughts on the matter, he kept them to himself.

"Speaking of commissions, Mr. Arnold, I should very much appreciate if you would relate to me how it is that you are no longer in uniform."

"Yes, certainly, sir. I was commissioned as a colonel by the Massachusetts Committee of Safety, with the understanding I would recruit and lead an expedition whose purpose was the capture of Fort Ticonderoga. That mission was ultimately accomplished in due course, with the cooperation of other patriot forces. Then, in an apparent bid to better secure and hold the fort, the Connecticut Colony, with no prior consultation with the Massachusetts Committee of Safety that I am aware of, sent a force under the command of one Colonel Hinman to take command of the fort, which I rightly refused, having been given no instructions to do so. But rather than back my claim, the Massachusetts gentlemen who'd initially sent me issued orders that I was to yield my command to Hinman. So, perceiving a lack of support and appreciation from the Massachusetts Colony government, I felt that honor demanded I resign my commission, which I did forthwith."

Washington said nothing, but leaned back in his chair, his fingers tented, and his brows furrowed in a thoughtful manner.

"General … if you would forgive my boldness," Arnold interjected, "though it is, as I said, an honor to be here speaking with you, I have to wonder—"

"Why I have asked you here, Mr. Arnold?"

Arnold smiled, and shrugged, "Well, yes, sir …"

"A reasonable query, but before we continue … you will understand, the matters we are about to discuss require the utmost discretion."

"Understood, sir. From the outset of the conflict, I have been the very picture of loyalty to the American cause. May I say, with all due humility, that the very artillery that must surely soon grace this encampment, when it can be brought here from Ticonderoga, will serve as mute testament to my trustworthiness."

"Indeed. And for the providential acquisition of those guns, we are certainly most grateful, Mr. Arnold."

Arnold bowed his head in acknowledgment.

"Then let us discuss the topic at hand, shall we? After I received General Schuyler's own report on the events at Fort Ticonderoga—which, by the way, reflect those you have just related—and his glowing recommendation of your actions, I received word that you had just recently returned to the Boston area. It occurred to me that you might be just the man I'm looking for to participate in a particular expedition, which I have been discussing with General Schuyler."

Arnold sat up straighter in his chair, and his eyes widened, "The Canadian invasion, sir?"

Washington winced, but nodded. "Yes, I suppose it could be deemed that, but myself and others in the Congress intend it more as an effort to aid our fellow North Americans in resisting the tyranny currently reigning over us all. I suspect that yoke is particularly oppressive amongst the French Canadians who were taken into the empire by conquest only a dozen years ago."

Arnold nodded, "Yes, certainly sir. I have no doubt they would also welcome being out from under His Majesty's thumb."

"But I do have to admit, there is a military advantage to be gained, nonetheless," Washington shrugged.

"Clearly, sir. Not only would it separate the British from a vast wealth of natural resources, but it would also deprive them of a base of operations, from which they could launch their own attacks into the colonies through New York."

Washington smiled, "I see you've already been considering the notion, Mr. Arnold?"

"Indeed, I have, sir. In fact, I recently discussed the very idea with General Schuyler before departing New York."

"Excellent. Then we are in agreement, that an expedition led by General Schuyler—with sufficient supplies and reinforcements from this camp—launched from Fort Ticonderoga north up through Lake Champlain has a good chance of taking Montreal? With the hopes that the French Canadians would rise up and ultimately create a fourteenth American colony?"

But to Washington's surprise, Arnold did not immediately answer. Instead, he stood, and strode over to the window, gazing out. Then he gasped, and turned suddenly back toward the general, "*Oh.* Forgive me, sir. That was most rude of me ... It's just, you have excited my marshal spirit with discussion of this momentous undertaking, and my thoughts are racing at the possibilities."

Washington waved his hand dismissively, "No harm done, Mr. Arnold. Please be at your comfort and remain standing, if you will, and tell me what is on your mind concerning this matter."

"Thank you, sir. As for your statement concerning the French-speaking people of Canada, I agree wholeheartedly, General. From all I've heard and from those I've spoken with personally, they would welcome us with open arms, and likely join us in a fight against their longtime enemy. That they will agree to the notion of a fourteenth American colony, I have no doubt.

"But ... you may be gratified to know, that since my last meeting with General Schuyler in New York, I've given the idea a great deal of thought, and I have come up with a plan of which I believe you may approve."

"*Oh?* Do tell, Mr. Arnold ..."

"Thank you, sir. First of all, let me say I do agree with the idea of General Schuyler leading a force against Montreal, even as you have said. But rather than reenforcing him from this camp, I've in mind a separate but coordinated expedition: an assault on Quebec City itself."

"*Quebec?*" Washington's typically stoic face took on a puzzled expression. "Well, of course it will need to be taken ultimately in order to control Canada, but Quebec is a heavily fortified city surrounded by water, on excellent, defensible high ground. And unless you hope to run the gauntlet of British warships patrolling the mouth of the St. Lawrence, with no gunships of our own, the road to Quebec must first pass through Montreal."

"Yes, sir, that's true. But only if you follow the normal route. I have in mind a different road. And as for the town being fortified, I suspect that the British will believe as you do, sir—meaning no disrespect—that we must first pass through Montreal. So they assume they will have plenty of warning before there is any need to reinforce Quebec, and will have positioned the bulk of their forces in Montreal. If I am right, we may find the Quebec fortress but lightly defended, and easily taken."

"Hmm ... go on ..."

"Um … have you a map, sir? It needn't be precise, just of the Quebec Territory in general …"

"Oh, very likely. Allow me to inquire." Washington stood and strode to the door, immediately pulling it open.

"Mr. Trumbull, a moment of your time, please," Washington called out down the hallway.

Seconds later, Trumbull appeared once again before the general. "Sir?"

"Colonel Trumbull, do we happen to have a map of the Quebec Territory in this headquarters?"

"*Quebec*, sir? Oh, I don't know … but I shall have a look."

"Thank you; please do so straightaway."

Washington returned to his seat, leaving the door ajar behind him. Arnold retook his seat opposite Washington. There was an awkward silence for a few moments.

"Tea, Mr. Arnold?" Washington finally asked.

"Oh, thank you, but no," Arnold gave a short laugh. "Ever since the so-called Boston Tea Party I have sworn off tea in protest against His Majesty's onerous taxes. I have tried switching to coffee, but must confess it tends to give me a bit of indigestion."

"Ah. Very noble of you, certainly," Washington nodded. The general considered asking Arnold about his travels, or initiating some other small talk to pass the time, but couldn't quite bring himself to do it. Being a man of action, and with a strong belief in talking only when meaningful and necessary, he had little stomach for the usual trite pleasantries that most people regularly indulged in.

Thankfully, they were saved from any additional discomfort by Trumbull's swift return. He strode into the office and breathlessly announced, "I've found it, sir."

"Ah, excellent, Colonel. Just spread it out here on the desk. Facing Mr. Arnold, if you please—I shall come around to his side."

Moments later, the two men stood gazing down at the map. Arnold said nothing for several minutes, running his index finger along the map, as if trying to get his bearings.

"It's not especially accurate," he finally stated, "and lacking in many important details. Fortunately, I've managed to acquire a detailed map of the route, along with a journal." He chuckled. "Ironically provided courtesy of His Majesty's own Royal Military Engineer by name of John Montresor. This information will be invaluable if and when it comes time to launch our expedition. But for now, this map will suffice for an overview.

"I have heard you are a great expert at maps, sir, so I will endeavor not insult you with too many details, though I do believe it is important to establish the critical reference points, since mostly they are lacking on this map."

Washington nodded, but said nothing, gazing intently at the map on the desk.

"Here, in northern New York colony, sits Fort Ticonderoga, on the southern end of Lake Champlain, which is denoted by this dark patch of ink. So, General Schuyler's expedition would presumably travel up-lake to the Richelieu River, retake Fort St. Johns there—just as we did previously— then cross a narrow strip of land to the St. Lawrence River just opposite Montreal."

"Yes, that is certainly the most expeditious route," Washington agreed.

"And here *we* are at Cambridge just outside Boston, of course ..." Arnold continued, moving his finger southeasterly toward the coast of Massachusetts. "But rather than marching overland to join the assault on Montreal via New York, I would propose we follow this route." He traced his finger up the coast to the north. "This squiggly line here that runs in a generally north by northwest direction is intended to represent the Kennebec River, up in the Maine colony. Then, here you see where the Kennebec peters out, there is a series of small lakes or ponds, and then a small hump of land before a larger lake called Mégantic. You can see another wavy line taking up the route flowing from the north end of the lake. This line is intended to represent the Chaudière River and it—"

"Empties into the St. Lawrence River directly across from Quebec City!" Washington exclaimed.

Arnold looked over at the general and beamed.

"Precisely, sir."

◄◄◄◄◄◆►►►►►

As Benedict Arnold strode briskly down the road from Washington's camp, headed back to his boarding house in Cambridge, he was not surprised when his young protégé, twenty-five-year-old Eleazer Oswald, suddenly stepped forward from where he stood leaning against an enormous oak tree, turned, and stepped in next to him, matching his stride. Oswald, like Arnold, was from New Haven, Connecticut, and had been briefly enlisted in the Connecticut militia before joining Arnold on the Ticonderoga campaign.

"Well?"

"Well, *what?*" Arnold answered, trying to be coy, but not quite pulling it off, as he couldn't keep a subtle grin from touching the corners of his mouth.

"Ah. I see it went *well!*" Oswald exclaimed, grinning broadly. "What did he want? What did he say? Did he offer you a commission?"

Arnold chuckled. "You are most perceptive, Oswald, as I have said before—one of the things I like best about you. To answer your last question first, *no*, he did not offer me a commission—not *yet*, anyway. As for the rest … the discussion went better than I had any right to hope for."

"How do you mean, Benedict?"

Arnold slowly shook his head, and was thoughtful for a moment. "The general is the most direct person I believe I've ever met. We'd only just said our greetings and shook hands when he says, 'What do you think about invading Canada?'"

"*No.* He didn't!"

"Yes, he most certainly did. As you can imagine, I was nearly flabbergasted. But I was able to keep my wits about me well enough to speak coherently on the subject, and present to him my plan for a march up through the Maine wilderness, such as you and I have discussed at length."

"Oh, that *is* good news. And what did he think of the idea?"

"He was intrigued, I am certain. But he did not commit to anything, concluding that he would have to think on the matter for a time. He did leave open the possibility of another meeting to discuss the notion further."

"That seems hopeful, at least …" Oswald concluded.

But Arnold turned to him and smiled, "Better than hopeful … I believe our plans are going to come to fruition on this. That General Washington is going to grant me a commission, a captaincy at the least, and … if I play my cards right, he may put me in command of the entire eastern arm of the expedition."

"That would be excellent news, sir. It would go a long way toward restoring your good reputation after the damage done by that scoundrel Ethan Allen. And *that* wouldn't hurt your commercial prospects for after the conflict, one must believe—assuming this whole war business has a positive outcome, of course."

"Exactly what I was thinking, Oswald. Exactly what I was thinking …"

But even as Benedict Arnold contemplated these happy, hopeful thoughts, a dark cloud seemed to pass in front of the bright rays of his reverie, as it always seemed to in the past several months—ever since his wife's untimely death while he was off capturing Fort Ticonderoga. *I wonder what it will take to ease the pain of losing Margaret*, he wondered, *or if anything ever will.*

◄◄◄◄◄◆►►►►►

Two days later, Benedict Arnold was once again summoned to meet with General Washington. This time, when he arrived, he was immediately ushered into the general's office where he was greeted much more warmly than on the previous occasion.

After exchanging brief pleasantries, both men took their seats. In keeping with his usual manner, Washington got right to the point. "Mr. Arnold, I've been mulling over your proposal from the day before yesterday, and—pending General Schuyler's agreement, which I have already taken the liberty of requesting by courier—I have decided to proceed with your plan."

"Ah, excellent, sir. That is very grand news indeed." Arnold smiled brightly. Washington returned the smile.

"Further, I would like to offer you a colonel's commission in the Continental Army, and place you in charge of the eastern branch of the expedition—with the clear understanding and agreement that General Schuyler shall retain overall command of the engagement."

"I am honored, sir, by your faith in me. I swear by all that's holy, I shall not disappoint you. And as for the overall command, I couldn't agree more. I shall defer to the general in all matters, without exception."

"Good, good man. It is agreed, then." Washington stood, and Arnold did likewise. They exchanged a firm handshake, after which the general added, "Congratulations, *Colonel* Arnold." This time, despite his lack of uniform, Arnold stood to attention and saluted his new commanding officer. Washington returned the salute, and then they resumed their seats.

Arnold immediately handed across a rolled parchment tied with a ribbon, and a sheath of papers in a leather pouch.

"The engineer's map and journal?" Washington inquired.

"Yes, sir. I presumed you would wish to see them … *if* you were of a mind to proceed with the expedition, that is."

"Yes, yes, good thought. Thank you, Colonel."

They spent the next several hours poring over the map, reading through the associated journal entries, and discussing various scenarios, plans, expectations, and contingencies.

Finally satisfied, Washington looked Arnold in the eye and said, "This route seems a good one to me, and not especially difficult or onerous, though of course there are always the unknowns."

"Agreed, General."

"There *is* one other matter, I wish to make plain with you, before we go further," Washington announced, gazing intently at Arnold, who returned the look with a curious expression.

"Sir?"

"I would remind you that the primary motivation for this mission is the liberation of the Canadian people—that military objectives are secondary."

"Yes, General. I do recall your words on the matter from our last meeting."

"And in keeping with these objectives, it is important to keep in mind that the French are of the *Catholic* faith, while we Americans are, for the most part, Protestant. There is always the possibility for animosity between our peoples in that regard, and I am of the firm belief that one of the critical liberties we must fight for is the freedom of religion. We must not, under any circumstance, antagonize or alienate our Canadian brethren on account of their faith. Is that clearly understood, Colonel?"

"Absolutely, sir. And I wholeheartedly agree. I shall make it clear to everyone under my command, from the officers to the privates, to the lowliest camp followers, that any such behavior will not be tolerated, and will be viewed as an intentional act of sabotage against our mission, to be punished as such."

"Good. See that it is so, Colonel. Now let's start our preparations straightaway, under the assumption that General Schuyler will concur, and then the Congress will provide the funding, as expected.

"Since this is presumed to be a dangerous mission into enemy-held territory, I believe it would be best to take only companies that volunteer. That being said, I believe we should keep the expedition relatively small so that it may travel lightly, move quickly, and maintain the element of surprise as much as possible. Say ... somewhere between a thousand and fifteen hundred men."

"That sounds reasonable, sir."

Washington smiled and shook his head. "With the lack of action here lately, I sincerely expect you will have more volunteers than you can possibly take with you."

"Seems likely, sir. Perhaps we should just choose by drawing lots amongst all commanders who volunteer to go."

Washington was quiet for a moment, then said, "Yes, a lottery would serve ... but with one exception. Though I don't normally believe in 'rigging the game,' I must insist that you ensure one particular company be included."

"Oh?"

"Yes. Captain Daniel Morgan's Virginia Riflemen. They are the most experienced and hardy frontiersmen in our camp, which you should find invaluable on your trek through the wilderness. And their leader, Daniel Morgan, is … well, he is as tough a man, and as fine a leader of men as you will ever care to meet. I have known him a long time, and I can honestly say he is someone I would trust with my life without a second thought. But …"

"But?"

"Morgan and his men are … a bit rough around the edges, one might say. Not especially keen on military protocol and etiquette, much like your old *friend* Ethan Allen. To be perfectly honest, they have not been a pleasure to have around camp: fighting, carousing, gambling, and generally making a nuisance of themselves. Other than their deadly accuracy with those long rifles of theirs—which has caused our friends in red no small amount of angst, I must admit—they are ill-suited to a siege such as we are currently engaged in here at Boston. In short, I will be happy to be rid of them."

Arnold smiled and nodded. "Understood, sir. We shall hold our little lottery, but I will ensure that Captain Morgan is one of the winners."

"Thank you, Colonel. That shall remain between the two of us, by the way."

"Most certainly, sir."

◄◄◄◄◄◆►►►►►

Saturday September 2, 1775 – Cambridge, Massachusetts Colony:

"I'm telling you, Colonel, them're the wrong kind of boat. Those big, flat-bottomed vessels—the *bateaux*, the French call them—won't handle well in the rough water of a wilderness stream, and they'll be heavy as hell to portage. Canoes would work much better," Daniel Morgan concluded, sitting back in his chair and folding his arms across his chest.

But Benedict Arnold had done his homework, and was prepared for the argument. "We'd considered canoes, Captain, and I don't entirely disagree with you on some of your points. But the truth of the matter is, canoes require a great deal more skill to build, not to mention more time and money—luxuries we don't have at the moment, especially given we need to complete this mission before the Canadian winter sets in.

"And, though they are lighter, they can't carry anywhere near the load we'll require to ferry all the men and materiel. They also demand more specific expertise to man them effectively, and most of our men have never even been in a boat before. Lastly, they are more fragile, and so likely to be broken apart if they hit rocks, which seems highly probable where we are going.

"Besides which, we've already consummated a contract with a shipbuilder up in Maine, a man by the name of Colburn, to build our small fleet of *bateaux*, per our specifications. He's already begun work on them, and promises to complete them by the time we arrive at the mouth of the Kennebec."

Morgan scowled, but then shrugged. "Well, that's all well and good, Colonel, but at least acquire enough canoes for scouting and foraging. And ideally recruit some experienced Indians to man them. They'll be able to move much faster and through tighter spots than your bateaux."

"Agreed," Arnold nodded his head, dipped his pen in the inkwell, and made a note on a piece of paper on the table in front of him.

General Washington, who sat across the room behind his desk, said nothing, and kept his expression unreadable, looking from one man to the other as they spoke.

"There is one other matter before we adjourn, Captain; there will be three rifle companies assigned to forge ahead and ensure a smooth passage for the remainder of the force: yours and two others. It is only common sense that they should have a single commander, so I intend to appoint one of you captains for the post. I shall announce which of you that will be in due time."

"I'll tell you one thing for certain, Colonel," Morgan scowled, glaring across at his new commanding officer, "I'll not put my men under the command of some city-dwelling captain. Not out in the wilderness. Not when my men's lives are at stake."

But if Morgan thought to provoke Benedict Arnold, he was quickly disabused of the notion. Arnold simply looked up at him and answered in mild, even tones, "It is not for you to decide the command of the various units of the expedition, Captain Morgan. I am the commanding officer. I will decide who my officers will be, and none other."

"Yes, yes … it's for *you* to decide all right. You'd just better decide it rightly, is all I have to say," Morgan answered, then stood to his feet. "Permission to return to my men now, *sir?*"

"Permission granted," Arnold answered, and Morgan pivoted on his heels and strode from the room, closing the door none too gently behind him.

Washington shook his head, "I warned you …"

But Arnold smiled. "I like him, despite his … *rough edges*, I believe you called it. He's got grit, that's clear. And I have no doubt, from all you've said, he can lead his men in the wilds. But … I believe I should not let him know that I hold him in high regard any too soon. Let him stew a bit, so he'll have no doubt as to who is in command."

Washington nodded. "An interesting strategy, Colonel. I shall leave *that* in your capable hands."

"Thank you, sir."

◄◄◄◄◄◆►►►►►

Three days after Morgan's meeting with General Washington and Colonel Arnold, Ethan was sitting in his tent sharing another meal with Levi when Sergeant Murphy poked his head in and said, "Cap'n wants to see you now, Ethan."

"Oh, all right. I'll come by your camp tomorrow, Levi," he said as he hopped up and headed out the tent flap.

"Are you ready for your next lesson, sir?" Ethan asked as he stepped into the captain's tent and removed his hat. "I was thinking we'd review the difference between vowels and consonants this time, then perhaps discuss nouns versus verbs …" But Ethan's enthusiasm faded and his words trailed off when he noted the frown on his captain's face, and the lack of response to his inquiries.

Morgan handed across a sheet of paper, "Orders from Colonel Arnold," he said. Ethan noticed the captain seemed agitated, so he wasn't surprised when Morgan added, "Likely wants to relieve me of command for how I last spoke to him. Never was good at keeping my mouth shut when it was needed. Well, he'll not get away with it … George, uh, that is, *General Washington*, knows what I can do. He'll stick up for me."

Ethan stood where he was, listening to Morgan and nodding. Then, during a pause in his captain's rant, he asked, "Shall I read it out, sir?"

"Oh. Yes, yes, of course. Sorry, Ethan. Colonel Arnold just gets under my skin, is all … strutting about all high and mighty in his fancy uniform. Well, what are you waiting for, Ethan? *Read it.*"

"Yes, sir." Ethan read aloud:

By Order of
The honorable Benedict Arnold, Esq.
Colonel, Continental Army
Headquarters, Cambridge, Sep. 5, 1775

Captain Daniel Morgan, Virginia Rifle Company—you are hereby placed in charge of the three rifle companies under my command; such authority to continue until further notice. These three companies to consist of your own Virginia Riflemen, Cumberland County Pennsylvania Riflemen under Captain William Hendricks, and Lancaster County Pennsylvania Riflemen under Captain Matthew Smith.

You will meet with your subordinate officers straightaway to coordinate your preparation and order of march, and to determine your new command's needs in terms of supplies and ammunition, for an extended march of a minimum of sixty days, and report same to me at army headquarters in three days' time.

Benedict Arnold

Ethan looked up at Morgan expectantly, and had to suppress a smile at his commander's almost comical expression of shock and puzzlement.

"Well, I'll be damned …" Morgan finally managed to say, before sinking back down into his chair.

◄◄◄◄◄◆►►►►►

Because of his peculiar circumstance as Daniel Morgan's clandestine scribe, Ethan knew much more about the impending expedition to Canada than any of the other soldiers in the rifle company—more than a private should know, in fact. And though he liked being in the know, it put a strain on his relationship with the other men, who began to grumble that he was getting special attention and treatment from the captain. But he was sworn to secrecy, both concerning the true nature of his work for Morgan and the details of the impending expedition.

It came to a head one day when Private George Merchant, a tall muscular fellow, intentionally bumped him—hard—while they were coming back from noontime mess. "Oh, *sorry*," Merchant said in a sarcastic tone. "S'pose you'll go runnin' to Daddy now, an' get me punished."

"What do you mean? My father's half a thousand miles away. And besides, I can fight my own fights," Ethan snapped back with a glower.

And he realized that he meant it, and that it was true. Despite his youth and lanky frame, he'd now been in enough brawls around camp that he felt confident he could hold his own in a fist fight when he had to. Although, he had to admit to himself, fighting Merchant would be a tall order.

But Ethan's glare at Merchant turned to shock when the latter answered, "I heard you was Morgan's bastard, which is why he brought you along, and why you spend so much time together."

"*What?* Of all the ridiculous … *no!* No, I am *not* Captain Morgan's bastard," Ethan shot back with a scowl. But in that moment, he realized he needed some excuse for his close association with Morgan, and that the honest truth was not an option. So he figured something that was close enough to the truth would suffice.

"Look here, Merchant ... the only reason I knew the captain back in Winchester before the war was because he rescued my father, who'd rolled our wagon out on the road and was nearly killed. I ... I am ashamed to admit it, but ... Captain Morgan told me that as he was getting ready to march to Boston, he realized he was going to need an errand boy when he got to General Washington's camp—an aide, to run courier duty, and to attend to his needs in camp, and whatnot. So, remembering me, and knowing I was in need of employment with my father hurt and all, he brought me along, even though I wasn't any kind of a fighter."

"Oh," Merchant said, no longer making eye contact. "Never heard that ... sorry, Ethan ... Sorry about your father."

Ethan shrugged. "Not something a *soldier* wants to talk about. But ... now you know." *And now, everyone else will know too*, Ethan thought, with some relief—and a little embarrassment, he had to admit, after all the effort he'd made to fit in with the *real* fighters in the company.

But then Merchant looked up at him and smiled, "Well, I must admit, for an errand boy, you're turnin' into a pretty fair hand in a fight, Ethan. And not too bad with a rifle, neither, now that I think on it." He grinned, broadly, displaying a dirty set of teeth, one missing in the front. Then he reached out and gave Ethan a pat on the shoulder, chuckled, and turned back toward camp.

Two other privates who'd been watching the encounter nodded, then also turned and continued on their way, likely disappointed that there wasn't going to be a fight after all.

◄◄◄◄◆►►►►►

Ethan carried an armload of goods away from the quartermaster's tent, silently chastising himself for not bringing along his knapsack to haul it all away in. He'd been issued a sturdy, plain civilian short jacket of wool, a new linen shirt, a belt, socks, razor, soap, comb, and so on. As he trudged through camp down the dirt path crossing the pasture between the rows of tents, he struggled to keep from dropping anything, realizing his arms would be aching before he reached his own tent.

Up ahead he could see others from his own company also heading back to camp carrying heavy loads. But he smiled wryly noting that those older, more experienced men *had* brought along something to carry their goods in. *Another lesson learned*, he decided, *and not the last one that I'll learn the hard way.* He groaned, but pressed on.

As he passed between two tents, a man stepped out and fell in next to him, matching his strides. Ethan glanced over, but didn't recognize the fellow—an older man in his mid-thirties, a little on the heavy side, with shoulder-length brown hair tied back behind his head. A rather handsome-looking fellow, though his face was marred by a large scar across his left cheek. Likely a private like himself, Ethan decided, based on the rough, workmanlike clothing.

"Hello," Ethan offered, by way of asking why the fellow he'd never met had decided to walk so close next to him.

"'Ello me good chum, let me lend ya a 'and wiv that load," the fellow offered.

And though the offer was tempting, given the growing ache in his arms, Ethan thought better of it. For one, he'd heard rumors of thieving in the camps, and he didn't know this fellow. For all he knew the man would take his goods and run.

But more than that, he was taken aback by the fellow's accent; back in Williamsburg he'd talked to enough of Governor Dunmore's servants and soldiers to recognize the sound: *Cockney*, such as working-class Englishmen spoke in London's east end.

"You're British," Ethan blurted out, before he thought better of it.

The man snorted derisively, "Well, I woz birthed and bred there, for sure. An' I *was* in the Brit Army, no denyin'. But I've legged it, and joined you Yanks."

"Oh. And why would you do *that*, may I ask?" Ethan was genuinely curious, having never heard of any British soldiers switching sides in the conflict.

"Well, it's on account o' me bein' a big believer in freedom an' opportunity, innit? You ain't got a problem with a Brit fightin' on yer side, 'ave ya?" The man seemed friendly and smiled broadly as he spoke, but Ethan thought something about him seemed disingenuous.

"No … of course not. I'm sure we can use all the help we can get," Ethan answered honestly. But he still kept ahold of his goods.

"So 'ow come your lot's gettin' all the loot and the rest of us ain't gettin' nothin'?" the man asked, still smiling.

Ethan just shrugged. He'd gotten used to deflecting questions about the expedition, knowing that his close association with Captain Morgan gave him knowledge he shouldn't share. He figured if the officers wanted to tell their men what was going on, they would do it, but he wasn't going to.

They walked along in silence a few more steps before the fellow tipped his hat and said, "Nice meetin' ya, mate. Maybe we'll have a natter another time."

"Likewise," Ethan answered, and the man turned and strode off in the direction they'd come.

But after a few dozen more strides, Ethan looked back over his shoulder, out of curiosity, and wasn't surprised to see the man walking along with a couple of other fellows of Captain Morgan's company who were coming along after. *I wonder if he really is a thief*, Ethan thought, *or … something else? Maybe I should report it to the captain.*

But by the time he reached his tent and unloaded his burden on onto the floor, the encounter with the British deserter was all but forgotten.

Sunday September 10, 1775 – Cambridge, Massachusetts Colony:

Lieutenant John André, Seventh Regiment of Foot, Royal Welsh Fusiliers, strode confidently into the King's Arms Tavern in Cambridge, presently filled to the brim with colonial rebels.

But despite being entirely surrounded by the enemy, his air of self-confidence was not faked—it reflected his true feelings concerning his present circumstances. Oh, he *was* excited, keyed up with adrenaline pumping, but he felt no fear or anxiety.

For one, he was not wearing his British officer's uniform. Instead, he was dressed in the elegant finery of a young European gentleman of the highest order. Since he'd arrived at Boston with only his officer's uniform, he'd been forced to borrow the attire for his little *ruse de guerre*. Commanding General Gage had offered a set of his clothes, but though the two men were of a similar height, the general apparently enjoyed his libations and had put on a few pounds over the years in the service of his king. Fortunately, Gage's subordinate officer, General Henry Clinton was a younger and—more to the point—thinner man, so the problem was solved.

André's handsome visage was accoutered with a wig, powdered white with just a whiff of lavender, and a touch of rouge upon his lips for some color.

A voluminous white silk shirt with ruffled front and cuffs was worn underneath a white waistcoat, intricately embroidered with a pattern of multi-colored fancifully designed flowers and swirls around the collar and down both sides of the front.

Over this he wore an elegant silk frock coat of a navy-blue color that stopped at the waist in front but continued to the knees in back, where a slit ran up to the waist, allowing the gentleman to sit or ride without becoming tangled in the garment. The coat featured the same flowery embroidery as the waistcoat, not only around the collar and down the front, but also around the broad cuffs, highlighting the pockets on the sides, and running up a foot or so from the waistline in back.

The outfit was finished off with knee-length breeches of the same dark-blue silk, with embroidered knee bands holding up white silk stockings running under highly polished dark-blue leather shoes with large silver buckles. The shoes were slightly smaller than he normally wore, but he gamely ignored the discomfort.

André had decided that the contrast between the dark blue coat and breeches and the white underneath looked particularly stunning.

His reasoning for the attire was that he believed the best way to not appear suspicious was the opposite of what one might expect. Rather than to try to blend in, he'd decided to make a spectacle. *That* would ensure no one would suspect he was anything other than what he appeared to be.

But the other thing he had going for him was that he would forgo his normal King's high English accent and instead speak English with a French accent—as an aristocrat from the countryside east of Paris, to be exact. He'd even invented a realistic persona and backstory for the occasion, though he doubted it would be necessary. Not unless he happened to meet another Frenchman.

André was even prepared for questions as to why a French aristocrat might find himself in the small, backwater town of Cambridge, Massachusetts—particularly at a time when the major city next door, Boston, was basically shut down. He was ready to respond to any such queries that he was in Cambridge in hopes of gaining an audience with General Washington in order to offer his services as an officer. André had heard that British spies in Paris were reporting a veritable flood of young French gentlemen queueing up at the door of the flat occupied by the American celebrity statesman Benjamin Franklin in hopes of getting an officer's commission in the new colonial army. Such a commission would not only be a boost to their reputation in their home country, but would offer them a chance for adventure, and to strike a blow against their ancient enemy, Britain.

André had even briefly considered actually attempting to speak with Washington—that might be extremely interesting. But he'd quickly discarded the idea as too dangerous; by all accounts the general was no fool, and there was a good chance he would see through the charade.

As he stepped into the crowded room, André slowly peeled off a pair of white silk gloves. He surreptitiously scanned the room for the fellow he sought, as if he were only looking for an open seat at a table, which in fact he was—that was one of the tells that would identify the man. André was not surprised to see many eyes turned his way, though none dared make actual eye contact. These were working-class men turned soldiers: common laborers, farmers, tradesmen. They were not used to seeing a fine gentleman in their midst. But he knew, despite the current rebellion, some traditions still held true, even in the colonies: commoners would always defer to aristocrats. No one would speak an ill word to him, and all would defer to him, of that he was certain.

After a few moments, he spotted the fellow he was looking for. Just as General Gage had described him: burly looking fellow, mid-thirties, dark hair, handsome face, but with a vivid scar on his left cheek. And, as expected, there was an open seat at the table opposite the man, though the rest of the place was packed to capacity. *Apparently General Washington feels no impending threat from our side if he allows his men such recreations,* he thought. *I shall have to inform General Gage of that …*

He turned and strode toward the table with the open seat, then paused and addressed the man with the scar. "Excuse *moi, monsieur,* but may I have this seat?" he asked with a slight bow.

The man glanced up at him but did not make eye contact, just as André would've expected, given that the man seated was actually a British soldier in disguise. Even if the man suspected that André was *not* actually a French gentleman, he *would* guess that he was a British officer, and so would naturally defer either way.

"Evenin' guv'nor. Turns out I'm a bit parched, but presently I'm skint. So I've been savin' this seat for a bloke wot'll buy me a pint."

André tilted his head as if considering, then nodded. It was the proper opening, and the man spoke the Cockney dialect of English as expected. So André responded, "Very well, *monsieur.* As this appears to be the only open seat at the moment, and I too am … how you say … *parched?* It would be my honor to purchase your libations, in return for said accommodations, no?"

The man grinned and gestured toward the seat. "Well, in that case, sit down and make yerself at 'ome, guv'nor."

"*Merci*," André answered, then made a show of brushing off the bench with one of his gloves before sitting. A skinny looking young fellow seated on the bench next to him slid down a bit to give the great man more room.

The soldier, who introduced himself as Thomas Whittingham, whistled and waved until the proprietor showed up with two pints of ale. Of course, in keeping with character, André asked if the ostler had any cognac in the house, or at least a good Bordeaux, but the man bowed his head and answered, "Sorry, m'lord … only ale. No spirits and no wine. My apologies, m'lord."

"Ah, well," André sighed, "then ale it must be. *Merci*, my good man." He made a show of pulling out a finely embroidered coin purse, retrieving two coins, and setting them in the proprietor's hand.

"Thank ye kindly, m'lord," the man answered, bowing as he backed away.

As the two men took a swallow, André prepared to give the code phrase that would initiate the exchange of information. That would've been the sensible thing to do: have a drink, get the goods, and get out quickly.

But André hesitated. Not out of any suspicion or fear; the man was clearly the deserter-turned-spy that General Gage had described. No, André's motives were now more personal and selfish; he found he was enjoying himself. It brought to mind the pleasurable months he'd spent in Paris before the present conflict. He was fluent in five languages, and many different dialects, and had decided to challenge himself to see if he could pass for an upper-crust Parisian in their very midst. And after a few stumbles, he was able to perfect the accent and dialect such that not even French natives could tell.

Aside from the fact that the French were still on reasonably good terms with the Americans, it was one of the reasons he had decided to use a French accent on this occasion. He'd not spent enough time in the colonies—yet—to feel confident he could fool a native. But no one could tell he wasn't French. Not even a Frenchman.

So, when he'd heard General Gage was looking for a volunteer to sneak across rebel lines to retrieve vital information from a spy, André had jumped at the chance. He always counted on his good luck, and the chance to impress the commander-in-chief was one of those rare events in life that could not have been planned and simply could not be refused, despite the risks.

André had only just arrived in Boston—after a long and arduous voyage at the request of the Governor of Canada, General Guy Carleton—starting from the Seventh Regiment's posting at Fort St. Johns just south of Montreal, up the St. Lawrence River to Halifax, and then by ship to Boston. His mission had been to confer with General Gage concerning the commander's expectations of another rebel attack on Canada now that they held Fort Ticonderoga. And to his surprise, the general had responded that he believed he might have just such information. But he was having trouble finding the right man to retrieve it from the spy he'd planted in Washington's camp.

André had always loved acting in plays, getting into character, and playing a role. And now he was doing it for a righteous purpose, not just for mere entertainment; if all went well, he would gather valuable intelligence on the rebels' activities and gain the favor of the commander-in-chief in the process.

And then it occurred to him that he could continue his present play acting not merely for personal pleasure, but with an actual, legitimate purpose in mind. He could test the general's spy to see how believable he was. This could prove useful, as it would speak to the reliability of the information he'd gathered. If the rebels didn't trust the man, it was highly unlikely he would've learned anything useful. Instead, he might just make something up to please the general.

"Out of curiosity, let me ask you, *monsieur* ... do I not detect a strong *English* accent, sir? From London, even, if I am not mistaken. Not *colonial* at all, to my ear ..."

"Blimy, but you're bang on, guv'nor. East-ender ... birthed and bred in earshot of Bow Bells, I was."

"Then am I misinformed, *monsieur?* I was made to understand there was currently … a *conflict* of sorts? Between the colonials and the English crown, *no?*"

"Aye, you have the right of it, sir. I even done me service in the King's army, I 'ave. But I've no love for the royals … meanin' no offence to yer 'onor," he answered, with an apologetic bow.

André waved dismissively.

Then the man adopted a more serious expression as he continued, "You see, I've taken a likin' to the way these Yanks think, innit? Freedom, respectin' the law, free market without all them bleedin' taxes, and all that malarkey. I couldn't in good conscience go in all guns blazin' to knock those beliefs, so when I spotted me chance to swap sides, I grabbed it."

Hmm, André thought, *the man is good. Very convincing … maybe a little too convincing. Wonder if he really has switched allegiance.*

But what André said was, "*Oui, oui.* Very commendable, *monsieur*, very commendable. And I, for one, agree. It seems to me the English have become … how you say … *oppressive* … in their governance of the colonies, no?"

The man nodded, then raised his glass. For the briefest of moments, he did make eye contact as he said, "To the colonies …"

André nodded, smiled slightly, and raised his own glass, "To the colonies, *monsieur* … May they gain that which they so richly deserve."

He enjoyed the irony of the statement, and it appeared to not be lost on his companion, who sported a quick grin before taking his swallow.

André then decided it was time to complete the transaction, so he gave the pre-planned code phrase: "May God's blessings smile upon you, my good fellow."

The man nodded and answered, "Oh, thankee, guv'nor. And may he hold you ever in the palm of his hand, Your Lordship." As he did so, André felt a touch on his knee. He already held his left hand under the table, so it was a simple matter to receive the tiny folded piece of paper and slip it up his frilly sleeve.

Then he raised the glass, downed the last sip, and stood. "Very refreshing, *merci*. I may acquire a taste for this American ale after all, no? *Monsieur … adieu.*"

Chapter 5. The Expedition

"Some journeys take us far from home.
Some adventures lead us to our destiny."
- C.S. Lewis
The Lion, the Witch, and the Wardrobe

Monday September 11, 1775 – the road to Newburyport, Massachusetts Colony:

As Ethan strode along, once again at the very back of the column of Captain Morgan's Virginia Riflemen, he was reminded of the grueling trek from Virginia to Boston. But to his astonishment, he found that he was actually enjoying the march this time, even though the load was much heavier, they were already several hours into it, and once again the sun beat down mercilessly on his back.

He smiled at the thought of how much he'd changed in just a few months. This time, there'd been no boyish excitement at the prospect of a grand adventure, nor the sudden sinking realization that the hike was much harder than he'd ever imagined possible. No, this time he only felt happy relief that they were finally on the move again, and that they were off to do something meaningful in the war effort after weeks of mostly idle siege routine.

Ethan was also pleased that—though he *was* still the last man in Captain Morgan's original company—he was *not* the last man in the entire column this time. Two other rifle companies from Pennsylvania followed along behind in a long, twisting line. Their original ninety-eight riflemen had grown to nearly three hundred. And because of his access to the captain's official correspondence, he knew that the entire expedition numbered well over a thousand, divided into four battalions: Captain Morgan's and three others.

It was a heady feeling to be part of something so big and so important, and he felt pride swelling in his breast. He imagined his father would be proud of him when he returned home again.

IF I return home again, he reminded himself. *This is, after all, a dangerous expedition into the unknown, against an unknown force of the enemy. But surely Captain Morgan knows what he's doing. Not to mention General Washington; he'd not send us out if he wasn't very confident of our success … would he?*

Ethan's reverie was interrupted when he sensed the sudden presence of a man marching behind him. The last time he'd looked back, the next rifle company was a hundred yards or more behind. *Surely they've not closed the distance so quickly?* he thought. *Captain Morgan is well known for setting a fast pace. Hard to believe the others would overtake us.*

He turned to see what was going on, then tripped and nearly fell in his surprise. "*Levi!*" he said. "What are *you* doing here?"

Levi smiled at Ethan's look of surprise, "Catching up to you, obviously."

"But … I didn't know your company was coming on this expedition."

"It isn't," Levi answered.

"But then—"

"I just decided to come," Levi responded, stepping up the pace so that he could walk next to Ethan.

"Levi, you can't just *decide* to come along."

"Why not? I wanted to, so why shouldn't I?"

"Well, because it's against the rules … you know, to abandon your company. They'll miss you, and think you're a deserter."

"Oh, *that*. Well, they can *think* whatever they want, but that don't make it true."

"What do you mean?"

"The truth is, Ethan, that I never enlisted in *any* company. Seth and I were standing around watching men march by with rifles, heading for Charles Town, when one of 'em looks at us and says, 'Come on along boys … you don't want to miss the fun.'

"So we looked at each other, shrugged, and followed along. Next thing you know, we're up at Bunker Hill behind a fence and a pile of dirt, getting shot at by British soldiers. And then Seth was—

"Well, anyway … I never signed up or nothin'. So nobody can say I'm a deserter, see?"

"All right, I see what you mean. But … not sure what the captain will say. He's mighty particular about who he takes into his Virginia Riflemen." Then Ethan chuckled, "Present company excepted."

Levi laughed with him. "Oh, I don't know, Ethan. I've been watching you. You look bigger now, or something. Like you fit in with 'em, though I never woulda believed it back at Winchester."

"Thanks, Levi … I guess."

They walked along in silence for a time. Finally, Ethan said, "I'll have a talk with the captain when we make camp … see if he'll allow you to stay."

"Thanks, Ethan."

"But, one question I have to ask first, Levi …"

"Yes?"

"*Why?* Why did you want to come on this march?"

"Because you're going, Ethan. I got nowhere else to be."

◄◄◄◄◄◆►►►►►

Later that evening, Ethan spoke with Daniel Morgan in the command tent. He was surprised at his captain's apparent nonchalance concerning Levi's wish to join the company.

"Can he shoot a rifle?" Morgan asked.

"Yes, sir. He's a farm boy from Winchester. He's been out hunting in the woods since he was old enough to walk. He's *way* better at shooting than me."

Morgan smiled. "There was a time not too distant where I would've laughed at that answer. But I seen some skill on you lately when it comes to wrangling the long rifle, so I'll just leave that be.

"Did he bring his own rifle and kit? I'll not have anyone begging for handouts, nor borrowing gear."

"Yes, sir—I checked his haversack myself. Rifle, ammunition, clothing, and enough dry food for several weeks."

"And you'll vouch for him? He'll keep up the pace, not shirk his duties, nor cause any undue mischief?"

"Yes, sir. I've known Levi for years. Though he has a sarcastic streak and a mean sense of humor at times, he's a good, reliable fellow. And he can fight; he was in that Bunker Hill battle. Fired his rifle into their ranks on several charges. Says he even shot one Brit up close, and likely killed another when he whacked him in the head with the rifle butt."

Morgan laughed, "Sounds like he'll fit right in. Tell him to come see me so's he can sign into the rolls."

"Yes, sir. Thank you, sir."

But Morgan suddenly had a serious look on his face. "You may *not* thank me later, Ethan, if you're starving out in the woods and you gotta share out yer last piece of meat with him."

Ethan thought this an odd statement, but didn't know how to answer, so he just saluted and went back to tell Levi the good news.

◄◄◄◄◄◆►►►►►

Thursday September 14, 1775 – off the coast of Massachusetts Colony:

British Vice Admiral Samuel Graves sat at the dining table in the captain's quarters of *HMS Preston*, a fifty-gun ship of the line commanded by Captain John Robinson, presently seated across from him. Graves felt quite sated after a pleasant meal of boiled fish, various spiced meats, and savory vegetables. He sighed contentedly as he leaned back in his seat, savoring a glass of claret and nibling on a generous offering of sweetmeats.

Graves held the wine glass up toward Robinson who raised his own goblet, mistakenly assuming the admiral was about to propose a toast.

"A fine vintage, wouldn't you say, Robinson," Graves said.

"Oh, yes—certainly, sir. From *Bordeaux*, isn't it?" Robinson replied.

"Quite. Liberated it, along with a great number of other bottles, from a French man o' war after the Battle of Quiberon Bay back in the great war with France, now some dozen years past. Ah, that was a glorious day, Robinson. I can still see the flames rising into the night above the devastated French fleet."

"Oh, yes, sir. Certainly one of the greatest victories in the long, storied history of the Royal Navy," Robinson agreed, nodding enthusiastically before indulging in another sip. "Wish I could've been there with you, sir."

As they chatted amiably, the two men paid little attention to the servants clearing away the dishes. But their pleasant exchange was interrupted by a knock at the door.

"Come, if you must," Captain Robinson called out, setting his glass on the table in front of him before turning to see what it might be about. A young ensign stepped in at the door, stood to attention, and snapped his hand to his forehead in salute. "Sorry to disturb you, sirs, but the packet just arrived from Boston …"

"Yes, yes, and what of it?" Robinson demanded. "I sincerely doubt there's anything in it that is so urgent as to disturb our repast."

"No, sir … uhm, I mean, yes, sir. It's just …" he extended his hand toward the admiral and held out a folded sheet of paper, sealed with wax. "There was *this* … it is addressed to your honor, Admiral. And it is annotated 'Most urgent – from General T. Gage, British Army Commanding, North America.'"

"*Oh.*" Graves responded, snatching the paper from the young man's hand, immediately breaking the seal, and unfolding the letter.

"You are dismissed, ensign," Captain Robinson said, waving his hand at the young officer.

"Thank you, sir," the ensign responded, backing away with a bow before turning to retreat from the room.

When Graves finished reading the page, he grunted and handed the letter across to Robinson.

Captain Robinson read:

General Thomas Gage,
Commander-In-Chief,
British Army of North America

Boston, Sep. 8, 1775

Vice Admiral Samuel Graves, Commanding Royal Navy,
North American Station:

I have obtained certain advice by a loyal subject posing as a deserter within the rebels' encampment that about 1,500 men have marched from Cambridge which are said to be going to Canada by way of Newburyport. I believe it is their intention to assault our naval station at Halifax by land.

I should think it exceedingly necessary that some small vessel would be immediately dispatched to watch their movements, such that it might give timely notice to the Naval Force you have in that Province in order to defeat any attempts the rebels may make by sea to come upon that land.

Thomas Gage

Robinson smiled wickedly as he looked up at Admiral Graves. "Ah, perhaps we shall finally have a little fun with these rebel vermin. I expect it will be some good sport to send several hundreds of the wretches directly to the bottom of the sea. After properly bloodying them, of course."

"Quite so," Graves answered with a curt nod. But he did not return Robinson's smile, instead downing the last of his wine in one long swallow.

Sunday September 17, 1775 – Newburyport, Massachusetts Colony:

As expected, Morgan's rifle battalion was the first to reach Newburyport, bivouacking in a field on the outskirts of town after a two-day march. Not only were the experienced frontiersmen the

95

hardiest and quickest travelers, but Colonel Arnold had intentionally staggered the march over the course of several days in an attempt to not raise British suspicions were they to observe a massed American formation on the move. Also, sending the three battalions the thirty-four miles overland piecemeal would allow each to seek out reasonable accommodations along the way and not clog the meager roadways.

Now, five days after Morgan's arrival, Arnold's entire expedition was finally assembled in a broad pasture outside town, including the colonel himself and his ever-present aide, the non-commissioned gentleman Eleazer Oswald, and the other members of Arnold's headquarters staff. Oswald was one of several young gentlemen who'd volunteered for the mission in hopes of gaining a commission afterward. Ethan had recently learned of the practice when he'd spoken to another such man who'd accompanied the expedition by the name of Aaron Burr. Burr, who was only a few years Ethan's senior, was a handsome, charming fellow who'd graduated from Princeton college just before the conflict broke out. Ethan admired Burr, as he too aspired to attend college himself one day, he hoped straight after the present troubles were over.

Ethan stood to attention, rifle at his side, two rows back from the front of Daniel Morgan's battalion. Their battalion had, as Ethan understood it, the traditional "position of honor" on the right side of the entire formation, with the other battalions off to their left. And though it might appear a motley, disheveled formation to an experienced military man—even the officers mostly wore civilian clothing, and all the soldiers carried mismatched weaponry including the various swords and short spears of the officers—to Ethan it was the grandest thing he'd ever seen. Row upon row of stern-visaged, vigorous looking men standing to attention, rifles or muskets at their sides, sunshine reflecting off brightly colored flags and pennants flapping in a light morning breeze. Though there was not yet any standard flag for the Continental Army, and the shapes varied from rectangular or square to triangular, many had bold slogans painted or sewn on them, including "Liberty," "Loyal Protest," and "An Appeal to Heaven" among many others.

And though they may not have been up to the "spit and polish" standards of the British Army, Ethan reminded himself that these were the same sort of regular fellows who'd given the empire all it could handle at Concord, and at Bunker Hill.

Civilians from Newburyport and the surrounding area had come out to see the show; hundreds gathered at the fence line surrounding the pasture, waving, shouting encouragement, and generally adopting a festive holiday spirit. Clearly the locals were in favor of the American cause, and had turned out to show their enthusiastic support.

In front of the formation strode Colonel Arnold himself in a dark-blue officer's uniform coat, gold-embroidered waistcoat wrapped in a scarlet sash, knee-length highly polished boots, and a tall, three-cornered hat perched jauntily upon his head. From the trim on the hat to the epaulets on his shoulders and the great row of buttons down each side of the front of his coat, all were trimmed in gold that sparkled in the sunlight.

By contrast, few of the other officers wore uniforms at all, and of those that did, most were red—leftovers of the British army from the French and Indian War. But those officers without uniforms could be identified by a gathered piece of brightly colored ribbon, called a cockade, pinned to their hats or a sash across their chests. Others could be identified simply by the fact that their civilian clothing was of a finer cut than that of the common soldiers.

Ironically, despite his seeming high access to officers at General Washington's camp, this was the first time Ethan had seen Colonel Arnold up close. In his courier duties, he'd always exchanged written messages with the headquarters aides. He noted that the colonel was short of stature, especially compared to the towering Daniel Morgan, but was sturdily built, like a man who could not be easily budged from a spot if he didn't wish to be. Ethan thought Arnold an especially handsome man, with a healthful, ruddy complexion, thick dark hair tied neatly behind his head, and the most intense eyes—like those of some kind of predatory bird—icy pale, piercing, and thoroughly intimidating. All in all, Ethan thought Arnold the very picture of what a high-ranking army officer *should* look like. Maybe even more so than General Washington, if that were possible.

Ethan felt a nudge at his left elbow, and took a quick glance in that direction knowing it was Levi standing there. His friend graced him with a quick grin and a wink, sharing in the excitement of the moment. Ethan returned the grin and a nod, *I know what you mean*, he thought.

He snapped his head back to the front just in time to see Colonel Arnold staring straight at him. *Oops.*

But after a quick frown, Arnold moved on by, continuing down the front of the formation to Ethan's left. Ethan breathed a sigh of relief.

After Colonel Arnold finished his review, the troops were ordered out by company to march in formation across the field, marching in step, drilling with their rifles: stopping, turning, then moving in various directions to the shouted commands of their officers. Fortunately for Ethan, Morgan's men had had plenty of time to practice back at Cambridge after General Washington had ordered a stop to the long-range sniping of the British. Captain Morgan, a firm believer in keeping his men productively occupied, had marched them for several hours each day, so much that Ethan felt like he could now do the maneuvers in his sleep.

At one point, Ethan's company marched close by a formation moving in the opposite direction: one of Colonel Greene's groups of regular soldiers, with smoothbore muskets mounted with bayonets slung over their shoulders. As they marched past Greene's men, something in the other column caught Ethan's eye, and he glanced in that direction; it was a man he thought he recognized: handsome, stout, with a wicked scar on the left side of his face. *Wait … is that the British deserter who quizzed me back at camp?* Ethan wondered.

But the man was already past, and there was no chance to get a better look. *If it was him, didn't he say his company wasn't getting the supplies doled out for the expedition, which implies they weren't among those selected? What's he doing here, then? I must mention this to Captain Morgan.*

But then one of the sergeants called out the next turn, and Ethan nearly missed it, so had to scramble to keep from bumping into Levi, who frowned at him. By the time Ethan had straightened himself out, the man with the scar was all but forgotten.

When the review in the mustering field was complete, the entire force turned and marched in parade formation along the road leading to town, and then continued down the main street to the First Presbyterian Church. There the companies took turns marching inside, colors flying and drums beating, standing to attention with their rifles at their sides as Chaplain Spring preached a short sermon before blessing them and the success of their mission.

At the end of the day, Ethan collapsed in his bedroll, exhausted. But he was so excited by the events of the day and the news that they would be loaded onto ships come the morrow, that it was a long time before he finally succumbed to sleep. But even as his mind slipped away, a faraway voice seemed to whisper, *But what about the man with the scar?* This last conscious thought as he drifted away seemed to bring on troubling dreams that disturbed his badly needed slumber.

◄◄◄◄◄◆►►►►►

Tuesday September 19, 1775 – Newburyport, Massachusetts Colony:

Ethan awoke at first light to the sound of creaking timbers and crying seabirds. In his first conscious breath he could taste the salt from a fresh, sea breeze.

He sat up in his bedroll and stretched, feeling sore in various odd places from sleeping on the hard planks of the ship's hold. Noticing Levi still slept soundly, he reached over and gave him a shake.

Levi sat up, rubbing his eyes. "*What?*" he asked blearily.

"Morning, sleepyhead."

Levi groaned and lay back down, "Go away. It's barely light out …"

It was a true statement, but gazing around the room, Ethan could see that most of the men were already awake and gone—presumably up on the deck of the schooner.

"C'mon, time to rise and shine." Ethan gave Levi another shake.

"All right, all right … I'll rise, but I sure ain't doin' no shinin'."

Ethan chuckled. "Fair enough. C'mon, let's see if they're serving out any breakfast."

When they climbed the stairs up onto the ship's deck, they were greeted by a magnificent sight: puffy clouds sailed by in a cobalt blue sky. Flags and pennants flashed in the sunlight over a fleet of eleven small ships tied up along the Newburyport wharf, each one packed to overflowing with the expedition's soldiers, approximately a hundred to a ship. And though the ships were all of a similar size, they, like their human cargo, were a hodgepodge collection of different configurations: single-masted sloops, double-masted fishing boats, and coastal traders—so named because they were used to transport loads of goods along the shallower waters of the coastline. There were also a few sleek schooners, including the one Captain Morgan and his original Virginians—including Ethan and Levi—were assigned to, named *Broad Bay*.

And to their great delight, Ethan and Levi discovered that breakfast was indeed being served out, and the smell of it finally brought Levi fully awake. The townsfolk, swarming along the shoreline, had feted the soldiers with all manner of cooked food to see them off on their journey: bacon, ham, eggs, sausages, boiled potatoes, and many different kinds of fruit. Ethan and Levi wasted no time queueing up in line to get their share.

When they'd finished their fine repast, the two friends parted company. By agreement, whenever Ethan went to check in with the captain, Levi would find something else to do—Ethan figured it wouldn't look good if Levi was also spending undue time hanging about their commander.

When Ethan located Captain Morgan up at the ship's bow and slipped up behind him, he was surprised to see Colonel Arnold was also there, and the two were conversing.

"… scout ships we sent up the coast day before yesterday have returned. They've had no sightings," Arnold was saying as Ethan stepped up within earshot, careful to stay behind Morgan and out of Arnold's line of sight.

"Don't mean they ain't there. Sea's a big place …" Morgan answered.

"Agreed, Captain. But it's at least some good news, as far as it goes. And we've a fair wind, blowing in a northerly direction. So I mean to launch within the hour."

"Very good, Colonel," Morgan answered, amiably.

Ethan thought it a positive sign that the two great men seemed to be getting along better, now that the expedition was underway. He assumed Arnold's decision to place Morgan in charge of the rifle battalion had gone a long way toward smoothing things over. But he also found himself wondering what the two men had been discussing. *Sightings of what?* he wondered.

So, after Colonel Arnold had stepped away, presumably to relay to his staff officers his orders to launch the ships, Ethan decided to press his position with the captain to see if he could find out what it was all about.

"Morning, sir," he said to Morgan's back, as the latter gazed out across the harbor. The captain turned and answered, "Oh, good morning, Ethan."

"Just checking if you needed me for anything, sir," Ethan prompted.

"No, no … not just at the moment, Ethan. But thanks for checking."

"Mind if I ask you a question, sir?"

Morgan tilted his head at him and gave him a wry grin. "Seems like you just did."

"Oh, yes. Sorry, sir. I couldn't help overhearing what the colonel said about scout ships, and that there were no *sightings*. Sightings of what? If you don't mind my asking."

"No, I don't mind, Ethan, though I'd think the answer ought to be as plain as the nose on your face. We're at war with the greatest empire on earth, which happens to have the biggest navy on earth. What you reckon'll happen if one of them big ol' warships finds our scraggly little armada of overloaded, unarmed ships out at sea?"

Ethan absorbed the question with a sudden, sick feeling. "Uh … nothing good, I imagine," he finally answered as the precariousness of their present circumstances began to sink in.

"Yep, that's right, son … nothing at all good."

An hour later, after much rushing about and shouted commands, which seemed like a foreign tongue to Ethan, the small squadron was underway. The large, enthusiastic crowd that had gathered on the waterfront to see them off waved handkerchiefs and shouted huzzahs.

And Ethan was gratified to see that Colonel Arnold, who was said to be an experienced sailor himself, having run a successful fleet of merchant ships before the war, had chosen to stay aboard the *Broad Bay*, designating it the flagship of the flotilla. And he seemed to take his role as commodore seriously, standing next to the ship's captain, giving him instructions to be relayed to the other ships via small, colorful flags the sailors called semaphores.

The little fleet of ships sailed briskly out of the harbor with drums beating, music playing, and banners flying. It was a glorious sight, which Ethan would've enjoyed a lot more if it weren't for the sudden, haunting question that his morning conversation with the captain had triggered: *But what about the British warships, waiting out there somewhere … just over the horizon?*

◄◄◄◄◄◆►►►►►

As morning wore into afternoon, clouds rolled in, obscuring the sun. Ethan felt a sudden cold bite to the wind that hadn't been there when they'd set out in the morning, so he went and fetched his jacket from his haversack.

Talking to the other men, he noted that Captain Morgan wasn't the only one concerned about the threat of British warships; it was the major topic of conversation among both soldiers and sailors, and many anxious eyes scanned the horizon in all directions, fearing the sight of sails in the distance.

And then, in the early afternoon, sails *were* spotted, and there was much shouting and pointing among the soldiers on deck. But after several tense minutes, one of the sailors called out, "They're just fishing boats, boys ... two of 'em. Nothin' to worry over."

Ethan could feel the anxiety draining from his body, and he realized he'd been clutching the ship's rail so hard that his hands ached when he loosened his grip.

When the fishing boats neared, *Broad Bay* bore up alongside the closest one, as the other ships of the fleet held back. Colonel Arnold hailed the newcomers, asking where they'd come from and if they'd seen any British warships. But the fishermen answered they'd come down the coast from northern Maine, and had encountered no British ships, neither warships nor merchant vessels, to the relief of all onboard.

So the fleet continued on, leaving the fishing boats behind.

By sunset, the clouds had thickened and the seas had become rough, rocking the small schooner violently from side to side as it heaved up rolling waves and dipped down into their troughs.

Many of the soldiers, most of whom had never been to sea, became ill, and Ethan watched dozens of men at a time leaning over the rails to relieve their tortured stomachs. He felt grateful he wasn't among them; for reasons he did not comprehend, the rough waters did not seem to affect him. The same could not be said for poor Levi, who gave up his lunch to the hungry sea before retreating to his bedroll, looking thoroughly beaten and miserable.

By nightfall, the high winds had become gale force, howling and screaming through the rigging, accompanied by a driving rain that forced the soldiers to seek shelter in the crowded cargo holds below decks. As Ethan made his way to the gangway, he noticed Colonel Arnold, his feet planted wide, still standing by the ship's pilot, a greatcoat wrapped around him, as if no amount of wind or weather could affect him. And towering over him was the unmistakable form of Daniel Morgan, arms folded across his chest. Morgan stood like an obstinate stone, as if daring the storm to move him and refusing to be outbraved by his commanding officer.

A few minutes later, as Ethan lay down to try and get some sleep, he pulled the blanket up over his nose in an attempt to block the strong smell of vomit that pervaded the ship. And despite the noise, motion, and stench, he quickly faded off. But sometime deep in the night, he felt a sudden change in the ship's motion and realized that they were no longer moving forward; they were at anchor. He said a quick prayer of thanks, then almost immediately fell back asleep.

◄◄◄◄◄◆►►►►►

The next morning, Ethan was once again awake just as the sun was rising, or at least the sky was a lighter shade of gray, he decided. He shivered as he pulled off his blanket, and immediately donned his coat. He looked over at Levi, but decided to let him sleep this time.

When Ethan came out on deck, he saw that there had been another dramatic change in the weather. The previous night's gale had apparently blown over, leaving in its wake a thick fog accompanied by a drizzling rain.

The ships were already underway, and Ethan could now see that the place Colonel Arnold had ordered them anchored during the night was a small island, which was now slipping past in the fog. Sergeants standing at the top of the gangway were passing orders to each man coming up from below to maintain silence so the sailors could call out soundings and land sightings to their captain.

Ethan went over to the rail on the landward side and gazed out through the thick fog, ignoring the raindrops streaming off his own hat. From time to time, he spotted through the gloom a glimpse of tall, dark pine or fir trees, towering over jagged rock outcroppings. He now understood the sailors' concern—they were hugging the coastline so that they'd not miss the Kennebec River mouth in the fog. But doing so was a very dicey business, with the chances of hitting a shoal or a jutting spur of land a very high probability.

Ethan could hear the unease in the sailors' voices as they called out to each other and to their captain. And once again, he had to remind himself to stop gripping the railing to the point of cramping up his hands.

Two anxious hours later, the sailor clinging to the tallest mast called out, "River mouth ahoy! Two points off the larboard bow!" to the great relief of all onboard.

They'd made it safely to Maine, somehow evading the ever-lurking British war fleet.

◄◄◄◄◆►►►►

The frightful night, and gloomy, tense early morning, gave way to warm, bright, cloudless sunshine as midday approached. The little fleet now sailed merrily up the smooth waters of the Kennebec River, flags once again flying and passengers lighthearted having left all fear of the British Navy behind at the river's estuary. Colonel Arnold himself ran up a flag he'd had made for this special occasion, to show his defiance of the enemy for all to see. It was a large, square scarlet flag with the word "LIBERTY" stitched on it in bold white letters. The soldiers and sailors all gave a cheer when it unfurled in the breeze.

A short time later, Levi finally made his appearance on deck, looking pale and shaken, but clearly on the mend.

"Come look at this place, Levi," Ethan said, waving his friend over toward the railing.

"*Oh my*, Ethan … When they said we were going to Maine, I pictured a raw wilderness: nothing but trees, water, and rocks. But this …" he whistled. "This is just … *beautiful*."

Ethan nodded his agreement. Against all expectation, the banks of the Kennebec were lined with cultivated fields and neatly maintained small farms nestled among the gigantic evergreen trees—spruce, hemlock, and pine—that towered over the rooftops. Deciduous trees lining the riverbank were already beginning to show bright fall colors of red, orange, and yellow. Ethan found this a particular wonder, as it was only mid-September. But then when he thought about how far north he'd traveled from his Virginia home, it actually made sense.

The occasional small village, inn, or church dotted the landscape on the shoreline. Along one stretch of river, they passed a row of stately homes on a high bluff overlooking the picturesque valley.

And the locals rushed to the shore and waved as they passed, clearly in support of the rebel cause. Others passed by in their own boats—coasters, fishing boats, and bateaux—headed downstream. These exchanged greetings and shouted words of encouragement to the soldiers. Ethan reckoned the locals knew enough about the course of the river to rightly guess the Americans were headed up the Kennebec to attack the Brits in Canada.

As sunset approached, they anchored for the night near an island in the stream, and all enjoyed a much more peaceful evening and night's sleep than on the previous stormy night at sea. Colonel Arnold, Captain Morgan, and several of the other officers went ashore and were welcomed into the homes of the inhabitants.

The next day, they weighed anchor once again and continued the journey upstream. But here the river narrowed, and became windier. The sailors clearly had to work harder to navigate the tricky currents. Throughout the day, the eleven ships gradually became separated such that Ethan could no longer see the ship directly behind them, even on the few longer straight stretches. Here there were still plenty of small farms, but now the rocky shoreline was nearly bursting at the seams with colorful birds of all description: ducks, geese, herons, egrets, and any number of small songbirds. And any time Ethan gazed into the waters, he could see that the stream was teeming with fish of all sizes, from minnows to veritable monsters. He was pretty sure he wasn't the only man aboard who wished he'd brought along a fishing pole.

In the late afternoon, they came to a very wide, relatively shallow still area in the river, which was surrounded by a marsh and swarming with waterfowl. A man fishing from a small canoe told them the place was called Merry Meeting Bay. Ethan thought the name appropriate, and apparently so did Colonel Arnold, who ordered a stop for the night, so that all the ships might rendezvous and regroup. By nightfall, all eleven vessels had arrived and anchored, and it was indeed a merry meeting.

In the morning, as they prepared to resume their journey, the sailors discovered, to their amazement, that the water level in the already shallow bay had dropped precipitously overnight. Since there'd been no change in the flow of the river, they finally concluded that the area was somehow affected by the ocean's tides, despite being some twenty miles inland.

After a brief discussion, Colonel Arnold decided to continue upstream, despite the risks. He was concerned if the waters continued to drain from the bay that the ships might flounder and become stuck or damaged.

And for a time, the decision seemed a good one, as *Broad Bay* and several other ships were able to successfully cross the wide, shallow marsh to reach the deeper, narrower stream beyond. But they'd not gone more than a few miles when a rider galloping along the shoreline flagged them down. He was a local who'd ridden ahead from the marsh to tell Colonel Arnold that two of the ships had become stuck in the bay.

So Arnold ordered one of the ships to turn back, offload the men, and tow the stranded ships back into the deeper stream with their row boats. This they were successfully able to do, but it made for a long day of little progress for the expedition.

Thursday September 21, 1775 – off the coast of Massachusetts Colony:

"Thank you for agreeing to meet with me, Admiral," British Army General Henry Clinton said as he sat across from Vice Admiral Samuel Graves in the captain's quarters aboard *HMS Preston*. "I am here at the behest of General Gage, who wishes to know the details of your interdiction of the rebel expedition, after they set sail from Newburyport on nineteen September. He has it from a reliable source that eleven small vessels left those shores carrying approximately 1,500 armed rebels, and he wishes to know how many of said vessels were destroyed or captured by the Royal Navy under your command, and approximately how many enemy combatants were either killed or captured."

Admiral Graves did not immediately answer the question, but crossed his arms and scowled as his face turned a dark shade of red. "General Gage has no authority whatsoever to *demand* a report of me or my activities," he growled.

General Clinton was taken aback by this response, as he had been expecting a simple, factual report of the action. "Oh, *no* sir. My apologies if I made it seem as if the general were *demanding* anything of you. And I was remiss in not first stating that he sends his highest regards and compliments. I should have said … General Gage respectfully wishes to inquire as to the status of the rebel ships and their passengers, if you should be so kind as to provide that information at this time, sir."

And though he was hoping this statement of contrition would mollify the admiral, Clinton was once again surprised by Graves's reaction. Instead of a begrudging acceptance of the apology, the admiral uncrossed his arms, placed his hands on the table in front of him, and seemed to suddenly deflate, sagging in his chair.

"I have nothing to report, General," he finally said in low tones.

"Excuse me, sir? *Nothing?* I … I don't understand …"

"You heard me, General. I have nothing to report. We have interdicted *no* rebel vessels."

"But, sir … General Gage sent you specific intelligence on the rebel expedition—numbers, dates, suspected destination and objectives, which he'd obtained at great cost from loyalists and spies in his employ. Did the rebels somehow manage to elude the ships you sent to watch for them?"

"There were no ships sent, General."

"No … *ships*, sir? But—"

"General Gage seems to think I have a simple task here: 'Just follow and intercept eleven small rebel vessels,' he says. But the truth of the matter is, I have only twenty-six warships with which I must patrol more than a thousand miles of coastline, from Nova Scotia to Florida. Most of those ships are too large to sail close enough to the shoreline to find and follow the small rebel vessels the general reported. I'm sorry, but our first priority must be interception of rebel commerce, as we are tasked with doing by Parliament and His Majesty."

"*Commerce?* You have prioritized capturing merchant vessels hauling wool, coal, or tea over military transports ferrying armed enemy troops? Hostiles intent on attacking the Empire and its soldiers?"

It was now the general's turn to become red in the face, as he could feel his temper flaring. He could easily envision the veritable thunderstorm that would rage back at headquarters in Boston when he informed General Gage of the admiral's response.

"I have given you answer, General Clinton. You may report same back to General Gage. You are dismissed." And before Clinton could respond, Graves stood, turned his back, and paced over to gaze out the aft window of the captain's quarters.

Clinton also stood, replaced his hat, clicked his boot heals together, and saluted. "Sir!" he snapped, then pivoted and marched from the room.

"*Merchant vessels* ..." he muttered to himself as he stepped out onto the deck of the warship, slowly shaking his head, "... of all the ridiculous, incompetent nonsense ..."

The boson, who was to ferry him back to shore in the ship's tender, asked, "Excuse me, sir?"

Clinton looked up at the sailor, embarrassed he'd spoken his thoughts aloud. "Oh ... nothing ... nothing at all, mister."

◄◄◄◄◄◆►►►►►

Thursday September 21, 1775 – Gardinerston, Maine (Massachusetts Colony):

As *Broad Bay* neared the pre-agreed rendezvous point at Gardinerston, Maine, Ethan once again felt an almost palpable sense of anxiety running through the ship—reflected on the face of their commander, Colonel Arnold, who paced back forth at the bow of the ship, with Daniel Morgan standing close by.

But this time, the anxiety had nothing to do with the British Navy, the tricky river currents, nor the weather; the small town of

Gardinerston on the Kennebec River housed Reuben Colburn's boatyard, and Colburn was the man who had promised Arnold and General Washington that he would build 200 small boats for the expedition less than eighteen days earlier. Neither Washington nor Arnold had heard a word from Colburn since the ambitious undertaking had been agreed upon and the contract inked.

So now, as they approached the town, no one knew if the boats Colburn had promised would be there, or if the entire expedition to this point had been for naught.

As usual on the voyage, Ethan stood as close to Captain Morgan as propriety would allow. This had been made easier and less controversial by his cover story that he was Morgan's errand boy, a story that had apparently even reached the ear of Colonel Arnold, who seemed to accept his regular presence along with his own aides and staff.

The ship's captain, a man named Samuel Banks, stepped up to Arnold and Morgan and said, "According to what I've been told by the locals, Gardinerston should be just around this bend. We'll enter a broad, relatively straight stretch of river, with most of the town to larboard. However, I'm told Mr. Colburn's house and boatyard will be to the starboard side. We should see it momentarily."

And then, to Ethan's surprise, Colonel Arnold turned away from the bow and faced the stern of the ship, directly in front of Morgan, who seemed puzzled by this and asked, "Colonel?"

Arnold gave Morgan a wry smile. "Captain, I find I am as tightly wound as a clock … not knowing if our bold expedition will have failed utterly before it could really begin. I prefer to learn the truth by the reaction on your face."

Morgan smiled, and nodded, then turned his gaze to the riverbank ahead, which was rocky, with large evergreens growing right down to the waterline, their thick branches overhanging the stream.

And though Arnold gazed intently at Morgan's face in order to gauge his reaction to the scene unfolding ahead, in the end it was not Morgan's visage that gave it away; after several tense minutes, a spontaneous cheer rose up from the crew, with hats waving, much pointing, and enthusiastic shouting. Arnold exchanged a smile with Morgan, then turned to take in the glorious sight.

Row upon row of small, flat-bottomed bateaux lined the gently sloping grass banks of the river to their right. In their midst stood a gentleman, stoutly built, his hat in his hand, waving it vigorously at the boat. Colonel Arnold removed his own hat and waved back at the gentleman, who gave a bow, then gestured toward his fleet of small boats. Reuben Colburn had been as good as his word and had pulled off the requisite minor miracle; to everyone's relief, the expedition's desperately needed boats had been completed on time.

Broad Bay anchored midstream in the Kennebec, and the ship's two rowboats were used to ferry Colonel Arnold, his staff officers, and Daniel Morgan to the east bank, and then groups of soldiers to the town on the west bank, to give them a respite from days aboard ship. As usual, the flagship had led the flotilla and was the first to arrive, with the remaining ten ships expected to catch up to her within the next day or two.

After confirming with Captain Morgan that his services would not be required anytime soon, Ethan decided to accompany the men, mostly so he could spend some more time with Levi.

After greeting Reuben Colburn, Arnold and Morgan went to inspect the boats. But as they walked up to the very first bateau—which was identical to all the others: flat bottomed with high sides and pointed at both bow and stern—Arnold's smile turned to a frown. He stopped and looked at Colburn a moment before striding over to the boat, standing at its stern, then pacing off the distance to its bow.

There he stopped and turned to Colburn. "Mr. Colburn ... these boats are only twenty-six feet long and quite narrow ... I was expecting thirty feet at the least, and much wider. Our contract clearly called for a boat big enough for six or seven men with all their provisions and baggage, of approximately one hundred pounds per man. These will hold only three or four men and not nearly the full amount of baggage. Please explain yourself, sir."

Colburn turned a bit red in the face, but did not turn from Arnold's severe gaze. "Well, yes, Colonel ... I will admit I exercised a bit of liberty in that regard ..."

"Liberty?"

"You see ... back at Cambridge when we met with General Washington, your specifications seemed reasonable to me, which is why I agreed to them. But then, once I got back here and met with my shipbuilders, I realized once we built them out, making their sides and bottom thick enough to withstand the pounding they're sure to receive on the rough waters of the upper river, they'd be far too heavy for your purposes. Even with these smaller boats, each one weighs nearly 400 pounds unloaded. Any more than that, and I felt the men would be unable to carry them when they needed to be portaged. And that doesn't include the cargo. It just didn't seem prudent to me, given the numerous rapids and waterfalls upstream. Not to mention, at some point you must carry them for some distance between the Kennebec and the Chaudière."

Arnold nodded, but continued to frown.

"So, since there wasn't time to return to Cambridge to discuss the matter further, I made the decision to build the boats slightly smaller than you'd asked for, which should work better for you under the circumstances."

"Easy for you to say," Arnold answered, still scowling. "With their smaller size, these boats will be insufficient to carry all of our men and cargo."

He turned to Eleazer Oswald, who stood a few steps behind. "Mr. Oswald, how many tons of supplies have we planned to take on the expedition?"

Oswald opened the flap of a leather satchel he carried and looked inside for a moment before extracting a sheet of paper and holding it up. He read aloud, "Basic foodstuffs for forty-three days, thirty-five tons. Ammunition at one hundred rounds per man, four tons. Rifles and muskets, five and a half tons. Tents, blankets, and other camp equipment, ten tons. Shovels, axes, and other tools, one ton. Personal belongings of officers and men, such as extra shoes and clothing at ten pounds per man, six tons. Other miscellaneous and sundry necessities such as medical supplies, nails, gunsmithing tools, and so forth, half a ton."

Arnold was thoughtful for a moment, then turned back to his aide. "Please take out a pencil and paper and begin the calculations on how many boats of this size we'll need to carry all the men and equipment. Have Mr. Colburn give you the calculation for the maximum load each boat will carry—"

"We'll need twenty more of these boats," Daniel Morgan said.

Arnold turned to him. "What's that you say, Captain?"

"I said, we'll need twenty more of these here small boats."

"But how do you know—"

"Look here, Colonel … based on the length, width, and draw of these boats, and figuring three average-sized men to properly wrangle each bateau, that leaves about 550 pounds for cargo, give or take. If you're fixing to carry all the supplies, you'll need twenty more boats of this size, and some of the men will still have to march upstream. That is, unless you mean to leave much of our materiel behind."

Arnold looked over at Colburn, who shrugged, then said, "The tonnage per boat seems about right …"

"But … Captain Morgan … how can you have done these calculations so quickly … and in your head, without pencil or paper?"

Morgan chuckled. Not bothering to tell Arnold he'd never learned to do math with a pencil and paper, he said, "Comes from long experience as an old wagoner, Colonel. Over the years, I got very good at figuring how much goods would fit into a given number of containers for hauling. Whether they be wagons on wheels, or ones that float on the water, makes no difference. The total tonnage of what Mr. Oswald just read off, is sixty-two. After that, dividing out the tonnage by the boats needed is a simple matter of 'rithmetic."

"Ah … yes, I see that now. Very good, thank you, Captain."

While Arnold had been speaking with Colburn, Morgan had been eyeing the boats with concern, so he turned to Arnold and asked, "Colonel, you've run a merchant business, so I expect you know a fair bit more'n I do about shipbuilding … What do you think o' these here boats?"

Arnold turned back toward the boat he'd been measuring, knelt down, and examined it more closely. "They were built using the simplest method, called *clinker-built*."

Arnold then smelled the boards and said, "Green wood, not properly aged. These things will leak like a sieve as the unseasoned wood losses its sap and starts to shrink. Not to mention they'll handle like a wild boar in the water. These boats were clearly made as quickly and cheaply as possible. But I would've been shocked to find anything else under the circumstances."

Then he looked up a Colburn. "And no aspersions on you, Mr. Colburn; clearly your options were limited given the short amount of time you were given. It is an impressive feat of manufacturing, certainly."

Colburn smiled and shrugged.

"I expect they'll mostly hold together," Arnold continued. "At least long enough to get us there. I don't intend to come back the same way, so we'll not have need of them after."

Arnold stood. "All in all, well done, Mr. Colburn. Please proceed to build us the additional twenty boats required, post haste. I will take the liberty of speaking on behalf of General Washington that the additional amount will be added to the contract. And speaking of monies, do you have a report for me from the men you were paid to hire to scout the route?"

"Oh, yes, certainly, Colonel. I have it laid out for you up at the house."

"Excellent. Thank you, sir."

And then with a short bow, and a gesture toward the fine, two-story house across the pasture from the boats, Colburn said, "Speaking of … would you gentlemen honor me by accepting the hospitality of my home, for rest and refreshment?"

But even as they turned away from the boats headed toward Colburn's residence, Benedict Arnold suffered his second unhappy news of the day. *Broad Bay's* ship captain, Banks, met the group about halfway to Colburn's house and immediately addressed the colonel.

"Colonel Arnold, sir … I am sorry to be the bearer of bad news, but … I'm afraid this is the end of the line for my ship—and the other ten vessels too, once they arrive."

"*What?!* What is the meaning of this, Mr. Banks? Are you quitting on me, after coming all this way, when we have but ten more miles to sail before reaching our staging point at Fort Western?"

"Oh, *no*, sir. Not at all … I would never do such a thing. It's just not possible to continue on, is all."

"Not possible? What do you mean?"

"It's the river, sir … It's just too shallow after this."

"Too shallow? How is that possible? We have been assured that men have been sailing this particular sized ship up to Fort Western for years—that it was used extensively in just such a manner during the last war, in fact. It's the main reason General Washington chose the fort as our forward outpost for the expedition."

"Yes, sir, and I agree with all you've said. But after my men reported their soundings, I went and asked some of the locals why the river was so shallow. They told me it was an unusually mild winter last year, with little enough snow up in the hills. And then that was compounded by an unseasonably hot spring, which melted all the snow there was all at once in several floods. Now that we're at the end of summer, there just ain't enough water left for the draft of these vessels. I'm sorry, sir, but there ain't no arguin' with Mother Nature. She does what she does, and no man can change her."

Arnold looked over at Morgan. "Well, *that's* a bitter pill."

Morgan nodded, but then shrugged. "Nothing to be done about it … we'll just have to figure another way of hauling the goods."

"Yes, I suppose you're right about that ... all sixty-two tons of it."

"One hundred and six tons, Colonel. You're forgetting the boats."

"Oh, yes, certainly. Though one might hope to *float* those ..."

◄◄◄◄◄◆►►►►►

Up to this point in his short life, Ethan considered the trek from Winchester to Boston as the most physically demanding and tiring thing he'd ever had to endure. But the three days after the company's arrival in Gardinerston made that earlier hike seem like a pleasurable walk in a park.

At first, Ethan and the other men were welcomed as heroes in the small town, and offered food and drink laid out on tables in a small pasture next to the river. The men accepted with great enthusiasm after days of bland, cold fare aboard ship.

But just as their celebratory feast was getting underway, Sergeant Murphy stepped up, stood on a table, cupped his hands around his mouth and shouted, "Finish up quick, boys—y'all have been called back to the boat straightaway, by order of Colonel Arnold hisself. So let's get a move on it." Ethan gulped his food down, swallowed the remains of his ale, and joined the throng headed back to the ship.

After that, with the exception of a short break for a cold meal of hardtack, he spent every minute carrying heavy barrels, boxes, and various odd—but always heavy—items up out of the ship's hold onto the deck. From there, other men lowered the goods down to the row boats for transport to the eastern shore, from which they were loaded into the bateaux or onto wagons they'd hired from the locals. The small boats were then sent upstream the ten miles to Fort Western with any men who claimed any sort of boating experience, while other boats were simply loaded to the top, then pulled up the stream by men walking along the shore pulling ropes. Somehow Levi had ended up being one of those men, so Ethan figured they would meet again up at the fort in a few days' time.

Daniel Morgan seemed to be everywhere at once, and not just supervising as one might expect of an officer; Morgan helped lift the heaviest barrels, assisted men wrangling the goods over the side, and even rowed the boats to the shore. At one point, Ethan saw the captain on shore, hip deep in the stream, helping men to rescue wooden crates from the water after a bateau had capsized. Ethan also noticed that Morgan's loud and steady stream of haranguing directed at his men was always good humored and encouraging, despite many foul-ups and stubborn obstacles. The man seemed entirely unflappable; Ethan suspected *that* was an effect from his long years of running wagons over the mountains of Virginia. Moving large quantities of goods was likely something he knew better than almost anyone, with the possible exception of Colonel Arnold, who owned a maritime shipping business.

Arnold was also seemingly everywhere during the unloading and shipping process, though more in a supervisory role; Ethan never saw the colonel lift any heavy objects. But he'd apparently taken Captain Morgan's advice and acquired a large canoe, which he personally used to run up and down the river and from the ship to the shore, accompanied by his ever-present aide, Eleazar Oswald. He'd also hired the services of a crew of Indians, of the friendly Penobscots, who expertly rowed and maneuvered the boat wherever the colonel wished to go.

By mid-afternoon, Ethan noticed that his arms, legs, and back no longer ached from the strain of all the heavy lifting, but he figured that was only because they were so tired they'd become almost numb. Finally, at about four in the afternoon, *Broad Bay's* hold was empty, so he sat down on the deck with his back to the railing, closed his eyes, and was almost immediately asleep.

Then, what seemed like only a minute later, someone was shaking him. He opened one eye and looked up at the grinning face of Sergeant Murphy. "Come on, lad … no time for shirkin'. Another ship has arrived, and after, the captain says we gotta help unload 'er."

Ethan groaned, but accepted the sergeant's outstretched hand for an assist to his feet. "No rest for the wicked," Ethan answered.

Murphy laughed. "There never is, lad. There never is, and there never will be."

◄◄◄◄◄◆►►►►►

Saturday September 30, 1775 – Winchester, Virginia Colony:

Elsie gave her hoop another quick tap with her stick, propelling the metal ring, whose previous life had been as a band around a wood barrel, to ever greater speed as it spun along the smooth dirt of the drive. She urged her own legs to greater effort to keep up with the hoop, and also in hopes of overtaking Nancy, who'd held the lead since early in the race. Betsy, the youngest of the three, already lagged a few paces behind.

And her exertions appeared to be paying off, as Nancy mistimed her own whack and had to readjust her grip and try again. This gave Elsie the opening she'd been hoping for, and she sped past her friend, gaining an advantage of several yards as she sprinted ahead.

But when she glanced back over her shoulder to see how her rival fared, she failed to notice she had reached the end of the drive and caught her foot on the edge of the lawn. She was soon tumbling head over heels across the grass. Nancy, noting Elsie's fall too late, also lost her footing and was soon tumbling after. The two girls ended in a tangle, spitting grass from their mouths and laughing hysterically. Betsy pulled up to a stop in time to avoid the collision, and stood looking down at them, hands on knees, joining in the laughter.

◄◄◄◄◄◆►►►►►

"*Oh!*" Abby exclaimed, jumping to her feet as she saw the two girls tumble to the ground. But once she'd determined that the girls were all right after all, she began to giggle and turned to smile down at Hannah, who'd remained in her chair but returned the smile.

"The girls do seem to get on splendidly," Abby said as she retook her seat.

"Yes. It's such a pleasure to see," Hannah answered, gazing out at the children as they retrieved their hoops and sticks in preparation for another race. The two ladies sat in rocking chairs in the shade of the veranda just outside the front door of the Morgans' farmhouse, enjoying a sip of cool cider.

They watched in silence for several moments longer, and Abby briefly closed her eyes, leaning back in her chair as she slowly rocked. She enjoyed the feel of the gentle breeze that wafted across the veranda, taking the edge off an otherwise hot, humid late summer day. She could hear the joyful sound of the children chattering nearby, and was about to drift off when she heard Hannah sigh. Abby opened her eyes and looked over to see a far away, thoughtful expression in her friend's eyes.

Abby had a pretty good idea that Hannah's angst came from one of two possible sources, so thought she'd broach the first subject: "Hannah, dear ... how is Gideon doing?"

"Oh ... he's doing much better, thank you for asking," Hannah answered.

But when Abby smiled at her reassuringly and offered, "That's wonderful news," Hannah began to tear up.

"No ... no, it's not true. I'm sorry, Abby," Hannah said, and put her hand over her eyes, before pulling out a kerchief and wiping them.

Abby said nothing, but reached over and gently patted her on the shoulder.

"It's true that his wounds are healing, and his overall health has improved, but ... he seems ... angry ... or sad. No, both, maybe. Oh, I don't know. He's ... It's as if he were a different person. Not the warm, gentle man I married. As if now that he can't work, he no longer knows himself, so he doesn't know how to deal with me."

"Oh, I'm so sorry, my dear," Abby said and leaned across to embrace Hannah.

When they separated, Abby said, "You know, I can recall there were several times when Daniel was badly hurt—in an accident, or out fighting in the wars—and came home in pain and was unable to do the things he normally did. He was *not* a pleasant man to live with then, I can tell you that. Like living with a bear inside your house."

Hannah smiled, appreciating her friend's attempt to comfort her. "And what happened?" she asked.

"Well, I just had to grit my teeth and 'soldier thorough it,' as the men would say. In time, as Daniel healed, he returned to his old self, and we were able to resume our happy life once again. I'm sure the same will happen with Gideon."

"I don't know, Abby … Daniel was able to heal completely … to get back to the way he was before, I presume. With Gideon it's different. The one arm he has left is crippled and nearly useless. Doc Adams says it may never return to the way it was before. That's the part that is hardest for him to accept. He was a man who worked with his hands, and now he has lost them."

"I'm so sorry, Hannah. We must just pray for God to grant him the wisdom and strength to overcome this tragedy and find a way to be happy again."

"Thank you, Abby. Amen to that … amen to that."

"*Oh.* I nearly forgot," Abby decided to broach the other subject, hoping it would turn their conversation in a more positive direction. "When we met at the dry goods store, you had mentioned you'd received a letter from Ethan, and that you'd tell me all about it when we were together."

"You're right, and shame on me … I meant to bring it along so you could read it, but I've completely forgotten and left it at home."

"That's all right. You can just tell me how Ethan is faring …"

"He is doing well, but … he suffered a terrible shock when he reached Boston. You'll recall me mentioning that two of Ethan's closest friends, Levi and Seth, had gone off to Boston several months before our men marched off?"

"Yes … *Oh dear*, did something ill befall them?"

"Well, Ethan met Levi there at General Washington's camp, but learned that Seth had been killed in the fighting up at Bunker Hill."

"Oh, no. I'm so sorry to hear it. Poor Ethan … and that poor family."

"Yes ... Ethan asked me to tell them what had happened. It was ... one of the most difficult things I've ever had to do ... to tell Annabel, Seth's mother, that he was ... *gone*." Hannah slowly shook her head and became choked up thinking about it, such that the last word came out in no more than a whisper.

Abby placed her arm around Hannah but said nothing. She knew what it was like to have to tell family a loved one had been killed in a war. Daniel had been in many fights, and not all of them had gone well for him and his men.

Hannah wiped a tear from her eye, then forced a smile as she looked up at Abby. "And I would be remiss if I didn't tell you that Ethan says Captain Morgan is also doing well, and meets regularly with General Washington and his other officers."

"Oh, praise the Lord. That's so good to hear," Abby beamed.

"Yes, and ... Ethan says Captain Morgan ... Daniel, I mean ... says to tell you he is composing a letter to send you, and that you should get it soon."

Abby smiled, knowing it meant Ethan was writing the letter on Daniel's behalf, but she kept that to herself.

"They are now in General Washington's camp at a town called Cambridge, which is just outside Boston," Hannah continued. "The British are inside Boston, and have thrown up barricades across the roadway, which neither side can cross. So other than some long-range rifle shots—which for reasons I don't quite understand, apparently the British are entirely ill equipped for— there has been no fighting at all."

"Well, that sounds hopeful."

"He did say there was talk of some kind of expedition up to the north that Mr. Morgan's men were expected to take part in. But since there is currently no fighting up that way, he believes it won't be anything too dangerous. Likely some sort of garrison duty at a fort up in New York, maybe."

"Oh. Well, then all is well, and we have nothing to worry about in that regard."

"Yes, so it would seem ... So it would seem."

But what Hannah did *not* tell Abby was that in Ethan's letter, he had apologized for not sending home any money; that he and the other soldiers had not yet been paid, and likely wouldn't be anytime soon—at least not until their current expedition was completed. And he had no idea when *that* might be.

It had been a bitter pill. With Gideon still unable to work, they had no money coming in. But the Morgans had done so much for them already. Hannah couldn't bear the thought of asking her new friend for more help; she couldn't stand the thought of becoming a permanent charity case.

Families must take care of their own, she decided. But the thought of family gave her a new idea—a new hope—something she would discuss with Gideon as soon as she returned home.

◄◄◄◄◆►►►►►

"Gideon … Gideon dear, please wake up now," Hannah insisted, as she sat on the edge of his bed and gently shook his shoulder.

"Hunh?" He opened one eye and gazed at her blearily. "What is it, Hannah? Why are you disturbing my sleep?"

"Gideon, it's three o'clock in the afternoon … Doc Adams says you mustn't just sleep all day. It's not good for your health and disposition."

"Pah! What does he know … He's never lost an arm," Gideon grumbled, and reclosed his one open eye.

"Gideon, you must wake up. There is something I need to discuss with you."

He groaned, but this time he opened both eyes, though he didn't attempt to lift his head from the pillow. "What is it?"

"You remember me telling you we received a letter from Ethan?"

"Yes, of course. What of it?"

"… and you recall he was unable to send any money …"

"Oh … is that what this is about? *Money?* You know I am incapable of working right now. What do you want me to do about it?"

"Well, you could sit up and help me figure out what to do about our present difficulties."

"Why not just ask Abby Morgan for more help?" he suggested with a frown.

"Now you listen here, Gideon Chambers … the Morgans have already helped enough. Have you no pride left? I'll not become their charity case. Besides which, I'm sure Daniel Morgan also has not been paid, and also hasn't been home to help run the farm, so there's no telling how their finances are faring. They too may be suffering under the circumstances."

He scowled at her and grumbled, "I'll not be spoken to in such a saucy manner, wife."

But though the words were harsh and reproachful, Hannah could tell there was no force nor venom behind them. She'd wounded his pride, and he was stung by it. *Good, she thought, maybe it will rouse him.*

"Gideon, I am bringing up our money problems not to burden you or to guilt you … but to tell you I have an idea."

"Oh?"

"Yes … I believe families ought to take care of their own, and I believe the time has come to call upon ours."

"Oh. I assume you are speaking of my brother James."

"Yes, that's who I was thinking of. He is your closest living relative, after all, and the only person on either side of the family who is well off enough to help without being overly burdened."

"Oh, Hannah … I don't know … James is … well, he is my older brother and has always lorded it over me—that he has been more successful, more important, of a higher class. Coming to him on bended knee … I don't know if I can do that."

"You won't have to; *I* will do it. Besides," she smiled for the first time in the conversation, "you can't write a letter anyway."

Her irreverent humor touched something in him, and made him chuckle and smile for the first time in weeks. "True, true … very well, wife. You write the letter, and we'll see what James has to say."

"Thank you, dear. Now … let's get you up and out of that bed. Here, take hold of my arm … come on now."

"Oh, all right, all right. You are such a stubborn woman!"

She smiled, "And you wouldn't have it any other way."

He smiled, and shook his head, but took her arm.

Chapter 6. Holding the Fort

"The aim of military training
is not just to prepare men for battle,
but to make them long for it."
- *Louis Simpson*

*Saturday September 16, 1775 – Île-aux-Noix (Walnut Island), Quebec
Province:*

"I am ashamed and appalled to leave you like this,
Montgomery," Continental Army Major General Philip Schuyler
said from where he lay on his cot, before a coughing spasm shook
his body for several moments. Brigadier General Richard
Montgomery could see that his commander was pale and looked
terribly weak, with dark rings around his eyes. A stark, frightful
contrast to the vigorous man he'd been when they'd first launched
their operation from Fort Ticonderoga just three weeks earlier.

"Nonsense, sir," Montgomery replied, and knelt down before
reaching out to take his commander's hand, which he found cold
and clammy. "They say the spirit is strong, but the flesh is weak …
We are all mortal men after all, and can only do as much as the
body will allow, no matter how strong the will," he continued,
patting his mentor's hand affectionately.

"Thank you for saying so, Richard. It is most kind and
understanding of you," Schuyler responded. "Though I can't help
feeling I have let you and the rest of the men down."

"Never even think on it, sir. There's still a lot more fighting to
be done after this. And you dying out here from the consumption
serves no purpose. Better that you get back to New York and
regain your health. Then you'll be ready to give the Brits hell
another day. Your country still needs you, so I believe it's your
duty to get well so you can continue the fight."

"Very well. I will relent and return home, as you suggest. But
before I go, allow me to inquire as to how you intend to proceed
on this front in my absence?"

"Certainly, sir, and I shall be happy to have your advice on the matter, as you see fit. I intend to launch an all-out attack on Fort St. Johns on the morrow. I hope to overrun her defenses, take the fort, their big guns, ammunition, and supplies, then immediately march on Montreal."

"Very good. And if you are unable to breach their walls?"

"Then we must face the necessity of laying siege to the fort, General," Montgomery answered.

"But we haven't the artillery to batter them into submission. A prolonged siege may take too long. I'm certain Colonel Arnold's expedition will be making good time through the wilderness. Likely they will arrive at Quebec any day now. If we aren't there to meet him, he will lose the element of surprise, and may even fall under attack himself and be forced to fall back."

"Then we will have to make sure we don't fail in our attack tomorrow," Montgomery countered with a frown.

Schuyler nodded, but closed his eyes, and seemed to drift off to sleep. After waiting a few moments to ensure the general still breathed, Montgomery left the room and immediately made the necessary arrangements for the general's transportation back home that he might recover his health.

Then he gathered his officers to discuss the attack on the British at Fort St. Johns.

◄◄◄◄◄◆►►►►►

Sunday September 17, 1775 – Fort St. Johns, Quebec Province:

British Major Sir Charles Preston, stood before his half-dozen staff and line officers gathered in his small headquarters office in Fort St. Johns, twenty-five miles south of Montreal. "Gentlemen, I have just received grave news. The wagon train we've been expecting, containing much needed supplies and ammunition, has just been captured by the enemy, who is now marching on the fort in full force, a well-armed column that outnumbers us two to one, at the least."

Nobody immediately spoke, though all held concerned looks as they digested this latest piece of bad news. The fort had successfully fought off numerous enemy attacks over the past several weeks, but the enemy had been steadily increasing their manpower and ratcheting up the pressure accordingly. The present crisis threatened to end the stalemate, but not in a good way for the British.

To no one's surprise, Lieutenant John André stepped forward to speak. Though André was the youngest and the lowest-ranking officer there, he carried a certain status as the commander of the fort's contingent of the elite Seventh Regiment of Foot, the Royal Welsh Fusiliers. He and his men had already proven their skill and effectiveness in several skirmishes with the enemy as they probed the fort's defenses. Because of this, the captains often deferred to him when it came to combat tactics and strategy.

"Major, I should like to volunteer to lead the Seventh on a sortie, with the goal of recapturing the supply wagons and driving the enemy back from our walls," he said in a calm, even voice.

But before the major could answer, Captain Brant of the Twenty-Sixth Regiment interjected, "But André, look here ... that's likely a *suicide* mission. Best to stay within the walls at this stage and ride it out. Though they may have us outmanned, we have them outgunned with our artillery. So far, they've shown little capacity in that regard."

André turned to the captain and answered in a mild tone, "I appreciate your concern, Captain. But I do not intend suicide, neither for myself nor for my men. I believe a bold, swift attack will catch the rebels by surprise. If the blow is struck hard enough and fast enough, we may be back within these walls—with our much-needed equipment in tow—before the enemy can react and regroup. If we delay ... then he has the opportunity to either overrun us now, or starve us out later with our dearth of supplies."

After a few minutes more of back-and-forth discussion, the Major held up his hand. "Gentlemen, if you please ..." All fell silent.

"Lieutenant André, please proceed with the sortie you have suggested straightaway. But do not take any undue risks. If the enemy is prepared, or responds in good order, fall back immediately. Better to take our chances on a prolonged siege than to lose your valuable services, and that of your men."

"Yes, sir. And thank you, sir."

Moments later, Lieutenant André stood before the one hundred soldiers of the Seventh Regiment assembled on the parade ground in front of the fort's north gate, their red tunics glowing in the sunlight and their muskets on their shoulders. He faced them as if for inspection, giving them his best stern British officer look. But inside, his heart soared; these were hard, brave men who trusted him, without question or doubt, to lead them in a desperate battle. It was a thrill he could not explain to another living soul: the feeling of being a part of a gallant, heroic mission with men whom he admired, and who admired him in return. Nothing quite compared, not even his many artistic and linguistic endeavors, nor his occasional foray into espionage, as he'd recently done in Cambridge, disguised as a French gentleman under the very nose of General Washington and his rebels.

No, nothing could compare to *this*, he decided. He took in a deep breath of satisfaction.

"Men of the Seventh, we are once again called upon to do what we do better than any other soldiers in His Majesty's service: meet the enemy on the field of battle, overwhelm him with deadly force, and drive him from the field in ignominious defeat."

He paused a moment, then called out, "Company will fix bayonets on my command ... *FIX ... BAYONETS!*"

One hundred soldiers inserted eighteen-inch-long, razor-sharp bayonets onto their muskets, and clicked them into place. So practiced were the veteran soldiers, and so precise their motions, that to a casual listener, it might have sounded as one single large weapon being readied.

"Company will prepare to follow me as we march out at the double quick to meet the enemy. Our objective is to engage and drive off the foe, seize back our stolen supply wagons, and return with same to the fort as exigencies allow."

Then he paused and gazed from face to face, making eye contact with each man in turn. He was gratified but not surprised to see grim determination, but no hint of fear. These were *his* men, loyal to the core. They would fight to the death for him, and he for them, and they knew it.

André turned about face, with his back now to his men, and unsheathed his sword. He signaled to the men manning the fort's main gate to throw it wide.

As soon as the gate began to move, André called out, "At the double-quick ... march!" Through the gate trotted 101 elite British soldiers, muskets on shoulders, prepared to engage an approaching enemy known to number more than a thousand.

Like the Spartans at Thermopylae, André decided. *Perhaps I shall write a sonnet about it after ...*

◄◄◄◄◄◆►►►►►

As they trotted out the front gate on the north side of Fort St. Johns, André turned and took a left-hand fork in the road—a roadway bending around the east side of the fort before heading due south. The scouts had reported that the rebels were taking the stolen goods south toward their main base at the island fort named *Île-aux-Noix*, from whence the main attack was coming. André hoped to hit the wagon train before it met up with the main American column, and then continue on in an attempt to blunt that metaphorical spear.

The countryside they now moved through was slightly rolling, with cleared farming areas separated by dense, heavily timbered acreages.

And though André was eager to fall upon the enemy, after a quarter hour of double-quick marching—essentially a trot—he called a halt. He never wanted his men to arrive at a battle out of breath with muscles strained. Better to arrive later ready to fight. But also, he never wanted to arrive in the middle of a fight without knowing how the enemy was positioned. So he called for two of his most trusted scouts, had them set aside their weapons and gear, and sent them forward to reconnoiter.

While they waited, he established a perimeter, and then ordered the men to take a knee but keep their muskets at the ready. Then he called over his two sergeants, John McCrea and

129

Roger Putnam. McCrea was a tough-as-nails grizzled veteran of twenty years, while the younger Putnam was a no-nonsense soldier, built like a bull. To André's mind, both men were formidable fellows, of the type you'd definitely not want to fight in a pub.

"Gentlemen, assuming the scouts report what I am expecting them to find, we should catch up to the wagon train before the main rebel column. If that is the case, I wish to fall upon them with bayonets only—no gunfire that may alert the approaching column—then Mr. McCrea, you take twenty of the men and start those wagons back toward the fort. Mr. Putnam, you and I will take the remaining men and continue south. I intend to fall upon the vanguard of their column like a hammer on an anvil: sow fear and chaos among them, drive them from their course, then fall back in good order before they can regroup.

"McCrea, once you've got the wagons back to the fort, you may return to reinforce our retreat. Any questions?"

Both men shook their heads. "No, sir," said McCrea. And then he grinned and added, "Seems a bloody good time for the likes o' me an' the boys, innit?"

To which Putnam added, "But not so much fun for them Yanks, I'm a thinkin'."

André smiled. "There's the proper fighting spirit. Good men, both of you."

The sergeants left to spread the orders among the men and to divide them into the two groups André had ordered, so that each man knew what was expected of him. André watched his men calmly getting themselves organized for a potentially deadly engagement with a growing sense of pride. *Such professionalism, such courage ... What a pleasure to be a part of*, he thought. Then he turned his gaze to the south once again, and then he too knelt down to await the scouts' return.

They hadn't long to wait. Before they'd totally caught their breath, the two scouts returned.

"Supplies wagons is just ahead, sir—maybe a quarter mile, and not in no hurry neither, to my thinkin'," the first scout reported. The other scout said nothing, but nodded his agreement with great vigor.

Then the first scout grinned. "Thinks they's safe as lambs … not knowin' us wolves is a comin'."

André returned the grin. "Just so, Mr. Hendricks. How many men guarding the wagons?"

"Less than a hundred, I'd say," he responded, then turned to his mate, "What you think, Willers?"

"Counted eighty-three," Willers answered, then shrugged when Hendricks rolled his eyes.

"And what of the main column?"

"No sign o' them yet, sir," Hendricks answered.

"Excellent work, men. Go ahead and collect your gear and report to your sergeants. Then we'll march."

A few minutes later, they crested a rise and saw the wagon train just ahead. Given the scouts' report, André wasn't surprised to see no rear guard, no skirmishers, nor any perimeter. Just a half dozen or so sloppy looking fellows trudging along at the rear of the column, their muskets hanging on their backs by their straps.

Amateurs, André thought, and shook his head in disbelief. He turned and gave the hand signal that said, "Pick up the pace." The men responded with a rush forward.

The men of the Seventh were on the rear of the train before the Americans were aware they were coming. These men were caught so completely by surprise there was never a thought of fighting back. They simply raised their hands in surrender, with several pleading, "Don't shoot, don't shoot!"

Leaving a few men to watch the prisoners, André sprinted on toward the front of the train. Taking a chance that he guessed right that the Americans had not bothered to swap out the British and Canadian teamsters for their own drivers, he called out as he passed each wagon, "Stop this wagon, in the name of the King!"

And to his satisfaction, the wagons began to come to a halt.

But the rebels at the front of the train had heard the shouting, and so they'd had a few moments to figure out what was happening. Several had unslung their rifles and were attempting to load them. And to their credit, others stepped up preparing to fight with nothing but the butts of their guns. But these were swiftly subdued either by threat, by musket butt, or by bayonet when nothing else would suffice. It had happened so quickly that no shots were fired on either side.

Those Americans who'd not resisted had fled, many throwing down their weapons as they did. This included the man who was clearly their commanding officer—identified by the bright red cockade in his hat—who went off at a gallop on the horse he was riding. When Sergeant McCrea stepped up and aimed his musket at the man's back, André reached over and lowered the gun. "No, Sergeant," he said. "We'll not target their officers in that manner … There's a good fellow."

McCrea nodded, seeming unconcerned about the implied rebuff. "Very good, sir," he answered, lowering the hammer to the halfcock and returning the musket to his shoulder. He turned and headed back to take charge of the wagon train as previously ordered.

André located Sergeant Putnam and shouted, "To me, Sergeant. And do just bring your men along, if you please …"

In moments, the eighty men not tasked with guarding the wagon train were once again on the move, heading south down the road, toward where they expected to meet the oncoming rebel army. But this time, André did *not* order the double-quick march, rather a brisk steady pace, in double file with himself in the lead. *No need to tire the men*, he decided. *Now that we've secured the wagons, it no longer matters where we meet the enemy. Better to have the men fresh …*

Once again, André sent the scouts ahead, this time to locate the front of the American column. He hoped to find a suitable place to set up an ambush, and for that he needed to know for certain if and when they were indeed coming, and to make sure they were marching up the road as he expected, and had not done something unexpected, like sending out scouts or a probing skirmish line.

Despite the fact they might now be warned by the escaping wagon guards, he doubted the Americans would be prepared for his attack. Likely they would assume his action had only been to recapture the wagons, since his numbers were so small. They would never assume such a miniscule force would engage their entire column on the march.

So far, the rebels had shown themselves to be amateurs at this war business, and he was counting on them continuing on in the same vein—for the time being, anyway. *At least until they have learned some hard lessons from their betters ... like the one I'm about to teach them,* he thought, and grinned.

Minutes later, with the scouts having reported back that the arrival of the American column was imminent, André chose a suitable place from which to launch his attack. He picked a small clearing on the right side of the road, just before the road made a sharp bend to the right. They were now positioned behind a small thicket of spruce trees which would serve to conceal them even as the enemy advanced around the curve. The position also had the advantage of elevation; the road sloped down toward the curve, so they'd be fighting their battle downhill.

The scouts had reported that the rebel column was coming on four abreast, with infantry in front and some men—presumably officers—riding in their midst further back.

Instructions for the attack had been given: he'd ordered a flying wedge this time, starting with bayonets, and then firing at will after impact with the column. This time it would be an all-out charge, making as much noise as possible and inflicting the greatest amount of damage. He hoped the noise and ensuing panic among the rebels in front would convince those further back that a major engagement was unfolding.

André peered out from around a large tree trunk, with Sergeant Putnam just behind him, while the men knelt behind him in a double row, their bayoneted muskets in their hands. André watched as the rebels appeared, turning the corner and coming up the hill. They wore no uniforms, their muskets and rifles held no bayonets, and they marched with no military synchronization. But there was no mistaking the determination in their faces. Though they were inexperienced soldiers, they did know how to fight. He would not underestimate them as the officers had done back at Bunker Hill. He would strike, and strike hard, then get out quickly before they could recover and destroy him.

He looked back at Sergeant Putnam and exchanged a nod. Then he raised his sword, the signal for the men to stand and get ready.

"CHARGE!" André shouted. He scrambled up onto the roadway, then turned and sprinted down the hill toward the oncoming enemy. He did not bother looking back, but could hear his men shouting at the top of their lungs, racing along behind him. He led with his saber as the point of a "V," his men flared out in wings to each side. As he drew closer, he saw the shock in the eyes of the men he approached as they scrambled to unshoulder their rifles.

André hit the front of the American lines at a run and plunged inside, not bothering to engage anyone at all until he was well inside their rows. The idea was to drive a wedge into the column and split it apart, creating chaos and confusion in the process. When the press of men around him slowed his pace, he began hacking with his sword, to the front, to the left, and to the right. Striking at heads, arms, upraised muskets, anything at all that presented itself. Now mixed with the shouting of the British soldiers were the screams and shouts of the Americans.

The men of the Seventh pressed forward, punching and slashing with their bayonets and firing their muskets at any rebel who raised a gun.

André slashed and thrust with his sword until his arm ached, and he feared he might falter. He'd just run a man through the chest and was trying to extract the blade when he saw out the corner of his right eye a man come at him with the butt of a rifle. He knew in that moment he would be too late to block or duck the blow. But as he turned, he saw the man impaled up under the chin by a bayonet. When it was yanked free, the rebel slumped to the ground. André saw it was the hulking form of Sergeant Putnam, who'd been next to him the whole battle, watching his back.

"Quite decent of you, Putnam," André said, to which the sergeant gave a quick nod and a grin before turning back to the business in front of him.

As their forward momentum slowed, André noted that it was not due to the enemy's resistance, but rather in their panic, they'd so clogged the roadway that they had nowhere to go. Many were streaming away from the battle off to the sides of the roadway, but the majority were trying to escape back the way they'd come and were now only getting in each other's way.

Time to make our exit, André decided, and turned to tug on Putnam's sleeve. Getting his sergeant's attention, he signaled the retreat. But as planned, they would not turn and run, but rather slow their forward movement to a stop, then slowly walk backward from the field, reloading and firing off their muskets as they went until they were disengaged completely from the battle. Then, and only then, they would double-quick it back to the fort.

As he slowly paced backward, he looked over his shoulder to make a quick survey and noted happily that they'd suffered only minor injuries and no casualties. He said a quick, silent prayer of thanks for that.

◄◄◄◄◆►►►►►

"Major Brown, for God's sake, what has happened? Where are the captured British supply wagons?" General Montgomery demanded as men streamed back past them—previously well-organized formations in utter disarray, including a large number of wounded being carried from the field. Major Brown had been in command of the company that had captured the wagons and was bringing them back to the American fort at *Île-aux-Noix*, but clearly something disastrous had just occurred.

"Lost, General … taken. They came on us without warning, hit us like a thunderstorm."

"Who did?"

"The Brits … an infantry battalion, bayonets fixed. They came on us at the run, firing no shots, making no noise until they was in our midst, stabbing away. Our men panicked and fled—most without firing a shot, many threw down their muskets. It was … a pathetic display. I'm sorry, General, but there was nothing I could do, so I came straight here to give you the news."

"Losing the wagons is bad enough, but *this* ..." Montgomery waved at the disheveled, tattered men of his command, now falling back from what he'd earlier assumed would be a certain victory.

"How many of the enemy?"

"There had to have been 500 or more ... fierce and disciplined. Never seen the like ..."

"Yes, yes, very well. Come, we must rally the men, and turn them about to face the enemy. Fierce or not, we have the Brits outnumbered, and must turn the tables on them and regain the initiative. Cut them off from their fort if we can."

"Yes, sir."

"Come, gentlemen ..." Montgomery called out to his staff officers, "Rally the men, and get them turned around. We must try to destroy these impertinent Brits before they can slink back inside their fort."

But hours later, despite a valiant counterattack, which forced the small British task force to leave behind several supply wagons before they could retreat behind the safety of their walls—Montgomery had to admit that his plans for a quick victory at Fort St. Johns were now in tatters.

He sighed in frustration. *I hope and trust that Colonel Benedict Arnold will have better success with his own venture,* he thought, even as he turned his attention to drawing up plans for the siege he'd desperately hoped to avoid.

Monday September 18, 1775 – Fort St. Johns, Quebec Province:

Lieutenant André stepped into Major Preston's office, stood to attention, and saluted. Preston, not bothering to rise or return the salute, simply gestured to the chair opposite his desk, so André obliged him and took his seat.

"Sir Charles," André began, without preamble, "the scouts have returned and are reporting that the Americans are *not* gathering for another attack, but rather have begun to dig in, building entrenchments surrounding the fort, including what appears to be a mortar battery just to the south."

"And the river?"

"Effectively cut off. The rebels control all the crossings between here and Montreal. It appears they are preparing for an extended siege."

"Good. That means we've done our duty and kept the colonists from attacking Montreal. It will buy time for General Carleton to reinforce the city, and then to send a relief column to our aid."

"Yes, sir, my thinking precisely," André nodded.

"How are our supplies?"

"With the return of the lion's share of the wagons, we have plenty of lead and powder, and food and other sundries for a month and more, though I should think it would be prudent to begin rationing."

"Yes, yes, makes sense. Let's also have the prisoners swear an oath not to raise arms against the crown—not that it'll do any good—and then turn them loose. Their scant numbers back among the enemy will make but little difference, and I'll not have them consuming our scarce rations, nor occupying men required to guard them."

"Seems wise, sir."

"See that it is so, Lieutenant."

"Yes, sir."

"By the by, Lieutenant … that was some good work out there yesterday."

"Thank you, sir." André had to work very hard to keep a stoic appearance and not to break into a grin at the rare praise from the stern commander of the Twenty-Sixth.

They were quiet for a moment before André had another, unrelated thought. "Sir … has there been any word on the rebel expedition I spoke of when first I returned from Boston? You recall, the fifteen hundred or so men under the command of one *Colonel Arnold*, who marched from Cambridge and then took ships from Newburyport headed north …?"

"Yes, I recall you mentioning it. But no … I've heard nothing on the matter since you first told me of it."

"Hmm … that's odd. Then there was *no* attack on Halifax Station, as had been expected? General Gage seemed quite certain that Washington intended to disrupt the Royal Navy's operations by depriving them of their primary base of operations."

"No, everything has been quiet in that regard. No rebel attacks in Quebec Province whatsoever. Other than *here*, of course."

"I don't understand it, sir. That many men don't just vanish."

"Perhaps there was a storm and they were lost at sea," Preston offered.

"Maybe … maybe. But I should think they would've hugged the shoreline in their small ships, hoping to elude our warships. If a threatening storm would've blown up, they could've sought shelter in any number of small bays or inlets along the route."

Preston shrugged. "Your guess is as good as mine, André."

André thought on the conundrum a moment longer, then an idea struck him. "My *guess*, you say … Well so far, I haven't *guessed* at all. But I think I shall give it a try, if you don't mind. Would you hand me that map on the shelf behind you, sir, please … the one of the entire province? Yes … yes, that's the one. Thank you, sir," André said as Preston handed him the large, tightly rolled map.

André stood and spread the map out on the desk, setting heavy objects at the corners to hold it flat.

"So … they took ship here, and sailed north, after which … we lost track of them …"

"Yes, thanks to that incompetent bumbler, Admiral Graves," Preston grumbled.

André nodded but said nothing, thinking it wasn't his place to criticize a superior officer, even if his own commander had already done so.

"… But they didn't attack Halifax," André continued. "I suppose they could've sailed on to the mouth of the St. Lawrence, thinking to run up stream and attack Quebec."

Preston snorted. "Even Graves isn't incompetent enough to allow *that*. The area around the mouth of the St. Lawrence is practically crawling with our naval vessels. I find it highly unlikely the Americans would be foolish enough to attempt such a thing … especially with small, unarmed ships. It would be utterly suicidal."

"Agreed. Then … *where* …?"

André gazed at the map for a long moment while Preston pulled out pen and paper and began writing something out.

"*Aha.* What is this? A river whose mouth is in the Massachusetts colony in the region they call 'Maine,' and whose source is in Canada, only a few miles from the source of another river, this one northbound … here … the *Chaudière,* it's called."

Then André chuckled. "And that river empties into the St. Lawrence just across from Quebec City. The rebels *do* mean to attack Quebec, but *not* down the St. Lawrence."

"Oh. Do you really think they intend to come *that* way? Forcing their way through hundreds of miles of raw wilderness, with fall fast approaching and winter on its way?"

"Yes, I do. In fact, it's what I would've done in their place." André smiled, and leaned back in his chair, continuing to gaze at the map. Now he was imagining the difficult and treacherous journey up the wilderness river, with over a thousand men and all their supplies. *A bold, daring move … the struggle, the sacrifice … a great, heroic adventure. I wish I could see it … I truly wish I could be there among them.*

He turned to Preston and said, "Major, if you are writing a message to Governor Carleton telling him of our predicament, as I suspect you are, may I ask that you include mention of my theory about this *Colonel Arnold's* expedition? That he may be leading his men through the wilderness intent on an attack against Quebec City?"

Preston was thoughtful for a moment, then nodded. "Very well, Lieutenant … I shall inform the governor of your thoughts on the matter. But I will leave it up to him as to what he may choose to do with that theory."

"Very good, sir. Thank you, sir."

Chapter 7. The River Road

"A river cuts through rock,
not because of its power,
but because of its persistence."
- James N. Watkins

Saturday September 23, 1775 – Gardinerston, Maine (Massachusetts Colony):

By the end of the third day in Gardinerston, all eleven ships of the expedition had been unloaded, and what goods weren't already on their way upstream to Fort Western were piled along the shore awaiting transport. As sunset was fast approaching, and they were near exhaustion from their efforts, Ethan and the other men of Morgan's battalion were ordered to spend one more night in the town before hiking the ten miles up to the fort the following morning.

Ethan was happy for another night in the welcoming little town, where the soldiers were treated to warm beds and home-cooked meals in the houses of the residents, not knowing when he would next enjoy that pleasure.

He was, to his annoyance, awakened in the middle of the night by the demands of his bladder, which insisted he drag himself out of his nice warm bed, pull on his britches, buckle up his belt with its requisite knife sheath, slip on and tie his shoes, and then brave the brisk outdoors just to use the outhouse. Fortunately, it was a moonlit night, so he'd not have to fumble about in the house's back alley to find the relief he sought.

When he'd finished his business and stepped out the outhouse door intending to return to the house, something caught the corner of his eye across the yard and its three-rail fence, out toward the road that led away from town. He turned toward the movement and was surprised to see a man walking along the road heading south. Ethan thought it odd that anyone would be out on the road in the dark in the middle of the night. And something about the way the man moved, glancing about in a furtive manner, made him suspicious. *What is this fellow up to, prowling about in the middle of the night,* he wondered. *Is he planning on stealing something? Likely there's still plenty of supplies lying about from the day's unloading, waiting to be hauled up stream come first light. Could be mighty tempting for an unscrupulous character.*

So, without any particular plan in mind, Ethan decided to follow from a safe distance until he could figure out what it was all about. If it turned out to be something innocent, then he'd not embarrass himself by having to explain to this fellow why he was following. If it turned out to be something *else* … well, he'd just have to wait and see, he decided.

It turned out that he didn't have long to wait. After a few hundred yards, the man paused next to a gate that led to a farmhouse on the lefthand side of the road. The man turned to look back up the road, as if to see if anyone was coming along. Ethan ducked behind a bush and held still, hoping his movement hadn't caught the fellow's eye in the darkness. He peered out between the branches and saw the man open the gate and step inside, closing it after.

Ethan rose up and moved as quickly as he could without making undue noise until he reached the gate. There he paused, kneeling down and peering through the slats. He saw the man he'd been following just a few yards away with his back turned. Another man was there, facing in Ethan's direction. He could not make out the man's face in the deep shadows.

The men were speaking in low tones, such that Ethan could not make out what they were saying. As the two men spoke, the one who'd been nearest the farmhouse stepped forward and stood next to the other on the path, so that Ethan now saw both men from the side. The one he'd been following extended his hand, holding out what looked like a folded piece of paper. The other man took it. *Odd*, Ethan thought, *I wonder what it could mean …*

And then the man Ethan had been following turned his head just enough so that the moonlight lit the side of his face, revealing a long scar down his left cheek. In a flash, Ethan realized what he was seeing and gasped. *The Brit with the scar ... he's a spy. Passing information on the expedition ...*

But he realized too late he'd given himself away.

"*Hey*, who's there?" the Brit said, and stepped toward the gate. The other man didn't wait to see who it was, but turned and fled into the night.

But the Brit seemed unconcerned, strolling casually toward the gate. "Evenin' mate. Havin' a restless night, like me? Nothin' like a bit of a stroll in the moonlight to bring on the ol' slumber, *innit?*" the man said with a broad grin.

But Ethan wasn't buying the nonchalance, and was more convinced than ever that the man was up to no good. "You're not out for a walk ... Who was that man you met, and what did you give him? Information on the expedition that he can bring back to the British? I'd bet money you're not a *true* deserter ... You're a spy."

But the fellow continued to smile as he came forward, finally reaching the gate and pulling it open. "Now, why would a fine young lad such as yerself, go sayin' a hurtful thing such as that to a dedicated fellow *rebel*, hunh?"

In the moonlight Ethan saw a flash, and instinctively moved his arm just in time to strike his wrist against the other man's arm—an arm Ethan could now see held a sharp blade! Without thinking, Ethan grabbed the man's wrist in both of his own, stopping it inches short. The man punched Ethan in the stomach with his free hand, then pressed forward with his knife hand. Ethan tried to retreat but tripped over something in the dark and fell on his back, with his assailant landing on top, knocking the wind out of him. The blade had just missed him during the fall, embedding itself in the roadway next to Ethan's ribcage. In a moment, the man raised the knife and brought it down, but Ethan squirmed to one side, and the knife missed, once again hitting the gravel.

With a sickening feeling, Ethan realized he was about to die. The man was stronger and quicker and he had a knife. It had only been luck that Ethan hadn't already been skewered. But in that instant, a thought flashed through his mind, *knife!* In the heat of

the moment, Ethan had forgotten his own belt knife in its sheath—
a small, six-inch blade he used for cutting ropes and cleaning fish.
He reached for it and pulled it loose.

As the man thrust down once again, Ethan stabbed upward
toward the center of the man's chest and felt the blade penetrate
to the hilt. The man inhaled, and his eyes widened. As Ethan
yanked the knife free, a gush of warm liquid ran down his arm
and splattered his chest. The assailant's knife fell from his lifeless
grasp as he collapsed on top of Ethan.

Ethan could hear his heart pounding in his ears as he pushed
the man's body off. He lay on the ground shaking, his breath
coming in gasps. His mind seemed to wander away to some
faraway place, and he could remember no conscious thoughts for
several minutes as he stared up at the full moon.

And then a bright light shown in his eyes, nearly blinding him.

"Hey ... what's going on here?" a voice shouted. In the light of
a lantern, Ethan looked down at his own hand, still clutching the
knife, now covered in half-dried blood. *This doesn't look good*, he
decided.

He looked back up and saw the lantern was held by a soldier
he didn't recognize, while two other soldiers pointed guns at him.
"You done murdered that fellow. What'd you want to go an' do
that for?" the man with the lantern asked.

Ethan tried to explain, but his mind didn't seem to cooperate
with his mouth, "He was—I was—Uh ... um ... I—" but then
something in the back of his mind told him he needed to speak
with Daniel Morgan.

"Take me to Captain Morgan," he managed, in a rasping voice
that was not much more than a whisper. "I ... I'm ... one of his
men. I must speak with him. Nobody else ..." He shook his head
emphatically, unable to get any more words out.

◄◄◄◄◆►►►►►

To his credit, Daniel Morgan did not appear especially
annoyed or upset about being awakened several hours before
sunrise, which Ethan took for a good sign. And Ethan was

143

impressed that Morgan did not even seem groggy with sleep, as most folks would be.

After quizzing the sentries for a few moments, Morgan sent them away. He told Ethan to sit in a camp chair while he sat across from him. The good news was, Ethan felt like he was coming back to himself; he could finally breathe properly again, and felt he could now put together a coherent explanation about what had just happened.

"So, Ethan … you had an interesting night, I'm told …"

"Yes, sir. *Interesting* is not how I'd say it, but I guess it's true as far as it goes."

Morgan grunted noncommittally. "They say you used your belt knife to murder one of your fellow soldiers—though thankfully, he was not one of our Virginians. Care to explain yourself? You two have an argument? Got into a fist fight that got out of hand?"

"No, sir." Ethan was ready to spew out his whole theory about the man being a spy, but before the words were out of his mouth, he thought better of it. *What if I was wrong about the man with the scar? Did I recklessly accuse him and cause the fight … Best just give the captain the facts and let him decide.*

So Ethan told his tale of the British deserter, the man with a scar on his left cheek, who had accosted him back at General Washington's camp, seemingly seeking information about the expedition. He also mentioned being surprised to see the same man later at Newburyport, though he'd thought that the fellow's original company wasn't one of those selected to go. Finally, Ethan described the evening's encounter, only leaving out the part where he accused the man of being a spy.

Daniel Morgan nodded but said nothing throughout Ethan's long narrative. When Ethan finished his tale, Morgan scowled and said, "The man was a goddamned spy. Reckon you caught him passing a note to a loyalist who'll take it straight to the Brits—I'd bet my life on it. He figured to knife you so's you couldn't turn him in."

"I think that's about the size of it," Ethan agreed. "I thought so at the time, but wanted to be sure—to see what you thought on it."

"What *I think*, is that you did some damned good work tonight, Ethan. Like as not, we'll never catch the accomplice, but at least we're rid of the traitor. We can send word back downstream for folks to be on the lookout for suspicious loyalists or Brits. You head on back to your bunk now, Ethan. I'll speak with the colonel in the morning so's there'll be no repercussions for you, and so's he can warn the other officers to keep a better watch for such doings."

"Thank you, sir. Though I doubt I'll be able to sleep after this. A bit … tightly wound … if you understand."

Morgan smiled. "Yep. Expect so. Natural. Happens to all of us after a close action. Tell you what, if you're agreeable—since we're already up and awake—let's have a writing lesson. No knowing when we'll get another chance, with the wilderness calling."

Ethan could hardly believe his ears. He'd just killed a man with his knife, was still covered in blood, and felt weak and shaky from the ordeal. But Daniel Morgan wanted him to teach a writing lesson. He shrugged. *Why not?*

"All right, sir. If you wish."

"Good, good. Thank you, Ethan. I been thinking on the different sounds letters make … vowels and constants, I believe you called them?"

"*Consonants*," Ethan answered. "Vowels and *consonants*."

"Yes, that was them," Morgan responded with a nod and a grin.

◄◄◄◄◄◆►►►►►

Sunday September 24, 1775 – Fort Western, Maine (Massachusetts Colony):

"Captain Morgan, you'll start upriver with your rifle battalion tomorrow morning," Colonel Arnold announced while gazing at the map spread out on the table in front of him. Daniel Morgan, Lieutenant Colonel Christopher Greene, commander of the First

Infantry Battalion, and Major Return Johnathon Meigs, commander of Second Battalion, leaned over the table on either side of Arnold as he spoke. Absent from the gathering of senior expedition officers was Lieutenant Colonel Roger Enos, of Third Battalion, as his force had not yet arrived at the fort and weren't expected for another day or so.

"Colonel Greene, you'll follow with First Battalion the day after tomorrow, then you, Major, will follow the next day. Colonel Enos will come along with Third Battalion one or two days later."

"Excuse me, sir," Greene said. "But do you think it's a good idea to spread our groups out so in a potentially hostile region?"

"It's a reasonable question, Christopher ... but I believe the risks are negligible until we cross over into Canada. The route isn't well known, and certainly hasn't been used in years. It's highly unlikely we'll meet any hostiles enroute, and I believe it's best to let our esteemed riflemen blaze the trail and clear any major obstacles before the bulk of the army comes through. No good getting ourselves bunched up and bogged down along the trail. I expect there will be limited good campsites as it is."

"I agree with that, Colonel," Morgan interjected. "Our rifles can handle any skirmishers or Indians they might think to send out along the trail—assuming their spy got his note passed through and the news made it all the way to Quebec ahead of us, which seems doubtful. But ... shouldn't we have a rendezvous point for the entire force once we cross the border?"

"It's a good point. Yes, the odds of being attacked increase greatly once we come down from the hills into Canada, so it would be wise to bring our four battalions together from that point forward. Let's rendezvous ... *here* ... at Lake Mégantic. We'll proceed as a united force thereafter.

"I've had a copy of this map made for each of you commanders ..." Arnold continued as he reached across the table to retrieve three rolled sheets of paper, handing one to each officer. "And we've already gone over the route in detail, so there should be no questions about that ...?" He looked at each officer in turn, but all three shook their heads. "Good."

Then he reached out his hand to Morgan. "Good luck and Godspeed, Daniel," he said, and the two shook hands.

Greene and Meigs also shook hands with Morgan, with Greene adding, "Good hunting, Morgan."

"Thank you, Colonel Greene. Colonel Arnold … Major Meigs, good luck to y'all as well. See y'all in Canada."

◄◄◄◄◄◆►►►►►

Monday September 25, 1775 – Kennebec River, Maine (Massachusetts Colony):

Daniel Morgan led the rifle battalion in the first bateau, and for reasons Ethan did not entirely understand, chose him and Levi to man the boat with him. Ethan suspected it was because they were the youngest men in the Virginia Rifle Company, and Morgan felt some responsibility for their safety—especially Ethan's, as the captain had brought him along for mostly selfish reasons against his mother's wishes. It likely also helped that Levi's family lived along a broad creek and owned a rowboat—Ethan and Levi had gone fishing together using it on several occasions, so they at least had some experience handling a rowboat, while many of the other men had no experience whatsoever.

Whatever the reasons, Ethan was grateful to be traveling in the same boat with Morgan; it gave him a sense of confidence—not quite of invulnerability, but the next best thing to it—that if something bad were to happen, he was certain he could not be in a better place than right next to the indominable spirit and imposing physical presence that was Captain Daniel Morgan.

Aside from getting to travel alongside the captain, Ethan felt elated that he'd get to ride in a boat rather than trudge along with those that were relegated to walking the whole way to Canada. At least he felt that way when he first got in the boat, until he realized that the Kennebec was not the smooth, gently flowing stream he'd experienced back home. This river was immense, powerful, and fast moving, and they would be rowing upstream the whole way.

The bateau had two long one-man oars that were threaded through oarlocks, one to each side. A man working one of these oars faced toward the back, or *stern* of the boat, so he could gain the most leverage by pulling the oar toward his chest while bracing himself with his legs. The third man would either sit in the stern of the boat and steer with a large paddle—when the water was slow moving—or paddle vigorously in swifter water to aid the oarsmen. When the water got rougher, he might move to the bow to watch out for and fend off rocks. The three of them took turns in rotation every hour or so, switching from one side to the other manning the oars or shifting to using the paddle.

After the first several hours, when his arms began to ache from the constant rowing, Ethan began to feel like he had on that day, now so long ago, when he'd marched out from Winchester at the tail end of Morgan's Riflemen—like there was no way he could possibly endure it.

Then he reminded himself that he'd survived that hike, and eventually it had gotten easier. He was determined he would survive this as well, and more importantly, he would not let Daniel Morgan down. So he continued to pull on his oar.

For his part, Morgan rowed with a strong steady pace, showing no signs of fatigue, as if he could do it all day long with effortless ease.

And when he glanced over at Levi, Ethan was gratified to see his friend was red in the face, and seemed to be just as beat as he was, or maybe more so. And then he chastised himself for enjoying Levi's discomfort. *Misery loves company, I guess.*

By the middle of the second day on the river, he found that it had gotten easier—aided by some useful pointers from the captain, though in camp at night he could feel soreness in muscles that he never knew he had.

At the end of the day, they stopped for the night at a place called Fort Halifax, though the decrepit, moldering buildings left over from the French and Indian War bore little resemblance to a fort, in Ethan's mind. The only memorable thing about it was that it was at the end of the old military road that ran up the shore of the river. This meant that all the supplies that had been carried by the wagons and carts that Colonel Arnold had hired out from Fort Western would now have to be unloaded, and those goods would now be distributed amongst the bateaux. That not only made the boats more cramped and uncomfortable, but also made them ride lower in the water, making them more burdensome to propel.

By the middle of the third day, the first day out from Fort Halifax, Ethan was starting to envy the men he could occasionally glimpse marching along the east side of the river, though those soldiers no longer had a road and had to make do with rough game or Indian trails that weaved in and out of the surrounding trees.

Although the river was broad and mostly smooth, twice during the day they came to rough water where the current was so swift they simply could not make headway against it, and their boat was bumped and jostled by unseen rocks under the surface.

It was then that Ethan understood why Captain Morgan had ordered the marchers to stay even with the boats and not to forge ahead, even though they likely could've outpaced the vessels. When the boats could progress no further, the men marching alongside came down to the shore, then pre-attached ropes were thrown out to them from the bateaux so that they could help pull the boats forward. In this manner, the boats' handlers were able to make it past the swift water and resume their unaided rowing thereafter.

◄◄◄◄◄◆►►►►►

It was the first time truly camping out on their expedition up the Kennebec, and the men set to work setting up A-shaped tents in a wide pasture. The canvas tents were held upright by two poles and secured with ropes. The men always looked for a smooth, level patch of ground, ideally situated between two trees to which the ropes might be attached.

Both officers and enlisted men slept in the tents, typically six to a tent, though the officers enjoyed the "privilege" of only having four men in theirs. Each group of men and their tent were often referred to as a "mess." These "messmates" were typically ones that spent the day together, either on the boats or marching, and then at the end of the day, pitched their tent, built their campfire, cooked their meal, and slept together, often bundled closely to share warmth.

Once again, Ethan felt privileged to be one of Captain Morgan's messmates, as it not only kept him in close proximity, but also afforded him the luxury of only have four men in the tent. Along with Levi, Morgan asked Sergeant Murphy to be their fourth—though he was one of the men marching rather than boating—as the sergeant could be relied on to relay any necessary orders or instructions from Morgan to the other captains in the evening or early morning. Sergeant Murphy's inclusion in their mess pleased Ethan as well; he'd liked Murphy from the start, and he'd already made a good connection with the jolly Irishman through their rifle training.

And Murphy quickly proved his frontiersman skills as well, getting their campfire put together and ready to light in just a few minutes after he'd finished showing the boys how to set up the tent.

Ethan noticed Murphy had gathered long branches for the fire, rather than chopping off shorter sections as one would typically toss on a fire, so he asked the sergeant why.

"Oh, saves time, don't ya see, lad. No need doin' all that choppin' when yer already gassed at the end of the day. Let the fire do the work for ye, and also dry out the wood as it goes. Watch and see …"

He proceeded to lay four or five branches across the place where the fire would be, with the branches crossing each other like the spokes of a wheel. Then he placed some crumbled up birchbark near the "hub," took a small, brass tinderbox from his haversack, and struck a spark into the tinder with the flint and steel. He leaned over and blew on it for a moment, then soon had a bright flame flickering, and a few moments later the fire was blazing merrily.

"Now, as the long sticks burn through, ye just shoves 'em further into the flame, and she keeps on burning. And when needed, ye throws another stick across the flame, easy as ye please; no choppin' needed."

"That seems good to me," Ethan said as he held his hands out over the warm blaze, enjoying the sensation in the quickly cooling evening air.

"On days we get a soakin', either of rain or of wadin' the stream, we'll string ropes across here to hang our clothes on for dryin'," Murphy said, as he poked at the logs to make a smooth spot for the large, iron cooking pot to rest.

He'd already filled the pot halfway with water, and when it was near to boiling, he tossed in their evening's ration of salted beef and some dried peas. Finally, he dumped in some flour. "That'll thicken 'er a bit, lads … turns it from soup into stew. More satisfyin' for an empty belly. Next time, we'll throw in some fish — either the dried ones or fresh if we catch some — then we'll call it chowder, though it's otherwise the same damned thing." He grinned. "Ain't much, but beats starvin'," he said, continuing to smile.

Captain Morgan, who'd been out speaking to the other companies' captains, returned just in time for the food to be dished out, and they all sat on the ground around the fire eating their meal with their fingers on simple, handmade wood plates. Ethan decided that after a long hard day on the boat, this simple meal felt like a feast.

The sun set shortly after their meal was consumed, and the four of them sat around the campfire as Sergeant Murphy regaled them with tales of his time fur trapping in the wilderness out west of the Shenandoah Valley.

As Murphy finished up a particularly humorous tale that involved a mule, three Indians, and a black bear, Ethan noticed Captain Morgan had nodded off, leaning his back against a tree stump, his arms folded across his chest.

"You sure do know a lot about the frontier life," Ethan said. "I've always admired men with that kind of experience, having been raised mostly in a town myself."

Murphy laughed. "Yep, sure do sound romantic an' all, don't it? But it's a hard life, me lads. Man don't live to an old age doin' it, I'll promise you that. And there ain't hardly no lassies out in them woods." He winked, and Ethan felt his face blush. "I'll tell you what … When this here war's over, I'm thinkin' on settin' me up a little farm somewhere back east. Maybe find me a fine, bonny lass to set up house with. Fellow I met on this expedition says he was one o' them as took Fort Ticonderoga from the Brits. Says there's some beautiful farmland just waitin' for the takin' up there in the north part o' New York Colony. May have to go have myself a gander one day …"

"Sounds nice," Levi said, nodding. "Always was partial to life on a farm, seein's how I growed up there, I reckon. Best o' both worlds, as they say … Get to be outdoors, hunting and fishing and mucking around, but still … enjoy a home cooked meal and sleep in a warm bed at the end of the day."

Murphy laughed. "And that's just what you ain't gonna git out here in this wilderness, laddie."

◄◄◄◄◄◆►►►►►

Early in the morning on the fourth day aboard the bateau, they encountered their first major obstacle. Looking ahead, they could see white water plunging down over a series of rock ledges, then swirling through an area of raging rapids. As they rowed toward it, Morgan turned to them and had to shout to be heard above the growing sound of the rushing waters ahead. "Map says it's Ticonic Falls; half a mile long … rapids and rock ledges that can't be passed by boat more'n the first few hundred yards. Portage is on the west bank. Keep to the left side. When I give the signal, pull for all you're worth until we hit the bank."

The two boys nodded their understanding, and within minutes were straining at the oars to keep up any forward momentum. Morgan tossed down his paddle and picked up a long "setting pole," a purpose-built, metal tipped sturdy length of wood used to propel a boat forward in places where a paddle would strike on rocks or get mired in mud. In this manner, they were able to move forward for several more minutes until, as promised, Morgan pointed toward the lefthand shore and they made for it with all they had.

Ten minutes of strenuous labor later, they rammed the front end of the boat onto a gravel bar at the edge of the water. The stream was calmer here, so they jumped into the frigid water and waded to shore, where Morgan tied off the boat.

They collapsed onto a grassy ledge just beyond the gravel bar and sat for a few minutes to catch their breath. But as soon as the next boat approached, Morgan ordered them to their feet again so they could catch the ropes that were tossed ashore in order to assist the other boats to the bank.

Even before all the boats were beached, they waded back out into the water to begin the task of unloading all the goods from their boat. The boats were simply too heavy to pull out of the water loaded with goods, and so everything had to be offloaded and stacked on the shore—food, tents, gunpowder, weapons, medical supplies, and other miscellaneous items—a process that took several hours.

If Ethan had any illusions that his exertions would be ended for the day once their bateau was pulled from the water, he was quickly disabused of the notion. By that time, the men who'd been marching up the east bank had been ordered to wade across to assist with the portage, so Morgan grabbed one of them to assist, and the four of them flipped the boat over so it was upside down.

Then they ran two of the setting poles under the boat from side to side, and the four of them lifted it to waist level. Ethan couldn't recall ever lifting anything so heavy in his life, but he was determined not to let the others down. He noticed some of the teams, clearly including stronger men than he, were simply lifting their boats onto their shoulders for the hike. *That looks unbearably painful*, he decided, and was once again grateful for the invaluable backwoods savvy of Captain Morgan.

They headed up the trail with their awkward, heavy load and quickly discovered that the portage trail was anything but a smooth path. It wandered over rugged terrain, where rocks and tree roots were a constant peril to the walkers, who could not easily see where they were stepping with their weighty burden. Several times, despite being led by Captain Morgan, they stumbled off the trail into the brush, or banged into the trunk of a tree, nearly causing them to drop their bateau. Even with his great strength and endurance, Morgan called a halt to set the boat down for a rest every few dozen yards.

In the end, after countless grueling hours, when they'd finally reached the large, cleared area where the river smoothed out again, even Captain Morgan sat back against the bottom of the boat with his eyes closed for several minutes. Ethan rubbed at his arms to try to get some life back into them, and resisted the urge to stretch is leg muscles for fear they'd cramp up on him. He decided that he had just endured the longest half mile of his life. And Levi, being smaller and lighter than Ethan, had clearly suffered it worse; he lay on the ground shivering, his arms wrapped around his legs and his eyes closed.

The good news was, Captain Morgan called a halt for the day, and ordered the men to make camp once all the boats and goods had been hauled upstream to the reentry point.

In the middle of the night, Ethan was awakened by two sensations. The first was that Levi had moved right up next to him in his bedroll. Under ordinary circumstances, that would've been annoying, and Ethan would've shoved him back to his spot in the tent, but given that the second sensation was of freezing cold biting at his ears, Levi's warm body next to him wasn't all that bad after all. But the reminder that winter came early in this northern environment caused Ethan some concern and made it difficult to regain his slumber.

◄◄◄◄◄◆►►►►►

Early the next day, Ethan groaned when he saw what appeared to be another set of rapids fast approaching. The thought of another grueling portage filled him with dread. But Captain Morgan, as if divining his thoughts, turned around and said, "These here rapids run for about five miles, but they say a boat can make it through, even fully loaded. We'll stay near the east bank this time, so if we need help, we can throw out the ropes. So, it's rowing and poling, boys." He grinned brightly, and the two young men in his boat couldn't help grinning back.

True to his word, though they were battered and jostled, and nearly tipped the boat over—twice—they eventually made it through the swift water with some timely help from the walkers along the shore.

This time, their efforts were rewarded by one of the most idyllic sights Ethan could ever recall. They entered a long, smooth stretch of water with scarcely a ripple. The calm water reflected an area of small settlements and farms, sparkling with the bright colors of autumn. The few inhabitants they passed stopped whatever they were doing to gaze in wonder as the fleet of small boats slipped past. And the men on the boats stared back, every bit as mesmerized by the raw beauty of this northern paradise.

That night, they pitched their tents in a beautiful green meadow of knee-high grass, surrounded by trees glowing in red, orange, and yellow on the landward side and the picturesque wilderness stream on the other. This night Ethan fell asleep to a tremendous sensation of peace and wellbeing such as he'd rarely experienced before. *If only this could last*, he thought as he faded off in slumber.

◄◄◄◄◄◆►►►►►

True to form, the fickle Kennebec did not disappoint when it came to providing its travelers with a steady series of dramatic changes and challenges. With almost no transition or warning, the beautiful tranquil river of the day before turned in a heartbeat to a raging monster.

As they rowed into what appeared to be a gentle, wide pool that simply ended with a heavily forested hillside, their first hint that something was amiss was a roaring sound that grew steadily louder as they moved forward. When they were nearly three quarters of the way across the pool, they could see above and to their right a narrow gorge, down which the river plunged in boiling rapids.

This time, Daniel Morgan did not look back at them, nor did he provide any instructions; he simply turned the boat with his paddle and headed toward the raging gorge, increasing his pace as he did so. Ethan and Levi exchanged a dark look, but there was little they could do but follow their captain's lead and begin to row harder.

They reached the swift water, and for a time made some headway, but they soon had to switch the oars for their setting poles so they could push and pry their way from one rock outcropping to the next.

Ethan looked to the shore to see if they might be able to throw out ropes to the marchers, but it was not to be; the chasm was too deep to get ropes to the men, who gazed down helplessly from on high. This time they were on their own, with no possibility of outside help.

Finally, they came to a place where they could simply go no further; the setting poles could not provide enough leverage against the raging waters to gain any headway. Without a word, Daniel Morgan tossed his pole into the boat, grabbed the rope tied to the bow, and went over the side into the water. Ethan gasped in surprise, expecting to see the captain swept away by the torrent. But in seconds he felt a strong jerk, and the boat was moving again. He scrambled up to the bow and saw Morgan, the rope over his right shoulder, straining forward, waist deep, with the frothing waters surging around him.

Before he could think better of it, Ethan was up and over the side, plunging into the icy stream up to his chest. He gasped at the shock of the sudden cold and stumbled, straining to keep his feet under him under the pressure of the water that threatened to toss him back against the sharp bow of the boat. But he managed to steady himself, then reached up, grabbed the rope, and did his best to help Morgan pull the bateau forward over the slippery rocks, pushing against the gushing water.

A minute later, Ethan sensed something large land in the water next to him and send a stream of frigid spray down the neck of his jacket. He looked over just in time to see Levi's horrified face slip under the water. Ethan instinctively reached out with his right hand and grabbed, coming up with a handful of hair with Levi attached to it. He pulled hard, lifting Levi's face out of the water, and with it his flailing arms.

"Get your feet under you, for God's sake!" Ethan shouted, while doing his best not to lose his own footing and continuing to pull Levi forward by the hair.

"Ow. Damn it, Ethan … that hurts!" Levi shouted back. "Stop pullin' on my hair!"

"Better than drowning. Get up here and grab the rope."

After another minute of thrashing, Levi was upright, and he too was finally tugging on the rope.

Though he was too busy to look back, Ethan heard Levi call out, "Thanks, Ethan. Reckon you saved my life there."

"Doubt it," Ethan called back. "One of the other boats would've fished you out downstream. Wasn't going to let you out of your share of the work *that* easy."

Levi laughed but said nothing more about it.

With the three of them now in the water, pulling, the boat began to make steady headway. After minutes that seemed like hours, Ethan noticed the river had become brighter. He looked up and saw they were coming to the end of the gorge. Morgan apparently noticed too, as he turned and shouted, "Levi, climb on back into the boat, and get ready to toss them ropes over to the men."

Levi scrambled to obey, but his waterlogged clothes, nearly numb legs, and the slick sides of the boat made it extremely difficult. Finally, Ethan had to let go of the rope and help lift Levi up so he could tumble over the side.

When they came into the clear, Levi tossed two ropes to the men waiting on the shore, who held them fast while Ethan and Morgan dragged themselves back aboard.

The stream was every bit as rough and swift in this section, but the addition of the men pulling from the shore made the going much easier.

After another half hour of being towed, they came to a place where they could simply go no further. Here, the river plunged over a twenty-foot-high ledge of rock, split in the middle by a large, rocky island.

"Skowhegan Falls," Morgan shouted. "The only portage is up the cliff face on that island in the stream. We'll pull up the boat on that beach there and wait for the others. Then we'll have to climb up and rig ropes and pullies to get everything to the top."

Ethan groaned inwardly, *Another portage ... and this one straight up a cliff? What next, we fly to the moon?*

But all he said was, "Yes, sir."

◄◄◄◄◄◆►►►►►

It was another long day of portaging, up and over the rock island in the midst of the waterfall, but fortunately for Ethan, he was not asked to do any of the difficult and dangerous rope work. Other men, like Daniel Morgan, had the experience with such maneuvers that he, thankfully, lacked. So he and Levi were only asked to carry supplies once they were pulled up over the falls ... and carry, and carry, and carry, back and forth to a wide, cleared space on the island atop the cliff. There they eventually made camp for the night.

In the morning, Ethan walked around with the captain taking notes with a pencil and paper as Morgan inspected each boat and ordered repairs to be done. All of the boats had damage of one kind or another from the battering they'd taken since their launch from Gardinerston, and most leaked in numerous places. Morgan paid little attention to the minor issues, only having Ethan write down the most serious problems, of which there were many. Mr. Colburn, who'd built the boats, had sent several of his boat makers along on the expedition to make repairs in the field as needed, and after Morgan completed his rounds, they went straight to work. The repairs took the remainder of the day, forcing the battalion to spend another night camped out on the tiny island in the midst of the stream.

◄◄◄◄◄◆►►►►►

The next week went by in a blur for Ethan, a seemingly never-ending, grueling series of portages around rapids or waterfalls, interspersed with long stretches of the most spectacularly beautiful, smooth, calm water imaginable.

The only memorable moment came just after they'd finished their portage around Norridgewock Falls. Ethan was once again making the rounds with Captain Morgan, inspecting the sadly beaten bateaux, when to their complete surprise, up strode

158

Colonel Arnold accompanied, as usual, by his aide, Eleazer Oswald.

After an exchange of salutes, Arnold said, "Captain Morgan … good to see you. I see you've made some good progress."

"Thank you, and likewise good to see you, sir, though we didn't expect you until Lake Mégantic."

"Well, with my experienced Penobscot crew, streamlined canoe, and little baggage, we were able to make good time, so that I could move between the four battalions as they progressed, yours being the foremost, of course. How're the men holding up?" Arnold asked.

"The men are holding up well, Colonel. Oh, they've been worked to the bone, that's certain. And we've had plenty of bumps, bruises, and several near drownings—not to mention plenty o' whining and carping—but so far, no serious casualties. Spirits are still high. Everyone's still itching to get on to Quebec so's we can take it to them Brits.

"All in all, they've done well, Colonel … I couldn't be better pleased." Morgan beamed like a proud father speaking of his well-performing sons.

"Good, good to hear. Excellent, Captain. Excellent. And the boats?"

"See for yourself, Colonel," Morgan answered, and frowned. "They're taking a pounding. Every boat has leaks, some worse than others. Most have cracked or missing boards. Others have damaged oarlocks or broken oars. Colburn's boat men are doing what they can, but we're like to lose more than a few bateaux before the end."

"Well, it can't be helped, I'm afraid. Do what you can with them," Arnold said as he gazed down inside the nearest bateau, shaking his head sadly. "The good news is, according to the map, you're now a third of the way to Quebec City, and the worst of the river is behind you. Within the week you'll be at the portage between the Kennebec and the Dead River, what the Indians call *The Great Carrying Place*. I've been assured that the portage is relatively easy, with three navigable ponds along the way to ease the passage. The only thing that should slow you is you'll need to take the time to widen the trail and remove obstacles as necessary for the other battalions to follow."

"Understood," Morgan nodded.

"After that, you'll reach the Dead River," Arnold continued, "And, as the name implies, it's a slow-moving, smooth-flowing stream. Then another short portage of five miles or so across a hilly section called the *Height of Land*, and you will find another stream that will drop you right into Lake Mégantic, at which point you will be in Canada."

"Good to hear, Colonel. We're looking forward to that."

Colonel Arnold then greeted Ethan warmly, shaking his hand, and asking after his health, which Ethan greatly appreciated, though he assumed he was just another soldier to the commanding officer. Then Colonel Arnold spent the rest of that day walking around the camp, chatting up the men, patting backs, shaking hands, and generally encouraging the riflemen with his contagious enthusiasm and dauntless spirit. Ethan was even more impressed with the man than he'd been at the start, and Colonel Arnold's effect on the morale of the troops was immeasurable and plain for all to see.

◄◄◄◄◄◆►►►►►

Monday October 6, 1775 – The Carrying Stream, Maine (Massachusetts Colony):

"It's like in one o' them old pirate storybooks, boys," Daniel Morgan said with a grin, as they rowed along the west bank of the Kennebec. "We're to look for a large mountain, shaped like a sugar loaf. Then the river turns eastward, still within sight of that mountain. Looking backwards, it will seem like the mountain rises right up out o' the stream. At that place we'll find a rocky brook, called the *Carrying Stream* that empties into the main river. That'll be the start of the portage."

The boys nodded, and from then on gazed at the skyline as they rowed.

"*There!* There it is." Levi suddenly called out from his present position on the bow of the boat. "The sugar loaf."

Morgan and Ethan gazed off to where Levi pointed, and sure enough, through the low clouds and misty haze in the distance, a tall, round-topped mountain loomed.

Then Morgan looked back along the river ahead of them and said, "And that there's our eastward bend …"

A half hour later, they stood on a sandbar gazing back across their beached bateau at the swift flowing river behind.

"Well, we made it, boys," Daniel Morgan said with a broad, satisfied smile. "We made it up the river road; beat old Kennebec at her own game."

They stood there taking in the sight even as the next bateau arrived, its men hoping out and wading to shore, pulling the boat after them.

"C'mon, boys, lets grab the gear and start making camp."

And even as he said this, a hard, icy cold rain began to fall.

Chapter 8. Death March

"A direful howling wilderness,
not describable."
- Dr. Isaac Senter
Journal of the Expedition to Quebec

Wednesday October 8, 1775 – The Great Carrying Place, Maine (Massachusetts Colony):

When Captain Morgan announced that the day following their arrival at the Great Carrying Place would be one of rest, as a reward for their hard labors on the Kennebec, Ethan was elated. So much so that he was having a hard time remembering the last time he had an entire day on which he had no work to do.

But the rain that'd begun when they'd first beached their boats intensified during the night, lashing their tent's canvas, making it rattle fitfully. By morning, a cold wind had picked up, driving the rain sideways in gusts, making for a miserable breakfast—and lunch … and dinner. There being nothing to do, Ethan, Levi, and Sergeant Murphy played cards, their usual game of Whist. Captain Morgan declined their invitation to join in, saying it wouldn't be fair for him to win every hand and take their money—though they had no money and only used odd tokens such as pebbles or buttons. Ethan wasn't sure if Morgan was joking or serious, but he suspected the captain was probably an expert at cards and gambling, like so many other things he did.

So Morgan spent much of the day napping, or sitting up staring out into the rain as his three messmates played cards, told jokes, and swapped stories—Murphy having the most of those, for obvious reasons.

And the next day was even worse; a howling wind sent blinding sheets of rain that threatened to snap the ropes of their tent. So Morgan reluctantly ordered another day of staying put in camp. And though Ethan's muscles were happy for another day of rest, the remainder of him was ready to get up and get moving again. Sitting in a dripping, drafty tent all day was beginning to wear thin. The only thing that happened to break up the miserable monotony of the day was when Levi sat down in front of Ethan and said, "Happy Birthday, by the way."

"What?"

Levi laughed. "Yeah, I had nothing better to do, so I started counting up the days since we left Boston. Just figured out that it's October 10th, your birthday." He grinned at Ethan's surprise.

"Well, I'll be … I totally forgot my own birthday," Ethan said, shaking his head. "Eighteen … Sure is different from last year when momma made such a fuss over me. Mmm … think of all that good *food* she cooked. I can still taste that apple pie she baked for me."

Levi groaned. "*Apple pie* … After all this bland travel food, I can't hardly remember what that tastes like."

"I can," Ethan answered with a dreamy look. "It was good, I'll tell you that … really, *really* good."

"Okay, now I'm sorry I brought it up," Levi said, rolling his eyes, which set Ethan to laughing. Levi laughed with him.

The weather finally broke sometime during that night, so that when the sun rose in the morning, they were able to break camp, pick up their bateau, and start the five-mile slog to the first carry pond. And a tiresome, muddy slog it was. The heavy rains of the past several days had flooded the trails, making the muck knee deep in places.

For Ethan, carrying the heavy boat was always the most difficult task they were asked to do on the expedition, even under the most ideal circumstances. And this day the conditions were anything but ideal; on the rough, twisting, slippery trail it seemed an impossible task.

An hour into their portage, as they pushed through knee deep mud that threatened to pull their boots off with each step, Ethan strained to hold up his corner of the boat, which was on the rear left side. He'd just extracted his left boot from the muck and was preparing to put it down again in front of the right one when the boat suddenly lurched to the right and the weight became unbearable. It drove him into the mud in a kneeling position with the lifting pole across his legs. After a few moments of squirming, he managed to extract himself, and leaving the pole lying in the mud, he stood up.

He heard a groan coming from the opposite side of the boat—Levi's position. He sloshed around the back of the boat and found Levi on his back in the mud, his body almost completely immersed, with the setting pole pinning him down. Fortunately, his head was still sticking out of the muck. Daniel Morgan was already there, lifting on the pole. He looked up at Ethan and said, "C'mon, Ethan, bear a hand and let's get him outta there. We'll have t'leverage this pole off in order to free him."

Ethan did as he was told, but it wasn't until Sergeant Murphy came around and lent his strength to the effort that they were able to lift Levi's side of the pole enough to drag him out from under it.

But rather than immediately yanking him to his feet, Morgan stood over Levi where he lay in the deep mud, gazing down into his eyes. "You hurt, son? Any broken bones?"

Levi just stared back with a blank look, as if he didn't understand the question. "I … I'm sorry, Captain. Sorry I spilled the boat. Foot slipped on a log I think … slick one … hidden under the mud. I'm sorry …"

Morgan frowned. "Have you been shirking, Private Miller, or did you do it o' purpose?"

Levi shook his head, "No, sir. I been … I been trying my hardest, though it's a durned heavy load, and mighty awkward."

"Well, then, Levi, you got nothing to be sorry *for*," Morgan answered. "Hell, every last one of us has slipped and fallen at some point. Done it myself plenty. Nothing to be ashamed of. Make sure you can wiggle your feet and arms so's we know you ain't busted nothing. Then we'll pull you up outta that muck. Reckon then we could all use a little rest 'fore we carry on."

And true to his word, they enjoyed a blissful quarter hour of rest before once again heaving up the heavy load and continuing on their way. Hauling the bateau the five miles to the first carry pond took most of the day.

And when they finally set the boat down and sat to rest at their destination, Morgan looked up at the sky, scratched at his chin a moment, then said, "Reckon there's still a couple of hours of daylight left, boys. Let's hoof it back to the start of the portage, and we'll pitch our tent there again. That way we can be up at first light, ready to carry another load o' goods over."

Even Sergeant Murphy groaned, but they all three got to their feet and said, "Yes, sir."

Halfway back to their starting point, they passed the crew of several dozen men assigned to clear obstacles from the trail and widen it so that men coming along after would have an easier time. They'd spent the entire day cutting branches, chopping down trees, and clearing away underbrush in an eight-foot-wide swath. Morgan stopped to spend some time with these men, sending his three messmates on to set up camp.

They were finishing up their evening meal back on the west bank of the Kennebec as the sun was setting when Captain Morgan arrived at camp. He smiled and greeted them warmly, thanking them for pitching the tent and for cooking. Ethan, who was so exhausted he could barely raise his food to his mouth, shook his head in wonder. After a whole day of slogging through the muck, carrying the heavy boat, Morgan seemed no more tired than he'd been at the start of the day.

◄◄◄◄◀◆▶►►►►

At the end of the second day of the portage to First Carry Pond—yet another back-breaking day in which they'd made two round trips carrying supplies—tempers had worn thin in camp, and Ethan was not surprised when a fist fight broke out. It started on the opposite side of a large bonfire the Virginia Rifle company had lit in the middle of camp, in a vain attempt to dry off clothing and equipment from heavy cloud cover that continued to rain on and off throughout the day.

Ethan was sitting near Morgan, as he often was, with Levi next to him with a steady stream of water dripping off their hats. They first noticed the fight when men started yelling, hooting, and scrambling to their feet on the far side of the fire.

Morgan, who'd been sitting on a log speaking with Sergeant Murphy, glanced up, looked across at the fight, shrugged his shoulders, and went back to talking. Fights were not uncommon, and Morgan was generally of the opinion it was best to let the men blow off a little steam and settle their differences quickly. But after several minutes went by, in which the sounds of fists pounding could be heard even above the usual shouts of excitement and encouragement, Morgan stood up and brushed himself off.

"Well," he said, "Reckon that's about enough o' that fun for today … Someone's like to break a bone … or a skull … and then it'll be a mischief tending to them. Or worse, carrying them." He strode around the campfire and forced his way through the men gathered around. Ethan, Levi, and Sergeant Murphy followed to see what the captain would do.

Morgan pushed through the last row of onlookers and stepped right up to the fighters, who were currently on the ground, with the man on top pounding his fist into the man on the bottom. Morgan grabbed the man on top, lifted him up, then held him at arm's length as he grabbed the other and pulled him to his feet. Morgan stood a full head taller than either man, and was also much stronger, so that he was able to hold them apart as he admonished them. "Enough for today, boys. Time to cool it off."

Morgan was calm and nonchalant about the whole business, and did not sound or act like he was particularly upset by the matter—but he *did* expect to be obeyed.

The man in Morgan's right fist immediately wilted and relaxed when he saw who it was that held him tight. He nodded at the captain, so Morgan released him.

But the man held in Morgan's left hand was still fighting mad, and resisted Morgan's grip, pulling and prying at the hand that held him to no avail. He finally tried punching at the arm, then swinging at Morgan's face—which he couldn't quite reach—all the while cursing and spitting.

Ethan exchanged a look with Levi that said, *Bad idea,* fully expecting the next thing would be a hammer-hard fist knocking some sense into the man, or maybe knocking him senseless. But Morgan remained calm, even holding an odd grin on his face. He stepped forward, gripped the man's shirt in front with both hands, then lifted him off his feet. Then, even as Ethan expected Morgan to slam the man to the ground, he simply laid the soldier down on his back, pinning him there with a knee to the chest. As the man squirmed and cussed, Morgan continued to hold him fast, such that he was unable to move. Inexplicably, Morgan never said another word, just gazed down at the man, smiling.

After several moments, the private stopped squirming, and his face relaxed as he gazed up at Morgan. For another moment, no words were spoken, and even the crowd gathered around had stopped talking so all could hear what would happen next. Finally, the man pinned to the ground said, "Sorry, sir. Lost my temper there. I … I sincerely beg your pardon, Captain … and promise to reform my behavior."

Morgan gazed into the man's eyes for another long moment, then chuckled and said, "Pardon granted, and no harm done; at least not to me. Now, on your feet. And I'll have you two shake hands and call the matter settled."

The two men then shook hands as ordered, and went back to their seats by the fire with fresh bruises, black eyes, and bloody lips, but otherwise no worse for the wear.

◄◄◄◄◄◆►►►►►

Though the weather had been wretched, and the work back-breaking hard, when Morgan's Virginia Riflemen had finished carting all of their boats and equipment to First Carry Pond, Morgan gave them the following day off to rest up before starting on the next leg of their trek, which would be to float across the pond, then portage everything to the second pond.

This free day led Ethan to experience two things he would not soon forget. The first was a grove of trees that had odd carvings in the trunks. Many of these had clearly been carved long ago, and were nearly healed over, while others were relatively fresh. He could make out images of many different animals: moose, otter, deer, and beaver were easily identified. And there were a wide variety of birds, along with many odd symbols whose meaning he could not discern. Captain Morgan said they were made by

Indians, likely to record successful hunts, or to give some kind of guidance or instruction to their fellows that only they could decipher.

Ethan found these carvings fascinating, and spent nearly an hour just going from tree to tree trying to puzzle out each one. Finally, just before he left the grove, he pulled out his belt knife and carved his initials "EC" and the year "1775" in one of the trunks. *There, let the Indians puzzle that one out,* he thought, and grinned.

The second thing that happened that day was the fishing. Men went down to the shore with spears, nets, and lines of string with hooks to see if there were any fish to be caught.

Levi had brought along several long lengths of spun linen line and a couple of bent hooks. The two of them quickly cut willow poles and tied the threads to the end. When they reached the shore, they could scarcely believe their eyes: men were pulling fish out of the lake as quickly as they could spear or cast a net. Large lake trout they were, shimmering and sparkling as they wriggled on the shore. Ethan and Levi immediately waded out into the pond and cast their lines in, not even bothering to bait the hooks. Within seconds they each had hooked a fish, and within an hour, dozens of fish were flopping on the shore behind them. Ethan had never seen anything like it before, and Levi, who'd fished the abundant streams around Winchester his entire life, admitted that he hadn't either.

That evening was the first time since they'd left Fort Western that everyone in camp ate their fill and then some. And unknown to Ethan, it would also be the last time for many days to come.

◄◄◄◄◄◆►►►►►

Tuesday October 10, 1775 – Second Carry Pond, Maine (Massachusetts Colony):

Daniel Morgan pushed the men hard, and expected a lot out of them, though Ethan considered him generally good-natured about it. He would suffer no shirking nor straggling on the trail. And though he didn't seem to mind grumbling and griping, it never changed his mind on anything, so men mostly stopped doing it in front of him.

But in private, Ethan overheard plenty of complaining about Morgan, especially from the men of the other two rifle companies made up mostly of Pennsylvanians—Captain Matthew Smith's company being the more vocal of the two. Ethan wasn't surprised by this, considering their commanding officer did not impress him in the least. Smith did not seem to be a serious, hard-driving officer like most of the others. He seemed happy to sit back and supervise, rather than pitch in to help like Captain Morgan. But the men of Smith's company seemed to like him, as he often allowed his men to goof off—"well-deserved rest," he called it—which only left more work for the other rifle companies.

Ethan wondered when Morgan and Smith were going to come to blows over this, but so far it hadn't happened. Then, as they were setting up camp at Second Carry Pond, after a much easier portage of only a half mile from the first pond, they heard a gunshot in the near distance.

Morgan, who'd been helping set up the tent, stopped, looked up, and said, "What the hell …?"

One of Morgan's more controversial orders to all three rifle companies had been no firing of guns without authorization. The purpose of this command was to save ammunition for when it would be needed in battle and to not needlessly give away their presence and position, should there be enemy scouts or hostile Indians in the area. And typically, the only reason for firing off shots, given that most of the game had been scared off by the presence of hundreds of men, was to easily unload one's rifle at the end of the day. Morgan considered this practice just plain lazy and wasteful, ordering instead the more tedious and time-consuming method of teasing out the lead with a screw rod, then carefully shaking out the powder and feeding it back into the powder horn.

But this time, someone had clearly broken the rules, and from the sound of it, someone from Captain Smith's company. Morgan dropped the rope and stomped off in the direction of the sound.

Sergeant Murphy looked over at the boys and grinned. He gestured toward Morgan's back and said in a low voice, "Think we'll want t'see this, lads."

So Morgan's three messmates followed along behind their commander.

They stepped through some bushes and into a small clearing where a half dozen riflemen were unloading their rifles—the hard way—but one was sitting down at his leisure, his rifle leaned against the log he was sitting on.

Morgan stepped up to the soldier and snatched up his rifle. Noting that the powder was gone, he flipped the rifle and smelled the end of the barrel.

"You just fired off this rifle, Private … against my orders," Morgan scowled.

But the man seemed unconcerned, not even bothering to stand, as would have been proper when addressed by an officer—though saluting wasn't generally practiced in the field. "Oh, no, sir. Not me … I never fired this gun. I'm just quick at unloading, is all." And then he grinned, like he'd just told some kind of joke.

Morgan scowled. "You're a liar. Don't tell me I don't know the smell of a rifle that's just been fired."

"Well, guess I reckon you don't, since I ain't fired this'n."

Ethan could see Morgan's face beginning to flush. He reached over, picked up a thick, three-foot long stick that was meant for the fire, and waved it in the private's face. "By God, you'll confess and admit what you done, or I'm fixing to give you a thrashing."

But then a voice called out, "Hey, what's all this, then?" And up strode Captain Smith. "What's going on, Morgan?"

Morgan frowned at Smith. "This man disobeyed orders and unloaded his gun by firing it. Now he denies it. I'll not suffer insubordination and lying in my command. I'll have his hide."

"You will do no such thing," Smith shot back. "These are *my* men, and I shall discipline them as I see fit, and no other."

Ethan was surprised, as he'd never seen Captain Smith display anything remotely resembling a backbone up to this point. And a fired-up Daniel Morgan, who towered over Smith, was not someone to be trifled with. Ethan surreptitiously eyed the other men gathered around, trying to decide if he and the other Virginians were about to get into a brawl on Captain Morgan's behalf. But Smith's men, as usual, seemed lackadaisical about the whole thing, as if there just wasn't much fight in them.

Morgan and Smith stared at each other for a long moment, and Ethan wondered what was preventing the captain from giving his subordinate a good, well-deserved whack.

Finally, Morgan nodded, dropped the stick to the ground and said, "Captain Smith, order your men to stop wasting rounds and giving away our position."

Then, without awaiting a response, Morgan turned and strode off, headed back to camp. After a quick look to make sure Smith's men weren't going to try anything, Ethan turned and trotted after, quickly catching up to Levi and Sergeant Murphy.

Sergeant Murphy looked back at Ethan and shrugged. "Oh well, maybe next time," he said, and grinned.

◄◄◄◄◄◆►►►►►

Thursday October 12, 1775 – Second Carry Pond, Maine (Massachusetts Colony):

"Ah, Doctor Senter, come in. I am anxious to hear your report on the maladies currently afflicting the men," Benedict Arnold said as he looked up from his seat on a section of log that served for a camp chair inside his tent next to the Second Carry Pond.

"I fear it is as Daniel Morgan's courier informed us before he pushed on to the *Third* Carry Pond: that the water here is foul, and is the cause of great gastronomical distress among the men—vomiting, cramps, diarrhea. A few of the worst cases are near death, I'm afraid. We must face the fact that many of our men will not be able to continue on, and must be cared for—with clean water and wholesome food—until they are at least strong enough to return back down the river."

Arnold was thoughtful for a moment, then asked, "How many men are we talking about, Doctor?"

"More than a hundred, I fear. I know it is a bitter blow to our chances of success, Colonel. I am sorry."

"Well, it can't be helped. We must do right by these brave men who have already suffered much on our behalf. I shall order a hospital be built immediately, on some dry high ground well back from this putrid pond. We can assign some of the men who are sick, but still mobile, to tend to those who are too ill to fend for themselves. We will send them back in groups as they recover. The rest of us must push on from this place as quickly as possible."

"I believe that plan is as good as we can do under the circumstances, Colonel. I thank you for that."

Arnold waved his hand dismissively, then nodded in acknowledgement.

"On the *other* topic we have previously discussed," Arnold continued, "have you finished your inspection of the food stocks?"

"Yes, Colonel. That's the other matter I've come to speak with you about."

"*And …?*"

"I'm afraid it's also not good, sir. I've taken the liberty of writing down some notes, so I'd not forget any of the essential points. Shall I read it out for you, sir?"

"Please do so, Doctor."

Senter pulled a folded sheet of paper from his pocket, unfolded it, and read:

> *The dried cod, which has generally been transported loose in the bottom of the bateaux, has spoiled through continuous exposure to dousing by fresh water running into the boats.*
>
> *The bread casks not being waterproof admitted the water in plenty, swelled the bread, burst the casks, as well as soured the whole bread.*
>
> *The same fate attended a number of fine casks of peas. These, with the others, were condemned and must be disposed of, making up a very valuable and large part of our provisions.*

Doctor Senter finished, then refolded the paper and slipped it back into his pocket. He and Colonel Arnold shared a grim look.

"I understand the implications of what you are saying, Doctor. I shall send word back to Colonel Enos to bring up the remaining food reserves forthwith. Once he arrives, we should have enough to make it to Canada, though we shall have to tighten our belts as we push on. Turning back is not an option. We must only look ahead, not behind, and do our best to acquire the necessary sustenance for the men once we move on into Canada."

"Yes, sir, as you say," Senter answered with a nod. "Colonel, though I have faith that you take me at my word on these matters, I very much believe it would be in order if you were to personally oversee the dumping of the condemned foodstuffs, that you may attest to the veracity of my report."

Arnold slowly shook his head. "Very well, Doctor. Please lead the way, and we shall complete the unpleasant task."

◄◄◄◄◆►►►►

The trail from the second pond to the third and last pond of the Great Carrying Place was only two miles, and should have been relatively easy as it climbed a few hundred feet up out of the swampy morass they'd been dealing with.

But nothing about the Great Carry had turned out to be easy, Ethan decided. This third trail, though not as muddy as the other two, was simply choked with large, twisty tree roots—roots so old and thick that the men assigned to widen the trail quickly gave up trying to do anything about them, figuring it would likely take weeks and many more men than they had to do the job. So the men hauling boats, baggage, and weapons had to clamber and stumble their way through one of the worst stretches of trail thus far.

The good news was, their efforts were rewarded by a spectacular sight at the end of the trail; the picturesque scene that greeted them at the third and final pond was breathtaking. Crystal clear and of a deep blue color, Third Carry Pond was surrounded by high peaks that reflected in the water whenever the wind died down, which it did just before the sun set in spectacular fashion.

They'd completed this latest portage in a single long day, and were looking forward to carrying on to the Dead River on the following day. But it was not to be, as a frigid windstorm kicked up in the middle of the night, continuing into the next morning. Gone was the smooth water reflecting mountains of the day before, replaced by frothing, white-capped waves. Morgan decided not to risk the already battered bateaux on the rough waters, so he ordered another day of rest. This time, he decided to take advantage of the respite to scout out the road ahead, so he sent out a group of scouts to survey the next leg of their portage, from the Third Carry Pond to the Dead River.

At the end of a long day of shivering in their tents, listening to the wind howl, and just as Captain Morgan's mess was finishing up their evening meal, the scouts returned.

The sergeant in command stepped up to Morgan to give his report. "The news ain't good, sir. The trail starts out well enough, with a short, steep hike of a couple hundred feet elevation gain, after which one comes upon a scene that appears most promising: a long gentle downward slope leading to a great, wide, smooth swath of green grass, ending in a tall evergreen forest off in the distance."

He paused, and stared at Morgan for a moment, as if waiting for a response. But Morgan just raised an eyebrow and said nothing, so the sergeant continued, "But looks can be deceiving, as we all know, Captain. Like the pretty, smiling barmaid who'll happily knife you in the back so as to pocket yer coins."

"So, Sergeant … I'm guessing your lovely, smooth grass is anything but …?"

"Yes, sir. When we hiked down to it, we discovered that-there is the devil's own playground, if you get my meaning: a waist-deep swamp, so choked with reeds that you'll never be able to drive a boat through it. They'll have to be carried as if you was on land, only you'll be wading deep the whole way.

"And then, if you was thinkin' the swamp might end at that lovely row of trees, you'd be sorely mistaken. The water carries right on into them woods, and now you're not only wadin'; you're tryin' to work your way through a tangle o' fallen branches, rotting trunks, and submerged roots—of cedar and spruce so thick you can scarcely squeeze between. Needless to say, we didn't go much further once we discovered that.

"All in all, Captain, I'd say over yonder is the last place on earth a man would want to go."

Morgan frowned and nodded. "Yes, seems so. But sadly, that's exactly where we have to go, starting first light tomorrow. Men … I suggest y'all get a good night's rest. Seems like tomorrow you're gonna need it."

◄◄◄◄◆►►►►

Crossing the swamp proved every bit as difficult as the scout had foretold; to Ethan, it was a nightmare blur of chest-high frigid water, icy cold rain falling, and reeds so thick they had to force their way through. Carrying the bateau upside down proved so painful and difficult that Morgan decided to flip it over and float it after all, even though that made it more difficult to force a way through the rushes. But with two men pulling on ropes in front, and two pushing in back, they were able to slowly work their way across the three and a half miles of grassland to the edge of the looming forest.

There they rested for a time, climbing up onto fallen logs or tree limbs and eating a cold meal of whatever they had with them before pushing on into the forest. All around them men of the Virginia Rifle Company were doing the same. So thick were the men in the trees thereabouts it made Ethan think of the stories he'd heard of monkeys filling the trees over in Africa. Only he imagined those monkeys were never this cold.

Since they'd started the day, the temperature had plummeted, such that they shivered in their wet clothes, and a thin layer of ice formed on the top of the swamp water.

Ethan wrapped his arms around himself and tried to stop his teeth from chattering, but to no avail. He and Levi leaned against each other where they sat on a slimy, moss-covered log in a vain attempt to keep warm. Ethan dreaded getting back into the numbing cold water. But when the captain gave the word to continue on, get in he did, along with the rest of the men.

And if he'd thought traversing the swampy savannah was the most difficult thing he'd ever done, he quickly discovered he'd been mistaken. Every step through the tangled, submerged forest was a battle. They continued to float the bateau, but to move it more than a few dozen feet at a time required them to chop branches and roots to clear the way. Thankfully, Morgan had planned for this and had ordered axes be carried by the forward-most men so they could cut a trail. When darkness fell, they were still at it, and Morgan had no choice but to order a halt that the men could once again climb into the trees in an attempt to find whatever comfort they could in this icy, foul, tangled hell. Ethan could not remember a sleepless night more miserable, nor being so grateful for daybreak, despite the horrific prospect of plunging back into the freezing muck.

And then, as Ethan dug into his pack and pulled out a piece of hard tack intending it for his evening meal, Captain Morgan looked over at him and said, "You may not want to eat that all at once, Ethan."

Ethan returned a puzzled look, but Morgan did not elaborate and had already pulled his hat down over his eyes, leaning back against the trunk of the tree they'd crawled up into.

Wonder what he meant by that? Ethan wondered. So he ate only half and put the rest back in his pack.

◄◄◄◄◆►►►►

Monday October 13, 1775 – Third Carry Pond, Maine (Massachusetts Colony):

The tired, soaked, and road-stained courier saluted Colonel Arnold, then handed him a letter, which had been wrapped in waxed paper, and sealed with a red blob of wax.

Arnold thanked the man, and ordered Oswald to get him food and a dry place to lie down, if there were any to be had.

He unsealed the letter, which was from General Washington's military secretary, Colonel Reed. The letter was in response to Arnold's last communication sent back to the commander in chief before departing from Fort Western.

He read:

An Official Communique by
Colonel Joseph Reed, Military Secretary
on behalf of
his Excellency George Washington, Esq.
Commander in Chief, Continental Army
Headquarters, Cambridge, Oct. 4, 1775

Colonel Benedict Arnold,
Quebec Expedition commanding.

I have his Excellency's directions to acknowledge your letter of the 25th September. He approves your disposition, and the order of your march, and hopes you will keep ever in your mind the lateness of the season, and the necessity of making the utmost dispatch.

In a letter written 20th September, General Schuyler reports his army is waiting for artillery and supplies of men and provisions before resuming his attack on Fort St. Johns, which has proven stubbornly resistant.

By a British brig sent from Quebec, captured enroute to Boston, we understand that the whole enemy force is drawn from Quebec to St. Johns, and that, in its present situation Quebec City must fall into your hands without firing a shot; that there is a great magazine of powder and other warlike stores at Quebec, and the French inhabitants and English merchants most favorably disposed to the American cause.

We hope this delay by Gen. Schuyler will be a happy circumstance for you, as it may keep General Carleton engaged at St. Johns; whereas, by his returning thence, and throwing himself into Quebec City, your enterprise would most probably be defeated. At present there is not a single regular at Quebec; nor have they the least suspicion of any danger from any other quarter than Gen. Schuyler.

Wishing you all possible honor to yourself, and success to your country, I remain, sir, your most obedient and humble servant,

J. Reed.

Arnold scoffed, then handed the paper across to Oswald, who had just returned from attending to the courier. "If only it will be so easy."

Oswald quickly read through the letter, then looked up. "Well, it sounds like good news, anyway. Seems like things are falling into place nicely, and that there should be little opposition."

"That's what worries me, Oswald," Arnold answered. "Nothing ever goes that smoothly."

◄◄◄◄◄◆►►►►►

The Dead River very nearly lived up to its name—calm and smooth flowing for the most part—though they were forced to portage several times, during which they continued to spend time widening the trails.

Meanwhile, Colonel Arnold had caught up with them and had assured Captain Morgan that their current dearth of food—they were now down to strict rations, mainly consisting of boiled oatmeal—would soon be solved, as he had ordered Colonel Enos to bring forward the remaining food reserves that Fourth Battalion had been transporting. Captain Morgan had answered, "That'll be good, Colonel, as I was about to order a halt on account o' every step forward now is a step further from any food for the men."

During one of the portages, Morgan's battalion had camped in a narrow, grassy field next to the river. Though rain clouds had thickened throughout the day, their tents were pitched eight or nine feet above the river, on good dry ground, such that there was little fear of the campground getting saturated.

As usual, Ethan had worked hard that day, and when he crawled into his bedroll he was almost immediately in a deep slumber, such that the sound of rain lashing against the tent's roof was unable to disturb his repose in the least.

"Sweet mother of Jesus!" a voice yelled in Ethan's dream. His eyes popped open, and he realized it hadn't been a dream, but rather Sergeant Murphy's voice. Murphy was standing in the tent, snatching at items on the floor as a stream of water flowed through.

Captain Morgan sat up and his eyes went wide, "What the hell?" He immediately stood up and pulled on his boots. Ethan and Levi scrambled to do the same, grabbing various articles of clothing that'd been lying on the ground.

Outside, a nightmarish scene of utter chaos met their eyes. What had started the evening as a nice, dry pasture had transformed during the night into a raging stream of brown water. All throughout the camp, men gathered up supplies and pulled down tents as blinding sheets of rain pelted them. Daniel Morgan surged forward into the darkness, immediately barking out orders for men to secure the boats and get the supplies loaded in them. The river had risen so high and so suddenly that they could now float their boats in what had previously been a dry portage.

By the time dawn lightened the horizon, they'd succeeded in making it onto higher ground, managing to salvage most of their equipment and supplies in the process. But the sight that greeted them that morning was unrecognizable from the day before. The smooth, sedate, picturesque Dead River had transformed overnight into a raging torrent of brown water that had so overflowed its banks that one could no longer tell where the original waterway had been.

Ethan could only shake his head in amazement. *What can possibly happen next?* he wondered.

There being nothing else to do, Morgan ordered the rifle companies to continue down the river, though it was now so inundated it was nearly impossible to navigate. The banks of the river had widened so severely that at places they stretched a mile or more inland. With the minor tributary streams also swollen, the men who normally marched on the bank alongside the bateaux were forced to wade alongside the bateaux, and when the waters became too deep to wade, they clung to the boats' sides as they drifted down the stream.

At one set of falls, the torrent was so strong the boats could not make it out of the current to attempt a portage, and were swept along and over. The raging flood swamped and sank a half-dozen boats, along with their precious supply of provisions, and the men had to be fished out of the waters downstream after nearly drowning.

In still other places, the flood was a blessing, as rocks and ripples that would've normally required portaging could be safely floated over with the added depth of water.

With the loss of much of their remaining supplies, and the flood making hunting and fishing impossible, the food shortage had become severe. "Where is Colonel Enos with the food?" became a commonly repeated question around camp.

And as they finished the last of their meager rations of oatmeal, Sergeant Murphy graced the boys with a wry grin and said, "Perhaps tomorrow, I'll introduce you young'ns to the pleasures of boilt shoe leather."

◄◄◄◄◆►►►►►

Wednesday October 25, 1775 – Dead River, Maine (Massachusetts Colony):

Benedict Arnold and Eleazar Oswald hopped out of the canoe into the ankle-deep, muddy water that now inundated much of the land surrounding the Dead River. Their Penobscot Indian crew had rowed them as far inland as possible before the bottom of the boat was scraping a few hundred yards short of where Colonel Christopher Greene and the Third Battalion had made camp. So Arnold and Oswald were forced to wade the rest of the way in.

Colonel Greene himself greeted them as they stepped up onto the higher dry ground of the camp. But after a quick exchange of greetings, Arnold noticed that Greene had an unusually serious expression.

"Christopher, is something amiss?"

"Yes, sir, it is … I have … most distressing news for you, I'm afraid."

"Oh?"

"Will you walk with me, sir?" Greene said, and made a quick glance toward Oswald.

Taking the hint, Arnold turned to Oswald, "Mr. Oswald, will you excuse us a moment? Perhaps you might find a campfire to dry your shoes."

"Certainly, sir," Oswald smiled, and nodded his understanding, then turned and headed into the campground.

Arnold and Greene turned and walked side by side along the edge of the camp, just beyond the reach of the flood.

"Colonel Enos arrived at our camp yesterday—" Greene began.

"*Oh.* That's good news," Arnold interrupted. "Did he bring the food reserves with him?"

"Well … yes … and no. He brought *some* food, but only a few barrels …"

"I … I don't understand. Perhaps I'd best hold my tongue and allow you to explain," Arnold said with a frown.

Greene smiled appreciatively, then continued, "Enos arrived yesterday afternoon, but not with his entire battalion: only himself and his staff officers. And they had brought with them just four barrels of food."

Arnold's expression darkened, but true to his word, he said nothing.

Greene continued, "He immediately asked for a council of war with the two of us and our officers. I told him I saw no need for such a council, and that you had not authorized any such meeting. But he argued that the matter was most urgent, and as neither of us knew your exact whereabouts it was not possible to obtain your prior consent. So, not knowing what it was about, I reluctantly agreed …"

"*And?*" Arnold prompted.

Greene scowled, "It turned out Enos wished to propose that we quit the expedition, and return back down the Kennebec!"

"He *what?!*" Arnold shouted, before catching himself, remembering he'd agreed to let Greene speak, and besides, it wouldn't do to have the men in camp overhear.

"Yes, you heard correctly, sir. Of course, I was dumbfounded, and asked him on what grounds he thought to take such a drastic measure. He answered that with damage, loss, and spoilage, food stocks were so low that continuing on would be suicidal. And then he said that you had *ordered* him to only send forward enough men as could be supplied for two weeks, and he argued that meant he could bring forward nobody, as he hadn't enough food to do so."

Arnold growled, "Yes … I did give him such an order, but clearly, I intended that as a temporary measure until more of the food reserves arrived up the river from Fort Western. He has taken my words and twisted them."

"Yes, so it would seem, Colonel. But at the time I did not know whether he spoke true or not. Regardless, *I* had no such orders from you, so I refused to turn back. But he insisted on a vote of our officers, so of course all of my officers voted a most vehement 'nay' to the notion. But not surprisingly, all of his voted for it, so there was an even split. Therefore, he determined to turn back.

"I begged him to reconsider, but he refused, making the excuse that he was duty-bound to follow the vote of his officers. Then, I must confess, I became angry with him, and berated him in a less-than-gentlemanly fashion in front of his own officers, for which I might feel some shame if it weren't for the dire seriousness of the circumstances."

Greene chuckled mirthlessly. "If he were any kind of a *man*, he would've struck me for my insults, but he simply turned away and left, which to my mind only reinforces his cowardice."

"Indeed. And no one can blame you for your angry words, I think." Arnold responded.

"Thank you for saying so, Colonel. In any case, not only did he depart straightaway, but he refused to even leave behind the four barrels of food he had brought with him, despite knowing the current extreme need of my men. I can tell you it took all of my self-restraint not to order my soldiers to open fire on his canoes as they departed."

"I can appreciate that," Arnold nodded while continuing to scowl fiercely. "I had always held doubts about his leadership abilities and his determination. But I had hoped, with the proper encouragement and good examples set by the other officers—such as yourself—that he would rise to the occasion. Clearly, my hopes have proven false. His was a most dastardly deed, and has struck us a deadly blow."

Arnold was quiet and thoughtful for several moments as they continued to walk.

"What now, Colonel?" Greene finally asked. "Fourth Battalion was our largest division ... With our growing number of sick, and several casualties from accidents, and so forth, his four hundred and some men represented nearly half our total."

"Yes, of that I am well aware, Christopher," Arnold answered. Then he stopped and turned toward Greene. The two men met eyes.

"But we must carry on. The campaign is too important, and the men have sacrificed too much already. I refuse to give it up on account of the shameless actions of a single man. And the news I have received from General Washington is that General Schuyler has the British well occupied over at Montreal, such that Quebec City is barely manned at all. Even with half our original force, if we can still arrive undetected, we may yet secure the victory."

"Yes, sir. *If* we can still arrive at all," Greene answered.

"Well, yes, there is that," Arnold agreed. "We must simply push on at a greater pace. The sooner we reach French Canada, the sooner we may expect to receive the aid we require."

"Agreed, Colonel. We must simply tighten our belts and push on. There is no other honorable choice."

◄◄◄◄◆►►►►►

Saturday October 28, 1775 – Height of Land, Maine (Massachusetts Colony):

Morgan's rifle battalion had finally reached dry land, at a portage place dubbed the "Height of Land" where they made camp.

Ethan had just finished laying out his bedroll when Daniel Morgan stepped into the tent and handed Ethan a sheet of paper.

"A courier just brought this from Colonel Arnold," he said with no preamble.

"Oh." Ethan responded, taking the paper and giving it a quick read.

His face must have reflected the dire news he was reading, as Morgan said, "What is it, Ethan?"

"Colonel Enos has abandoned us … taking Fourth Battalion and all our food reserves with him. Colonel Arnold says we are now entirely out of food, and with Fourth Battalion gone and all the men in hospital back at the carry lakes, we are now half the force we were at the start."

"Damn Enos. That God-forsaken, cowardly bastard!" Morgan swore. "What does Colonel Arnold order us to do now?"

"He says … well, he basically says to hurry along and get to Canada where we can expect to find food and other supplies from the French civilians there. The good news is, he says we can now abandon the boats if we wish … that we can simply march and carry the remaining supplies from this point forward."

"Oh …" Morgan said.

He was quiet and thoughtful for several minutes until Ethan finally asked, "What now, Captain? What shall we do?"

But Morgan turned to him as if he'd just asked the oddest question imaginable. "What d'ya mean, Ethan? We do as our colonel has ordered. We carry on … only faster, now."

"Yes, sir."

A few minutes later, Captain Morgan ordered the men of his command to gather next to the great bonfire they'd lit in the center of camp. He did not mince words, but told them straight out of Colonel Enos's betrayal and Colonel Arnold's orders to hurry on to Canada, which was now their only hope of resupply.

The news was greeted with sullen, downcast looks, but nobody spoke. All knew the implications; they were already hungry, and would now have to carry on without knowing when their next meal might come, if ever.

"What do we do now, Captain?" someone called out.

"We do as we're ordered. And … pray for our safe and timely arrival at our destination," he answered.

Then, to Morgan's surprise, Sergeant Murphy stepped up to him and said, "Excuse me, sir, but I'd like to offer a proper Irish prayer, fitting unto the circumstance, if you don't mind."

"By all means, Sergeant. Pray away …" Morgan said, gesturing him forward.

"Thank you, sir."

Murphy stepped up in front of Morgan and faced the men gathered around.

"Men, those that know me know I'm a good, God-fearin' Irishman … for whatever that's worth," he chuckled, and there were a few laughs in the crowd, but the mood was too serious for much levity.

"Anyway, we Irish seem t'always have a proper blessin' for nearly everythin' and every occasion, and this here's no exception. So, here goes: *May God bless and keep Colonel Enos and his men …*" Murphy began in a solemn, pious tone, then paused a moment.

There were groans and grumbles in the crowd at this opening; nobody held any warm feelings toward those who'd abandoned them to their fate, much less wished to bless them.

But then Murphy scowled and barked out, "*… in such a manner as they might meet with some disaster as to equal the dastardly manner by which they abandoned their comrades in arms in their hour of need. Amen.*"

And at "amen," the sullen looks on the men's faces brightened up and they lifted their hats, waved them in the air, and shouted, "*Amen! Amen! Amen!*"

Murphy turned back to Captain Morgan, winked, and grinned. Morgan nodded and returned the grin, before reaching out and patting Murphy on the back.

◄◄◄◄◄◆►►►►►

The Height of Land crossing was the most difficult portage yet. The path was slick with ice and snow, which served to obscure hidden rocks, fallen logs, and tree roots as they trekked over the greatest elevation gain of the journey.

And to make matters worse, Daniel Morgan had made the unpopular decision to bring the bateaux along, despite Colonel Arnold's suggestion that they could now be abandoned. Captains Hendricks and Smith, of the two Pennsylvania rifle companies, had argued against it, and in the end, they'd compromised: Morgan's Virginia Riflemen would carry all of their remaining seven boats, while the other two companies would carry only one each, in which they could ferry supplies later on when they reached Lake Mégantic and the Chaudière River.

There was, of course, much grumbling about carrying the heavy boats. The men were becoming weak from lack of food and from the seemingly endless journey, and the knowledge that Captain Morgan had overridden Colonel Arnold's permission to leave them behind was not well received. Even Ethan questioned it, and inwardly cursed the decision, though he dared not say anything aloud to his commander.

When they reached the end of the portage, at yet another swamp, this one thankfully with a small, navigable stream running through it, they set down their bateau and collapsed on the ground from exhaustion. For nearly an hour nobody attempted to get up and start working to set up camp, despite the freezing temperatures.

Then Captain Morgan stood, stretched his limbs, and announced, "Heading back up the trail ... need to encourage the men ... let 'em know we made it, so they can too."

Then he gazed at his three companions and said, "You men stay here. Get a fire started so's you don't freeze solid ... then ... start working on the camp."

All three of them were too tired to even respond beyond a nod of the head. Morgan returned the nod, and then with likely nothing beyond pure willpower and determination, he started his feet moving back the way they'd come. Ethan watched him as Morgan staggered away; even his great strength and endurance had clearly reached its limits, and yet he soldiered on.

It was then, while leaning his back against the boat, trying to summon up enough energy to stand, that Ethan realized for the first time that they had just crossed into Canada.

◄◄◄◄◆►►►►►

Though they were all exhausted from the Height of Land portage, which all agreed had been the worst yet, the next morning they broke camp at first light. Since there was nothing to eat, and thus no need to cook breakfast, they immediately headed into the swamp. Hunger drove them such that there was no need for Captain Morgan to say a word.

And immediately Ethan saw the wisdom of Morgan's decision to bring along the bateaux despite his men's grumbling and the other captains' objections. With the boats, they were able to follow the stream and make steady progress through the mire, with the marching men clinging to the sides of each boat. And since the other two rifle companies had only brought one boat each, their men came forward and tightly crowded around the boats of the Virginians in groups numbering as many as could lay a hand on the side of the boat.

The good news of this arrangement for Ethan was that there was no need to paddle or to pole the boat to move it forward—in fact with the marchers surrounding the boat, they couldn't have if they'd wanted to—the men wading propelled the vessel along by dragging it through the water.

And when they reached the end of the swamp and saw Lake Mégantic spreading out into the distance before them, there was no celebration and no respite. The bateaux were immediately put to work ferrying men and materiel the ten miles to the north end of the lake, where the Chaudière River emptied out from its waters.

Sunday November 2, 1775 – Chaudière River, Quebec Province:

Although Colonel Arnold's original plan, agreed to way back at Fort Western, had been for the four battalions to rendezvous at Lake Mégantic before moving down the Chaudière River toward Quebec City, Daniel Morgan decided the rifle companies could not wait; the men were starving, and if that situation weren't rectified in short order, good, brave men were going to die.

So after only a single hungry, cold night camping on the shores of the lake, near the place where the river flowed out, they were up at first light, stumbling about in their emaciated state, loading as much of the equipment on the remaining bateaux as they could and shouldering the rest. This time, there would be no coming back. Anything that couldn't be carried would be left behind. But the good news—such as it was—was that there was no more food to carry, which considerably lightened the load.

As they packed in the equipment, Ethan had to force himself to ignore the sorry condition of their bateau. Multiple boards had cracks, and water seeped in so regularly that whoever wasn't manning one of the oars had to spend nearly half his time bailing out water with a bucket. Even the keel of the boat was beginning to show cracks. Ethan decided he'd be happy—very happy, indeed—when the day came that he'd never have to get back into the decrepit, barely-sea-worthy vessel.

As they'd done since the beginning of the trek up the Kennebec, Morgan ordered the marchers to keep pace with the boats, in case they needed to throw out ropes or once again had to portage around rough water. The good news this time was that for the first time on the journey, they'd be floating downstream, so there'd be a lot less need to row, for which Ethan was grateful. His stomach felt twisted into knots, and lifting even the least heavy load seemed monumental. He doubted he or anyone else, with the possible exception of Captain Morgan, would be able to row against the swift river current of the Chaudière at this point. And then, remembering the French his father had taught him, he thought about the odd name of the river: Chaudière translated to "Boiler" in English. *Odd name for a river*, he thought. *Wonder if it gets very hot in the summertime. Certainly anything but hot now, brrrr.*

And when they shoved off into the swift stream, Ethan's expectations for light rowing work seemed to be bearing fruit; there was no need of the oars whatsoever for the first several miles as the river rushed on in a smooth, steady flow. Morgan ordered the boys to ship the oars while he guided the boat from the stern using the paddle.

But then, as they rounded a bend, they quickly learned the downside of riding the river's current: the water turned rough, and their speed increased dramatically. In every case before, both on the Kennebec and the Dead River, they'd been able to see rough water ahead of them with plenty of advanced warning, and could maneuver the boat into the best channel and choose strategically when to engage with the rapids or to head for shore and portage around them.

But suddenly, the bateau was swept forward, and now Ethan and Levi had to use the oars to try to slow down their momentum. Morgan shouted at them to steer to larboard as he poked and shoved with a setting pole to keep them off the rocks. Ethan could tell that the captain meant to steer them to the western shore, but it was too late; the boat was rocking and bouncing off huge rocks, both seen and unseen, as water splashed over the gunwales and drenched them with icy cold water. Ethan rowed with all his strength, but as he glanced down, he could see the boat was nearly halfway full of water, and nobody had time to bail.

As they pitched over a particularly large swell, the boat dropped with a sickening lurch and slammed against something hard with a loud *crack!* The spine of the boat heaved up in the middle, split in half, and the last thing Ethan saw before plunging into the water was Daniel Morgan falling backward off the stern of the boat, his pole flung skyward as he went.

Water frothed and boiled around him as he was swept along under water, bouncing off huge rocks and rushing downhill with no control, fighting and clawing to get his head above the surface to catch a breath of air. Then, suddenly his head sprang above the water and he gasped in a breath before being swept over another fall and deep down into the bubbling water. And in that moment, as he struggled to live, in a strange, surreal instant of serendipity, it came to him what the French had meant by calling the river the Boiler; it wasn't because it was hot, but rather because it raged like a boiling cauldron.

For minutes that felt like eternity, Ethan fought to protect his head from being bashed against the rocks, taking any chance he could to catch a breath.

And then, suddenly, everything changed; he was still moving swiftly underwater, but there were no more rocks. He desperately swam for the surface and broke through to the air, taking it in with great gasping lungfuls as he thrashed the water to stay afloat. Looking around and seeing the shore, he headed in that direction. But then, remembering that the marchers were on the western bank, he luckily still retained enough presence of mind to realize he was going the wrong direction, so he turned around and headed for the opposite shore.

As he swam, his right arm hit something in the water. At first, he thought it must be a log; then he realized it was a man. He grabbed at the cloth of the man's jacket and pulled him along. A moment later, he felt his feet touch the bottom, so he stood and tried to pull the man up with him. But the man was large and heavy, his weight nearly tipping Ethan over. The man coughed and spluttered and stood up. He shook the water from his head and looked at Ethan. In shock, he realized it was Captain Morgan. And then, to Ethan's further surprise, the first thing the captain did was reach inside his frock shirt and pull out a heavy leather bag and shake it.

Coins, Ethan decided. No wonder he was so heavy and nearly drowned.

"You oughtn't to have kept those coins on you, Captain," he said. "You nearly drowned."

But Morgan shook his head and said, "Better'n losing all our hard money, Ethan. These coins'll buy us food where we're going. Without it …?" he shrugged.

But then the Captain seemed to have a whole new thought and immediately looked around. "Where's Levi?" he asked.

"Don't know," Ethan answered, and also gazed all around, but could see nothing of his friend.

Then they heard a shout, "Hey! Hey! I'm over here!"

They both looked toward the bank and saw Levi clinging to a barrel that'd come loose when the boat split apart. The barrel had lodged in a fallen tree snag and was rolling and bobbing precariously as Levi scrambled to stay atop his uncooperative mount.

In moments, they'd pulled him off the barrel, and all three had waded to shore. But after only a minute's rest, Morgan turned to them and said, "Quick, boys. Grab the longest stick you can handle and let's wade back out. If *we* lost our boat and went into the water, you can bet the others are sure to follow. We'll fish them out as they float by."

And fish they did, pulling the other boaters out as they floated down the stream. Ethan thought it the oddest kind of fishing he'd ever done, and he remembered the Bible talking about Christ being a "fisher of men"; he had to smile at the thought.

At the end, all the boaters were rescued except one pour soul who was pulled ashore unconscious with his head covered in blood. Clearly, he'd bashed his skull against one of the rocks as he'd rolled downstream. Captain Morgan pronounced the man dead and ordered an abbreviated burial detail, consisting of placing the fellow in a low spot on the bank and piling rocks over top.

By the time they finished the burial, the men marching caught up to them. For once, the boats had outpaced the walkers. They'd now lost all the bateaux, and all the equipment and supplies they'd carried, save a few odd barrels and boxes they were able to rescue from the water.

The weather was frigid, so Morgan ordered a large fire be built to warm up those that'd been thrown into the river. But after an hour or so, he ordered the march to continue.

"No sense being warm just so you can starve to death," he said, and nobody argued the point. Soon they were on the move again, though it was slow going, as many of the men had been badly battered in the rapids and stumbled along, Ethan included. Throughout the long, hard, exhausting journey, this was the most drained he'd felt, and he knew he was not alone in that. Levi staggered along next to him, and several times seemed to fall asleep on his feet, such that Ethan had to reach out and shake him.

As darkness fell that evening, nobody bothered to make camp; most of the tents and camping equipment had been lost to the river. Instead, they simply lit a large bonfire and men slept huddled around it.

The next morning, cold and stiff, Ethan rose to his feet. He could barely stand or walk, but the good news was he'd not have to carry much. He'd lost everything except the rifle that Morgan had lent him. It was another of the captain's strict rules: whatever else was happening, every man had to carry his rifle on his back at all times, except when sleeping, and then it would be next to him as he slept. Even in the bateaux, rowing or poling, they wore their rifles on their backs in case something happened, like what just had.

But Ethan knew Levi was in a bad way. He had started the journey out leaner and smaller than Ethan, and so it was likely that the lack of food hit him all the harder. Ethan helped his friend to his feet and got him moving, but when it became clear he would not be able to make it much further, Ethan ordered him to grab onto the back of his coat so he could help drag him forward.

And so it was that the ragged, starving, bedraggled rifle battalion of Daniel Morgan limped their way down the trail running alongside the Chaudière in the direction of Quebec City, with no idea of when they would reach a place where they might find food and shelter. And all the while as they marched, Morgan alternated between leading the way and staggering up and down the line of marchers, joking, cajoling, pushing, prodding, and ever encouraging—refusing to let anyone give up and die.

As they stumbled forward, Ethan kept himself going by watching his captain's feet in front of him and just moving his own feet to match. And he could feel Levi's hand clutching at his coat in the back, the only way his friend could keep moving. It was a sore test of Ethan's willpower, and love for his friend, to not slap the dragging weight off his back. He ruefully remembered Captain Morgan's words when Levi first joined their company back in Massachusetts: *"You may not thank me later, Ethan, if you're starving out in the woods and you got to share out your last piece of meat with him …"*

And then, suddenly Morgan's feet stopped, so Ethan's stopped as well, as if they had a mind of their own.

"What the …?" he heard Morgan mutter. Ethan forced himself to step forward until he stood next to the captain, with Levi still clinging on behind. At first, Ethan could see nothing in the failing light. His strength seemed to be failing as well; his eyes didn't seem to want to focus. But then he saw movement … Large shapes moving on the trail ahead. He squinted and tried to focus his

mind. *Why ... those must be ... cows*, he decided. And then it hit him: it was a small herd of cattle, being driven up the trail straight toward them. They were not going to die of starvation after all.

When the cattle came closer, Ethan could see they were being driven by a half dozen young men, walking all around them with long, slender sticks that served as whips.

When the young men reached Daniel Morgan, the one in the lead stopped, removed his hat with a bow, and said, *"Bonjour, monsieur."*

And though Morgan spoke no French, he recognized the language. "Well, by God, they're French. *Hallelujah*. Hey, Ethan, do you know if anyone in the company speaks French? Guess I shoulda thought to ask *that* before now ..."

"Well, yes sir. *I* do. My father taught me starting at a young age ... Said he thought it might be useful one day, though he never said why. Haven't used it much, but I still remember ..."

"Well, damn, Ethan. That's fine, just fine. Please tell them I want to buy those cattle, that my men are starving."

"Yes, sir."

Ethan looked over at the young man and said, *"Bonjour, monsieur. Je m'appelle Ethan, et je suis le Capitaine Morgan."*

"Ah ... Ravi de vous rencontrer, Ethan. Je m'appelle Michael."

They shook hands, then Ethan told him the captain wished to purchase his cattle.

But Michael shook his head vigorously, and answered in French, "No, no ... you needn't purchase them; they are already yours. Sent to you by your Colonel Arnold, who has visited our village earlier in the day and purchased them on your behalf."

Morgan, who'd been listening intently, understood nothing except Arnold's name. "What'd he say about 'Arnold'?"

So Ethan translated, and Morgan grinned brightly. "Well, then, in that case, let's get these creatures butchered and get a cooking fire set up straight away," he said.

Sergeant Murphy, who'd stepped up behind them as they spoke, said, "I'll gladly relay *those* orders, sir ..."

But then a strong, firm voice called out in English, "Belay that order ... Those cattle are not for you, Captain Morgan." Benedict Arnold stepped forward with Eleazar Oswald behind him.

Daniel Morgan stepped up and embraced the colonel in a great warm hug. "Damn ... it's good to see you, Colonel," he finally said, stepping back and patting the colonel on both arms.

"Likewise, Daniel," Arnold answered, smiling but looking slightly embarrassed by the exuberant greeting. "Happy to see you're still alive. I have been fearing the worst, as I had lost track of your company altogether and had heard nothing for days."

"Well, here we are, and still alive ... *barely*. But what did you mean just now that these here cattle ain't for us?" Morgan asked.

"They are not for you because you and your men are even now but two miles from salvation. The French village where I purchased these cattle is just down the road. They await your arrival and will feed you and give you shelter. You and your men are already saved, by your own great courage and willpower.

"But the other battalions still lag behind, and are in great need, I fear. These cattle are intended for them.

An hour later, Ethan sat inside a house at a table with a plate of hot food set in front of him saying a quick, silent prayer of thanks to God, Jesus, and any listening saints for their timely salvation.

Monday October 30, 1775 – Winchester, Virginia Colony:

Hannah came to the end of the row and held up the knitting needles, examining her work. Deciding the scarf was finished, she tied off the yarn, pulled loose the needles, and cut the thread with a small, sharp pair of scissors she kept for just such a purpose. She ran her hands across the soft wool, the last of the fine yarn from London that Gideon had acquired for her several years ago down in Williamsburg. She wondered when they'd ever see such wool again, with the conflict now raging and money so tight.

She sat back and admired her work for a few moments, enjoying the contrast of light and dark yarn combined in an intricate pattern using the ridged feather stitch—one of her favorites, though it was tricky to do and required extra concentration. She'd made the scarf as a gift for Gideon, hoping to cheer him up, and perhaps to inspire him to venture outdoors in the cool autumn weather—a thing he'd not done for many months.

And then, for the hundredth time, she wondered if Gideon's brother James, up in the New York Colony, had received any of her letters. It had now been a month since she'd sent the first, and she'd written similarly worded letters every week or so after, not knowing if the post was functioning at all. When she'd asked the local postmaster if the mail was still getting through to the northern colonies, he just shrugged. "Sometimes it does, and sometimes it don't. There just ain't no knowin' these days, ma'am."

She sighed again … They were down to scraps in the cupboard. It seemed likely she'd have to swallow her pride and ask Abby for more help after all … or starve. But then a knock on the door interrupted her dark reverie, making her jump in startlement.

When she opened the door, she gasped.

"Well, don't look so surprised, my dear," a large broad gentleman said, sporting a wide grin. He removed his fine, wool three-cornered hat with a bow. "After all, you did ask for my assistance, did you not?"

"*James!* Well, yes, I did ask for your help, but received no reply … I never expected you to just appear on my doorstep." She took in his features, which she hadn't seen in half a dozen or more years. Though he was much taller and heavier, and slightly older—his hair was now almost completely gray—Hannah noted the unmistakable Chambers family resemblance to both Gideon and Ethan. He was dressed as a proper gentleman, with finely embroidered silk coat, waistcoat, and shiny black knee-high riding boots.

And then, remembering her manners and recovering from the shock, she returned his smile and opened wide the door. "Please,

please do come in. I am appalled that I have not already said 'welcome, most welcome, brother James.'"

"Thank you, my dear. Don't mind if I do," James answered, stepping through the door. Hannah saw a fine, black carriage with two horses tied to the hitching post by the front gate. A man was there, presumably James's driver, unloading various items of luggage. *Guess they'll be staying here,* Hannah thought with a silent groan. *Well, we've the one extra room with Ethan being gone ... and I suppose Elsie can sleep in our room on a pallet for now.*

And then she remembered that she must be grateful and not resentful; after all, James was a man of means who had traveled a great distance to help them in their hour of need. Presumably he would now ensure their survival through the coming winter, and that was not something to be taken lightly.

"You look well, Hannah," James said, and then chuckled. "Much better than Gideon, I suspect. Speaking of ... where is my disreputable younger brother? Gideon! Are you hiding from me, like you used to when we were onery little brats, scurrying about father's farm?"

And then Gideon came shuffling out from the hallway, blinking and rubbing his eyes, as if he'd been sleeping, though it was nearly noon.

"Ah, there you are, Gideon ... Oh my, you have suffered a bit of a spill, haven't you?" James asked.

"James ... good to see you again. And so good of you to come," Gideon answered. Then, acknowledging his brother's comments about his injuries, he looked down at his arms and shrugged. Hannah noted the usual lack of enthusiasm from Gideon toward his older brother. She was aware that theirs had not been a peaceful relationship when they were children, with James always the domineering, physically dominant older brother, and Gideon suffering the typical boyhood result of that scenario.

Hannah had hoped the two might put all that childhood trauma behind them, given the present dire circumstances. But now she wasn't sure that would be possible; some roots just went too deep.

Elsie peered out from the hallway, seemingly hesitant to approach the large, loud man she could not remember ever meeting. But he caught sight of her and called out, "Well, now. There's the sweet little princess. My goodness, but she's grown, Hannah. Why, when last I saw her, she was only about yay tall. And look at her now. C'mon here, my darling niece, and say hello to your old uncle James."

Elsie stepped up to him, gracing him with a shy smile and a quick curtsy, saying, "Hello, Uncle James."

He beamed in answer. "Well, if you aren't just the cutest little aphid, I don't know who is." Then he looked over at Hannah, "Clearly gets her good looks from her mother, thank God," then he laughed, reaching over to give Gideon a pat on the shoulder. Hannah grimaced as she saw her husband flinch, but she said nothing.

"And where's that boy of yours? Ethan must be nearly as tall as his daddy by now. He's now, what … fifteen … sixteen?"

"Seventeen," Gideon answered, "and he's already taller than me. And likely not done growing."

James beamed, slowly shaking his head. "Imagine that … little Ethan all grown up. Where is the lad, anyway? Out doing chores?"

But neither Hannah nor Gideon immediately answered. Though they hadn't spoken to James on the subject, they were fairly certain he was a loyalist, still maintaining close personal and business relationships with the mother country. They'd agreed not to mention Ethan's present circumstances to James, so as not to alienate him. But that was when they believed he would only help them from afar by sending money or other goods. Now … now, there'd be no disguising that Ethan was gone.

"He's … not here," Gideon finally answered.

"Oh? Gone off to school, has he? I recall you mentioning he wanted to follow in your footsteps and attend the college down in Williamsburg … William and Mary College, wasn't it?"

"Yes, William and Mary. But … he's not there. He's … he's up at Boston."

"Boston ...? But ..." James looked from Gideon to Hannah, seeming to suddenly comprehend that things were not as he'd expected. "What's the lad doing up at Boston, may I ask?"

Gideon slowly nodded, then sighed, "He's joined up with those helping General Washington."

"A *rebel?* Oh, dear ... I ... I can hardly believe it. My nephew ... a traitor to the crown? Gideon, you know full well that our family have always been loyal Englishmen. Faithful to the crown. Our father was, as was our grandfather ... and his father before him, going all the way back before the time they came over from England.

"*No!* I'll not stand for it. We must speak to the lad ... talk sense into him. No Chambers would ever betray our king. Gideon, you must write the boy immediately—tell him to come straight home. I'll convince him to change his ways—return to the fold—never you fear."

Hannah could think of nothing to say, but expected Gideon to stand up for their son, to defend his actions as brave, honorable, and justified. But to her chagrin, all he said was, "Yes ... yes, of course I will write to him. But the post ..." he shrugged. "Well ... you know."

◄◄◄◄◆►►►►►

Friday November 3, 1775 – Fort St. Johns, Quebec Province:

"Perhaps we should attempt a breakout," Lieutenant André suggested to the room full of sullen faces. "We can fire off the remainder of our artillery rounds, targeted at the Americans dug in to the north, then throw open the gates and rush out with bayonets, punching a hole through their lines. After the breakout, we can make for Montreal."

But the officers in the room just stared at him as if he'd lost his mind, and he knew he would not win them over. They'd been surrounded and besieged now for forty-five days—bombarded, half-starved, running out of supplies and ammunition. And they had to endure the disheartening news of the fall of nearby Fort Chambly, including the other part of André's own Seventh

199

Regiment of Foot that'd been stationed there, and then the recent failed relief attempt by Governor Carleton. Daily the Americans received more troops and more artillery. And daily the bombardment continued.

It had become a thoroughly hopeless situation. So much so that the rebel General Montgomery had sent Major Preston a letter this morning via a prisoner requesting his surrender. Preston had called the present meeting to discuss the matter.

Preston looked at André and said, "Lieutenant, you and your men have fought bravely and well, for which you should be proud. In fact, I intend to recommend you for promotion … whenever it becomes possible to do so. But look at yourself: your uniform is in tatters … God knows you've lost weight your slim frame could ill-afford. You've been fighting almost non-stop for the last … what's it been, forty-five days now?"

André glanced down at his uniform and noticed for the first time its shabby condition; no longer the elegant attire it had once been, it was now torn, stained, and blood splattered. *Most of that is from other men, thankfully*, he thought. He looked back up at the Major with a wan smile and shrugged.

"You certainly should hold your head high," Preston continued. "And you ought not feel ashamed for having been forced to surrender. Also, you needn't fear any maltreatment by our enemies—I know their general, Montgomery, and have served with him in *our* army in the past; he's a good, honest fellow, and will not tolerate any mistreatment of prisoners, I can assure you."

"Thank you, sir, for the compliments," André responded. "But I have no fear of maltreatment at their hands. In fact, I hold no animosity toward the Americans whatever. I find them quite fascinating, really, and admirable in many ways, though often crude and uncouth to our eyes.

"Though, of course, I'd prefer my freedom, if I must be held prisoner, I mean to make the most of it—polishing my American accent and learning all their odd English colloquialisms and mannerisms. It should prove quite informative.

"Incarceration will also give me time to write poems, script plays, and compose music, which I've had little time for of late, for obvious reasons.

"And I'm certain, at some point in the not-too-distant future, the warring parties will conduct a prisoner exchange, and I shall be back in the fight." He graced the officers with a sincere smile. And despite their present dire circumstances, his personality was so winning that the other officers could not help but reflect his happy visage.

Even Major Preston smiled, one of the rare times André had ever seen the gesture on the typically severe man. "You are a wonder, Lieutenant," he said. "I can't say I've ever met anyone quite like you—a gallant, fearless soldier on the one hand, and a highly capable scholar, artist, and philosopher on the other. And always of a good humor, despite the unpleasantness of the circumstances. Godspeed to you, sir."

"Thank you, Sir Charles. And likewise to you. And the rest of you. Thank you, and Godspeed."

Chapter 9. Opening Moves

"Every battle is won before it is fought."
- Sun Tzu

Sunday November 5, 1775 – Chaudière River, Quebec Province:

Colonel Arnold chaired a ragged-looking group of officers—unshaven, dirty, clothes stained, torn, and mud-splattered—seated around a dinner table in a small French-Canadian village along the Chaudière River. All three remaining divisions of Arnold's command had finally arrived at the village, and all of the expedition's officers gathered for the meeting felt thankful to be alive—none more so than Colonel Christopher Greene, whose gaunt, haunted appearance was in stark contrast to the robust, vigorous man he'd been at the start of the expedition.

"I feel a great deal of responsibility for what happened to you and your men on the approach to Lake Mégantic," Arnold addressed Greene. "According to the map, you should've had an easy, dry march to the lake's shores. Instead—"

"Yes … instead we became lost in a quagmire, what the men took to calling 'Spider Lake' on account of it's many 'legs' that we were forced to circumnavigate, and eventually became lost and completely turned around, headed in the wrong direction. What should've taken hours took days. And even right to the end we did not know how far we yet had to travel. For men on the verge of starvation, wandering through an impassible, wretched bog is a death march. I am still hopeful that some additional men may yet wander back out of the swamp, but I fear they will not. We have lost thirty-seven men thus far, either to starvation or exposure, and a dozen more are still missing. It has been a devastating blow, both to my command and to me personally."

"I now curse my order allowing you to leave the *bateaux* behind at the Dead River," Arnold said. "Captain Morgan, I commend you for your prescient decision to bring your boats along, so that you and your men had a relatively easy time of crossing that last swamp. Doubtless your hard, unpopular choice saved many lives among your men."

Morgan shrugged. "Maybe. Though it nearly got us all drowned later, going down the Chaudière."

"But it didn't, and here you are," Arnold argued.

Morgan nodded his head in appreciation of the compliment. But when he looked back up at Arnold, he held a thoughtful expression. "Colonel … I been thinking about that map. Odd that it'd be missing something as vital as the spider lake … I was just remembering that I have a fellow in my company who did surveying and mapmaking before the war. How's about we have him take a look at that map and tell us what he thinks of it?"

"Certainly, why not?" Arnold answered. "Send for your man, if you would, and let's see what he has to say. I'd like to get to the bottom of this matter, for which I feel a good deal of responsibility and more than a little shame."

◄◄◄◄◆►►►►►

Moments later, Ethan stepped into the room, believing he had been summoned by Captain Morgan, but now realizing that he had just been invited into a meeting of the expedition's senior officers, led by the colonel himself. He forced down a feeling of panic by looking at Morgan, who gave him a calm, reassuring nod.

But it was Colonel Arnold who rose to greet him, stepping up and offering him a seat. "Come in, come in and be at your ease, Private …?"

"*Chambers*, sir. Ethan Chambers."

"Private Chambers," Arnold concluded. He then retook his own seat and immediately handed across his original copy of the map they'd used to plan the entire expedition.

"Chambers, I understand from Captain Morgan that you are an expert in mapmaking … though I must confess I'd assumed you would be a bit … older?" he glanced over at Morgan, who returned an unreadable look.

Ethan was about to correct the colonel, telling him he was still only an apprentice, but he glanced at the captain first, who gave him a subtle shake of the head, so he decided it was best not to disagree, which might make the captain look bad in front of all these important men.

"Yes, sir. It's true that I am young ... but my father has been in the business back in Virginia since before I was born, and I reckon I've been around it as long as I can remember. Most recently surveying and mapmaking in the Shenandoah Valley of Virginia, commissioned by the Royal Governor Lord Dunmore, before volunteering for Captain Morgan's rifle company."

"Ah. Excellent, excellent. Now, Private, the reason I have asked you to come here, is I have been quite surprised at how our map seems to have been ... well, *inaccurate* might be the best way to put it. The map was made by a British Military engineer by the name of John Montresor back during the French and Indian War. To the best of my knowledge, this is the original map, along with the journal of his exploration of the area. I'd like you to have a look at the map and its accompanying journal, then give us your expert opinion on them."

Ethan got a sudden, sinking feeling that he was in way over his head, and that he'd not be able to have any opinion on the map, expert or otherwise. But what he said was, "Yes, sir. I'll be happy to take a look at it for you."

Ethan unrolled the map, and the men sitting nearby assisted him by placing heavy objects on the corners: two metal cups, a pocket watch, and a knife. Ethan gazed at the map for a moment, feeling entirely inadequate and overwhelmed. Then he forced himself to relax, took a deep breath, and tried to remember everything his father had taught him about mapmaking.

Before he took in any geographical details, he focused on the quality of the rendering. At a glance, he could see that this map had been crafted by an expert cartographer. Ethan's own father, Gideon, was a highly skilled professional mapmaker, and yet this map was of a quality surpassing anything he'd done. Though drawn in the typical two-dimensional perspective, the subtle use of brown and green watercolors had given the illusion of depth, including a feel for the topography, elevation, and vegetation. Lakes and ponds had been colored using subtle shades of blue, and mountain ridges had been drawn in, artistic flourishes that added to the sense of realism. *So ... a map of the highest quality, drawn by man who was clearly a master at the craft. Then why did Colonel Arnold complain that it was woefully inaccurate?*

First thing, verify the scale, he remembered his father saying. Fortunately, the map included a scale of miles, in five-mile increments up to thirty miles. *Well, it's a starting point, anyway ...*

Ethan looked up and, for the first time, noticed that Colonel Arnold was gazing at him intently, as were all the other officers gathered around, as if expecting some sudden pronouncement. Ethan fought down an overwhelming sense of self consciousness. "Uh ... sorry, Colonel. I guess I should've said that this might take some time ... to do it properly, I mean."

"Oh. Yes, of course. Gentlemen, let us resume our seats, and continue discussing our next course of action while Private Chambers studies the map."

There was a general nodding of heads and movement back to the chairs gathered around the table.

"Um ... one more thing, Colonel, if you please ..."

"Yes?"

"Have you a ruler about you, sir?"

Arnold raised an eyebrow at this like it was the oddest request, and all of the officers either shook their heads, shrugged their shoulders, or answered some variation of "Not me," or "I haven't any."

But Arnold's aide, Eleazer Oswald, stepped up and handed Ethan a neat, twelve-inch wooden ruler. "Will this do, Mr. Chambers?" he asked.

"Oh, yes, perfectly. Thank you kindly, Mr. Oswald. Oh ... and would you happen to have a pencil, and sheet of paper I might borrow?"

Oswald produced the requested items, bowed, and stepped back to his place, hovering just behind Colonel Arnold's chair.

Then, as the officers reconvened their planning for the journey downstream and what might come after, Ethan began his detailed examination of the map.

First, he measured the scale of miles on the ruler so that he could use it to measure distances on the map. Next, he had to verify that the scale of miles was in fact accurate. Remembering that Daniel Morgan had at one point stated that Fort Western was twenty miles upstream from the mouth of the Kennebec, and seeing that the river ran relatively straight in a northerly direction on that stretch, Ethan decided to use *that* as his verification, and so he laid down the ruler on the map to measure it. *Looks to be about eighteen miles … With the slight bending and curving of the river, twenty miles ought to be about right. So, the scale appears to be correct, as I had expected. Now … what?*

He pondered for a few moments and then noticed that the mapmaker—whose name, Montresor, was written at the top—had noted his camp sites as he surveyed, sequentially numbered on the map as "Camp 15," "Camp 16," "Camp 17," etc.

This gave him an idea. Using the known distances, such as between Fort Western and old Fort Halifax, and how long it took to paddle upstream between them, he could get an idea of the time it took to travel one mile upon the river. And given that the portages were, though difficult and tiresome, relatively short stretches—typically no more than five miles—he was able to plot out their various campsites versus how long it should've taken between them, and thus the distances. He did this all the way up the Kennebec to the Great Carrying Place, putting tiny marks on the map and jotting down notes and calculations on the paper.

He then worked his way across the Great Carrying Place, thinking back on all the events and circumstances, such as when they were delayed several days by the torrential rains, so that these could be denoted on his list.

From time to time as he worked, he could see Colonel Arnold glance over at him and stare at his sheet of notes. It was an odd sensation to have the great man looking over his shoulder, so he tried his best to ignore it and concentrate on what he was doing. When he had nearly filled his sheet of paper, he discovered that Colonel Arnold was not the only one watching his progress; Oswald slipped up next to him and placed another blank piece of paper adjacent to the original one on the table. Ethan looked up at him and exchanged a smile, and a nod of appreciation, then went back to work.

When he reached Lake Mégantic, he picked up Montresor's journal of his expedition and began reading through it. It was many pages long, and much of it wasn't applicable, as the engineer had explored the areas for miles around their route in every direction, which was of no concern to Ethan's present task. But in the places that were applicable, Ethan again took notes and compared Montresor's words to the map and to his own recollections of the journey.

When he was finished, he read back through his own notes and re-checked all his own calculations to make sure he hadn't missed anything critical.

Then he set down his pencil and looked up. He realized that he'd been so focused on his own task that he'd paid no mind to what the officers had been discussing. Major Meigs was presently speaking, going over the logistics of the number of boats that would be required to cross the St. Lawrence River to get at Quebec City on the other side.

Colonel Arnold must have noticed Ethan was no longer working, as he turned and gazed in his direction. The other officers, noticing their commander's change of focus, turned toward him as well. Even Major Meigs, noticing that no one seemed to be paying attention to him any longer, trailed off mid-sentence, and looked his way as well.

Colonel Arnold broke the silence, "Private Chambers … have you completed your task?"

"Yes, sir, I have."

"And?"

Ethan couldn't help a quick glance toward Daniel Morgan, who gave him a thoughtful, but otherwise unreadable, expression.

"I have come to several conclusions concerning the map and a number of detailed observations," Ethan answered.

"Please, proceed," Arnold responded with a wave of his hand.

"Yes, sir. Firstly, this map was clearly crafted by a mapmaker of the highest caliber, which should not be surprising from a

Royal Military engineer, I suppose. This leads to my second point: I believe that everything on this map is accurate, both in distance and in content."

"*What?*" Colonel Greene gasped. "Surely not. I have lost several dozen good men due to the shortcomings of this map."

Ethan's face turned red, but he shook his head and raised his hand in an attempt to calm Greene.

"Sorry, Colonel Greene … I have not spoken clearly … When I say 'everything *on* the map is correct,' what I failed to say is that there are also important things that are *missing*."

"Oh," Greene responded in a calmer voice, "… sorry, please do continue, Private."

Ethan was surprised to find he actually *did* know more than he'd ever realized about maps, in fact, apparently much more than any of these officers. The thought gave him more confidence as he continued his narrative.

"Thank you, sir. As I was saying, everything on the map appears to be correct, but there are a number of critical things that are *not* on the map, such as the 'spider lake' that your men encountered. I also noticed, from my own personal recollections of the journey, that a number of important things like streams, ridges, waterfalls, and swamps, were also not denoted on the map. And further, these same missing features were not mentioned in Montresor's journal.

"At first, I assumed that they were simply excluded because they were minor details, insignificant in the overall scheme of the map. But that didn't explain the spider lake. And not just the lake; the entire vast swamp at the south end of Lake Mégantic was missing as well. The only thing that shows on the map in that area, and the only thing mentioned in the journal, is a stream running from the Height of Land to the lake, making it seem to be an easy passage.

"And then I began to notice that words were sometimes left off from the journal. Like here, on page ten. It says, 'Our course was …' And then there is nothing more. The very next sentence says, 'After walking about,' and then there's a gap, concluding with 'we came to a beautiful lake.' Clearly there are missing words here that would've indicated the distance or time."

"I'd noticed missing words like that in the journal," Arnold interjected, "but assumed they were just errors made when the journal was being copied."

"Maybe, sir. But isn't it curious that the missing words occur at critical junctures where an accurate distance or obvious landmark might spell the difference between taking the correct route, and wandering miles off course?"

"Interesting point, Chambers. Go on …" Arnold prompted.

"Then, thinking on the missing features, I recognized that very few waterfalls or rapids are denoted on the map. Odd, considering these obstacles would've been major impediments to Montresor's expedition, same as ours. And then I kept coming back to the spider lake … Why was it missing?"

"And?" Arnold asked.

"Sir, I believe it was intentionally left off. In fact, I believe it was left off to serve as a trap."

"A trap?"

"Yes, sir. The British must've feared the French might get their hands on the map and journal, then use them to launch their own invasion southward. So they intentionally made altered copies of the originals that made it look like the route between the lake and the highland was a dry, open plain, when in fact it was an impassable morass, and that the journey down the river would be swift and easy. If the British decided to use the route, they would provide their officers with the *real* map and journal, so they could avoid the obstacles."

"So … my men fell into a trap laid by the British more than fifteen years ago?" Greene said, slowly shaking his head.

"Yes, but not a trap intended for us, ironically," Arnold answered. "Good work, Private Chambers. Thank you kindly for your service."

"Thank *you*, sir. It was … my pleasure," Ethan answered. Then, taking it as his cue to depart, he rose and stepped toward the door. But as he left, he caught Captain Morgan's eye. Morgan nodded and gave him a quick smile, which he chose to interpret as high praise from his commander. *Or at least I didn't embarrass him in front of those other officers*, Ethan thought with a wry grin as he stepped out the door.

◄◄◄◄◄◆►►►►►

Thursday November 9, 1775 – Chaudière River, Quebec Province:

If Ethan thought the remainder of the journey to Quebec City would be easy now that they'd made it to the Chaudière River, had finally rid themselves of the burdensome bateaux, and were marching downhill the rest of the way, he was sorely mistaken.

The weather continued to plague them with frigid temperatures, and the clouds couldn't seem to decide between pouring rain and swirling snow down on them. The result was a trail of thick, frigid muck up to their knees and beyond that sucked at their feet with every step.

The good news was, though they were still a ragged, unshaven, motley looking lot, they were now rested and well fed, which made the slog seem less insurmountable. They also had reasonable shoes on their feet once again, though mostly hand-made moccasins to replace the worn-out or missing boots and shoes they'd started the journey with. The moccasins were the quickest and easiest thing for them to make, lacking the proper tools and skills to manufacture anything sturdier.

And Levi's recovery from exhaustion and near starvation had seemed almost miraculous to Ethan, a thing for which he felt a good deal of relief and gratitude. So greatly had his friend recovered that he was now outpacing Ethan on the march. This gave Ethan the mischievous idea of grabbing onto the back of Levi's jacket to let *him* pull for a change. *Would serve him right and let him see how it feels*, he thought with a grin.

But just as he stepped up right behind Levi and reached out to seize a handful of jacket, Levi stopped, and Ethan bumped into his back, grabbing onto him to keep from tipping over.

"*Hey* … what'd you stop like that for?" Ethan asked in annoyance.

"Look …" Levi said, pointing ahead.

Ethan looked out, but all he could see was a cloud of swirling snow. But he noticed all the other men had stopped marching as well and were staring out ahead.

"What—" he started to ask but cut himself off; through a break in the swirling snow, he caught a glimpse of water—a great, wide, smooth-flowing waterway, the largest he'd seen since they'd left the Atlantic at the mouth of the Kennebec. And beyond the water … a fortress city high on a hill: they'd reached Quebec City at last.

◄◄◄◄◄◆►►►►►

Friday November 10, 1775 – Point Levis, Quebec Province:

Ethan and Levi returned from picket duty and stepped inside the door to the cavernous, abandoned warehouse that now served as the barracks and headquarters for Daniel Morgan's command at Point Levis, a sparsely populated area to the east of where they'd first reached the St. Lawrence River at the mouth of the Chaudière. The warehouse was sited due south and directly across the river from Quebec City.

They'd only just stepped up to the fire, squeezing their way in between the men gathered round and stretching out their frozen fingers, when Sergeant Murphy stepped up to Ethan. "Seen anythin' interestin', Chambers?" he asked.

"No, sir, Sarge. Just snow, and those two British gunboats anchored next to the city. No sign of any redcoats, except on those ships. We kept out of sight, as ordered, and I've seen nothing that says they're aware of us yet."

"Good, good. Let's hope it stays that way."

"Yes, sir."

"Oh … I nearly forgot," Murphy said, as he'd begun to turn away. "Cap wants to see you. Said t'send ya in soon as you got back. Didn't say why."

"Oh. All right. Thanks, Sarge."

Ethan turned and exchanged a nod with Levi, then headed toward the northeast corner of the building and up a flight of stairs to the captain's "office," a small room with its own stove and a window overlooking the river.

He climbed the stairs to the office, knocked, then entered after hearing, "Come on in," through the door.

"Sir … Sergeant Murphy said you wanted to see me."

"Yes, come on in, Ethan, and have a seat. If you're cold, pull the chair up by the stove."

"Thank you, sir." Ethan took advantage of Morgan's offer and slid the extra chair up next to the stove, then turned it so it faced the captain where he sat behind a small, wood table that served for a desk.

"Ethan, Colonel Arnold was impressed by what you did the other day with that map of the Kennebec route. So was I, for that matter."

"Thank you, sir. I was … a little surprised that I could see what was wrong with it. Still think of myself as just an apprentice, with so much to learn … But, I guess I *do* know more than I thought I did."

"Hmph … I suspected as much, which is why I stuck my neck out and called you an 'expert' in front of the colonel. I'm happy you proved me right, though it would've been no shame on you if you hadn't.

"In any case, the reason I asked you here is on account o' *this* …" He handed Ethan a large, rolled up sheet of parchment.

"Another map?"

"Yep. The colonel asked me to give it to you. It's a map of the city and its defenses from back during the French and Indian War. After the fiasco with the Kennebec map, he wants to make sure we have it right this time."

"Oh … I see. But … how does he expect me to do that with the city over on the far side of a mile-wide river that's guarded by British gunboats?"

Morgan chuckled and rolled his eyes. "Oh, you are a bright one, Ethan. No, he doesn't expect you to fly like a bird, or swim like a fish. For now, he just wants you to draft an exact copy of the map, so he doesn't risk losing the original. Then, after we cross the river—which we're still discussing the means of—you can take your copy and make all the necessary changes to make sure it's as accurate as it can be, with the understanding that you'll be limited to what you can observe from outside the fortress walls."

"Oh, all right," he said and unrolled the map to have a look. He gazed at it for several moments, then said, "Shouldn't be too difficult to make the copy. I'll need a large parchment, of course, pens, ink, and a ruler …"

"Already done. The colonel sent the necessities over with the map. You can sit right here and work on it. Hell, Ethan, you already read and write out all the orders around here, so I don't reckon there's anything that'll be said in this office the next couple of days that you can't hear."

Ethan returned the captain's grin. "Yes, sir. I reckon that's true. I'll get started straightaway."

"Good man."

◄◄◄◄◄◆►►►►►

Saturday November 11, 1775 – Point Levis, Quebec Province:

Ethan worked diligently, staying up late into the night working on the map then getting up at first light the following morning, finishing it up before noon. It was now early afternoon, and as he shivered out on picket duty, he chastised himself for finishing up the map work so quickly.

"What was I *thinking?*" he asked Levi and the five other privates who were hunkered down behind a brick wall, taking turns peering out at the distant city when they weren't huddled up in a vain attempt to keep warm. "I could be in the captain's nice warm office right now working a pen, rather than out here freezing my backside off working a rifle."

Levi smirked. "Yeah, for such a smart fella, sometimes you act pretty dumb, Ethan."

The others laughed. Private Merchant said, "Sometimes it's best not to work too hard or too quick, Ethan. All's it gets you is more work, in my experience."

There were nods of agreement from the others, and grins.

"For once, I agree with you shirkers," Ethan responded with a wry grin, which caused Merchant to nod and chuckle.

"Hey, guys … shush. Lookie here … what's this?" Private Carland, whose turn it was to look out over the wall, interrupted their banter with a serious tone. "A rowboat … comin' our way. And it's full o' redcoats … with muskets and all!"

"Lemme see," Merchant said, starting to stand.

But Ethan grabbed his jacket. "No! We can't all stand up at once and start gawking … They'll see us. One at a time."

Merchant nodded at Ethan and sat back down.

"Who's got the spyglass?" Ethan then asked. There were only a handful of spyglasses in Daniel Morgan's command. These were the personal property of the officers, so were carefully doled out, one per group of pickets, and then jealously reclaimed at the end of each tour. But up to this point, they'd not needed it, as there'd been nothing interesting to see. Only the usual bored redcoats pacing guard duty on the two warships on the river. After a few tedious minutes of watching *that* action, nobody was interested in seeing it again. So the spyglass had been all but forgotten.

Nobody answered, so Ethan looked over at Private Kurtz and said, "Hey Adam, didn't you have the spyglass when we left the warehouse?"

"Oh. Yeah, you're right, Ethan. I do have it." He reached inside his haversack, then pulled out a long brass tube. "Here you go." He handed it across to Ethan as if never thinking to question who it ought to go to. Ethan took it, then met eyes with Kurtz, who was still standing, and they switched positions so someone watching might think there was just a single man there looking out in simple curiosity.

Ethan stood and held the brass spyglass to his right eye, ignoring the stinging coldness of it. But it immediately fogged up, and he had to bring it down, blow hot breath on both ends, then wipe it with his sleeve before trying again.

This time, he could clearly see what Kurtz had reported. A British long boat was coming straight toward the warehouse. He couldn't make an exact count, but it appeared to hold nearly a dozen red-coated soldiers, each one holding a musket with a fixed bayonet. It had four oars, each being worked in a swift, steady motion by a sailor. An officer, dressed in bright red coat with sparkling brass buttons and tall peaked hat, stood in the stern, gazing in their direction.

"It's a British long boat, all right. Ten or twelve soldiers ... muskets with bayonets. An officer out front. Headed right at the warehouse."

Ethan dropped back down. He looked around at the other privates. All were wide-eyed, and several looked downright fearful. Other than the long-range, relatively risk-free sniping they'd done back at Boston, this was their first encounter with a fully armed enemy patrol.

"What should we do?" Kurtz asked, looking around. There were shrugs, but nobody had an answer. In that moment, it occurred to Ethan that there was nobody in charge and that someone needed to step up. In that same instant, he realized if he didn't do it, nobody would. *What would Captain Morgan do right now if he were me?* he wondered. And then he answered his own question: *He would fight!*

"George, run over and tell the captain what's happening," Ethan said. He knew that Private Merchant had the longest legs, so he likely could navigate the treacherous, snowy terrain the quickest.

"All right ... I'm going," Merchant said, then scrambled back from the wall and moved off, ducking down so he'd not be seen by the British boat, which was now only a few hundred yards from shore.

Levi looked over at Ethan. "He ain't gonna get to the captain 'fore that boat comes ashore, Ethan. Our men in the warehouse are gonna get caught by surprise."

Ethan nodded, then rose up for another look, first at the boat, then over toward the warehouse, more than a hundred yards off to their right through a twisting, muddy trail that took some time to traverse.

"Yep ... reckon you're right about that, Levi. Except the part where they catch our men by surprise. Load your rifles, boys. I'll keep a watch, and when they're almost to shore, I'll give the word, y'all stand, and we'll give 'em a volley. That'll at least slow them down, and it'll give our guys fair warning."

"Okay, Ethan," Kurtz said.

"Yep, sounds good," Levi agreed.

The others nodded, and all began loading their rifles, including Ethan, who ducked down just long enough to get his own rifle ready. Then he leaned the weapon against the wall next to him and stood back up, but he no longer needed the spyglass to see the fast-approaching vessel.

"Just a few more minutes … Gonna let 'em hit the sandbar first. That'll distract them a bit, trying to steady the boat and whatnot. That's when we'll let 'em have it … Just a little further …"

Ethan watched as the boat stroked closer … closer … closer. Finally, it slowed and came to a stop, and the officer in the prow leapt from the boat, landing in water up to his knees.

"Now!" Ethan called out, reaching down to pick up his own rifle. Then, remembering the proper words, he said, "Like we've been taught, boys … *Present arms … aim … fire!*"

Boom! Smoke swirled in the air above the six rifles. The effect of the volley was immediate, and extremely satisfying to Ethan. Though there were no obvious casualties among the enemy soldiers, the oarsmen reversed course and pulled in the opposite direction as quickly as they could. The soldiers inside the boat ducked down below the gunwales, making no attempt to return fire.

And from the warehouse, the Americans came pouring out, weapons in hand, led by Captain Morgan himself, charging toward the water with his sword outstretched. It was then that Ethan noticed the British naval officer was down on his hands and knees in the water, scrambling to get to his feet, even as his comrades sped away, abandoning him to his fate. He stood, then seemed to notice Captain Morgan and his men racing toward him. The young ensign turned and saw his own boat moving swiftly away. He began slogging through the water in a vain attempt to return to the boat, but it was too late. Morgan stopped at the shore, then waved on a few of his men to wade out and take charge of the prisoner, the first British captive of the expedition.

Sunday November 12, 1775 – Point Levis, Quebec Province:

"Gentlemen, this is Mr. John Halstead, late of the New Jersey Colony, who's been transacting business in Quebec these several years past," Colonel Arnold announced to his gathered senior officers. "Needless to say, Mr. Halstead is a proponent of our cause, though of necessity he does so in secrecy, as one would expect. He has recently come from the city, and has graciously consented to provide us with a report on conditions therein. Mr. Halstead."

"Thank you, Colonel. Gentlemen. As the colonel has alluded to, I am an avid proponent of your current expedition, and am at great risk coming here, as I suspect I am already under some suspicion being known as hailing from the colonies.

"Though I have given the colonel a more detailed report of everything I know about the current state of the city's defenses, I shall provide you officers with a brief summary.

"In short, Quebec City is ripe for the taking, in my opinion, especially with Governor Carleton away at Montreal, dealing with General Montgomery's advance. The man he has left in charge, Lieutenant Governor Cramahé, is a weak, ineffective man. And the soldiers left in his charge are mainly English loyalists rather than army regulars. He also ostensibly has at his disposal the captains and crews from the two Royal Navy vessels anchored in the river. But there seems to be some sort of rift between him and them, so that the seamen are rarely seen ashore.

"There is also, theoretically, a local militia made up of several hundreds of conscripted French Canadians. But who they would side with in a fight—if they would fight at all—is anyone's guess.

"I will not presume to advise you military men on the best course of action, but if it was me, I think I would be inclined to act before Governor Carleton is aware of your presence and can move to reinforce the city. It could be that you would encounter but token resistance."

After Halstead departed, Arnold opened up the discussion by stating his intention of moving on the city as quickly as possible.

Daniel Morgan and Colonel Greene immediately spoke in favor of the notion, but several others were more reticent, suggesting it would be more prudent to await the arrival of General Montgomery's army.

But in the end, Colonel Arnold could not be dissuaded, and announced his decision to cross the river the following evening under cover of darkness, utilizing the forty-some boats and canoes they had managed to acquire since arriving at the St. Lawrence. These had been hidden in a small bay back upstream inside the mouth of the Chaudière, and would be brought down to the crossing point as soon as the sun set the following day. They would also bring out the large number of scaling ladders they'd hired the locals to build in secrecy, which had been hidden in Morgan's abandoned warehouse. After the men were all gathered, the operation would commence.

◄◄◄◄◄◆►►►►►

Monday November 13, 1775 – Quebec City, Quebec Province:

Though it was chilly, there was no breeze, so the river flowing lazily from left to right was glassy smooth. And with the clouds covering the moon, it was so black out that it would've been impossible to see anything at all if not for the night-watch lamps aboard the two British warships anchored in the river next to the city.

It was these warships that caused the most anxiety among the hundred and fifty Americans moving across the river in forty small boats and canoes. The crossing, which had begun just after nine o'clock in the evening, required the small flotilla to pass within yards of the two lurking gunships, so absolute quiet was the order of the day. Even the men manning the oars and paddles did their best to limit the noise they produced.

Ethan felt like he was holding his breath from his spot just behind Captain Morgan on the left side in the lead boat as they slipped between the two warships, each less than a hundred yards distant.

Colonel Arnold was also in the boat, sitting next to Morgan to his right. Though Ethan could feel his nerves on edge, once again he was grateful to be in the company of those two formidable men. It always gave him the sense that whatever happened, he was in the best place he could possibly be.

They reached the shore, and the men debarked as quickly and quietly as they could, hopping out into the shallow water of a sandbar, then pushing the boats back into the stream. They hadn't enough boats to bring all 600 men across at once; the boats would need to make the journey three more times, and on the last journey, they'd need to also bring the scaling ladders.

Ethan felt for the men manning the boats; it was a nerve-wracking, tiresome, dangerous duty. He said a quick, silent prayer for their safety as he watched them slowly paddling back toward the distant shore. Then he turned and trotted after Captain Morgan with his rifle and haversack flung over his shoulders.

He could feel his excitement building as the walls of the city loomed high in the distance, illuminated only by small lamps in the watchtowers becoming ever more obscured by the snow that had begun to fall from the thickening clouds. Ethan glanced over at Levi and the two shared a grin. After more than two months of hard travel, deprivation, and even starvation, they were finally ready to begin the attack on Quebec.

◄◄◄◄◄◆►►►►►

Five British privates and a corporal sat in the small log guardhouse around a rough wooden table playing at cards while a fire blazed gaily in the corner, giving off just enough light to see the contents of their hands.

Just as Private William Mayes leaned forward in his chair to lay down a card, the door burst open, sending an icy blast swirling through the room, knocking cards off the table and sending several caps flying.

"On yer feet, ye slovenly rascals!" a deep voice bellowed. In the doorway stood a strongly built, stern-looking middle-aged man in the distinctive Black Watch uniform of an officer in the Royal Highlander regiments, complete with bright-red, gold-trimmed tunic, distinctive Scottish cap, and green tartan kilt, though the officer wisely wore full-length leggings underneath due to the frigid weather. Behind him stood two tall, scowling soldiers holding rifles with mounted bayonets, though these men wore simple green uniforms.

The soldiers at the table all stood and snapped to attention. "I'm Lieutenant Colonel Allan Maclean," the officer growled in a heavy Scottish accent. "And by God, I'll suffer nae dereliction o' duty under my watch. Load yer weapons, and man yer firing slits; this city's under attack! Even now a damned rebel army marches across the Plains of Abraham, and we hae only just outrun 'em t'Quebec after bein' turned back at Montreal. Stiffen up and show a little pride, won't ye? Prepare for the fight, by damn! Now ... who's in command o' the city?" he asked, stepping up to the closest man almost nose to nose, staring him hard in the eyes.

"Uh ... that'd be the lieutenant governor, Hector de Cramahé, I suppose ... what with General Carleton off to Montreal," the man answered.

Maclean backed away toward the door. "By damn, I'd better hear ye men did yer duty and fought, or there'll be God's holy hell tae pay when I come back here!" he shouted. Then he turned and was gone. The soldiers scrambled to don their tunics, load their rifles, and man their posts, preparing for battle.

Moments later, Colonel Maclean arrived at the St. John's Gate on the city's west side, and to his utter shock, found it still wide open and but lightly manned. The gate guards suffered the same harsh haranguing as had those at the guard post; the gate was swiftly pulled shut and bolted with a loud *clang*.

Maclean dispersed his men to the walls in preparation for the expected attack. These hardened veteran soldiers included 120 volunteer Scotsmen—veterans of the Seven Years' War against the French—that he'd recently recruited in America to form a Highlander Emigrant regiment, plus a company of eighty members of the Royal Fusiliers of the elite Seventh Regiment of Foot, whose other members had been cut off and surrounded at

Fort St. Johns, now reportedly captured by the Americans. It was a small but formidable force, such as hadn't been seen in Quebec since Carleton's departure for Montreal.

Maclean himself continued on to the governor's palace, determined to have a word with the lieutenant governor. His dander was up at the complete lack of preparation he saw at the fort with an enemy assault imminent, so he was pretty sure it wasn't going to be a nice, polite word.

◄◄◄◄◄◆►►►►►

It was a somber meeting in the great hall at the governor's palace, situated on the highest point in Quebec with a grand view of the river below. Lieutenant Governor Cramahé sat with Governor Carleton's ministers discussing their next course of action, which appeared to be the imminent surrender to the approaching army of the Americans. The news of late had not been good: Fort Chambly had fallen, followed almost immediately by Fort St. Johns. And then the shocking news that the Americans had taken Montreal and that Governor Carleton had been forced to flee with the few men he had left. But rumor had it the Americans also controlled the waterway, so it seemed highly likely Carleton would be cut off and captured. It was, all in all, a thoroughly dismal and depressing set of circumstances.

Cramahé had no significant fighting force at his disposal: only the half-hearted militia made up of French Canadians, whose loyalty was highly suspect, and the crews from two gunships, a sloop of war named *Hunter* and a frigate named *Lizard*, moored in the river, and their captains, Thomas Mackenzie and John Hamilton, respectively—not exactly a force to be reckoned with. Cramahé had just asked his aide, Joseph Duggan to draw up the document of surrender when the large, oak double doors to the meeting room flung wide with a clatter.

In strode a barrel-chested officer in full Highlander uniform. He stomped up to the table, a scowl on his face.

"Which one o' ye is Cramahé?" he demanded.

The lieutenant governor gazed up at him, blinking. "I am Lieutenant Governor Hector de Cramahé," he answered.

"Governor, I'm Lieutenant Colonel Allan Maclean, Royal Highlanders. Who's the senior officer in command o' this fort?" he asked.

Though it was highly rude behavior, Cramahé was so taken aback by the colonel's bluster and domineering presence that it never occurred to him to protest. "Why … there are no army officers of high rank present, so I suppose Captain John Hamilton of the Royal Navy, commander of the frigate *Lizard*, is the most senior officer in the city at the moment. Oh, I suppose … now, that would be *you*, Colonel."

"Good. Then I'm now officially takin' command o' this post and its defense. Where can I find Hamilton?"

"Oh … I think he has quarters down the lane somewhere. My servants can likely tell you."

"I shall go there straightaway. My first order will be for him to bring his cannons into the fort and up on tae the walls."

"But … I believe he intends to use them to prevent the Americans from crossing the river from Point Levis," Cramahé argued.

"Tae late for that, Governor … They're already here. I entered the gate with 'em on m'very heels. We'll be attacked or under siege come mornin'."

"*Oh*. But dear Colonel … you should know … I was preparing to issue a declaration of surrender when they arrived. Thinking to prevent loss of life and destruction of the city, you understand."

"Belay tha' order. I just brought you tae hundred veteran soldiers who don't know the meanin' o' the word quit. And along with the marines off the gunships anchored in the river, we'll give these rebel rascals a fight, ye can bet on that."

"Well, I must say it's a relief to have a man of your experience here to guide us," Cramahé said. "But you should know, at this very moment the citizens of the town are holding a meeting to decide whether or not to refuse their duty to serve as militia, and to throw open the gates to the Americans."

"Oh, they are, are they? Where is this meeting? I must go there immediately! By damn, they'll not shirk their duty. Nae on my watch."

Colonel Arnold ordered Captain Morgan to lead his rifle battalion up to the city walls to reconnoiter and verify the state of its defenses.

Ethan and Levi were in Sergeant Murphy's company, as usual, trotting along in silence, loaded rifles in hand, just to the left of the captain, who was in the lead. They'd come to a place where various neat-looking houses and buildings lined both sides of the street, but there were no people about, as if the area had been recently evacuated. Their shoes ploughing through the freshly fallen, foot-deep snow and the soft jingling of various metal objects they carried were the only sounds to be heard, lending the scene an eerie, surreal feel. The snow that'd begun to fall when they'd first landed had stopped, along with the breeze, leaving in its wake an uncanny stillness. *It's as if the land itself is holding its breath, waiting to see what will happen next*, Ethan thought.

As they made their way down the street, Ethan could see the snow-topped city wall towering in the background, now only a few hundred yards away. And beneath the wall, where the roadway led, was a large, solid iron gate. Not surprisingly, the gate was shut.

Ethan could see that the buildings were about to come to an end, with the last one being a large, grand-looking brick manor house to the right of the road. His gaze was fixed on this impressive structure, such that he nearly missed the signal to halt given by the captain.

He looked over at Morgan and was surprised that the captain was not looking at the manor house, but rather at an unassuming log building on the opposite side of the road. Morgan signaled a movement in that direction, and Sergeant Murphy's company obeyed, trotting down a heavily treed lane running in front of the building.

They'd just passed the log building when they heard a voice shouting out from that direction: *"Present arms … aim … fire!"*

Nobody had to tell them the meaning of those words, and Ethan hit the ground along with the rest of his company as bullets buzzed by overhead, followed by a loud *boom!*

But Daniel Morgan was immediately on his feet, sword drawn, racing toward the building. "C'mon men, let's get 'em before they reload!" he shouted.

With no conscious thought, Ethan was on his feet, racing forward, watching Captain Morgan reach the front door and, without pause or backward glance, thrust his boot at the center of the door, bursting it inwards. Ethan, who had outpaced his fellows, was the next man through the doorway. He entered, rifle at the ready, prepared to open fire.

But he immediately saw that the fight was over, and lowered the hammer on his gun. Daniel Morgan stood with his sword raised toward six British soldiers who had already dropped their rifles and had their hands in the air.

◄-◄-◄-◄◆►-►-►-►

Moments later, Daniel Morgan stood in front of the six redcoats, arms folded across his chest and a scowl on his face. He towered over the nervous looking young men, and with his broad shoulders, muscular physique, and thoroughly intimidating demeanor, Ethan was happy he was on the American side.

"Now … so far you boys are still in one piece … which I assume you're happy about. But if you wish to *stay* that way, I suggest you tell me what I want to know."

Nobody answered, but Ethan thought the statement had produced the desired effect; the soldiers looked even more fearful than before, if that were possible.

Morgan stepped up to the corporal and said, "Now … I want to know about the fort's defenses … how many men are on the walls, what kind of artillery they have, who's in command, and so forth. If you answer me honestly, it'll go easy on you. If not …" He left the sentence unfinished, allowing them to imagine the rest.

But the corporal was apparently not of a mind to find out what "hard" might look like, so he answered, "Well, sir, up 'til an hour ago, I'd say you could just walk right in, and nobody'd raise a finger. Gate was wide open, and the men on the walls were mostly for show. No cannons to speak of. Supposedly there's a militia o' locals, but never seen anythin' o' them. French, *pah!* Why would they wanna fight for the likes o' us anyhow? And ... rumor was that the lieutenant governor, name o' Cramahé—bit of a fancy dan, to my mind, and thoroughly spineless by all accounts—was ready to surrender at the first sight o' you Bostonians."

"Oh? And what happened an hour ago?"

"A regular army officer shows up. Never seen 'im before. Highlander ... kilt an' all. A colonel, he was ..." He looked at the man next to him. "What'd he say his name was?"

"Maclean," the private answered. "Aye, and he had a whole pack o' regular soldiers with him. Veteran types. Hard cases ... no humor in 'em at all," he continued in a heavy Welsh accent, slowly shaking his head as if saddened by the thought of such thoroughly serious men.

Then the corporal added, "Yes, that was it. Lieutenant Colonel Allan Maclean. It was him as made us open fire on your men, sir ... Sorry about that, but he threatened to personally come back here and give us a good thrashing if'n we didn't put up a fight.

"But I ... well, I'll beg of you never to repeat this, sir, but ... I told the boys to fire over your heads and not to try'n hit anyone. That way we done our duty, but you'd have no reason to come in here an' kill us all."

The other privates nodded their agreement to this.

"Very pragmatic of you, Corporal. And ... just how many men did this Maclean bring with him?" Morgan asked.

"Oh ... couple hundred, I'd say," the corporal answered. "Most were them Scottish Highlander types—Black Watch, they call them. The others looked more like Londoners," he glanced over at the private next to him again.

The private nodded. "Oh, aye ... Brits for sure ... Heard someone mention Seventh Regiment of Foot. Fusiliers they are ... Men as live for a good fight, I heard."

The corporal shook his head. "Never found there to be nothin' good about a fight. 'Cept if one wishes to be dead."

The private nodded his agreement.

Morgan turned to Ethan. "Private Chambers, run back to Colonel Arnold and let him know what these prisoners just told us: that some veteran redcoats just arrived, but they are still few and have no artillery. Tell him I suggest we launch an attack straightaway and not wait for the remaining men to cross the river. Likely this Brit colonel has not yet had time to organize his defense. If we move quickly, he may never get the chance."

"Yes, sir. I'm on my way," Ethan answered. He then turned and headed back toward Arnold's position at a fast trot.

◄◄◄◄◄◆►►►►►

Colonel Arnold listened to Ethan's report with rapt attention, asking a few pointed questions before standing and pacing the room for several minutes, his head down as if examining the floorboards. They were a mile back from the city's walls in an abandoned farmhouse that was being used as a staging area until the remainder of the American forces arrived from across the river. Eleazer Oswald sat in a chair near Arnold's, as usual.

Finally, Arnold stopped, turned toward Ethan, and looked up. "Damn the luck … If we'd only arrived an hour earlier … But I fear I must decline Captain Morgan's suggestion. With the element of surprise gone, the veteran British officer and his soldiers now within the walls, less than half our men on this side of the river and none of the scaling ladders, plus General Montgomery yet to arrive, I dare not assault the fortress. Tell the captain we shall await the arrival of the remainder of our men. In the meantime, he is to invest the fortress. Place pickets outside the western gates and prevent anyone from coming or going."

"Yes, sir. I will tell him," Ethan answered, then left and returned to give Captain Morgan the unhappy news.

But when he returned to give Morgan the colonel's answer, he was surprised at the nonchalant response he received. He suspected that Morgan already knew what the answer would be, but like a small child wanting one more piece of candy, he felt obliged to ask anyway.

"All right, Ethan. Thank you for that," was all Morgan said in response. "Hey, have you seen this place?" he then asked, waving his hand around the room. Since Ethan had left to visit the colonel, Morgan had entered the manor house across from where they'd captured the British soldiers, and that's where Ethan had found him.

"Yes, sir. It's … very nice," was all Ethan could think to say. But he knew it was a monumental understatement. Elegant wood paneling lined the walls and the ceilings, and the floors sparkled with rich hardwoods and marble. Brightly colored draperies with fanciful embroidery adorned every window. It was the very picture of a fine, aristocratic mansion. The only thing Ethan had ever seen that came close was the Royal Governor's palace back in Williamsburg, Virginia that he'd once visited with his father.

"Glad you like it," Morgan smirked. "Find yourself a room to bunk down in for the night. But don't get too used to it. If I know Colonel Arnold, he'll want to use this place for his headquarters starting tomorrow."

Morgan's words concerning the colonel would prove prophetic, but that night Ethan and the rest of the Virginia Riflemen were nevertheless treated to one night sleeping in the most luxurious quarters any of them had ever enjoyed.

Wednesday November 15, 1775 – Quebec City, Quebec Province:

With the situation before Quebec City quickly devolving into a state of siege, Colonel Arnold decided to try to bluff the city's defenders into surrendering and at the same time terrify its citizenry into abandoning their support for the British.

So as a bright sun rose, sparkling off the snow, Arnold's entire command of nearly 600 men marched in formation, rifles on their shoulders, to within 800 yards of the main gate to the city. There they halted and stood to attention with Colonel Arnold, Daniel Morgan, and the other senior officers standing out front.

From there, Eleazer Oswald stepped forward carrying a white flag and accompanied by a single drummer, who beat the international "call to parley." The two strode forward to within hailing distance of the wall, and then paused.

Oswald placed the flag under his left arm, then pulled out a single rolled sheet of paper. He unrolled the paper and held it up toward the parapet. He could see a tall thin man dressed in fine civilian clothing, accompanied by a more robust looking officer in red. Along the walls, red-coated soldiers gazed out expectantly.

Oswald read out in a voice intended to project to the top of the wall and beyond:

> *I am ordered by his Excellency General Washington to take possession of the town of Quebec. I do therefore, in the name of the united American colonies, demand immediate surrender of the town, fortifications, etcetera, of Quebec, to the forces under my command.*
>
> *On surrendering the town, the property of every individual shall be secured unto him. But if I am obliged to carry the town by storm, you may expect every severity practiced on such an occasion, and the merchants who may now save their property will most probably be involved in the general ruin.*
>
> *Colonel Benedict Arnold*
> *Commanding Officer*
> *American Expeditionary Forces*

Oswald lowered the paper and inserted it back into his jacket. As if on cue, the American soldiers watching gave out three lusty, "*huzzahs*" that echoed off the city's walls.

Oswald was still gazing up at the wall when he saw the British officer wave his arm in a sharp downward motion. The next instant, Oswald and the drummer were splattered in mud and snow, followed immediately by a resounding *boom!*

Oswald, startled and besmirched but otherwise unharmed, brushed ineffectually at his soiled coat, then looked up to see a small cloud of smoke rising above a single cannon.

The British had given their answer.

Lieutenant Governor Cramahé looked away from the departing Americans and turned toward Colonel Maclean. "What now, Colonel?"

Maclean returned Cramahé's look with a frown. "First, we evacuate the lower town, erect barricades, and demolish any buildings close tae the walls as the enemy may use t'harbor his snipers. Captain Hamilton has agreed to bring two-thirds o' his cannons and their crews into the fort, which is bein' already underway. We've sent word out for all loyalists bearin' arms in the surrounding countryside to make their way to the fort; they can still get to it from the water side—for now. Next, we must roust out the French militia, get 'em positioned and ready, check they have workable firearms and ammunition. And we insert our own men for their officers, so's there's nae chance o' them switchin' sides on us."

"Well, that all sounds good. Anything else after that, Colonel?"

Maclean scowled and folded his arms across his chest. "Aye … then we fight, Governor. Then we fight."

Chapter 10. Gathering Storms

"God's peace is not the calm after the storm.
It's the steadfastness during it."
- Dr. Michelle Bengtson

Wednesday November 15, 1775 – Winchester, Virginia Colony:

True to his word, James Chambers had been more than generous in his aid to Gideon and his family. He'd spared no expense in providing food, clothing, shoes, and anything else the family required. He'd even repaid a small loan that Gideon had taken out the previous year to purchase badly needed surveying equipment and tools.

But Hannah was beginning to wonder if it was worth it after all. James was now a constant in the middle of their lives, as was his ever-present driver and all-around servant, Cyrus Simpson, a thirty-something year old man of extremely limited intellect, from what Hannah could tell.

But at least Simpson was quiet and polite, almost painfully shy. James, on the other hand, was loud, boisterous, and highly opinionated. He was a man well used to being in command of his circumstances; a man used to ordering people about and used to being obeyed.

Though that was bad enough—making Hannah feel like a servant in her own house—she decided it was *not* the worst thing about the situation. His constant pontification and harping on the idiocy of George Washington, the "so-called Continental Congress," and other "traitors" as he called them was beginning to wear thin. And almost daily he asked if there'd been any word from Ethan. And despite herself, Hannah found she was actually hoping they would *not* hear from their son, under the present circumstances.

And the worst part of it was when James discovered that they'd become friends with Daniel Morgan and his wife Abby, and that Morgan was probably the most notorious "traitor" in

Winchester, who'd led a hundred or so men, including Ethan, off to fight against the king. James absolutely *forbade* Hannah having anything more to do with Abby Morgan.

And when Hannah complained to Gideon about it, and asked him to intervene on her behalf, he was sympathetic but hesitant to confront his brother, saying, "Let's not antagonize him just now … After all the help he's given us. Best just to not see Abby for a while."

"*What?* Just cut her off? After all she's done for us?" Hannah answered, dumbfounded. "And what of Elsie? She's become best friends with the Morgan girls."

"Just for a time … until James calms down about it. Or goes on to some other concern and forgets about her. Then you two can see each other again, and Elsie can visit her girls."

Thursday November 16, 1775 – Quebec City, Quebec Province:

"Come in, Ethan, take a seat," Morgan said, gesturing to the sawed-off section of log that served as a guest chair in his tent.

Ethan took the proffered seat, then looked up expectantly.

"Given that the colonel's attempt to convince the Brits to surrender has clearly failed, and he's ordered a siege, reckon it's time for you to go out and update that map of the city," Morgan said in his typical, no-nonsense manner.

"All right. I'll … do my best, sir. Can I … take Levi with me? You know, to watch my back and so forth while I'm working on the map?"

"No. Levi's more like to distract you than to guard you."

"Oh … all right. Then I'll just … be careful, I guess …"

Morgan scowled, "You mistake my meaning, son. I don't expect you to go it alone … Personal feelings aside, your mission is too valuable to risk it. For one, we can't afford for that map to fall into the enemy's hands. We don't want them to know what we know about their defenses, especially once you've made changes to the original map.

"I'm sending a patrol with you, including Sergeant Murphy."

"Oh, that's sounds fine. Thank you, sir. I'll get started straightaway. Was there anything else?"

"Yes, there is. I've been thinking on this little mission of yours, and after discussing it with the colonel, we've decided to grant you a field promotion to the rank of lieutenant, effective immediately."

"*Lieutenant?* You mean ... I'll outrank the sergeants?"

"Well, yes, that's generally what it means, all right," Morgan answered with a wry smile.

"Oh. I ... I don't know about that, sir. Doesn't seem right ..."

"Listen here, Ethan. If I say it's right, and the colonel agrees, then who are you to argue?" Morgan frowned, crossing his arms across his chest.

Ethan's eyes widened at the reproach, but then he saw Morgan's expression soften.

"Look, son ... there are plenty o' good reasons for it. First, you'll need to be able to tell the men on your patrol where to go and what to do, without worry over someone overriding your decisions. And ... well, I hesitate to mention it, but ... it's a risky mission; it's possible you may get captured by the enemy. If you do, you'll receive better treatment and may be exchanged quicker if you're a commissioned officer rather than an enlisted private."

"Oh. That makes sense. Thank you for thinking of it, sir."

Morgan shrugged. "No need to thank me ... It's the simple truth is all. And one more thing weighed into it ..."

"Sir?"

"Yes. How you acted the other day when you were on picket duty ... when the enemy longboat attacked. Without orders or authority, you took charge, got the men organized, and fought the enemy. That was well done—showed leadership ... the kind we'll need in the coming fight."

"Thank you for saying so, sir. But ... what will the other men say, I wonder? Will they do what I say when they know I started as a private ... even as an 'errand boy,' back in Boston?"

"Let's find out," Morgan answered, then stood to his feet, stepped to the tent flap, leaned out and hollered, "Sergeant Murphy. Come here, if you please."

Morgan returned to his seat, and a moment later, Sergeant Murphy stepped into the tent.

"Yes, sir?" he asked.

"Sergeant. Colonel Arnold and I have decided to promote Ethan here to lieutenant. He's been assigned a mission to update our map of the city, and you'll be assigned to provide his guard detail while he does it. Do you have a problem with any of that, Sergeant, or do you reckon any of the men will?"

Murphy grinned, and shook his head. "No, sir. I been after watching our boy here for some time, and it seems to me a good fit. He's a sharp fella, aye … and has a bit o' backbone—which to me is about all a good officer needs. And if any o' me boys have a gripe on it … well, let's just say I ain't opposed to crackin' a few heads if it comes down to it."

"Good. Then get a patrol organized—say five or six privates plus yourself—and report to Lieutenant Chambers within the hour to get started."

"Yes, sir," Murphy said. He turned and gave Ethan a wink before exiting the tent.

Morgan stood, and Ethan did likewise.

"Do me proud out there, son," he said, extending his hand.

"Yes, sir. I will do my best," Ethan answered, shaking the captain's hand.

"No, Ethan … don't just do your *best*. Do what you *have* to do, no matter what it takes; do your duty," Morgan answered with a stern look.

"Yes, sir." The two met eyes for a long moment, then Ethan nodded and left the tent.

For two days, Ethan and his patrol scouted the perimeter of Quebec City. While he tried not to be too obvious in his observations and note-taking, with American forces controlling the exterior of the city, there was generally very little danger from the enemy. Though he still found it baffling, the British soldiers in Quebec, as in Boston, used no long-range rifles, so were of little threat beyond a hundred yards—their smooth bore muskets having no accuracy whatsoever beyond that range. And apparently, they'd been ordered to save ammunition, which, when Ethan considered it, did make sense with their city besieged. So the British made no attempt to target the Americans roaming around just outside their great, towering walls on the west side of the city—what they called the "upper town," due to its position up on a high plateau.

By contrast, the "lower town," on the curving east side of the city, was down at the river level and outside the great walls. And though it had no fortress walls, the British had built ten-foot-tall barricades across the main street. This area was more dangerous to approach, as the enemy soldiers that manned the barricades were much closer, and so much more likely to take a shot at an unwary American soldier who came too close.

Ironically, this thin stretch of land between the high fortress walls and the river frustrated Ethan's efforts to circumnavigate the city for his map. It was here, while approaching the lower town from the south end, where Ethan's platoon had its first taste of danger.

They'd come to a small house, which was presently occupied by some of their fellow Virginia Riflemen who were keeping a watch over that area of the town.

"How far from here to the British barricade?" Ethan asked the sergeant in charge.

"Oh, three or four blocks down, I'd say," the sergeant answered. "But we got no reason t'go thata way, see … Cap'n ordered us to keep anyone from coming to the town, or gettin' out. This here's a good spot to do that. See … there's this nice open courtyard in front of us. Ain't nobody crossin' that without us seein' 'em. No need of us goin' any further up the street and riskin' a bullet."

"Yes, that makes sense," Ethan answered. "But I can't see anything of the walls from here. Just this high cliff off to our left with a little piece of the wall showing above it. I need to see what the fort looks like further north."

"Oh, I can't let you do that, Ethan. Too dangerous. I'm in charge here, and I don't let nobody go no further, see. It ain't safe."

"Oh … I see," Ethan said. He had just about decided to accept that he could accomplish nothing further in this part of the city when he remembered that Captain Morgan had said he needed to get the job done, whatever it took. *And besides, I'm a lieutenant now, aren't I?*

"*I see* … that you are just trying to do your duty, Sergeant. But *my* duty is to map these walls, and as it turns out … I outrank you, sir."

The sergeant scowled and opened his mouth to speak, but then snapped it shut again and shrugged. "Well, it's your neck … *sir*," he replied in what could only be interpreted as a disrespectful tone.

Then Ethan thought about how Daniel Morgan might handle this situation, or possibly Colonel Arnold, and decided if the men were to respect him, he would need to force the issue.

"Sergeant … in future, you will address me with the proper respect due to a lieutenant. Is that clear?" he said. Ethan tried to look stern, but he had no idea what he would do if the man pushed back or argued the point with him.

But to Ethan's surprise, the older, more experienced and physically tougher sergeant's eyes widened, and he said, "Yes, sir. I beg pardon for soundin' sassy just now. Only tryin' to keep you safe, is all. Meanin' no disrespect, sir."

"Pardon granted, Sergeant. Now … tell us what you know of the streets ahead," Ethan said with a silent sigh of relief.

Minutes later, Ethan, Murphy, and their men were trotting down an abandoned street lined on both sides with houses or small stores. They kept to the east side of the buildings to their left, as this kept them out of sight of the city walls, which loomed on the hillside above. They were so close to the walls that even a smoothbore musket might hit them. At the far corner of each building, Ethan motioned the men to stop, then glance around the corner to the left and up the hill to see if there were any soldiers watching. So far, he'd seen none, so they continued on.

They'd just passed the fourth building, and now Ethan could see the great Citadel of Quebec, the heart of the military fortress, towering atop a cliff to their left. So distracted was he by the awe-inspiring sight that he was not looking carefully ahead. As he stepped in front of the next building, he noticed the door was open and there were loud noises coming from inside, as if someone were doing construction. He looked in the doorway, and there stood a red-coated British soldier, staring back at him.

"*Hey!*" the soldier shouted as he reached for a musket leaning against the wall next to him. Ethan could see hammers, saws, and pry bars, piles of broken boards lying about the floor, and broken-down walls—not to mention a dozen or more soldiers, several in only their undershirts. He immediately deduced these soldiers had been in the process of demolishing the house. Probably to prevent the Americans from using it in the coming fight.

Ethan scrambled back, bumping into Sergeant Murphy who'd been following close behind him.

"Redcoats!" Ethan shouted as he turned and waved his men back from the building. They all scrambled to obey, heading for the house on the far side of the street.

Ethan was the last to make it through the door, slamming it shut behind him and leaning his back against it, breathing heavily. The next instant, the wood next to his head exploded inward, spewing splinters into the room and leaving a bullet-sized hole in the door.

"Get down, ya damned fool!" Murphy shouted. Then added, "Uh ... *lieutenant* fool, I mean."

But Ethan was already moving away from the door, unslinging his rifle from his back as he did so. To his relief, he still clutched the map and his notes in his hand, despite the sudden terror of the moment. Murphy crawled up to one of the windows, raised up and punched out the glass with the butt of his rifle. He ducked down just as bullets impacted the outer wall next to the window frame and sailed on through to smack into the far wall behind him.

Private Merchant crawled up next to Murphy, the two met eyes, then Murphy said, "One ... Two ... Three!" The two of them rose from cover, leaned their rifles out the window, and fired at the Brits across the street.

Ethan and the other four privates broke out two more windows and also returned fire on the enemy.

More bullets impacted against the house, but fortunately it was made from thick boards and beams that prevented any of them from penetrating.

Ethan glanced out another window that'd been pierced by two bullets but was not yet entirely broken out. He could see another troop of redcoats coming up the street from the direction of the British barricade, obviously drawn by the sounds of gunfire.

"The neighborhood's getting crowded," Ethan said. "And the neighbors don't look too friendly. Kurtz, see if there's a back door to this place, and if so, check if it's clear outside."

"Yes, sir." Keeping crouched down, Private Kurtz moved out the back door of the room. A moment later he shouted, "There's a door, sir. And nobody's outside."

"All right, Sergeant, let's give 'em a volley, then reload and get out that back door. We'll head back to that last outpost of ours and hopefully get some help from our friends. I'll take the lead, Sergeant; you'll have rear guard."

"All right, you heard 'im, boys. Everyone loaded?" Murphy said, looking around to make sure everyone nodded. "We're gonna shortcut things this time. When I say 'now,' just raise up in the window and fire after. Don't much matter if ya hit anythin', just so's you make 'em get their heads down. Ready … *now!*"

All seven Virginians, including Ethan, rose up into the windows and fired.

They immediately dropped down and reloaded, then headed for the back door, Ethan in front and Murphy coming along last.

Ethan pulled open the door and made a quick look to the right and left to make sure the street was still clear. Straight ahead was the river, and that was presently empty of any boats. He turned right and headed out at a fast trot.

As he moved, he resisted the urge to look back over his shoulder. *No need for that; Murphy will watch our back trail and warn me if there's trouble.* But he suffered an almost palpable feeling that a bullet was headed straight at his back—a feeling he couldn't entirely shake until they'd made it back to the American outpost and were safely inside.

◄◄◄◄◆►►►►

The next day, Ethan decided to try getting into the lower town again, this time by going around the north end of the city along the St. Charles River, then coming down the east side of town heading south. But once again, after spending most of the day hiking about, trying various possible avenues, he was again stymied by the British barricades that blocked the entrances to the town.

The good news was that the sergeant on this side, by the name of Livingston, who was one of the Pennsylvanian riflemen, was much friendlier and more cooperative than his counterpart on the other side of town had been. Livingston was happy to assist Ethan in his mission, if there was anything he could do. But unfortunately, it seemed as if there wasn't.

Ethan, Murphy, and Livingston stood in the doorway of the house that served as the forward American guard post on this side of town, gazing out at the British barricade less than two hundred yards away blocking the main road that ran that direction.

Off to the left was the St. Lawrence River, which Ethan had considered trying to somehow use to gain access to the town, but had decided against it when he thought about the British longboats prowling about. He had no desire to get into a gunfight with one of those while out in the water in a defenseless rowboat or canoe. But as he gazed out in that direction, he noticed a fairly steady stream of small boats, manned by civilians, coming and going.

"What're those small boats doing there?" he asked Sergeant Livingston.

"Oh, them're the local merchants, bringing in goods to sell to the folks in the city. Though we're supposed to be stopping them, as you can see, there's little enough we can do about it. 'Less we was to start shootin' civilians, but I doubt the captain or the colonel would approve."

238

"Yes … likely not," Ethan answered, but was already pulling out the brass spyglass he'd borrowed from the captain to get a better look at the boats. "The redcoats seem friendly with them … even helping them unload, from the looks of it."

"Yes, well, I reckon even redcoats got to eat," Livingston said and chuckled.

"True enough," Ethan responded, lowering the glass. But even as he did so, an idea began to form in his mind.

◄◄◄◄◄◆►►►►►

"Well, you're the boss, Ethan. But I'm tellin' you right now, I'm against it, for whatever *that's* worth," Murphy said with a frown, his arms folded across his chest.

"It's worth plenty … But the captain said to get the job done, whatever it takes."

"Well, I understand that. And the captain ain't a man one wants to displease. But I doubt he had *this* in mind. Goin' around with an armed company eying the enemy's walls from the outside is one thing; sneakin' around inside them is quite another. They'll know you for an American as soon as you open yer mouth. And *when* they catch you … well, I reckon you already know what they do to spies."

"The Brits won't know I'm American if I speak only in French. Though some of them also know it, I'm sure they won't be able to tell French spoken with an American accent from French spoken by a Canadian."

"I don't know, Ethan … That seems mighty risky. Maybe run it by the captain first. Or at least sleep on it tonight. If you get up in the mornin' still wantin' to give it a try, then we'll work on the plan, startin' with findin' a boat and some reasonable lookin' goods to sell."

"All right. I'll sleep on it," Ethan agreed.

But that night, as he lay in his bedroll, sleep seemed as far away as home, way back in Winchester, Virginia. *No use getting homesick now,* Ethan scolded himself. *Too much to do.*

With a conscious will, he shoved thoughts of home aside and focused on the idea he'd had, of posing as a French merchant's delivery boy bringing goods into the town, and then seeing how far he could get on his scouting mission. Though he suffered a little trepidation at the thought, he also felt excitement; he'd be doing something important, but risky, that would ultimately please the captain and the colonel.

But thoughts of the captain kept coming back into his head, and it was now the one thing that troubled him most, more than the danger; he felt guilty for undertaking such a risky venture without first telling the captain.

Finally, he got up and left the tent, slipping gingerly past the five other men snoring away on the floor all around him. He knew the way to the captain's tent even in the dark and was soon standing outside its flap. He was pleased, but not surprised, to see a light glowing within.

"Captain, sir? May I come in?" he asked at the tent flap.

"Yes, come in … Hello, Ethan. Can't sleep?"

"No, sir. And it's on account of a matter I need to discuss with you."

"Well, then, have a seat and tell it out."

"Thank you, sir."

Ethan went on to explain his frustration at being unable to access the lower town due to the British barricades, and his observation of the small merchant boats coming and going in defiance of the American siege. Finally, he told of his idea of posing as one of those merchants in order to complete his mission.

Morgan said nothing for several minutes, just gazing intently at Ethan and slowly nodding his head.

"Well, Ethan, it does you credit that you'd think to do such a thing … Shows some smarts … and guts. I assume Sergeant Murphy warned you that they'd hang you for a spy if you were caught?"

"Yes, sir. He did."

"I admire your courage, son. But I'll not let you do it. It's too risky for an unknown benefit. For all we know, the town hasn't changed since the French army left, and the colonel's map will work just fine. You said yourself that the outer wall hasn't changed much."

"That's true. Then you are ordering me *not* to do it?"

"Yes, I am. And I think you've done enough with the map work, so write up what you have tomorrow, and I'll get it back to the colonel. Now … I'm ordering you to get back to bed and get some sleep. And I'll try to do likewise."

"Yes, sir. Thank you, sir … and good night."

"Good night, Ethan."

◄◄◄◄◄◆►►►►►

Sunday November 19, 1775 – Quebec City, Quebec Province:

Ethan was in command of a patrol of riflemen charged with keeping a watch on the British warships along the river. It was a tedious but necessary duty. Though many of the ships' cannons had been carted to shore and installed on the fort's walls, Colonel Arnold still wanted to know if the ships moved or if any others arrived. The warships were an odd anomaly in the siege, Ethan decided. Though the Americans ostensibly controlled the area surrounding the fortress walls, the ships, with their dangerous cannons, still controlled the narrow strip of land along the south shore of the city. And because of this, their men and materiel could come and go into the city unimpeded by the Americans, who dared not come too close except in small numbers that would not elicit an artillery response, such as when Ethan scouted the walls with his men.

Ethan shivered as he lowered the spyglass from viewing the larger of the two ships, a frigate named *Lizard*. The only slightly entertaining aspect of the whole thing was that the Royal Navy officer of the watch, whoever he happened to be at the moment, would invariably be gazing back at Ethan through his own spyglass. So finally, Ethan decided to wave to him, and was surprised when the officer waved back. It had now become the routine: two sworn enemies sharing a mutual, tedious duty.

And though the day was chilly and dull, the news running through camp was anything but: it was reported that General Montgomery and his men, of the western branch of the Canadian expedition, had conquered Montreal, completely routing the garrison there and sending Royal Governor Carleton to flight, along with his staff and remaining soldiers. The expectation in camp was that Montgomery would appear any day now at the head of a great army, at which point the conquest of Quebec would be a foregone conclusion.

Ethan couldn't help but smile as he envisioned that heady time to come, and he waved vigorously at the British officer who'd just taken the watch. *Yep, wave and smile, my good fellow, but your days here are numbered now*, he decided.

And then he noticed the officer suddenly turn and face the river, then call out orders of some kind, though it was too far to hear what they were. Ethan lowered the spyglass and looked out at the water.

A medium-sized merchant vessel, its sailors already lowering the sails, was pulling up preparing to anchor near *Lizard*. Ethan turned his attention to the new arrival and saw a naval officer, likely the ship's captain—which was odd for a merchant vessel manned by ordinary seamen. He was gesturing and shouting orders to the men while a tall, lean, middle-aged man in fine civilian clothing stood next to him gazing out toward the city's walls. And then Ethan noticed that the captain bowed to this man and seemed to treat him deferentially. Ethan was curious who this man was.

It wasn't until several days later he learned he had witnessed the arrival of the Royal Governor of the Quebec Province, General Guy Carleton, commander of all British forces in Canada. The governor had disguised himself as a civilian and boarded a merchant vessel to escape capture by General Montgomery.

◄◄◄◄◄◆►►►►►

Once relieved of their stint watching the warships, Ethan and his platoon were put to work performing two very disparate tasks: long-range targeting of the British manning the walls, on the one hand, and endeavoring to sow good will amongst the local French civilians on the other.

The first task was one they knew well from their time in Boston, where General Washington held the British army besieged within the town. The main difference this time was that the riflemen dared not stay in one place more than a few minutes, as the British would invariably move a cannon into position and begin lobbing cannon balls in on top of any structure the riflemen occupied.

The other difference was that Colonel Arnold, unlike General Washington, was not morally opposed to the practice of long-range sniping at British soldiers and officers. The only things he forbade were the targeting of unarmed civilians and the targeting of sailors on or near the British warships anchored on the river.

As Ethan understood it, there was some sort of unspoken truce between the ships, with their mobility and their deadly, highly destructive long-range cannons, and the Americans on shore, with their more precise, but equally deadly long-range rifles. Both sides knew they could make things extremely uncomfortable for the other side, but with no real effect on the outcome of the conflict. So they'd mutually agreed not to engage without ever saying so.

The other task was unfamiliar to the soldiers, but in some ways more enjoyable. They were tasked with trudging out to the surrounding farms and villages, where they would attempt to engage the locals, purchase their foodstuffs and other supplies, and distribute fliers containing a message of peace and brotherhood written out by General Washington. Ethan was particularly successful in this endeavor, as opposed to the other American officers, due to his ability to speak the language. He found the interaction with the generally friendly French-Canadian farmers and merchants very satisfying and uplifting — a pleasant counterpart to the violence he was otherwise engaged in.

But one afternoon, when he returned to camp, he heard a rumor that Colonel Arnold had called a halt to the long-range sniping. When Ethan went to ask Captain Morgan why, he chuckled, shook his head, and answered with a wry smile, "Ironically, for the same reason General Washington gave: that we are running dangerously low on ammunition. Only in this case, the colonel's right. We did an audit and found we're down to only five rounds per man. And ammunition is the one thing we can't buy in any large quantity from the locals. The colonel has sent couriers to General Montgomery over to Montreal for his aid, but that'll take some days at best."

"Oh," Ethan answered. "Then I guess we'll just have to hand out more fliers."

"Yep, you do that Ethan. It can't hurt … And you never know, it may help."

◄◄◄◄◄◆►►►►►

Wednesday December 6, 1775 – Quebec City, Quebec Province:

When Brigadier General Richard Montgomery rode unannounced into the American camp at the head of a column of 400 fully equipped American soldiers, a festive, celebratory mood spread like wildfire. *Not exactly a feeling of salvation*, Ethan decided, *but certainly elevated hopes of success.*

Adding to the men's excitement, three armed sloops, which had been captured from the British at Montreal, arrived at the same time, loaded to the brim with warm clothing, blankets, food, muskets, and ammunition. They also brought with them several dozen cannons, though these were of the smaller six to twelve pounder size—not potent enough to breach Quebec's massive walls.

And if the addition of manpower and materiel was a boost to morale, General Montgomery himself was even more so. Tall, handsome, and genteel, with an easy agreeable manner, the general inspired almost instant admiration and respect from the men.

And despite some reported trepidation on both sides before the event, Montgomery and Arnold apparently had an almost immediate rapport once they met, from what Ethan heard, which could only be to the benefit of all.

The only detriment the general's arrival served was that Arnold's men had assumed the western column would be two or three times larger than it was. But apparently, the siege of Fort St. Johns and subsequent conquest of Montreal—along with mass enlistment expirations and an outbreak of smallpox—had taken their toll on the number of troops Montgomery was able to muster for the attack on Quebec. And to add further consternation, it was soon discovered that many of those he'd brought with him were raw recruits, just come north from the colonies with no previous combat experience.

◄◄◄◄◄◆►►►►►

That evening, General Montgomery called a council of war for all his senior officers. Colonel Arnold, being the host, introduced the general to the Kennebec Expedition officers, during which he made it clear to all concerned that he had officially relinquished overall command of the operation against Quebec to General Montgomery.

"Thank you, Colonel Arnold," Montgomery began. "It is an honor to meet you all. And I cannot express in strong enough terms my respect for your recent conquest of the Maine wilderness. It is a feat unparalleled in the history of this continent, and speaks volumes concerning the courage, determination, and dedication of you officers and your dear men.

"By God, if you aren't iron-hard men, seemingly immune to the ravages of starvation, weather, and extreme terrain! You have proven yourselves under the most dire conditions— circumstances that would've crushed lesser men, clearly. For that, I offer you my undying admiration and congratulations."

And to put words into action, he proceeded to circle the room, meeting each man, shaking his hand, and personally congratulating him on his unprecedented victory over the elements. He was followed around the room by his own group of senior officers, who likewise congratulated the men of Arnold's expedition. And catching on to the general feeling of camaraderie that the general was clearly intending to inspire, the Kennebec officers began to congratulate Montgomery's officers in turn for their own victory over the enemy at Fort St. Johns and Montreal.

When introductions were complete, Montgomery once again addressed the group. "Gentlemen ... I am well aware that you have now been stationed here for some weeks ... have been waiting patiently for our arrival, and meanwhile keeping the enemy pinned down within his own fortress. For this, I once again thank you.

"But if you were thinking my arrival might signal an impending all-out assault … or perhaps, conversely, the beginning of a severe, extended siege, then I fear I must disabuse you of both those notions.

"I am sorry, but we simply haven't the manpower for an immediate assault; the enemy has an extremely strong defensive position, and from what Colonel Arnold tells me, just enough professional experience and mettle to carry off an effective resistance. And even though the large chunks of ice we currently see floating in the river presage a time when the stream will be entirely frozen over, and thus our enemies entirely cut off from re-supply, I fear they already have stores enough to last through the long winter.

"And speaking of … With winter now upon us, I must imagine none of us relishes the thought of suffering through that with dwindling supplies and insufficient shelter. There is also the ever-present threat of disease ravaging our numbers.

"And finally, Colonel Arnold informs me that your men who toiled their way up the Kennebec were only enlisted until the end of the year. No one can predict whether or not they will stay and fight or simply give up and go home once their enlistments expire on January first."

There were murmurs of assent following this statement. It was an ever-growing topic of concern among Arnold's officers.

It was Colonel Christopher Greene who first spoke: "What then do you propose, General? Surely, we have not suffered so much and come so far just to give it up now?"

"No, Colonel Greene, I do not intend to give up. But we must face reality. We need an advantage … something to help put the odds in our favor.

"First, I intend to study the maps of the city, and working with Colonel Arnold and each of you, evaluate the best capabilities of each of our companies, and come up with a detailed plan, so that when the right opportunity arises, we will be ready to strike, and strike hard."

"And … what opportunity would *that* be, General?" Colonel Greene asked.

"We must regain the element of surprise for our assault, gentlemen. We must wait for a dark and stormy night."

◄◄◄◄◄◆►►►►►

Wednesday December 6, 1775 – Quebec City, Quebec Province:

"Come in, Colonel," Royal Governor Guy Carleton said, not bothering to rise from his seat. He gestured toward the elegantly carved, gold-trimmed and heavily lacquered chair opposite him, and Colonel Maclean sat.

Maclean noticed the governor had changed from civilian garb back into the elegant red and gold military uniform of a commanding general. He took that for a good sign.

"I assume you've heard the news, Colonel," Carleton began.

"Aye, sir. Our sources say the American General Montgomery, who, um … forced your withdrawal from Montreal … has arrived at the head o' an American column," he said. He'd tried to think of a delicate way to frame Carleton's humiliating defeat, but suspected he hadn't fully succeeded. He mentally shrugged it off; he was a soldier after all, not a diplomat.

"Yes … just so," Carleton answered cooly. Then the general leaned back in his chair and tented his hands, gazing at them intently. He seemed deep in thought, so Maclean resisted the urge to say anything, though he could think of several important topics that needed discussing. With the American general's arrival, the situation had clearly changed dramatically.

But finally, Carleton lowered his hands and sat up, locking eyes with Maclean. "They can't hope to assault us directly. The reports are he has brought only four hundred some men with him, and many are raw recruits. And he did drag along some artillery pieces—nine and twelve pounders, from what I saw—but no heavy siege guns capable of breaching our walls, plus a few mortars, and rockets. In short, he hasn't the men and guns he needs for an all-out assault against this fortress—especially now that you and your men are here, along with the other loyalists who have continued to stream in and the artillery we've brought up from the warships."

He was quiet again for another long moment, then said, "And … he dares not engage us in an extended siege. He knows as well as we do that we can be re-supplied from the river up until it freezes over, and by then, we'll have stockpiled enough food and supplies to last the winter. And he knows we will better endure the harsh winter indoors than he'll be able to do out in a camp, which will shortly be inundated with smallpox, typhoid, and all other manner of pestilence."

There was another long silence, and finally Maclean could no longer restrain himself from asking. "Then *what*, General? What will Montgomery do?"

Carleton looked Maclean in the eye and said, "He will wait for the darkest night he can find, with the harshest, most blinding blizzard. *Then* he will attack."

Maclean thought about this and slowly nodded, then said, "And when he does … we'll be ready for him."

Carleton returned the nod, and for the first time that evening, he smiled.

◄◄◄◄◄◆►►►►►►

Friday December 24, 1775 – Winchester, Virginia Colony:

Hannah stood to answer a knock on her door. She opened it and suffered a start; Abby Morgan stood there, wrapped in a fur coat, flakes of snow settling softly on her blonde hair.

"Hello, Hannah," she said, then glanced up at the falling snow. "May I come in?" she asked.

It was not lost on Hannah that Abby was not her usual, glowing self, and that her greeting had not been overly friendly. And the worst part was, she knew she deserved the coldness and had expected no less.

"Yes, of course, dear … please come in," Hannah answered, before even considering the ramifications of Abby coming face-to-face with James. But fortunately, her brother-in-law was out of the house at the moment, having gone into town for more supplies.

After Hannah had relieved Abby of her coat and ushered her into the living room, the two ladies sat and gazed at one another in awkward silence. Finally, Abby frowned, sat forward in her chair, and said, "Hannah … I feared you were ill … but I see now it is not true."

"No, I've been of good health, thank you for your concern," Hannah answered, and immediately felt ashamed and foolish talking such abysmal platitudes to a woman who deserved so much better of her.

"Oh, Abby … I'm sorry … it's just … just—"

"What has happened, Hannah? I felt we were becoming such fast friends. And our dear little ones were getting along so famously … and then, you stopped visiting … and you never answered my messages. And I … I just don't understand … Is it something I did or said?"

"Oh no, oh no, my dear Abby. You've done nothing wrong. Nothing at all. On the contrary, you've been the greatest friend … to me, and to our entire family."

"Then why, Hannah? Why have you cut me off so?"

Hannah made up her mind in that moment that only the truth would do, regardless of what James or Gideon thought about it. This wonderful woman deserved that much, and more.

"You see, Abby, what happened was—"

The door opened and James stepped in, followed closely by Simpson, his arms loaded down with packages.

The women stood, and James stopped in his tracks when he saw Abby. She was a lovely young woman, and Hannah knew a man like James would not resist speaking with her. And she dreaded what might happen when he did.

"Oh, I see we have a visitor. Hannah, dear, won't you introduce us?" James said, beaming as he removed his hat and shook off the snow.

"Yes, certainly, James. This is my good friend and neighbor Abby. Abby, this is Gideon's brother, James. James has come to visit us from the New York Colony."

But James's bright smile suddenly dimmed, and a curious expression replaced it. "Do you have a surname, Miss Abby?" he asked in a mild tone.

"Why yes, certainly, Mr. Chambers. I am Abby Morgan. If you've been in town a while now, you may have heard of my husband, *Daniel* Morgan."

Hannah's heart sank, as Abby had, in complete innocence, just announced herself as the sworn enemy of James.

James scowled and withdrew the hand he'd begun to hold out to take hers. "Madam … I would be remiss and disingenuous, if I didn't state straight out, that I believe your husband is a villainous traitor to our king and his legitimate government. As such, you are not welcome in this house."

Abby's eyes widened in shock and she stood. "How dare you disparage my husband, sir? Daniel is the greatest man I've ever known, likely the greatest in all of Virginia, and I'll not have his good name besmirched by you or any other man. If I was strong enough, I would strike you with my bare fist for such an insult." And as if to emphasize the point, she made a dainty fist and shook it at him.

But he only scowled, turned, and stepped to the door, pulling it open and gesturing outside. "As I said, you are no longer welcome in this house."

Abby stalked across the room, grabbed her fur coat, and stepped to the door's threshold. There she turned and gave Hannah a glare.

"I … I'm so sorry, Abby," Hannah said, fighting off the tears welling in her eyes.

But Abby said nothing. She just turned and strode out into the snow.

Hannah turned to James, who continued to gaze after Abby for a moment longer before closing the door.

"You have no right to be rude to my guest and send her away," Hannah said in a voice choked with emotion.

"Calm yourself, Hannah. Such a childish display of emotions does *not* do you credit. As for your so-called guests … Well, with

Gideon … let's just say, *incapable* … I am the man of this house. I will decide who comes and goes. Is that understood?"

Hannah was so upset she found she had no voice. But a strong, deep voice behind her answered James's question.

"No. No, that is *not* understood, James. Not understood, because it is *not* true. *I* am still the man of this house, and as long as I continue to draw breath, I shall remain so."

Hannah turned and saw Gideon standing in the doorway to the hallway. He looked frail, still in his bedclothes with his hair disheveled from sleep. And with one arm missing, and the other bent to the point of being nearly useless, he was not much of a physical presence. But Hannah saw a scowl on his face and a fire in his eyes that she'd not seen in many long months. Then, despite the tension in the room, she smiled. *That's the man I remember … the man I married.*

Gideon crossed the room and stepped up in front of his brother, who was a head taller and many pounds heavier. Yet, Hannah saw a look of surprise and puzzlement on James's face.

"I will allow no one to speak to my guests, nor my wife, as you have just done. This is *my* house, and if you wish to stay here, you will obey my rules and keep a civil tongue, *sir*," Gideon said, staring into his brother's eyes. "I shall ask that good woman to return here, that you might apologize to her, face-to-face, for your rude treatment. And further, neither her husband, Daniel Morgan, nor my son is a villain, or a traitor; I have been a despicable coward for not saying so before. They are both brave, honorable men, who are only doing what they believe is best for this country. Whether or not you or I agree with it."

For a long moment, the two just stared at one another.

Then James slowly nodded. "So, *that's* how it is … After all I've done to help. *Ingrate.* I shall not apologize to that shameless trollop wife of a scandalous traitor. Never in life. Nor shall I agree that anyone who fights against the king is admirable or honorable.

"I can see where I'm not wanted nor appreciated. I believe it's time for me to return home."

"Yes, I believe that would be for the best," Gideon nodded, still staring his brother in the eyes. "Though I would be remiss if I didn't thank you for your largess, in our hour of desperate need ... It has been ... greatly appreciated."

An hour later, James departed with no word of farewell. As a last parting blow, he ordered his man Simpson to gather up all the food he'd just purchased and load it back into the carriage. But when James's back was turned, Simpson slipped several parcels behind a chair, then winked at Hannah, who returned his kindness with a grin and a nod.

After James departed, Gideon looked at Hannah and said, "I owe you an apology for *that*, my wife. I should've never let it go this far. I just ... never was used to standing up to him, though I often wished to. But when I heard him speak to you and that lovely, selfless woman like *that*, something inside me finally snapped. And a voice inside me seemed to say, *No more. Enough is enough.*"

"Thank you for that, Gideon. I know it took a great deal of courage to stand up to him."

He nodded. "Well, better late than never, I suppose."

They were quiet for a moment, then Gideon said, "Hannah, do you remember me teaching you how to hitch up the wagon, and to drive it?"

"Yes, of course—you seem to forget I have done it several times before, and since Ethan has been gone and you've been ... Well, anyway, yes, I can hitch it up and I can drive it. Why? Where is it you wish to go?"

"I wish to go straight to Miss Abby's house, that I may beg her forgiveness ... on bended knee, if necessary," he answered with a frown. "She deserves no less, and likely much more, though it's all I have to offer."

Hannah smiled, wiping back tears. "The good news is, the snow has stopped falling, and none has stuck to the road ... I shall have the wagon ready within the hour. Will you please make sure Elsie is properly dressed?"

Chapter 11. The Battle of Quebec

"The true soldier fights
not because he hates what is in front of him,
but because he loves what is behind him."
- Gilbert Keith Chesterton

Friday December 15, 1775 – Quebec City, Quebec Province:

"Gentlemen, this is the plan Colonel Arnold and I have worked out. Mr. Aaron Burr has volunteered to drill and train a group of fifty men on the use of scaling ladders, so that when the time comes, they will scale the wall, then open the gate. We will launch attacks against four gates at once, but all save one will be feints. On the main attack, which will be on the southernmost gate, we will concentrate the bulk of our forces, including placing Captain Morgan's riflemen in position to target any British soldiers attempting to dislodge the scaling ladders. And for good measure, we will bring up a couple of twelve-pounder guns on sleds to knock down the gate, should the scaling ladder mission prove untenable."

After some discussion and minor refinement, the plan was agreed upon.

"Let us be prepared so that when the proper weather arrives, we can strike on the instant," Montgomery concluded.

Friday December 22, 1775 – Quebec City, Quebec Province:

"Colonel, have you that report on our numbers I requested?" General Carleton asked in his usual straightforward manner even as Maclean stepped up to his desk.

"Aye, sir. Shall I read it out?"

"Please do, my good sir," Carleton answered, gesturing for Maclean to take the seat opposite him.

Maclean sat, pulled out a sheet of paper, unfolded it, and said, "The following is the tally of our current effectives, as of one hour ago:"

70 Royal Fusiliers (7th Regiment of Foot)
230 Royal Highlanders
22 Artillerymen
330 British loyalist militia
543 French-Canadian militia
400 Seamen
50 Ships officers
35 Royal Marines
100 Artificers from the ships

Total of 1,780 officers and men under arms.

"Oh, that does nae count you and I … So I suppose that makes it 1,782, sir," Maclean concluded with a faint attempt at a smile, which Carleton did *not* return.

Carleton nodded. "Well, that sounds a bit more promising than the few hundred we had when I first arrived."

"Aye, sir. *Much* more promisin'. Though I still worry tha' we have too great a perimeter to be able to defend everywhere at once. Even with a force roughly half our own, the Americans can still concentrate an attack on a single point and may well break through."

Carleton slowly nodded his head as he gazed down at the desktop in front of him.

"Sir," Maclean continued, "I been thinkin' … Now tha' we have them outnumbered, what if we gathered the men, sortied out, and swept them from the field? One big push, overrun their camp and be done with 'em?"

Carleton looked up and met eyes with Maclean. "Colonel, though I appreciate your fighting spirit and gallantry, there are several reasons why that is a *very* bad idea.

"First, though we may have numerical superiority, the majority of our men are untrained and inexperienced at warfare, while most of theirs have at least proven their mettle by their unfathomably difficult trek through the Canadian wilderness."

"Aye, sir … and to yer point, we must consider tha' the French militia may well be less than reliable, and might well turn against us in the middle of the fight."

"Yes. More to the point, it would be foolish to give up our greatest advantage, which is this highly defensible fortress. Much better to defend with inexperienced, untrustworthy troops than to attack. I was here with Wolfe back in '59 when the French were in our position, and we were the ones out on the Plains of Abraham, where the Americans are now. The French general, the Marquis de Montcalm, foolishly sallied forth from the fortress to do battle with General Wolfe. The Marquis not only lost the battle; he lost his life in the process. No, Colonel, I will not make that same mistake, thank you very much."

"Aye, sir. I respectfully withdraw the suggestion."

Carleton waved off Maclean's reply dismissively. Then he said, "Perhaps it will set your mind more at ease, Colonel, if I told you that I have spies in the enemy's camp. If they do their job, then we should know ahead of time exactly when and where the Americans will strike."

"Oh. Aye, that does help ease my concern somewhat. Thank ye for telling me that, sir."

◄◄◄◄◄◆►►►►►►

Wednesday December 27, 1775 – Quebec City, Quebec Province:

The day dawned with a heavy snowstorm, so General Montgomery announced that the attack would commence at nightfall.

Ethan, upon hearing the news, felt a sudden surge of excitement mixed with more than a little trepidation. He'd never before been in a real life-or-death battle, much less been expected to lead men in one. But now that he was an officer, he was responsible for several dozens of Morgan's Virginians, with the help of Sergeant Murphy, of course, for which he was thoroughly grateful.

He made the rounds of the men in his platoon with Sergeant Murphy, making sure each man packed only the bare essentials he would need for the assault—ammunition, water, and hardtack—and ensuring that each rifle was well oiled and in good working order.

But as the sun began to set, Ethan noticed that the snow had let up considerably. And an hour later he knew what the new orders would be even before they were made official when he looked up at the moon shining brightly through a nearly cloudless sky: there would be no battle this day.

Thursday December 28, 1775 – Quebec City, Quebec Province:

"General … good morning," Colonel Arnold said as he trudged up through the snow to where Montgomery stood gazing out at the gate they'd planned to attack the night before. The day had dawned bright and clear, though so bitingly cold that Arnold's breath came out in steamy gusts as he walked.

"Ah. Good morning, Colonel," Montgomery answered. He turned and held out the spyglass. "Have a look … Tell me what you see."

Arnold took the glass, held it to his right eye, and gazed along the battlements. "I see … one … two … three, four, five, six … hmm … at least ten large guns. And … aside from the gunners, dozens of red-coated soldiers with muskets …"

He lowered the glass and the two men met eyes.

"General … those guns were *not* there the day before yesterday."

"Yes, Colonel. And neither were the men. And if I'm not mistaken, those uniforms are of the Seventh Regiment of Foot— their best soldiers. Which means—"

"They *knew* we were coming … We have a spy in our midst."

"Yes, I'm afraid so," Montgomery agreed.

"What then do you propose we do, sir?" Arnold asked.

"We must make a new plan, clearly. Only this time, only our most senior officers must know of it. Everyone else will have to be ready to move on a moment's notice, and then simply follow their officers' lead," Montgomery answered.

Saturday December 30, 1775 – Quebec City, Quebec Province:

The two days following the aborted attack had dawned fair and clear, though bitterly cold, frustrating Montgomery and Arnold's plans for an assault and bringing Arnold's troops to the very brink of their enlistment expirations. Nobody knew what would happen when that day arrived—whether Arnold could convince some or all of them to stay longer, or whether they would all pack up and head for home, was anyone's guess.

Ethan knew he would do whatever Captain Morgan said to do, regardless. He'd never much thought about the enlistment ending, only about doing whatever needed doing that he'd volunteered for. But he'd tried to feel out the other men on their thinking. Most of his fellow Virginians were of the same mind as he: that they were Daniel Morgan's men and would follow him regardless. But the men of the other rifle companies and regiments were less committed to their officers. Many felt they'd served their duty, and other patriots ought to volunteer to come fill their place. Others were non-committal, adopting a wait-and-see attitude.

But on the afternoon of December 30th, heavy winds began to blow from thick clouds that turned day into night. It was the kind of storm the New Englanders called a "nor'easter," but to Ethan, it was simply the most terrible storm he'd ever been in. Snow came swirling down in blinding sheets, bringing visibility to almost zero. Ethan knew this was the weather General Montgomery had been waiting for, that this was the storm he needed to launch his attack. Ethan told his men to be ready; to sleep on their arms. But nobody slept that night.

At midnight, the order was given to form up and move out. Colonel Arnold led the four hundred some remaining men of the Kennebec expedition around the north end of the town to gather in a suburb called St. Roch and await the signal to attack. Ethan understood from a quick briefing of the officers by Captain

Morgan that they were to attack the lower town along the river from the north while General Montgomery would lead an attack on the lower town from the south. The two armies would then join forces and fight their way into the upper town from that point on. Meanwhile, diversionary attacks with scaling ladders, mortars, and rockets would be launched against the gates on the west wall in hopes of confusing General Carleton and his defenders.

At two o'clock in the morning, a sudden flare of red light high in the sky off to their right caught Ethan's attention. He gazed out through the thick snow and watched as five streaks flashed through the sky, briefly illuminating the ice-encrusted ramparts of the city. *Five rockets—the signal to be prepared, that the attack is on,* he remembered. He unslung his rifle, checked to make sure the small, waxed sheet of paper was still firmly in place, keeping the powder dry. All he could do now was wait for the signal to move forward. And pray.

◄◄◄◄◄◆►►►►►

Daniel Morgan, just in front of Ethan, also saw the rockets flashing through the sky. He thought it an eerie sight. *Like the very fires of hell,* he decided.

And at the thought of hell, it struck him that he might very well be on the brink of going there, and it occurred to him that might *not* be a good thing. So he took a few steps out into the snow, several yards away from the other men, and went down on one knee. Through all they had endured since departing Winchester, all the dangers, toils, and depravations, he'd never once stopped to say a prayer. He figured this was the time. He closed his eyes and spoke softly under his breath, "Dear Lord, I know I ain't always been the best o' your servants, but you of all people know my heart is in the right place, even if my actions and words don't always show it. On this day of all days, I ask only that you preserve me and my men from death, if you would, that we might prevail in a sorely needed victory for our country. Amen."

◄◄◄◄◄◆►►►►►

General Carleton paced back and forth in his command post at the Recollect Monastery. As had been his habit of late, he was dressed in his military uniform. But this night, he also wore his sword and had his two pistols out, fully loaded, lying on the table.

"The rebels will attack this night," he said, stopping to glare over at Colonel Maclean. "I can taste it! Such a wretched storm … Montgomery will not pass up the chance to use it for cover. Colonel, I *must* know what's happening. Where are the Americans?"

Then something flashed outside the window. They stepped out the door, ignoring the snow swirling around them, gazing up into the sky at the red streaks off to the west. The bright red lights were followed by distant popping sounds.

Maclean looked over at the governor and said, "There they are, General."

◀◀◀◀◆▶▶▶▶

For Ethan, gun in hand, waiting in the frigid, snowy darkness, the earth took on an eerie, other-worldly quietness. He thought it the strangest experience of his life, sitting and waiting in silence out in a storm with 400 other armed men, waiting for a signal that would not only break the silence, but hurl them into the cacophony and chaos of battle.

The only thing of interest during the waiting was when men came around handing out slips of paper and straight pins. Each slip of paper had the words "Liberty or Death" written on it in bold letters. Colonel Arnold had ordered all the men to pin these slips to their hats, so that in the heat of battle, with likely large numbers of men dressed as civilians on both sides, it would be possible to tell friend from foe.

And then it came: two streaks of red light arcing high above in the darkness, illuminating a cloud of snow encircling the cold, hard bastion ahead of them. He knew these two rockets were the pre-arranged signal for the battle to commence.

Immediately, thunderous artillery fire could be heard rumbling in the distance, along with the distinctive popping sound of musket fire. These, Ethan knew, were the sounds of the false attacks against the western gates, intended only as a distraction from the main thrust into the lower town, of which they were the major component.

Colonel Arnold led the Kennebec men forward with a "forlorn hope" of twenty-five of his officers and hand-picked volunteers; a *forlorn hope*, in military parlance, being a band of soldiers in the vanguard of an operation, such as a suicidal assault through the breach of a defended position, where the risk of casualties is high.

Next came a gun crew pulling a brass six-pounder gun on a sled that they intended to use for battering down the British barricades. Then came Captain Morgan and his Virginians, starting with Ethan and his platoon, including Levi and Sergeant Murphy. Lieutenant Colonel Greene's men came next, followed by all the remaining units of the expedition.

Now that they were on the move and no longer hunkered down, Ethan and his company were pelted in the face by heavy snowfall driven by gale-force winds. He pulled his scarf up over his face, leaving only his eyes exposed, and trudged on.

Their first task was to traverse a narrow trail that ran between the river and the cliffs upon which sat the fortress walls. The path was so narrow that men were forced to move in single file. It was a dangerous passage, as they were visible to the sentries above on the walls, despite the darkness and weather. Gunfire rang out, and several men were killed or wounded. But fortunately, the sentries were few, and return fire drove them back from the wall.

Though the element of surprise was now clearly lost, Colonel Arnold did not hesitate, but pressed forward even after the sled carrying their cannon slid off the trail and became hopelessly lodged in an icy ravine.

They turned a sharp corner to the right, and here the trail widened out and they could see the British barricade ahead. It was ten feet high and manned with several dozen men.

◄◄◄◄◆►►►►►

Colonel Arnold led his forlorn hope forward, sword in hand. As they neared the wall, the defenders opened fire. And though their firing was generally erratic and to little effect, Colonel Arnold was struck in the leg, just below his left knee.

It was a ricochet, rather than a direct hit, and Arnold did not fall to the ground. Rather, he attempted to continue on, though now limping badly. He could feel blood streaming down his leg, pooling in his boot, and his head began to swim. He feared he would faint into the snow, but willed himself to remain standing. He could not let his men down.

◄◄◄◄◄◆►►►►►

"Colonel, without the six-pounder gun, I think we ought to—" Daniel Morgan cut short what he was starting to say as he saw the look of pain on Colonel Arnold's face, then glanced down and saw the blood streaming down his pant leg.

"Sir, you're wounded. We must get you to the hospital."

"No, no … I'll be fine," Arnold insisted. "I can still walk." He strode out a step to demonstrate, but Morgan caught him as he began to collapse.

Morgan looked behind him and saw Ethan standing there, wide-eyed.

"Ethan! Er … I mean, Lieutenant Chambers … the Colonel's been hit. Take him back to the hospital, straightaway."

"But, sir … I—"

"No time to argue, Lieutenant." And then spotting Levi next to Ethan, Morgan added, "And take Private Miller with you."

Ethan thought to argue the point, feeling obliged to stay and lead his men in the battle, but seeing the stern look in his captain's eyes, he thought better of it. He turned to Sergeant Murphy and said, "Take charge of the company, Sergeant. I shall return as soon as I'm able."

"Yes, sir," Murphy responded. "And good luck, sir."

◄◄◄◄◄◆►►►►►

"Forward, men!" Daniel Morgan shouted, and the Virginians rushed forward, firing through the loopholes, throwing up ladders, and clambering over the top of the wall. Virginian Rifleman, Sergeant Charles Porterfield was the first man to leap down onto the other side, followed closely by a flood of others. And though they'd lost their big gun in the snow, to their credit, the artillerymen led by Captain Lamb joined in the fight, firing muskets and wielding swords.

Though the fighting was intense, it was over in moments with the defenders quickly routed, either surrendering or fleeing back into the city. The men who'd scaled the wall unlocked the iron gate and flung it open for the men following to pour through.

"Riflemen, with me!" Morgan shouted. He headed up the street at a run, followed by a few dozen men of his company. French-Canadian militiamen, many wearing the traditional white uniform coats of the Royal French Army, threw down their weapons and attempted to surrender to the Americans in the street, calling out *"Vive la liberte!"* But Morgan ignored them and hurried past, figuring those units following after could deal with the prisoners. He had more important things to worry about.

They reached a second barricade across the street but saw no one atop it. So Morgan cautiously approached the iron sally port door, turned the handle, and pulled it open. After a quick glance inside, he threw the door wide open and strode through. His men immediately followed.

They gazed around them at the surrounding buildings and were shocked to see no one.

"Come, men," he said, and trotted up the street, rifle in hand, prepared for an ambush, gazing all about. But they soon reached the large, open, lower town square with still not a soul in sight.

He turned to his men. "Quickly now, we must hurry back and fetch the others. The town is open to us, if we but seize it!"

Ethan and Levi held Colonel Arnold between them, his arms over their shoulders. He was bleeding steadily, but not profusely. Ethan reckoned if they could get him to the hospital quickly, Dr. Senter could stop the bleeding and keep him alive.

But helping the wounded man along the treacherous, icy trail, dodging gunfire from the British in the fort above, was not an easy task. And since he'd been in the front of the American column when he'd been hit, they had to squeeze past their own troops headed in the opposite direction. And though Colonel Arnold did the best he could to lighten their load by hopping on his one good leg, he was quickly losing strength and often tripped and faltered, such that they were forced to bear his entire weight. To make matters worse, he was not just any ordinary wounded soldier; he was the commanding officer, and felt obliged to stop and urge on each officer and each company of men as they passed, assuring them that he would quickly return to lead them to victory. To press on, to keep fighting, and so on, and so on.

By the time they finally reached the hospital, all three of them were exhausted, and Colonel Arnold was pale as a sheet. But Dr. Senter, in his calm, reassuring manner, eased their fears, telling them the colonel should make a full recovery, but needed treatment straightaway. Ethan, remembering how he'd assisted Doc Adams back home amputate his father's arm, offered to help, which Senter accepted.

So Ethan held Colonel Arnold's leg still as Dr. Senter operated to remove the splintered musket ball from below the knee and sew the wound closed. Ethan decided this medical experience had been much easier than he'd faced with his father; Colonel Arnold had never flinched nor cried out as Senter worked on him, though he was wide awake the entire time.

When it was over, and the colonel was put in a bed to recover, Ethan sat down next to Levi on a bench to rest. Dr. Senter came over and thanked Ethan. "You were a good steady hand just now. I could use your help when they bring in more wounded," he said.

Ethan appreciated the compliment, but it occurred to him that the doctor might just be trying to keep him away from the fighting due to his youthful appearance. And then it hit him like a load of bricks: Captain Morgan was still out there fighting, and here he was sitting in the hospital, resting.

He jumped to his feet. "No! I must get back to the battle. Captain Morgan needs me. Come on, Levi, we've got to go back!"

When Morgan returned to the area just inside the first barricade, he encountered a chaotic scene. Dozens of prisoners were being rounded up and guarded, and wounded men were streaming in from the ever-more dangerous path under the city's walls. Hundreds of Americans were still outside the barricade, including Colonel Greene and Major Meigs.

And when Morgan demanded the other rifle company commanders, Captains Hendricks and Smith join him in taking the second barricade, which was currently unguarded, they balked, arguing that it was likely a trap, that they must wait for the rest of the column to pass through the first barricade before proceeding, and finally, that they should wait here until General Montgomery arrived from the south, shouldn't they? Besides, they now had prisoners to deal with.

When Morgan tried to order them to come, they refused, arguing that his command over them had ended once the expedition reached Quebec. That he had only been in command of them during the trek, but not during the present battle. And since Colonel Arnold wasn't available to decide the issue, there was nothing Daniel could do to persuade them.

An exasperated Morgan gathered his own Virginians and rushed back to the second barricade, arriving there just as the sun was rising, serving only to make the stormy sky a lighter shade of gray.

But when they arrived back at the gate, they found it was now occupied. British soldiers in red lined its parapet, bayoneted muskets bristling. And they could see the barrels of two cannons protruding from large portholes at the barricade's base.

Morgan knew that he could not attack the strongpoint now with the few troops he had; to do so would be suicidal. He would now have to wait for the rest of the column to come forward. Or for Montgomery to arrive from the other side and take the enemy from the rear.

And then a sinking thought occurred to him: *He should've been here by now. We should be hearing the sounds of his gunfire close at hand, and yet I hear ... nothing. Where is General Montgomery?* he wondered.

But to that question, the swirling snow gave no answer.

◄◄◄◄◄◆►►►►►

General Montgomery led his 300 men of the First New York Regiment forward along the southern edge of the upper town. They pushed their way through the deep, drifting snow, and had to navigate up and over treacherous chunks of ice that had been forced ashore and onto the trail from the river.

Though they'd yet to meet any resistance, their informants had warned them of a heavily defended blockhouse fifty or so yards beyond a sturdy picket fence.

When they reached the fence, they could see what they assumed was the blockhouse several dozen yards beyond. There were no lights shining from the building, and no movement could be seen.

The engineers came forward and began sawing at the boards of the fence. But after a few moments, General Montgomery became impatient. He stepped up to one of the engineers and said, "Give me your axe."

Montgomery took the axe, stepped up to the fence, and proceeded to batter a hole large enough for several men to pass through abreast. He then led the men forward through the gap, moving cautiously toward the building, followed closely by the officers of his command. There was still no sign of life inside the building. He paused and looked at Aaron Burr, who stood beside him, as if trying to decide what to do next.

Then Montgomery turned back toward the house, unsheathed his sword, and shouted, "Quebec is ours, men!" and charged forward. His men followed with a shout.

Then a thunderous, concussive roar shook the earth, accompanied by a blinding flash of light. A thick cloud of smoke swirled up from the blockhouse to mix with the falling snow.

Aaron Burr picked himself up from the snow and brushed himself off. The concussion from the cannon had knocked him down, but miraculously he was unharmed. But then he gazed about and realized others had not been so lucky. Dozens of men lay scattered about in the snow, their bodies torn and bleeding from the deadly grapeshot fired from a cannon at close range. As he looked about, his eyes came upon a sight that made his heart sink: General Montgomery lay dead upon the ground, a gaping hole in the side of his head. His young aide, a man named Macpherson, lay dead beside him.

And then Burr winced, and ducked, as musket fire began pouring from the blockhouse. To their credit, the New Yorkers quickly recovered from the shock and began returning fire, moving forward to press the attack on the defenders in the house. Burr joined them, firing into the loopholes, reloading, and moving forward again.

But to Burr's shock and consternation, the man left in charge by the sudden death of General Montgomery, quartermaster Colonel Donald Campbell, lost his nerve. Instead of pressing the attack, in which the Americans had the clear advantage, he suddenly ordered a withdrawal.

"Colonel Cambell," Burr beseeched him, "we have them outmanned … If we push forward, we can join forces with Colonel Arnold and secure the victory!"

But Campbell was unmoved. "No, Mr. Burr. The General is dead, and with him, his designs on the city. We *will* withdraw."

Then, with tears streaming unashamedly down his face, Burr went to General Montgomery's body and attempted to lift him, intending to carry him from the scene. But musket fire continued to pelt the snow around him, and he realized that Montgomery was a large, heavy man, and it was beyond his strength to carry him. If he tried, he would quickly join the general in the afterlife. So he reluctantly set Montgomery back down into the snow, then turned and ran to catch up with retreating New Yorkers.

"All right, Colonel Maclean, tell me what we know about the rebel attack," General Carleton demanded.

"Sir, Captain Caldwell reports some musket fire and one burst of artillery—ours, presumably—along the south shore. But tha' has since faded away, so if it *was* anything serious, it has apparently been repulsed.

"I have personally just come from the St. Louis gate, and though there are some fires burning, mortars being lobbed, and random musket fire, this seems to me nae more than a noisy demonstration—nae at all serious. That appearin' t'be the case, I ordered the thirty men stationed there—good, reliable men of the Seventh Regiment of Foot—to follow me here, that we may decide how best to redeploy them.

"The northwestern gate also seems to be a lot o' smoke and noise, but not much action. The only place experiencing any serious fighting at the moment is the northern end of the lower town. I'm receiving reports o' heavy gunfire along the Dog Lane and in and around the outer barricade there."

"Hmm ..." Carleton paced the floor, staring at his boots. "I suspect you are correct about the western gates, nothing more than noisy feints. The *real* attack is the one against the lower town ... No, make that *attacks* ... They intended to catch our men there in a pincer, coming in from the north and south at the same time. A clever strategy ...

"But somehow their attack to the south has faltered ... The rebels in the north end are now left to their own devices, but likely they don't yet know it."

"Colonel, gather every man you can quickly muster and get down to the lower town. We must stop them from breaching those barricades, or all will be lost. There is not a moment to lose!"

"Sir!" Maclean saluted, then turned and raced out the door.

Colonel Maclean signaled for the thirty fusiliers he'd left outside the monastery to follow him at the double quick. As they trotted, he shouted out to the sentries lining the square, ordering them all to fall in and come with him.

Remembering he'd stationed a company of Royal Highlanders near the Hotel Dieu in the northwest corner of the upper town, he headed there next. After that, he went to the rue de la Montagne and gathered up fifty sailors positioned there, along with their officer. Then he raced for the lower town, a force of some two hundred men trotted along behind him, bayoneted muskets in hand.

When he arrived at the lower town, Maclean turned to the north, leading his men toward the inner of two constructed barricades blocking the road. When he arrived, it was but lightly defended by a dozen or so soldiers atop the parapets.

But speaking to the officer in charge, an aggressive young lieutenant named Matthew Anderson, Maclean learned that the Americans had breached the outer barricade, and at least some portion of their column was just outside this inner one, presumably waiting for reinforcements to arrive.

Quickly assessing the situation, Maclean positioned half of his best soldiers on the street, a hundred feet back from the barricade. These he ordered to wait and hold their position until the enemy scaled the wall. Then they were to open fire on anyone reaching the top. The other half of his men he deployed to the highest floors of the houses lining either side of the barricade. These he instructed to rain fire down on the Americans as they approached the barrier. After ensuring that the two cannons were primed and loaded with grapeshot, he decided there was nothing more he could do but to wait for the assault to begin.

After the better part of an infuriating hour of waiting for the rest of the column to arrive, Morgan decided he finally had enough men and ladders assembled to attempt the assault. The remainder would just have to join in the fight as they arrived. Colonel Greene and Major Meigs were there with most of their men, but both agreed to let Morgan lead the assault. So he ordered the ladders brought forward and the men to prepare for the attack.

But even as he turned toward the wall and opened his mouth to shout the order to advance, an inexplicable thing happened. The sally gate suddenly opened, and out strode a lean, young British officer accompanied by a half dozen soldiers with rifles. The officer advanced a few paces, then stopped, gazed about at the gathered Americans, then called out in a loud, clear voice. "I am Lieutenant Matthew Anderson of the British Army, a royally authorized defender of this station. I do hereby demand your surrender, in the name of his majesty, King George III, of England."

Morgan shook his head in amazement, then muttered, "I've no time for this nonsense." He pulled a pistol from his belt, aimed it at the lieutenant, and fired. The British officer dropped like a stone. The Americans gathered round cheered. Then, taking it as the signal to attack, they rushed forward with the ladders. The British soldiers who'd accompanied their lieutenant on his ill-advised sortie, dragged their dead officer back through the door and slammed it shut.

Daniel Morgan himself scrambled up one of the ladders. Reaching the top with no resistance, he turned and shouted back at the men on the ground, "C'mon, men … Quebec is ours!"

And then his world exploded.

Colonel Maclean could only shake his head in wonder and complete bafflement as the soldiers dragged the body of the young lieutenant back through the sally door. The colonel had not had any inkling that the young man had such a rash notion in mind, or he would've forbidden it. *Damn fool*, was all he could think of on the matter.

But Maclean had other concerns, as he could hear the Americans shouting as they rushed the wall. He called out the pre-planned order for the men on the parapet to retreat down the ladders on this side so they'd not be in the line of fire.

Then he strode out in front of the men he'd assembled on the street. Standing off to one side, he waited a moment, then called out, "Company will volley fire, three rows at a time, on my command. First three rows, *present arms!*" He waited a moment, trying to gauge how long it might take a man to climb a twelve-foot scaling ladder, "*Aim!*" He waited until a half dozen or more Americans had crested the wall, "*Fire!*" The volley roared out, filling the falling snow with smoke and clearing the top of the wall of the Americans who'd stood there only a moment earlier.

"Second three rows ... *Present arms!*" Maclean called out.

◄◄◄◄◄◆►►►►►

Daniel Morgan lay on his back in the snow with a heavy wooden ladder across his chest. For several moments, he tried to breathe, but he simply could get no air into his lungs. But he was an old wagoner who had taken many falls before, so there was no panic in him. He knew the breath would return soon enough. He also knew to test all his extremities before trying to move or rise. He'd seen plenty of men try to get right back up after a serious fall only to injure themselves worse in the effort. So he calmly wiggled the fingers on his right hand, and then his left. Then he carefully raised and flexed his right arm, followed by the left. Next, he wiggled his toes, and his legs. But before he could complete the exercise, men were above him, leaning down and shouting at him, pulling the ladder off and dragging him to his feet. He could see they were shouting, but his ears rang so badly he could scarcely hear them.

"All right, all right, enough of that," he said, concluding that he was not seriously injured after all, thankfully. Then, noticing his hat was missing, he bent down and picked it up out of the snow and brushed it off. It now had a neat round hole in the front at the top of the crown and a matching one at the back. He shrugged and put it back on his head. Then he looked down at his clothes and saw another hole in the flap of his jacket, about waist high.

Morgan looked around to reassess the situation and saw that the British had men in the upper stories of the buildings surrounding the wall, so he shouted orders for men to break into the houses on their side of the barricade, climb to the top, and return fire against the enemy. This they did, and shortly a gunfight was being waged from housetop to housetop.

Morgan then ordered another attempt with the scaling ladders, but this attempt, too, was turned away with great loss.

And just as he was contemplating organizing a scouting party, to attempt slipping past the British in order to ascertain what had happened to General Montgomery, Major Meigs came trotting up.

"Morgan, the enemy has retaken the first barricade. Even now they advance toward us in great force. We are cut off," he announced.

"Then we must retake it, Major, and reopen our supply lines. If we can't push forward, we must fight our way back out."

But Colonel Greene came over at that moment, and hearing Morgan's response, said, "The risk is too great, Captain Morgan. They've now a large company of Highlanders and sailors, and have brought up several cannon, presumably loaded with grapeshot. Our men will be cut to pieces. Better to wait here for General Montgomery to arrive to the rear of the second barricade. Then the enemy will be forced to withdraw, and the lane into the city will be open."

"Colonel, there's no sign nor sound of the General's approach," Morgan replied. "I fear the worst: that he may never come. We *must* break out back through the first barricade ..."

But the colonel and the major could not be persuaded, continuing to insist that they wait for the general.

So Morgan returned his focus to the second barricade, knowing that *everything* now depended on breaking through.

Sergeant Timothy Murphy reloaded his rifle from his position kneeling behind an open door on the left side of the street. The noise from hundreds of gunshots, punctuated by the occasional cannon blast, shook the ground and made his ears ring.

When the reloading task was complete, he leaned out around the door and aimed up toward British soldiers firing from atop the barricade, trying to find a target through the falling snow. But before he could pull the trigger, and despite the ongoing cacophony, he heard a loud crash back inside the house.

He turned in time to see a group of British soldiers pouring into the building, having apparently kicked in the back door. One redcoat aimed a musket right at him, so he dove into a drift of snow to one side of the door even as a bullet zipped past where he'd been an instant before.

Then, before he could pull himself up, he saw a movement out of the corner of his eye, coming from the street behind him. He looked up to see Daniel Morgan himself, sword in hand, roaring as he rushed to the house and into the open doorway Murphy had just vacated. Morgan was closely followed by a half-dozen of his Virginians, rifles in hand, also yelling as they came.

Murphy jumped up and followed. For the next several minutes, they fought their way through the house, first to the back door, then up the stairs where the British had retreated. The fighting was fierce, first with rifles and muskets, and then—once both side's bullets were expended—swords, bayonets, and rifle butts. On the top floor, Captain Morgan cornered the last Brit, knocking aside his bayonet thrust, then pinning him to the wall with his sword.

Morgan yanked the sword free, and even as the redcoat slumped to the floor, the captain turned to his men and said, "You men stay here and target them Brits across the way. Sergeant, you're with me … We've got more troops to rally."

Without waiting for reply, Morgan was heading back down the stairs. Murphy scooped up one of the British muskets and followed. He was nearly out of ammunition, and decided he might soon need to use the bayonet.

When he reached the front door, Daniel Morgan was standing there looking about. Murphy stepped up beside him and followed his gaze. Over to their right, in the direction leading back toward the first barricade, he could see entire companies of Americans standing with their hands in the air. *That's not good*, he thought.

But Morgan just growled and rushed out into the melee, shouting, "To me, Virginians, keep fighting!"

So Sergeant Murphy followed him across the street. A dozen Virginians, hearing his shout, rose from their positions and fell in as he reached the far side of the street. There, a new group of Brits had broken through, and these now targeted the Americans from inside a storefront. Once again, Morgan led the charge with his sword, and once again the combat devolved into hand-to-hand carnage, with Murphy tossing aside his rifle and using the British bayonet.

But when they'd cleared the building and returned to the street, they were confronted by a ring of a dozen or more red-coated soldiers, bristling bayonets pointing straight at them. The men behind Captain Morgan dropped their rifles into the snow and raised their hands. Sergeant Murphy, with a heavy heart, tossed down his own musket. Then he, too, held up his hands in surrender.

A silence fell over the battlefield. Sergeant Murphy gazed about, taking in the full scene of their disaster. Every American was either dead, wounded, or had surrendered to the enemy.

Every American save one: Daniel Morgan.

Morgan stood alone, now backed against the storefront wall, face red, tears streaming down his face in his wrath and frustration, still holding out his sword.

British soldiers who'd begun herding the prisoners realized that Morgan had not yet capitulated, so they surrounded him with rifles, bayonets pointed inward threateningly.

But despite their demands, he refused to surrender, waving his blade at them and shouting, "If you want my sword, come and take it, you cowards!"

One of the soldiers laughed derisively. "Why, we'll just go ahead an' shoot you, and *then* we'll take your damn sword."

But then a burly, fierce-looking officer strode up and said, "No, you'll *not* shoot him. Nobody shoots him unless I say so."

Morgan glared at the newcomer, "Who're you?" he demanded.

"I am Lieutenant Colonel Allan Maclean, Royal Highlanders, officer in command. Will ye nae yield, sir?"

"No. If you want my sword come take it. Unless you're too much the coward."

"I'm nae coward, but neither am I a fool. You're bigger, younger, and stronger than me. Plus … I have all the guns. Why would I let you run a sword through my guts? Just so you won't call me coward? I dinnae think so.

"Again, I say, will ye nae yield, sir? Or will ye force me to order my men to shoot ye down, like a dog in the street?"

Morgan glared at the colonel for a long moment.

Sergeant Murphy cried out, "Please, Captain! Please! Don't throw your life away. Give it up, and after … you can fight another day."

Others of Morgan's command quickly took up the cry, pleading with him to surrender and not force the Brits to kill him.

But Morgan ignored them, stubbornly refusing to capitulate to his enemies. Maclean shrugged, and said, "All right then, have it yer way. But it's a damn shame and a waste, to my thinkin'. Men—"

◄◄◄◄◄◆►►►►►

Daniel Morgan shook with anger, frustration, and a horrifying grief for all the brave men he'd lost. So dark and hopeless was his humor in that moment, that he determined it would be better to die. So he'd decided to go out fighting, to charge forward, blade swinging, forcing the British to end his life.

But then … a vision of Abby and his little girls came sharp and clear into his mind, and inexplicably, he smiled. Then he remembered the prayer he'd said before the battle, asking God to spare his life and that of his men. He had to admit the Lord had mostly come through on that count, saving him and at least some of his men. And then he began to wonder if perhaps it was *not* his place to throw away a gift God had so graciously granted.

It was then that he noticed a priest a few yards away, kneeling down to comfort a dying man. Thinking still of God and his answered prayer, Morgan made his decision. He reversed the blade, and holding the handle forward, he pushed through the soldiers, who cautiously backed away. He stepped up to the priest and handed him his sword, hilt first.

The priest looked up and took the proffered sword with a puzzled expression. Morgan said, "This is for God. Tell him I said 'thanks.'"

◄◄◄◄◄◆►►►►►

The sounds of gunfire, which had been intense but distant as Ethan and Levi trudged back toward Quebec City, had begun to die out. By the time they came within view of the narrow path leading to the first British barricade, a silence had settled over the city.

The two of them exchanged a look of surprise, but neither knew what the silence meant. At this stage, all outcomes were still possible.

But fortunately for their purposes, the snowfall had not abated; in fact, if anything, it had increased, such that they were able to traverse the icy trail below the fort's walls with little fear of being seen from above.

When they reached the point where the trail widened out and made a sharp right-hand turn to the south, they ducked behind a large chunk of river ice and peered out. The snow was still falling so thickly that they could barely make out the British barricade, though it was now less than fifty yards distant.

Ethan watched for any movement upon the wall, but there was nothing. Then a gust of wind cleared the view for a moment, and his heart sank. He could clearly see red-coated soldiers pacing along the parapet at the top of the wall; and worst of all, they were all facing inward. Clearly, the Americans were still inside the town, but the British were back in control of the gate.

"What does it mean, Ethan?" Levi asked, having seen the same thing.

"I don't know, but I think ... I think it must *not* be good. If our attack against the lower town had been successful, we'd still need to fight through the upper town. There ought to be sounds of a gunfight. And ... I think these redcoats wouldn't just be standing here on the wall."

Levi nodded but said nothing. He wrapped his arms around his own shoulders and shivered. He wore a scarf wrapped around the lower half of his face, such that only his eyes showed. It occurred to Ethan that if he didn't know the person next to him was Levi, he would not be able to tell. Since Ethan also wore a scarf, he knew the same could be said of him. This thought gave him the inkling of an idea.

"Captain Morgan is in there," Ethan began. "And Murphy, and all our other men. I have to know what happened to them—if they're alive and captured or ..."

Levi's eyes went wide at the implication, so Ethan left the sentence unfinished. Levi continued to shiver, and Ethan realized his friend was nearly spent.

"Levi … you must return and report what we've seen to Colonel Arnold. Warn him that our attack has failed, and that our men have likely been captured."

"All right … But what are *you* going to do, Ethan?"

"I'm going to try to sneak in there and find out what has happened."

"No, Ethan. No! I can't let you do it. They'll shoot you for sure. Or take you prisoner. Don't do it, *please!*"

Ethan's heart ached for his friend, and he realized in that moment that Levi would be totally lost without him. But he needed to know what had become of Captain Morgan and the others.

"Don't you worry, Levi. I have a plan … You know how I can speak French? Well, I'll just wait around until some of the civilians start coming out, and then I'll merge in with them, and the Brits won't know the difference."

"Ethan, no … I can't … I can't leave you here."

"Now listen here, Levi. We've both got a job to do, and there's no use arguing about it."

Levi looked down at the snow but didn't answer.

"Here, take my rifle," Ethan said, handing it across. Levi took it reluctantly. Then, noticing the *Liberty or Death* paper pinned to Levi's hat, he remembered his own and reached up to pull it off.

"Now listen to me, 'cause this is important," Ethan said, waiting until Levi looked him in the eye. He could see Levi's eyes were red and watery, but he wasn't sure if that was from the swirling snow and wind or something else.

"I will meet you back at the camp in a few hours. If I'm not back by tomorrow night, assume I've been captured. Our enlistment is up tomorrow, so then you'll be free to decide what to do next: either stay here and help Colonel Arnold and his men, or go back to Winchester. It's up to you."

"But … I don't want to go *anywhere* without you, Ethan. Please …"

"Well, hopefully you won't have to, and I'll see you back at camp. Go now ... go. *Please.*"

"All right. But you come back, Ethan, you come back."

"Okay, I will," Ethan answered, praying it would turn out to be true.

◄◄◄◄◆►►►►

After Levi departed, Ethan continued to watch the gate for several minutes. But though the sentries continued to look mostly inward, occasionally one of them would turn and gaze out in his direction. And the gate remained closed, presumably locked from the inside, with nobody coming or going.

So he decided he'd just have to take the difficult and dangerous route of clambering over and through the great piles of ice chunks along the shoreline. The British had not bothered to block that route, as it would be impossible for a large formation of soldiers to pass through it without getting slaughtered by the men up on the walls. But a single man in a blizzard might go unnoticed, he decided.

An hour later, during which he'd nearly slid into the icy waters of the river on two occasions, only saving himself by digging his belt knife into the ice to stop his slide, Ethan reached a point that was several buildings down from the barricade. He decided to try his luck here, as just ahead was a new obstacle; many different small boats were beached here, and the ropes securing them to the land stretched tightly across the river's edge, tied to pilings along the shore. Crawling over and under these frozen ropes in the ice and snow held little appeal.

He scrambled across the ice chunks onto dry land, though he thought the idea quite ironic, considering everything was blanketed in several feet of snow. He crept across the short stretch of open ground toward a narrow alleyway between two buildings.

But then it occurred to him he should just walk normally and casually. If he snuck along fearfully, he would give himself away as one of the American invaders trying to avoid capture. But if he strode calmly, like he belonged there ...

277

So he forced himself to walk at a steady pace—at least as steady as one could in the deep, drifting snow. When he reached the end of the alleyway and peered out at the street, he could see the remains of a battle and winced. At a quick glance, he saw more than a dozen bodies scattered about in the snow, the dark red splatters of blood contrasting sharply with the white ground. But he saw no living soldiers, so he turned to the left and headed up the street. As he walked, he glanced at the strewn bodies to see if he recognized anyone. He was gratified to see that most of the dead were either British soldiers, with their red uniforms, or French militia, typically wearing white uniform coats and black, three-cornered hats. In this area, at least, there were few American dead, and of these he did not recognize any faces.

He'd walked only a few dozen yards when he saw the second barricade in the distance, though it too was obscured by the snowfall. He continued to gaze at it as he walked, and in several brief glimpses, he confirmed what he had feared but expected: this barricade was also manned by redcoats who were looking inward.

But even as he walked, he tripped over something in the snow and nearly fell. He caught himself, and noticed he'd tripped over the outstretched musket of a soldier, half buried in the snow. He saw that this soldier was one of the white-coated French-Canadian militia, and that the poor fellow had taken a bullet to the head that had left a gaping hole where his left ear had been. Ethan grimaced at the gory sight, but at that same moment, the idea he'd been mulling over since even before Levi departed solidified in his mind: he'd need to convince the British that he was French, not American, if he was to have any chance of avoiding capture. And what better way to do that than to dress as a French militiaman.

A quick glance in both directions confirmed that he was still alone on the street. So he picked up the musket and slung it over his shoulder. Then he grabbed the dead man by the collar and dragged him across the snow into the nearest building. The door had, thankfully, been kicked in and hung crookedly on its hinges, so he had no problem entering.

Fortunately, the man was of a similar size as Ethan, and the only uniform he wore was the white coat and black three-cornered hat. Underneath, the man wore ordinary civilian clothing, similar to what Ethan himself wore. So he'd not need to do anything but swap coats and hats with the man, *And viola! I'm a French militiaman*, he thought, then grinned. But his self-congratulations were short-lived as he remembered a sobering thought—the thing Daniel Morgan had told him when he'd proposed sneaking into the city previously, when he was working on the map: "If they catch you in disguise, they'll hang you for a spy." If he walked in and was caught in his regular clothes, they'd just throw him in with the other Americans. With these clothes on …

But he was determined to carry on, so he suppressed the evil vision of his neck in a rope and stepped back onto the street. As he walked, he thought about what he would say when he encountered the British sentries. He decided on a ploy, and to help sell the story, he began walking erratically, dragging the butt of his musket in the snow behind him. He stopped next to another dead soldier, this one British, and scooped up a handful of bloody snow, smearing the blood on the side of his face, which helped explain the splatter of blood on the coat's collar from the dead French militiaman. But as he stood he noticed for the first time that this area in front of the second barricade was littered with bodies, a handful of British and Canadians, but mostly Americans. He made a quick scan of those around him and winced when he recognized the face of one of his own men, Private Adam Kurtz. And though he ached at the sight, and burned to retrieve the body for a proper burial, he knew he had to continue on.

When he reached the iron door, it was closed, of course. So he banged on it with the musket. A small port hole opened, and a man gazed out.

Ethan tried to act dazed, shaking his head from side to side, and said, "*Ouvrez la porte s'il vous plaît. Je gèle*," asking them to please open the door, as he was freezing, shivering to help make the point.

The port hole closed, and the gate was pushed open.

"*Merci*," he continued. Then, "*J'ai été frappé à la tête dans le combat. Je me suis réveillé et tout le monde était parti*," explaining that he'd been struck on the head in the battle, and when he awoke, everyone was gone.

"What'd he say?" the man in front of him, who'd opened the door, asked the soldier next to him.

"Well, my French ain't so good, but I think he said he got bonked on the head in the fight."

"Well, it don't take no scholar to see that, mate. The fella looks a mess … blood everywhere," the first soldier answered, opening the gate wider. "Come on in, Frenchy. Your mates have already headed up the street, herding the prisoners."

Ethan acted confused, so the second soldier pointed vigorously down the street and said, "Uh … *Les Français* … went … um … what's the word … oh, *descendirent … la rue*."

"Ah. *Merci*," Ethan answered, then shuffled off down the street in the direction indicated. *So far, so good*, he thought.

But as he stumbled along, it occurred to him not to overdo the wounded act; the last thing he wanted was to be shuttled off to the hospital, where his ruse would be quickly discovered. So he slung his rifle over his shoulder and walked with a steadier pace.

As he passed down the street, he saw an open area through an alleyway off to his right. There he could see a crowd had gathered, so he headed in that direction. When he stepped out of the alley, he saw he was in a broad square, likely the center of the lower town, he decided. Facing away from him, lining the square, were a smattering of British soldiers and a long row of French-Canadian militia.

Ethan paused and took a deep breath. This would be the most dangerous part, he knew; fooling the British with his French was relatively simple, but fooling a Frenchman? He knew he could never pull that off; they'd recognize his American accent straightaway. But he could see men moving from his right to left through the square, heading in the direction of the main road leading up the hill to the upper town.

So he wrapped his scarf around his face and stepped forward into the square, moving toward the row of Frenchmen. Spotting a gap in the line, he stepped up into it and stood to attention, musket butt rested on the ground at his side, same as the others. He noticed the man next to him glance over and start.

The man asked if he was wounded, "*Êtes-vous blessé?*"

But it was loud in the square, so Ethan just lowered the scarf, gave the man a wan smile, mimed being hit on the head, then shrugged.

The man returned the smile and nodded, turning back toward the square.

Ethan breathed a sigh of relief, then turned his attention to the men walking by in front of him. As he'd expected, it was the Americans of Colonel Arnold's command. Clearly all had been killed or captured, and the survivors were now being marched off to whatever they used for a prison in the upper city. Ethan watched the men's faces as they passed, trying to memorize the ones whose names he knew so he could report these to the colonel later.

He saw Colonel Christopher Greene, and Major Meigs, along with many of their officers, whose names he knew. Of course, there were many soldiers whose faces were familiar, but whose names he did *not* know, them being from the other divisions of the Kennebec Expedition. Finally, the rifle battalion passed, led by the Pennsylvanians. Ethan knew many of those, and did his best to commit their names to memory as they passed.

Finally, the Virginians passed, all of which he knew well. In their case, he tried to think about who was missing, rather than who was there. *So many missing* ... he inwardly groaned, as the last of their company shuffled past. But he was pleased to see some of his own men, Sergeant Murphy, George Merchant, and several others. He so badly wanted to call out to them or to make eye contact, but he dared not, and kept the scarf pulled up over his nose.

To Ethan's relief, Captain Morgan was the very last man in the column. He was trailed by four British regulars, who followed with bayonets leveled, as if he were some kind of dangerous animal. *Which is likely true,* Ethan decided.

As Morgan walked past, Ethan saw that his head was down, and though he'd not wanted any of the other men to see him, for fear their reaction might give him away, he desperately wanted the captain to know that he was there. He was already thinking that he would try to somehow affect an escape, for Morgan, at least. But he could think of nothing to say that might catch Morgan's attention and not give himself away.

And then it came to him. He pulled down his scarf from his face, mimed getting ready to sneeze, then faked a sneeze, while loudly shouting, "*Winchester!*"

The militiaman next to him leaned in and said, "*à tes/vos souhaits,*" the common French response whenever someone sneezed. Ethan realized the phrase oddly translated as "to your wishes" in English.

He nodded acknowledgment at the man, but again chose not to respond. But when he looked back at Morgan, he saw the captain had heard the familiar name of their hometown, and now locked eyes with Ethan, nodding in recognition. Morgan's eyes were stern and determined, but Ethan noticed they were oddly red and swollen, as if he'd been crying. But he quickly dismissed the notion; Captain Morgan certainly did *not* cry.

Ethan returned the nod, then made a motion with his head toward the upper town, trying to convey his intention to follow along.

But Morgan shook his head, emphatically, then mouthed, "*No. Go … Home.*"

Ethan reluctantly nodded his understanding.

Then as he stepped up even with Ethan, about to pass by, Morgan looked straight ahead and called out in a loud, clear voice, as if shouting to the men in front of him, "Godspeed, Ethan. You're a good man. Give my best to Abby and the girls."

And then Daniel Morgan was gone, and Ethan wondered if they would ever meet again.

◄◄◄◄◄◆►►►►►

Fortunately, getting back out of the city again was not as difficult as getting in; he'd simply fallen in with a French patrol being sent out to collect the fallen, and then he'd slipped away into the snowy darkness. He figured the white French militia coat helped, as it not only made for good camouflage in the snow, but if a British soldier saw him leaving the city, he'd likely just take him for a deserter and let him go rather than shooting him. One less unreliable mouth to feed, he'd probably figure.

When Ethan arrived back at camp an hour after darkness, he went straight to the hospital to report to Colonel Arnold. Arnold was downcast by Ethan's news, the first concrete information he'd received on the outcome of the battle, but was effusive in his praise for Ethan and his sneaking into the city to reconnoiter.

Arnold told Ethan to bring him his sword and pistols that were stacked in the corner near his bed. Then he called for Dr. Senter, ordering him to arm all the wounded in the hospital, in case the British thought to sally out and attack the American camp.

Ethan left the hospital and went to find Levi. He found him next to a glowing campfire outside their tent.

Ethan stepped up to the fire and said, "Hello, Levi. I'm back."

Levi jumped to his feet, stepped up and hugged Ethan tightly. Ethan returned the hug, and for several minutes neither of them moved or spoke, until Ethan felt Levi's body shuddering with sobs, and he gently patted his friend on the back.

Chapter 12. The Return

"When I die and go to heaven
to St. Peter I will tell,
'One more soldier reporting for duty,
sir, I've served my time in hell.'"
- Hal Popplewell

Monday December 24, 1776 – Winchester, Virginia Colony:

Abby Morgan sat slowly rocking her chair in the sitting room. She felt thoroughly downcast. It was Christmas Eve, and she was all alone. The girls had gone to bed, and Daniel was still away in the war, somewhere off to the north. *God knows where Daniel is*, she thought, *but I must trust that He will watch over my good husband.*

But the thought gave her little comfort in her loneliness. She couldn't remember ever feeling so blue. A woman she thought was her best friend had turned her back, allowing her brother-in-law to act the bully … casting her out of the house in a shameful manner. It was infuriating, true … but mostly she just felt sad about it—like she had just lost something new but precious.

And then, in the midst of her dark reverie, there came a knock at the door. She sighed … She was in no mood for visitors. But she'd given all the servants the evening and the next day off, since it was Christmas. So she'd have to get up and answer it herself.

She opened the door and suffered a surprise. *"Gideon!"*

"Miss Abby," he said, removing his hat, "I won't mince words, ma'am. I expect you don't have any good feelings about me just now, and I can't say I blame you. My family has behaved in a disgraceful manner toward you. You who deserve so much better from us, who owe you so much for your selfless kindness."

Abby didn't know what to say to this, so she just stared at Gideon.

"Anyway, I just came here to tell you that I have sent my brother away for the despicable manner in which he treated you, and I have come here simply to apologize as sincerely and humbly as a man can." And then, true to his word, he knelt down on one knee and gazed up at her.

"Miss Abby, I beg your forgiveness. And … I also wanted to tell you that this was all my fault, and I beg you not to blame Hannah for any of this. She loves you dearly, and never wanted to shun you; she was forced into it by the unconscionable men in her household."

"Well, for heaven's sake, Gideon. Please get up and come in out of the cold. Where is Hannah, anyway?"

"Oh, she's …" he turned back toward the drive, and Abby saw Hannah sitting on the driver's seat of the wagon, with Elsie cuddled up next to her. Abby waved at them and gestured them to come inside.

After welcoming her guests, Abby roused Nancy and Betsy from their beds, then warmed up the food left over from their evening meal. Then, for the next several hours, the Morgan and Chambers families enjoyed a simple but joyous Christmas celebration more memorable than any that had come before, only dampened by the obvious absence of their two men off fighting in the war.

And when it came time for the evening to end, Abby gave them guest rooms so they'd not have to drive home in the dark, and so they might continue the celebration come the morning.

Monday January 1, 1776 – Winchester, Virginia Colony:

Abby woke early on New Year's Day in a happy mood. She was still basking in the warm glow of her reunion with Hannah and their joyous Christmas celebration that had continued throughout the day on the twenty-fifth until the Chambers family finally departed that evening, inviting Abby and her children to their house on New Year's Day.

But as she moved about the kitchen gathering various food items to take with her for the day's dinner—a cooked ham, sweet potatoes, bread, fried okra, and black-eyed peas—a sudden thought occurred to her: that James had not just been a domineering annoyance to them, he had also been their main benefactor since his arrival. Whatever else he was, he was clearly a gentleman of means. And now that she thought about it, he must've been providing them with all the necessities of life in her absence. *Why didn't they just ask me for more help?* she wondered.

But after a moment's reflection and a wry smile, she answered her own question: *Because they are proud people, and don't want to continue receiving charity, at least not from outside their own family — thus the brother stepping in.*

She stewed on this conundrum for several minutes as she continued to load up her picnic basket. *How can I help them, without it seeming like charity?*

And then it hit her, and she smiled. *Of course, that's the solution ... and it will also benefit me ... in so many ways.*

Abby, finally finding herself alone with Hannah as the two ladies cleaned up the dishes from the New Year's meal, decided it was time to broach the subject that was foremost in her mind. "Hannah, dear, I wish to ask something of you ..."

"Oh? Certainly, if there's anything at all I can do for you, I will surely do it without a moment's hesitation."

"I'm happy you say that, because I've been thinking ... we had such a wonderful time at Christmas ..."

"Yes, it was just lovely, wasn't it?"

"Truly. I felt so down and lonely until you arrived, missing Daniel and all ..."

"Yes, you poor dear. Though of course we miss Ethan, at least we have each other. I'm so happy we could come cheer you up."

"You certainly did ... and it got me to thinking ... what if you came and lived with me on the farm? Always. I mean all of you, Gideon and Elsie too."

"Oh. I ... I don't know, Abby. If it were only up to me, I'm sure I should jump at the chance. I have always loved our visits, and your farm is so lovely and peaceful. But I'm afraid Gideon ... Well, he's a proud man, and won't like the idea of being your guest all the time."

But Abby just smiled, "Just tell me you will do it, Hannah. Then leave Gideon to me."

"Oh, do you really think you can convince him? Then yes, yes, I will do it, if you can get him to agree."

Abby reached out and embraced her friend. "You have made me so happy, my dear."

Then she stepped back, and the two exchanged bright smiles.

When they'd finished up the dishes, they returned to the living room, where Gideon sat talking quietly with the girls, who were working a wooden puzzle on the floor in front of his chair. He looked up and smiled as they entered, "All done?"

"Yes, dear," Hannah answered. "But Abby has something she wishes to speak with you about."

"Oh?" He gazed at Abby questioningly as she stepped in front of him and looked him in the eye.

"Yes, Gideon … I wish to speak to you because, I'm in need of your help, and I am wondering if you would be willing to come to my aid."

"Well, of course, Miss Abby … Anything you need, as long as it's within my power to give." He held out his bent left hand, then shrugged.

"I'm so pleased to hear it. The truth is, with Daniel being gone for so long, and no end of the war in sight, I have been struggling to run the farm by myself. I was not raised a farmgirl, and Daniel has always run things. But now that it's all up to me, I find I am not always up to the task."

"Understandable, and certainly no shame in it. But how can I help?"

"Well, I have a business proposition for you, Gideon. As you are not at present able to carry on with your surveying business, as I understand it, and as I need help running my farm, I was wondering if you would consent to running it for me."

"Oh. I don't have any experience running a farm," he answered. "And besides …" he once again held out his near useless hand, "I doubt I'd be able to do much farming."

Then she frowned at him. "You're a well-educated, highly intelligent man, who's been running his own successful business for years. A farm needs a man to oversee it, to make sure the *business* side of it is profitable, just like any other enterprise. As for the other issue … I don't need you for your *arms*, Gideon; I have plenty of strong farm hands for lifting heavy objects. I need you for your *mind*—your intelligence and leadership, two things the farm is almost entirely lacking at the moment."

"But how can I properly run a business when I can't even write?"

"Never fear; I am excellent with a pen, sir. If you need anything written out, just tell it to me, and I shall write it down for you; problem solved.

"But … there is one requirement of the job, and I'm afraid I must insist on this point: you and your family must live on the farm. I'll not have you wasting time traveling back and forth each day, through all sorts of treacherous weather. I would worry over you, and I'll not have it. Besides, with the present troubles, there's no sense in our families paying to run two households when one will do. Perhaps you can even rent out your place for a time."

Gideon slowly nodded and gazed down at the floor for a long moment. Then he looked back up at her. "And you say you *really* need my help?"

"Oh, yes, most certainly. I have been nearly at my wits' end trying to keep everything running—paying the loans, purchasing the seeds, paying the workers, and on and on … I never expected Daniel to be gone so long, and I really don't know anyone else who can help me with this. If you don't agree to help … I'm just not sure what I shall do."

"Well, after all the kindness you and Daniel have shown us … it would be ungrateful of me to refuse you. So … the answer is *yes*, I will help you with the farm. To the best of my abilities, though with the understanding I've never done it before, and will have much to learn."

"Agreed. And thank you so very much, Gideon. You have made me so, so happy." She beamed, and he returned the smile. Elsie squealed with delight, then hugged her momma as the two Morgan girls danced around them, sharing in the happiness of the moment.

Several hours later, as the Morgans prepared to depart, Hannah once again asked Abby to join her in the kitchen, where they conversed in quiet tones.

"Abby … what you have done tonight," Hannah said, slowly shaking her head with tears welling in her eyes. "… what you have done for Gideon … giving him a chance to feel useful once again … Why, that was likely the kindest thing I think I have ever had the pleasure of witnessing."

Abby smiled, "Nonsense, my dear. Every word was true. Though of course I had considered that it would surely benefit him to have something important to accomplish, I was not entirely altruistic in my designs. I truly can use his help, and I believe it will help to lift a great burden from me. And besides, it makes it so you and Elsie can be with me always."

Hannah returned Abby's smile before stepping forward for a warm, heartfelt embrace.

◄◄◄◄◄◆►►►►►

Tuesday January 2, 1776 – Quebec City, Quebec Province:

Two days after the battle, Ethan was summoned to Colonel Arnold's bedside in the hospital. It was the first time he'd seen the colonel since the night after the battle, and decided his commander looked much improved, though understandably he had a downcast look about him. Ethan, however, was elated to find Arnold sitting up in bed, sipping hot tea, and gazing at a map.

Arnold greeted Ethan warmly, once again thanking him for his timely and even heroic actions on the night of the battle. Ethan shrugged it off, saying he'd only done his duty. But he knew he'd gone above and beyond at the end, sneaking into the city to reconnoiter.

Then, before Arnold could explain the reason for the summons, they were interrupted by an unexpected arrival. Major Meigs, whom Ethan had seen marching with the captured men along with Daniel Morgan, strode up to Arnold's bed.

"Meigs. You've escaped!" Arnold exclaimed happily.

But Meigs sat down heavily in a chair next to Arnold's bed. "No, Colonel, I'm sorry to say it, but I have *not* escaped. Governor Carleton has magnanimously agreed to allow me to return to our camp to gather clothing and other personal items of our captive officers and return with them to the city. I have sworn an oath, on my word of honor, to return promptly to captivity. I have also sworn not to divulge anything I may have seen within the fortress concerning its defenses."

"Ah, I see. I would not ask you to break your word, Major … but can you not at least provide us with an accounting of our men? The numbers of killed, wounded, and captured, and the specific deportment of our officers? Lieutenant Chambers here, who gallantly snuck into the city shortly after the surrender, has provided us with some details, but his view of the men affected was understandably limited."

Meigs looked at Ethan and nodded in appreciation for the effort. "Yes … I believe that would be appropriate, and I can see no reason why the governor would object. According to what I have been told, 426 of our men were killed or captured; of these, sixty were said to have died in the battle, including three of our good officers: Captain Henricks, Lieutenant Humphreys, and Lieutenant Cooper.

"Of the remaining men who were captured, one hundred were wounded to various degrees, including Captain Hubbard, whose injuries may yet prove mortal.

"Happily, Lieutenant Colonel Greene, Major Bigelow, and Captain Morgan are all in good health, along with a number of other officers of lower ranks. I shall write you out a list before I depart. Oh, and your aide, Eleazer Oswald, is also held captive and bears no wounds."

Meigs went on to describe the battle in detail from the point after Arnold was carried from the field up to the moment of their surrender. Arnold, in turn, informed Meigs of General Montgomery's tragic death and the subsequent failure of his attack, as reported by the returning New York regiment.

Meigs then departed and went to gather what goods he might for the incarcerated officers before returning to captivity. Ethan felt a great sadness for Meigs, but also admired him for keeping his word and selflessly returning to confinement.

Colonel Arnold gazed down at his boots for a long moment without speaking. Ethan was trying to decide whether he should just depart and come back another time when the colonel seemed to remember his presence and looked up at him.

"Chambers … I asked you here because I have a very important, specific task I require of you."

"Yes, sir?"

"I need someone sensible, and of great fortitude to deliver my report of the recent action here at Quebec to General Washington. You men of Captain Morgan's Virginia Riflemen have proven yourselves the most resilient and reliable of our troops when it comes to a difficult and dangerous journey through the wilderness. And you are its last officer not killed or captured. You may take one or two companions with you, if you wish, but keep your numbers small, as I wish you to travel light and swiftly. Toward that end, I will lend you my canoe and my trusted Penobscot Indian crew to man it. I intend for you to take the more straightforward route southward—which also has the advantage of being under the control of our forces—by water through Montreal, down Lake Champlain, to Fort Ticonderoga. There, you may give over a copy of my written report to the fort commander that he might forward it on by swift courier to General Washington. You will then proceed on foot to Cambridge where you will hand deliver the other copy, on the off chance the courier does not make it through.

"Though I will not include it in the written report, lest you are captured and the enemy gets their hands on it, I will ask you to tell the general that I intend to continue the siege, and will ask General Wooster, who is now in command at Montreal, to send reinforcements that we may look for another opportunity to take the city by storm. I ask that General Washington also send as many reinforcements as possible, to renew the offensive. Now, state this message back to me, if you please …"

Ethan quickly did as he was bid.

"Good, very good. I will write out my official report for the General shortly, and have two copies of it delivered to you this evening, that you may depart in the morning at first light. Good luck, Godspeed, and thank you, Lieutenant."

"Thank you, sir. And Godspeed to you as well, sir ... and a quick recovery from your wounds."

◄◄◄◄◆►►►►

As Ethan trudged back to his tent through the well-beaten path in the snow, he passed two officers who were standing off to one side near a large tree trunk. They appeared to be engaged in a deep conversation. He recognized them as Major John Brown, one of the officers who'd come from Montreal with General Montgomery, and Captain Oliver Hanchett from Major Meigs's division of Arnold's army. He did not personally know Brown, though he had a reputation as a good officer.

He didn't especially like Hanchett, though, but he had to admit it was only based on rumors he'd heard that Hanchett and Colonel Arnold did not see eye to eye and had exchanged heated words at various times during the Kennebec expedition.

Odd place to hold a conversation, out here in the bitter cold, he thought.

Then he noticed the two men stopped talking and watched him intently as he passed by. He tipped his hat to them, and Brown nodded in return. Hatchett did not acknowledge Ethan at all, but turned back toward Brown.

Yep, I'd call that odd, Ethan concluded, but then his thoughts turned to the happy image of what Levi's reaction would be when he heard the news that they were finally going home.

◄◄◄◄◆►►►►

"See that young rascal?" Captain Hatchett said as Ethan Chambers passed out of sight.

"Yes ... what about him?" Major Brown asked. He did not know the young fellow's name, though he did recall seeing him about camp from time to time.

"He's an example of what I was talking about—Arnold playing favorites. The boy started out as a mere private back at Boston. But Arnold jumped him all the way to lieutenant just because the boy is some sort of family friend of Morgan's."

"Ah … yes, that would be Benedict Arnold's style, all right," Brown agreed. "But … getting back to what I was saying before … I believe you and I have a common bond concerning our Colonel Arnold. He and I had a falling out back at Ticonderoga when he refused to recognize my legitimate command of the fort. And I understand you too have felt the unfair capriciousness of his commands …?"

"Indeed. He has treated me with the utmost disrespect on the trip up the Kennebec. You can be sure I have no love for the man."

"Seeing's how it's brutally cold out just now, let us conclude for the nonce with an agreement on the matter. With his current heroics fresh in everyone's mind, and us being stuck up here in this Godforsaken frozen wasteland, this is not the time to act. Let us bide our time on the matter. But once we are all back in the colonies, I'm sure we can put our heads together and come up with a plan to knock our *beloved* colonel down a few pegs."

"All right, but how do you propose we do that? I understand he is tight with General Washington himself."

"True, but I have certain friends in the Congress … I have already appealed to them once to elevate Ethan Allen and his men in their view at Arnold's expense. It does not take a great deal of imagination to picture that happening again. For instance, I see Arnold as a man who will not mind taking advantage of his station to line his own pockets."

Hatchett shrugged. "It is a common enough practice in the military. Men often cash in on their circumstances so they can dole treasure out to their men. Helps insure their loyalty. No great shame in that."

Brown smiled. "True. You know that, and I know that, along with pretty much any experienced officer. Certainly, General Washington knows it. But … what do you think our fine gentlemen in the Congress know about the practice?"

Hatchett thought about it a moment, then answered, "Nothing at all, I'd guess."

"Exactly," Brown replied with a wicked grin.

◄◄◄◄◀◆▶►►►►

Thursday February 1, 1776 – New York City, New York Colony:

When James Chambers returned to New York after his tiresome journey from Winchester, he was shocked to learn that his long-time friend, colonial governor William Tryon, was no longer in residence at the governor's mansion. Fearing for his safety, and that of his family, from the radical rebels calling themselves the Sons of Liberty, the governor had fled to the safety of the British sloop of war, *Halifax*, anchored in New York Harbor.

Have things gotten that bad even here in New York? James thought in disgust.

So James had sought passage to the ship and was now sitting at tea opposite Tryon at the captain's table with the ship's captain, a man named Bowers, and the governor's long-time secretary, Edmund Fanning.

"I was just thinking, William, how badly things have deteriorated here in New York in my absence," James said as he forked a piece of cake with finely crafted silver flatware.

"Yes, my dear James," Tryon shook his head slowly, "hard to believe it has come to this … me, the royal governor of the colony, forced to seek shelter on a floating gun battery to ensure my very safety. It was rumored their so-called 'Continental Congress'—a group of uncouth ruffians, if you ask me—had issued a warrant for my arrest. Can you believe it! Apparently, their General Washington refused to allow it, to his credit, though it made my dear Margaret so nervous she could no longer sleep at night. And so, here I sit, bouncing about in the harbor."

"Disgraceful, Your Honor," Fanning interjected. "And where is the army in all this, I'd like to ask?"

"Penned up in Boston, I'm afraid," Tryon answered, shaking his head. "Of course, I have appealed to Lord Howe for troops, but to no avail."

"But William," James said, "surely there is nothing more to be gained by the army staying in Boston. They are besieged in the town, from what I've heard, with the rebels holding the high ground surrounding. Very little chance of a breakout."

"Precisely," Fanning nodded, taking another sip of his tea. "Look here, Mr. Chambers," Fanning continued, "it seems we are of a mind here ... that it is only a matter of time before the army must admit the inevitable and abandon Boston."

"Humph ... agreed. And I pray they burn the town down around the ears of those Godforsaken radicals when they do," James answered.

"Hear, hear," Tryon agreed, snorting a chuckle.

"The point is," Fanning gestured with his fork, after swallowing another bite of cake, "that when the army leaves Boston, it must go somewhere, and I think we can all agree that the logical place for them to go is—"

"Well, right here in New York, of course," James finished the sentence for him. "The majority of men here are loyalists, though the radicals presently have them cowed by their strident voices and their threats of violence."

"Undeniably," Tryon nodded.

"And when the army *does* arrive here," Fanning continued, "those of us who have remained loyal to the king will flock to their banner, ready to take up arms without fear of reprisal by these villainous so-called 'Sons of Liberty.'"

"Agreed," James and Tryon said at nearly the same moment, then smiled at each other and raised their teacups in salute.

"Gentlemen," Fanning also raised his cup. "I propose that when that happy moment arrives, we take command of a new loyalist regiment as its commissioned officers. Your honor, I believe it is within your purview to issue such commissions in time of emergency ...?"

"Oh, yes, indeed. And I agree wholeheartedly, Edmund. We gentlemen here at this table, excluding the good captain, of course, no slight intended ..." He turned to Captain Bowers and raised his cup. The captain bowed his head in acknowledgment.

"... Are best qualified to lead the loyal resistance. And in recognition of our loyalty to the crown, I propose we call our new fighting force the *King's American Regiment.*"

"To the King's American Regiment," Fanning said, and all four men clinked their teacups, then took a sip to consummate the agreement.

It was only on his way back to shore, on the ship's tender, that the full impact of the event hit home to James. He'd just agreed to lead men into battle in an actual war, a thing he'd never before contemplated in life. And it also occurred to him that he would now be in armed opposition to the other branch of his own family, his brother's side in Virginia. But the thought of their ingratitude drove out all previous warm feelings, and strengthened his resolve to prove that the Chambers family were loyal king's men after all. If that put him at odds with his own brother, then so be it.

◄◄◄◄◄◆►►►►►

Friday January 19, 1776 – Fort Ticonderoga, New York Colony:

It took Ethan and Levi more than two weeks to reach Fort Ticonderoga, with their days spent shivering in a canoe and their nights spent shivering in a tent.

But their Penobscot Indian companions—whose names they soon learned were Soncier, Eneas, Sebatis, Metagone, and Sewanockett—bore the brunt of the labor, with Ethan and Levi occasionally spelling them on the paddles.

They found their ride in the sleek, lightweight canoe more enjoyable than the heavy, awkward bateau had been, but they also found it temperamental and touchy, which caused them to be clumsy with their paddling efforts, to the amusement of their highly skilled and experienced counterparts. Sewanockett seemed particularly inclined to tease them, often saying such things as, "You boys ride her like pig. Must treat her gently, like woman," to which both boys simply smiled and shrugged; after all, they knew something about pigs, but little to nothing about women.

And though this journey might have overawed them before they'd started out for the Kennebec all those months earlier, it now seemed no more than an extended—though frigidly cold—holiday, with plenty to eat, short easy portages, and little real danger.

But despite the relative ease of their return journey from Canada, by the time Ethan and Levi reached Fort Ticonderoga, they were more than ready for a warm, dry bed by a roaring fire in the fort's barracks.

The commander of the fort feted them as heroes, though he was saddened to hear about the results of the battle, especially the death of General Montgomery, whom he'd greatly admired. He immediately sent a courier ahead with Colonel Arnold's written report to deliver it to General Washington.

But despite completing that aspect of their present mission, Ethan felt obliged to push on in order to deliver the verbal portion of the message, as instructed by Colonel Arnold. So after only a few days of rest, Ethan and Levi once again ventured out into the cold, this time headed back to General Washington's camp at Cambridge, still some two hundred miles away.

◄◄◄◄◄◆►►►►►►

Wednesday January 31, 1776 – Quebec City, Quebec Province:

Daniel Morgan strode along between two British soldiers, who'd fetched him out of the American officers' prison, a converted seminary in Quebec's fortified upper city. They'd not told him where he was going, and he'd not thought to ask. And though he had little doubt that he could overpower these two guards—he was not bound, and they foolishly escorted him with their rifles on their shoulders rather than pointed at his body—he didn't think about doing that, either; he would never abandon the other officers and men in order to make his own escape. He'd only escape if they all did.

His boots crunched through the crusty snow of the street, beat down by many feet until it was as hard as ice. They turned a corner and marched him up to what appeared to be a small pub, but there were no patrons about. The soldier in the lead stepped up to the door and knocked. A voice called out, "Enter."

The soldier pushed the door open and said, "The prisoner you requested, sir."

"Send him in."

The two soldiers took positions on either side of the door, facing outward, and gestured for Morgan to enter.

He stepped into the dimly lit room and noticed it was filled with a dozen or so tables spread out across a dark hardwood floor. But the tables were empty, with chairs stacked atop them. All except one, where a man sat gazing up at Morgan expectantly. And not just any man; this man was dressed in the elegant red and gold finery of the very highest-ranking British officer. And Morgan recognized him immediately, though until now he'd only seen him from a distance: here sat General Guy Carleton, Royal Governor of Quebec Province.

"Captain Morgan, please come in and be seated," he said, smiling warmly and gesturing toward a chair opposite him at the table.

Morgan stepped up to the table, pulled out the chair and sat. "Governor. To what do I owe the ... *pleasure*, would be the proper term, I suppose?"

Carleton gave out a quiet laugh. "Yes, I'm sure you have little reason to desire my company. But I wished to meet *you*, sir. I have heard much about you—your valor and unquenchable gallantry during the battle, the very last American to surrender, as I understand it. And ready to go down fighting, rather than give up your sword."

Morgan shrugged, but could think of nothing to say to this. It was not something he'd thought much about since the end of the battle.

"Indulge my curiosity, if you would, sir," Carleton continued. "What made you do it? Finally decide to surrender your sword, I mean."

Morgan thought about that a moment, then said, "I wasn't going to ... Then a vision of my dear sweet wife Abby suddenly came into my mind ... and my two little darlin' daughters, Nancy and Betsy, back home in Virginia. Guess I decided I'd like to see them again … in *this* world."

Carleton nodded his head. "I *like* that answer … No bravado, no braggadocio, just simple, human kindness and love. Surprising for a man of your demeanor and reputation."

"What reputation would that be, sir?"

"A reputation as a tough character; quick to anger, and ready to fight at the slightest provocation."

Morgan nodded and looked down at his hands, feeling more than a little shame at the governor's implication. The worst part of it was, he knew it was true.

"I … wasn't always like this," Morgan finally answered.

"Hmm … I expect for a man of action like yourself, confinement must be the worst sort of hell. I imagine you'd rather be whipped and worked hard than to just sit and stare at a wall."

Morgan looked Carleton in the eye, and what he saw there was sincerity. The man wasn't trying to get anything from him, and seemed to have no hidden motives. But Morgan wanted to be sure.

"If you're trying to get me to switch sides, like some of your other officers have done, you're wasting your time, Governor."

Carleton smiled. "No … I wouldn't insult you in that manner, though I might try it on some of the others. No, Captain Morgan, I figure you for a man who is firm in his convictions. Though I may disagree with your loyalties, and consider them misplaced, I respect your resolve and would not seek to sway you from it."

"Why, then? Why am I here today, sir?"

"Captain, you may not believe this, but for a soldier, I am a compassionate man. I do not believe in making prisoners suffer, especially officers who've fought bravely and with honor. For instance, you may be pleased to know that I ordered your General Montgomery to be buried with full military honors after the battle. As for you, Captain, I come here because I am concerned about the fighting between yourself and some of your own fellow American officers."

Morgan nodded. "In my defense, I've only fought with those few who are total scoundrels, and a disgrace to their country."

"I'm sure that's true, but … I do feel responsible for the safety of *all* of my prisoners, even the *scoundrels*. I should hate to see the violence escalate to the point where someone gets killed. I'm sure your so-called Continental Congress would have a jolly time berating me in your American newspapers if that were to happen. I can only imagine what sort of monster they'd make me out to be."

Morgan looked at Carleton for a long moment, as if seeing the man for the first time. "But … you're not a monster, are you, Governor?"

"No, I'm not. And neither are you, Captain. That's why I'm here today. To make sure you remain an honorable man, and don't become a monster due to the frustrations of your incarceration."

"That is … decent of you, sir. But … how do you propose doing that? I don't expect you're going to turn me loose."

"No. Not yet, anyway. Not until the present crisis is entirely resolved. You are too dangerous an opponent for me to consider that. But I would propose a truce … between yourself and the other *scoundrel* officers. In return, I will allow you to get out for fresh air on a regular basis, such as you are doing today. I may even join you, from time to time—on your word of honor, of course, that you won't try to escape during those outings."

Morgan gazed up at the ceiling for a moment, then took a deep breath. "Getting outside … would be good." Then he chuckled, "So, yes, I agree. Unless that offer of a whipping and hard work is still on the table."

Carleton smiled. "I'm afraid not. Well, I must go now; I have other duties, as you can imagine. But the guards have been instructed on a specific route you may walk that will afford you some exercise and fresh air, but will not grant you a particularly interesting view of our defenses."

"Seems more'n fair. And … thanks for this, Governor. It is a kindness unexpected, and it speaks volumes as to your good character."

"You are most welcome. And I will expect you to speak kindly of me to your wife and children, whenever you return to Virginia."

"That I will, sir. That I surely will."

◄◄◄◄◄◆►►►►►

Wednesday January 31, 1776 – Lancaster, Pennsylvania Colony:

While Daniel Morgan suffered his imprisonment in a cold lockup in Quebec Province, British Lieutenant John André of the Seventh Regiment of Foot, who'd also been taken prisoner during the Canada campaign, found he was actually enjoying his incarceration at the hands of the Americans. But not just for the reasons he'd expected—time for his personal pursuits of language, arts, and music.

After the British surrender of Fort St. Johns, back in early November, André had been taken prisoner and transported back to New York, where he was held in a military blockhouse for a short time before all the prisoners held there were dispersed to various other towns around the colonies. André was paroled, awaiting prisoner exchange, and sent to the small town of Lancaster in Pennsylvania. As the town had no prison facilities, he found lodging in the home of a man named Caleb Cope, where he was placed under house arrest. Cope was a Quaker, and like many of his denomination, was a passive loyalist, and thus was sympathetic to the young British officer's plight.

Cope and André hit it off from the first, finding they had many interests in common, including poetry and music. One day, after several weeks had gone by, Cope asked André to join him for tea in the sitting room.

"John, I find I have thoroughly enjoyed your company since your arrival," Cope began.

"Likewise, Caleb. I can assure you the pleasure has been all mine, sir. And young Thomas has certainly been a delight; his drawing skills are coming along quite nicely, I must say."

"Thanks to you, John, for taking him under your wing, so to speak—giving him lessons on the subject."

301

"Never mention it, my good man; happy to do it."

They sipped tea in silence for a moment before Caleb broke the silence. "John … I've been thinking on a matter …"

"Yes?"

"I would like to offer you a proposal which I hope you will find agreeable; if you will swear on your word of honor, as a British officer and a proper gentleman, that you will not attempt to escape, then I should like to grant you freedom to come and go about the town as you wish—in civilian clothing, of course. Some of the neighbors are … *sensitive* in that regard."

"Why, my dear Caleb, I am touched and deeply honored by your kind and generous offer, and the trust you have placed in me. Of course I accept, and I swear on my honor I shall not betray you and attempt to escape, nor to do anything else that might impugn your good name. Thank you, sir. Thank you so very much for that."

"You are most welcome. Good, good. Now that that's settled, shall we continue our discussion from yesterday? I should very much like to hear your thoughts on the writings of Voltaire."

"With pleasure, sir. With pleasure."

◄◄◄◄◀◆▶►►►►►

Thursday February 1, 1776 – Cambridge, Massachusetts Colony:

Ethan and Levi trudged along the deeply rutted, muddy road. They were footsore and weary, but these physical woes were offset by a growing sense of anticipation—that they were very close to their long-sought goal.

Ethan gazed down at the mud in the road and noticed a growing hole on the top of his right boot. *May need to mend that soon, or the whole thing will fall apart*, he thought. And then he noticed that Levi had stopped, so he also stopped, and looked over at his friend to see what had happened.

But Levi was not looking at him; rather he was staring out ahead as he pointed, "Look, Ethan."

Ethan turned, looked forward, and gasped. There, spread out before them, was General Washington's camp at Cambridge just as they had left it five months earlier. Thousands upon thousands of tents of all sizes and descriptions lined the fields in neat rows. Uncounted campfires sent thin streams of smoke rising lazily in the still, cool air, and hundreds of men could be seen walking about singly, in small groups, or marching in columns, muskets on their shoulders.

But Ethan noticed that all was *not* as it had been. He saw that there were now large berms at the far edge of the encampment, in the area closest to Boston—the very same place where he and the other riflemen from Virginia had taken pot shots at the British behind their barricade so many months earlier. But these berms were now filled with artillery. Dozens of large, black cannons, aimed at the enemy below.

He decided those cannons must be the most beautiful sight he could ever remember seeing. And it struck him that *that* thought was a sure sign something had changed inside himself.

He turned toward Levi, who was already facing him. "Well, I guess we made it," Ethan said.

"Yep, guess we did," Levi answered, trying to sound nonchalant about it. But then his face wrinkled up, and tears began to stream down his cheeks. "I can't hardly believe it … We made it home alive, Ethan," he said in almost a whisper.

Ethan stepped forward, wrapped his arms around his friend, and held him for a long moment, as he too felt the tears welling.

◄◄◄◄◄◆►►►►►

Two hours later, after he and Levi had scrounged a midday meal at the mess tents, Ethan sat in a room in General Washington's headquarters writing out his report on the Quebec expedition. To his disappointment, he had not been allowed to give his report directly to the general, as he had imagined doing, but rather had been asked to transcribe it by one of the general's aides–a non-commissioned volunteer name Robert Harrison—in as much detail as possible.

Washington's headquarters already knew about the expedition's failure, of course—the courier from Fort Ticonderoga had beat the boys back to Cambridge bringing Colonel Arnold's written report bearing the unhappy news. The only thing General Washington wanted from Ethan was the finer details of the expedition and of the engagement against Quebec.

So Ethan scratched away at the parchment in front of him. It had seemed a monumental task at first—he felt like it must surely fill a book—but after he began, he found the words flowed quickly, so that he had already filled a half dozen pages and had had to ask the aide for more paper.

He also found that it felt good to get the story down on paper. It seemed somehow satisfying and correct that those who were so courageous and had given so much—in many cases their very lives—should be recognized officially to their commanding general who had sent them.

When he was finished, he walked out into the hallway, handed the stack of papers to Mr. Harrison, and departed. On the way out the door, another of Washington's aides suggested the boys might find a room at a local inn, and handed them enough money in coins to pay the rent. Then he instructed them to report back to headquarters the next day in case the general wished to ask any questions of them.

As Ethan strode down the path and through the tents, quickly joined by Levi, who'd been loitering outside, he felt that their homecoming had been oddly anti-climactic. He'd not expected a parade or anything, but had hoped for some sort of recognition after the ordeal they had endured on behalf of their country. When he tried to explain how he was feeling to Levi, the latter just shrugged and said nothing, as if such considerations held no significance to him whatsoever.

As they walked into town to look for the inn, Ethan briefly considered penning a letter to his mother, to tell her of his return to Boston. But he immediately decided that if he mailed a letter— the mail service being disrupted by the war—it was likely he would arrive in Winchester well before the post, if it ever arrived at all. It was in that moment he realized he had, with no conscious thought on the matter, already decided to return home as soon as possible. He'd not discussed it with Levi, but he assumed his friend would want the same.

They awoke the next morning to a loud knock on their bedroom door at the inn.

"Young sirs ... are you awake?" a voice called out. "There is an important person here to speak with you."

"Oh?" Ethan answered. "We are ... just getting dressed ... give us but a moment ..." He rolled out of the bed, his feet hitting the floor with a thump, then he turned back to give Levi a shake. "Up and at 'em, sleepyhead," he said, to which Levi only groaned. But he did roll out of bed, his eyes still half closed.

Ethan stretched and immediately had to fight off a cramp that threatened to lock up his left calf muscle. He realized he ached all over from the long weeks of hiking.

When his clothes were pulled on, and Levi was at least reasonably presentable, he opened the door.

As expected, the proprietor was standing there, smiling and bowing. "Good morning, young sirs."

"Good morning, Mr. Sullivan," Ethan answered.

"Mr. Chambers, may I present *uh* ..."

"George Baylor." A young gentleman, neatly dressed, stepped forward and extended his hand. "From General Washington's staff."

"Oh." Ethan said, taking the proffered hand and shaking it. Levi also stepped forward and shook hands with the young gentleman.

"Mr. Harrison tells me y'all are Virginians, Daniel Morgan's men, from over to Winchester. I'm from New Market, myself."

"Ah, good to meet a fellow Virginian, Mr. Baylor."

"The pleasure is all mine, Mr. Chambers."

"Uh ... What can I do for you, Mr. Baylor?" Ethan asked, as Baylor just stood in the hallway smiling.

"Oh, yes ... *that.* Well, you see, I have come to fetch you, of course, Mr. Chambers."

"Fetch me?"

"Yes, the general has read your report and wishes to speak with you."

"To me? In person?"

"Yes, certainly. I am sent to escort you to his office."

Ethan turned back toward Levi, who just waved him off. "You go on without me, Ethan. I'll just go back to bed for a spell," he said, and with no further ado, did just that.

Ethan shook his head, then turned back toward Baylor. "Very well. Lead on, Mr. Baylor, if you please."

A quarter hour walk later, during which Ethan was treated to the sights and sounds of a thunderous barrage unleashed upon the British by the encampment's large guns, he stood behind Mr. Baylor as the latter knocked on a door in Washington's headquarters, then pushed it ajar without waiting for an answer.

"Private Chambers here to see you, sir," Baylor announced, then stepped to one side and, with a bow, gestured Ethan to enter. Ethan wondered about being announced as a private—wasn't he now a *lieutenant*? But he shrugged it off, assuming the man had simply misspoken.

When he entered the room, General Washington was seated at his desk, but he rose when Ethan entered. Ethan took one step forward, then remembering the proper protocol, came to attention and saluted. Washington snapped a quick salute in return, then said, "Be at your ease, Mr. Chambers," and then to Ethan's shock and joy, extended his hand. "Welcome back to Cambridge after your long, hard journey."

"Thank you, sir," he said, taking the general's extended hand. It was large, strong, and firm—just as he'd remembered from their one chance meeting back before the war, which now seemed ages ago, though it had not yet been a whole year.

"Please, do have a seat." Washington gestured toward the guest chair even as he retook his own seat.

Then the general gazed at Ethan thoughtfully for a moment and said, "You look familiar somehow, Mr. Chambers. Did we speak before you left on the Quebec expedition?"

"No, sir. But you are correct that we have met before, and spoken, though only briefly. It was back before the war, in Richmond. My father and I were passing through and happened to meet you at St. John's Episcopal Church, just when Mr. Patrick Henry was about to make his now-famous speech."

"'*Give me liberty or give me death* ...' Ah yes, now I recall ... you're Gideon's boy. How is your father?"

"Not well, last I saw him, I'm sorry to say. He suffered a terrible accident; rolled the wagon on top of himself and crushed his arms. Lost one completely and crippled the other. It was actually Daniel Morgan ... uh ... *Captain* Morgan, I should say ... who came along the road and pulled him out. I'm sure my father would've perished right there beside the road if Mr. Morgan hadn't been there. Anyway, father can no longer do surveying or map making, as you can well imagine."

"Oh ... sorry to hear that. He's a good man."

"Yes, sir. Thank you, sir."

"Ethan ... I asked you here because I wished to express my gratitude for your most excellent report on the expedition. I have to admit I was dreading reading it when I saw how lengthy it was; imagining it to be the hen scratching of some half-literate soldier, with endless, tedious detail concerning the tons of flour loaded and the number of bullets expended. But your narrative reads like an adventure novel, my dear boy. True, it does contain the necessary details one might want and expect—dates, places, numbers, and so forth—but I found myself nearly breathless reading it. The heroism, the courage, the self-sacrifice of the men and their officers—especially Daniel Morgan and Benedict Arnold—was heartwarming and inspiring.

"I began reading it last evening and must confess to burning a bit of the proverbial midnight oil in order to finish. Well done, Mr. Chambers ... well done."

"Thank you very much, sir. I can't imagine a better compliment than to hear those words coming from you, sir."

"It is really quite good, Ethan. If I weren't already flush with aides, I'd ask you to join my staff; you're just that good at writing.

"So much so, in fact, that I have asked one of my aides to copy it out and give you back the original. If you decide to become an author after the war, this may make the basis for a fine book one day."

"Thank you, sir. That is most kindly and thoughtful of you."

"Never mention it, dear boy; never mention it. Now, I know you and your fellow soldier, uh …"

"Levi, sir. Levi Miller."

"Yes, Private Miller … you and Miller currently find yourselves without a company, given that the rest of Daniel Morgan's men are at present unhappy guests of His Majesty. So, if you wish to re-enlist, which I would greatly beseech you to do, I have asked Mr. Harrison to sign you onto the roles with a promotion to the rank of corporal effective immediately, on the roster of one of the other Virginia companies … with the understanding that you will be returned to Daniel Morgan's command as soon as we can arrange his exchange."

Ethan's elation at the general's glowing words and warm reception suddenly soured. Though the general believed he was promoting Ethan from private to corporal, in fact it was a demotion from the lieutenant rank he'd received from Daniel Morgan out in the field.

But Washington had read the report, after all. And though Ethan had not tried to embellish his own role, he hadn't omitted anything either. He had made it clear that he had served as a lieutenant for Daniel Morgan, hadn't he? And, despite his initial lack of confidence, he'd grown into the role, and had even thrived in it—Captain Morgan had even said so. Colonel Arnold had also treated him with respect and acknowledged his rank as an officer. *But if General Washington says I'm to be a corporal, then who am I to argue?*

And then something welled up inside him, the same spark of courage he had felt when it had come right down to it and he had to lead his men toward that frightful, towering wall, in the swirling snow, at Quebec City …

"*No*, sir."

Washington tilted his head, "What's that you say, son?"

"I said, *no*, sir. Though I started out as a private, I finished the Quebec Expedition as a *lieutenant*."

Washington frowned. "Yes, I read that in your report. Officer's commissions may be temporarily granted in the field as circumstances require, but once the crisis is over, the soldier must revert back to his previous rank. Permanent officer's commissions must either be approved by the Congress or by the commanding general—which in this case, would be me.

"I am offering you a promotion to the rank of corporal in recognition of your commendable service during the campaign."

"With all due respect, sir, I'll not accept enlistment as a corporal. Captain Daniel Morgan, who to my mind is a great military man, promoted me to lieutenant, and I have faithfully served at that rank since. I'll not insult Captain Morgan by accepting a lesser rank."

Washington continued to frown, but said nothing, gazing at Ethan for a long moment. Not knowing what else to do, Ethan gazed back, willing himself not to break eye contact with the thoroughly intimidating general.

And then he thought he detected a smile touch the corner of Washington's mouth, and the general said, "Very well ... *Lieutenant* Chambers ... I shall have the aides speak to the commanding officers of the other Virginia regiments to see which may have need of a *lieutenant*. You may take Corporal Miller with you to whichever company that may be. Will *that* be satisfactory, sir?"

"Yes, sir. And thank you very kindly, sir. *But ...*"

"Yes? Is there something *more* you'd like to request?" the general asked with a raised brow.

"Yes, sir ... sorry, sir, but I've been away from home such a very long time now, and with my father in bad shape and all— after I've rested up for a few weeks here in camp, I'd like to receive my back pay, and then take leave long enough to visit Winchester for a few days so I can help out the folks."

Washington nodded. "*Done.* I will have Mr. Harrison draw your back pay and write up your furlough papers, effective in two weeks' time. After that, you can be on your way. We'll see you back at camp by ... the end of May, shall we say?"

"Thank you very kindly, sir."

"Oh ... and one more thing I nearly forgot to mention, Lieutenant, that you may appreciate ..."

"Sir?"

"Though they likely don't know it yet, when it was learned that Colonel Arnold and Daniel Morgan had successfully made it to Quebec with their men, and even before the battle commenced, Congress was so elated that it voted them both promotions. They are now *Brigadier General* Arnold, and *Colonel* Morgan."

"Oh. That *is* wonderful news, sir, and couldn't be more highly deserved, to my thinking. Thank you very kindly for telling me, sir."

◄◄◄◄◆►►►►►

After Lieutenant Ethan Chambers's departure, Washington mused on the interview for several moments, quietly chuckling to himself. *The boy has spunk, that's certain*, he decided. Washington knew he could be hard and intimidating, and it took courage for the boy to stand up to him. *A boy no longer*, he reminded himself. *The fellow is now a man in every respect. And having actually led men in battle, that makes him one of my more experienced combat officers, ironically, despite his age.*

Then his thoughts turned to his current dilemma. The siege of Boston had dragged on and on. He'd never expected to still be encamped at Cambridge when men from the Quebec Expedition returned. To a man of action like himself, it was a bitter pill, being forced into a long, drawn-out stalemate.

But how to break it, he wondered for the thousandth time. He stood from his desk, walked to the door, and grabbed his hat from a peg on the wall, placing it on his head. He strolled out into the foyer, then out the front door of the headquarters building, original long-time purpose of which had been as a simple farmhouse. He was not surprised that three of his staff officers had scrambled to grab their hats and follow, though they stayed behind at a respectful distance, understanding that he needed time for thought and that he would call on them if needed.

Washington walked a short stretch across the slope of the hillside to a place where he could see his dug-in artillery with the rooftops of Boston in the near distance. Though it had been a godsend to receive the cannons and their tremendous supply of ammunition—a testament to the genius and tenacity of Colonel Henry Knox, who'd dragged them down from Fort Ticonderoga through all kinds of bleak midwinter weather—they'd not been enough to break the stalemate. The big guns could hit the town, all right, but all *that* accomplished was to damage a few roofs and batter down a few walls. Though there were undoubtedly casualties on the British side, it was not sufficient to induce the British to capitulate. He needed something more.

He turned and gazed about the vista, from left to right and all the way back around again, searching the landscape for an idea … something … anything …

But there was nothing that stood out—no unguarded neck of land from which he might launch an amphibious assault, no higher ground than what they already occupied which might allow them to better target the British garrison in the town.

And then the thought of high ground made him gaze across the rooftops of Boston once again. In the far, hazy distance, he saw …

He turned around and said, "Mr. Harrison, has anyone a spyglass about him?"

"I have, sir," Mr. Baylor answered, and stepping forward, pulled the small, collapsed copper tube from his coat pocket, handing it to the general.

"Thank you, Mr. Baylor," Washington said. He extended the spyglass to its full length and once again turned toward Boston, looking for what he'd seen beyond. It was a high ridgeline on the opposite side of the town from Cambridge, but located across the water from the Boston peninsula which contained the British. In his mind's eye, he pictured a map of the city. "*Dorchester Heights,*" he whispered, and then he panned the spyglass from that hill leftward, over to where the British fleet was anchored, their high masts visible in the distance out in the harbor, safely beyond the range of the American guns at Cambridge. *But … not out of range from—*

"What's that you said, General?" Mr. Baylor asked.

"I said, *Dorchester Heights*, Mr. Baylor. We shall place our artillery on Dorchester Heights."

Washington lowered the spyglass, refolded it, and smiled at his aide.

"And may I ask what *that* may accomplish, sir?"

"Yes, you may … *That* will allow us to bombard and destroy the British fleet."

"Oh. Well, that ought to stir them up, I should think," Baylor responded.

"Precisely, Mr. Baylor … Precisely."

◄◄◄◄◄◆►►►►►

Monday April 1, 1776 – Winchester, Virginia Colony:

Abby Morgan poked her head in at the door of the sitting room, and Hannah could see that her friend was beaming, but strangely, she also had tears streaming down her cheeks.

"What is it, dear?" Hannah asked, coming to her feet. Ever since James Chambers's unhappy departure, the Chambers family had been living at the Morgans' farm just outside town, which had turned out to be a godsend for all concerned.

Abby's loneliness at the continuing absence of her husband— made even more acute by the news of his capture by the British, sent by General Washington—had been abated by Hannah's presence. And Gideon had taken her request seriously; he had applied all his intelligence, education, and ingenuity to running the Morgan farm. This had the dual benefit of making the farm run more efficiently while relieving Abby of its burden, and allowing Gideon to see himself as a useful, productive man once again. His health and his demeanor had improved accordingly, and Hannah was overjoyed at the return of Gideon's old, happy self. He'd even begun to use his bent left hand for simple tasks, such as teaching himself to write once again.

Now Hannah approached Abby and put her hands on her friend's shoulders. "What is it … What has happened, Abby?"

But Abby continued to smile through her tears, "Oh, Hannah … I'm so happy for you … Someone special is here to see you."

And then a man walked into the room. He was tall … taller than she remembered him being … and though still lean, he seemed more muscular, somehow. But more than that, his face had a hard, tough look to it that hadn't been there before.

She gasped, "Oh, my dear God! *Ethan!*" she reached out and embraced him, burying her face in his chest as she sobbed.

"Hello, Momma. I'm home," he said.

<END OF BOOK 1>

If you enjoyed *The Road to Revolution*
please post a review.

The Road to Revolution – Facts vs. Fiction

I get asked all the time whether this or that person or event in one of my books was factual or invented for dramatic effect. This volume, like those in my *Road to the Breaking* series, contains a good number of interesting historical facts and circumstances that may, at first, seem made up. I thought you might enjoy the following enumeration and explanation of these details. – *Chris Bennett*

- **Ethan Chambers** – is the fictional great grandfather of Nathaniel Chambers, featured in the Road to the Breaking series, which takes place just before and during the America Civil War. Ethan's son, Daniel, is the fictional founder of Mountain Meadows Farm in western Virginia, which his son Jacob expands and enhances until it is finally inherited by Nathaniel in the year 1860.
- **Daniel Morgan** – is a real-life figure who was already a local legend in the Shenandoah Valley of Virginia before the American Revolution. He went on to become one of the most important officers in the Continental Army, ultimately commanding one of the most brilliant tactical victories in American military history, at the Battle of Cowpens in South Carolina. This action helped turn the tide of the war, leading directly to the American victory at Yorktown which secured independence for the new nation.
- **American invasion of Canada** – members of the Continental Congress, along with key military figures such as **George Washington**, envisioned bringing the disaffected, French-speaking citizens of Canada (at the time officially named the **Quebec Province**) into the war as the **Fourteenth American Colony**. By doing so, they would not only broaden the scope of the war, but would deprive the British of critical military bases and sources of supply in North America. **Washington**

recruited the brilliant and aggressive **Colonel Benedict Arnold** for the assignment.

- **Expedition up the Kennebec** – More than 1,000 Americans worked their way up the wilderness river and into Canada, an arduous journey of over 300 miles. Overcoming numerous obstacles and hardships, including starvation and the onset of the deadly Canadian winter, they ultimately arrived at their destination, Quebec City. This incredible journey has been described by historian Arthur S. Lefkowitz as "one of the greatest adventure stories in American history."

- **British Lieutenant John André** – is a real-life figure, who, as depicted in this series, was a man of many talents, including leading men in battle, conducting espionage operations, speaking multiple languages, and indulging in numerous artistic pursuits at which he excelled. His most historically noteworthy action, however, was his involvement in the ultimate subterfuge of Benedict Arnold (to be told in future volumes of this series.)

- **Brigadier General Richard Montgomery** – was the beloved and highly respected American commander of the western arm of the Canadian expedition who led his forces northward from Fort Ticonderoga. He first took **Fort St. Johns** by siege, then captured **Montreal**, forcing **General Guy Carleton, Royal Governor of Quebec Province**, to escape to Quebec disguised in civilian clothing. Montgomery's death at the beginning of the **Battle of Quebec** was a major contributing factor in the Americans' defeat.

- **Aaron Burr** – is a real-life figure. Young, handsome, highly educated, and energetic, he is best known as the future United States Vice President who shot and killed Alexander Hamilton in a duel. Burr served as a volunteer officer during the Quebec expedition, as he had yet to gain a commission (this was a common practice at the time among young gentlemen wanting to prove their worth and hoping to gain an officer's commission.) He gained some positive national renown during the Quebec battle for his heroic, but ultimately unsuccessful, attempt to retrieve General Montgomery's body under a hail of enemy gunfire. He later rose to the rank of Lieutenant Colonel in the Continental Army.

- **Battle of Quebec** – As described in this book, if any number of things had turned out differently, Canada might very well be the northern half of the United States today. These odd contributing circumstances included:
  - **If Benedict Arnold's army would've approached the open gates of Quebec a few hours earlier**, before the unplanned arrival of the experienced and combative **Lieutenant Colonel Allan Maclean** and his Royal Highlanders, **Lieutenant Governor Hector de Cramahé** almost certainly would've capitulated without a fight.
  - **If Benedict Arnold hadn't been wounded** at the beginning of the battle, he likely would've followed Daniel Morgan's recommendation to immediately overrun the unguarded second British barricade, despite the absence of General Montgomery's force. This would've allowed the Americans to penetrate deep into the city's fortress with little opposition. Without Arnold's presence, Morgan lacked the command authority to override his reluctant fellow officers and order the attack.
  - **If General Montgomery hadn't been killed** at the outset of his attack on the British guard post at the southern end of the lower town, his advance probably would have succeeded,

resulting in his force assaulting the second barricade's defenders from the rear and routing them. The combined American force would've then been able to attack the nearly defenseless upper town.

- o **If Montgomery's second in command, Colonel Donald Campbell**, had ordered his New York regiment to press the attack after the general's death, the greatly outnumbered British defenders would've been overrun, and again, the Americans would've been able to complete the attack from the south. Instead, Campbell inexplicably ordered a withdrawal, effectively abandoning Colonel Arnold's force to their fate.

- **Daniel Morgan's surrender** – as described in this book, Morgan was in fact the last American to surrender, refusing to give up his sword to the "cowardly" British surrounding him. For reasons known only to himself, he did finally capitulate, but only after surrendering his sword to a priest rather than the British soldiers. By his own account, he was treated with kindness and respect by **Governor Guy Carleton** during his captivity.

INDEPENDENCE
ROAD TO REVOLUTION — BOOK 2

Ethan Chambers's arduous expedition to Canada may be over, but his adventures are just getting started—find out what happens next in volume two of the series …

Spring 1776. With Captain Daniel Morgan captured in Quebec, Lieutenant Ethan Chambers returns home burdened by guilt but determined to carry on his mentor's cause. As the colonies push for freedom from the English crown, he raises a company of riflemen—farmers, tradesmen, and boys barely old enough to hold a musket—and leads them north to join General George Washington's battered army, defending against a massive British assault on New York.

Thrust into a nightmare of chaos and retreat, Ethan and his men are outnumbered, outgunned, and relentlessly hunted through rain, mud, and snow by British redcoats and Hessian mercenaries. Each step tests his resolve as he learns to lead under fire and begins to understand, for himself, the true meaning of independence. He discovers that courage is not found in glory, and freedom is not won through speeches, but through determination, discipline, and the willingness to endure when defeat seems inevitable.

As the Revolution falters and winter closes in, Ethan and his soldiers march beside Washington to the frozen banks of the Delaware River where they risk everything on one final, desperate gamble that will either save the cause or end it forever.

A sweeping tale of brotherhood, sacrifice, and a young officer's rise to command during the darkest days of the

American Revolution, when the future of a nation depended on the willingness of ordinary men to claim their *Independence*.

Don't miss the next great adventure in the *Road to Revolution* series by Chris Bennett:

INDEPENDENCE – ROAD TO REVOLUTION BOOK 2

To start reading now, scan the QR code below:

◄◄◄◄◄◆►►►►►

And don't miss the free short story prequel to *The Road to Revolution*, to find out how Ethan and Daniel met when Ethan's father Gideon was nearly killed, even as the colonies hurtled inexorably toward a devastating confrontation with England in:

TROUBLES

A SHORT STORY
FROM THE
ROAD TO REVOLUTION SERIES

To download your **free copy** of the short story **TROUBLES**, please use the web address below:

https://www.chrisabennett.com/troubles

And be sure to check out my Civil War series, featuring Ethan Chambers's great grandson, Captain Nathaniel Chambers in:

ROAD TO THE BREAKING

Nothing survived "The Breaking" unchanged; lives and fortunes, love and hate, freedom and slavery …

It's early 1860, and war hero Captain Nathaniel Chambers, commander U.S. Army Fort Davis in the west Texas wilderness, has received shocking news: his father is dead. He must return home to Virginia and claim his inheritance before a maniacal neighbor can murder his widowed mother and seize the family plantation.

But he's torn by a terrible dilemma – to stay in the army and turn his back on his fortune, his mother and his beloved childhood home, or to become the thing he despises: a slave master! Is there no other choice?

An epic journey across a young nation seething with debauchery, brutality, corruption, and political intrigue, unwittingly on the brink of an unimaginable disaster: the American Civil War. Nathan Chambers has left the violent army life behind in Texas, never imaging he's on the very *Road to The Breaking.*

Get started today on book one of the series:
ROAD TO THE BREAKING

To start reading now, scan the QR code below:

Acknowledgments

Special thanks as always to my editor, Ericka McIntyre, who keeps me honest and on track, and my proofreader and fellow Tolkien fanatic Travis Tynan, who makes sure everything is done correctly.

And, as always, I can't thank her enough for all she does for our writing and publishing team—our "head coach" and my most excellent partner in crime, Keri-Rae Barnum. *You are the best!*

Recommended Reading

There are a number of good non-fiction accounts of the events in this book, including:

- *Daniel Morgan: A Revolutionary Life*, by Albert Louis Zambone

- *Daniel Morgan: Forgotten Hero*, by Ronald Hamilton

- *Benedict Arnold's Army: The 1775 American Invasion of Canada During the Revolutionary War*, by Arthur S. Lefkowitz

- *Through a Howling Wilderness: Benedict Arnold's March to Quebec, 1775*, by Thomas A. Desjardin

And for an excellent and highly compelling historical fiction overview of the American Revolution from start to finish, I highly recommend Jeff Shaara's two-book series (***warning, spoiler alert:*** if you're not highly familiar with the war and don't want any battle spoilers or Daniel Morgan spoilers, you may want to wait until the end of the *Road to Revolution* series to read Jeff Shaara's books!):

- *Rise to Rebellion: Book 1*
- *The Glorious Cause: Book 2*

GET EXCLUSIVE FREE CONTENT

The most enjoyable part of writing books is talking about them with readers like you. In my case, that means all things related to my two historical fiction series—the stories and characters, themes, and concepts. And of course, American history in general.

If you sign up for my mailing list, you'll receive some free bonus material I think you'll enjoy:

- An exclusive short story introducing the characters in my **Civil War history series, Road to the Breaking**. "Advent" tells the story of when Captain Nathan Chambers first arrived to take command at Fort Davis in west Texas, and introduces readers to his particular "band of brothers" who follow him throughout the Civil War.
- **Cut scenes from my books.** One of the hazards of writing novels is word and page count. At some point, you realize you need to trim it back to give the reader a faster-paced, more engaging experience. However, after you've finished reading a book, wouldn't you like to know a little more detail about some of your favorite characters? Here's your chance to take a peek behind the curtain (don't worry, I do warn of any potential plot spoilers!)
- I'll occasionally put out a **newsletter with information about my books**—new book releases, news and information about the author, etc. I promise not to inundate you with spam (it's one of my personal pet peeves, so why would I propagate it?)

To sign up, visit my website:
http://www.ChrisABennett.com

323